WIDOW'S WEB

"Most of the characters in Estep's riveting series suffer from serious emotional baggage. What makes this ensemble so compelling is their determined struggle to build new lives."

—*RT Book Reviews* (Top Pick!)

"Filled with such emotional and physical intensity that it leaves you happily exhausted by the end. . . . I can't wait to see what happens to Gin in *Deadly Sting*."

—*All Things Urban Fantasy*

BY A THREAD

Goodreads nominee for Best Paranormal Fantasy Novel, and *RT Book Reviews* nominee for Best Urban Fantasy World Building

"Filled with butt-kicking action, insidious danger and a heroine with her own unique moral code, this thrilling story is top-notch. Brava!"   —*RT Book Reviews* (Top Pick!)

"*By a Thread* is a ride and really fun to read."

—*Yummy Men & Kick Ass Chicks*

SPIDER'S REVENGE

RITA nominee, and *RT Book Reviews* Editor's Choice for Best Urban Fantasy Novel

"Explosive . . . outstanding. . . . Hang on, this is one smackdown you won't want to miss!"

—*RT Book Reviews* (Top Pick!)

"A whirlwind of tension, intrigue, and mind-blowing action that leaves your heart pounding."   —*Smexy Books*

TANGLED THREADS

"Interesting storylines, alluring world, and fascinating characters. That is what I've come to expect from Estep's series."

—*Yummy Men & Kick Ass Chicks*

"The story had me whooping with joy and screaming in outrage, just as all really good books always do."

—*Literary Escapism*

VENOM

"Estep has really hit her stride with this gritty and compelling series. . . . Brisk pacing and knife-edged danger make this an exciting page-turner." —*RT Book Reviews* (Top Pick!)

"Gin is a compelling and complicated character whose story is only made better by the lovable band of merry misfits she calls her family." —*Fresh Fiction*

"Since the first book in the series, I have been entranced by Gin. . . . Every book has been jam-packed with action and mystery, and once I think it can't get any better, *Venom* comes along and proves me completely wrong."

—*Literary Escapism*

WEB OF LIES

"The second chapter of the series is just as hard-edged and compelling as the first. Gin Blanco is a fascinatingly pragmatic character, whose intricate layers are just beginning to unravel." —*RT Book Reviews*

"One of the best urban fantasy series I've ever read. The action is off the charts, the passion is hot, and her cast of secondary characters is stellar. . . . If you haven't read this series, you are missing out on one heck of a good time!"

—*The Romance Dish*

SPIDER'S BITE

"The fast pace, clever dialogue, and intriguing heroine help make this new series launch one to watch."

—*Library Journal*

"Bodies litter the pages of this first entry in Estep's engrossing urban fantasy series. . . . Fans will love it."

—*Publishers Weekly*

JENNIFER ESTEP

DEADLY Sting

AN ELEMENTAL ASSASSIN BOOK

POCKET BOOKS

New York London Toronto Sydney New Delhi

Pocket Books
A Division of Simon & Schuster, Inc.
1230 Avenue of the Americas
New York, NY 10020

This book is a work of fiction. Names, characters, places, and incidents either are products of the author's imagination or are used fictitiously. Any resemblance to actual events or locales or persons, living or dead, is entirely coincidental.

First Pocket Books paperback edition April 2013

POCKET and colophon are registered trademarks of Simon & Schuster, Inc.

For information about special discounts for bulk purchases, please contact Simon & Schuster Special Sales at 1-866-506-1949 or business@simonandschuster.com.

The Simon & Schuster Speakers Bureau can bring authors to your live event. For more information or to book an event contact the Simon & Schuster Speakers Bureau at 1-866-248-3049 or visit our website at www.simonspeakers.com.

Manufactured in the United States of America

10 9 8 7 6 5 4 3 2 1

ISBN 978-1-4516-8899-3
ISBN 978-1-4516-8903-7 (ebook)

To my mom, my grandma, and Andre—
for everything

To my grandma again, for saying,
"Why ask for one million if you can ask for two?"

To my papaw—
you will be missed

ACKNOWLEDGMENTS

Once again, my heartfelt thanks go out to all the folks who help turn my words into a book.

Thanks go to my agent, Annelise Robey, and editors, Adam Wilson and Lauren McKenna, for all their helpful advice, support, and encouragement. Thanks also to Julia Fincher.

Thanks to Tony Mauro for illustrating another terrific cover, and thanks to Louise Burke, Lisa Litwack, and everyone else at Pocket Books and Simon & Schuster for their work on the cover, the book, and the series.

And finally, a big thanks to all the readers. Knowing that folks read and enjoy my books is truly humbling, and I'm glad that you are all enjoying Gin and her adventures.

I appreciate you all more than you will ever know.

Happy reading!

DEADLY Sting

1

"That would look *fabulous* on you."

Finnegan Lane, my foster brother, pointed to a tennis bracelet in the middle of a glass case full of jewelry. The shimmer of the gemstones matched the sparkle of greed in his eyes.

I looked at the price tag beside the diamond-crusted monstrosity. "You do realize that the cost of that bracelet is within spitting distance of my going rate as an assassin, right?"

"You mean your going rate back when you were actually killing people for money," Finn said. "Or as I like to call them—the good ole days."

Finn gave the diamond bracelet one more greedy glance before moving over to a display of shoes. He grabbed a purple pump off a shelf and waggled the shoe at me before holding it up and inspecting it himself. He gazed at the shoe with a rapt expression, as though it were a work of art instead of merely overpriced pieces of leather sewn together.

"It's the latest style," he said in a dreamy voice. "Hand-stitched lavender suede with custom-made four-inch heels. Isn't it marvelous?"

I arched an eyebrow. "Have I ever told you how scary it is that you know more about shoes than I do?"

Finn grinned, his green eyes lighting up with amusement. "Frequently. But my impeccable fashion sense is one of the many things you love about me."

He straightened his gray silk tie and winked at me. I snorted and moved over to look at some dresses hanging on a rack near the wall.

The two of us were out shopping, which was one of Finn's favorite things to do. Not mine, though. I never paid too much attention to what I was wearing, beyond making sure that my jeans and boots were comfortable enough to fight in and that my T-shirt sleeves were long enough to hide the knives I had tucked up each one. As an assassin, I'd learned a long time ago not to invest too much money in clothes that were only going to end up with bloodstains on them.

But here I was, along for the consumer ride. Finn had shown up at the Pork Pit, my barbecue joint, just after the lunch rush ended and had dragged me all the way up to Northtown, the part of Ashland that housed and catered to the wealthy, social, and magical elite. We'd spent the last hour traipsing from store to store in an upscale shopping development that had just opened up.

Now we were browsing through Posh, the biggest, fanciest, and most expensive boutique on this particular block. Racks of ball gowns and evening dresses filled the store, starting with all-white frocks on the left and darkening to midnight-black ones on the right, like a rainbow of color arcing from one side of the store to the other. There wasn't a dress in here that was less than five grand, and the shoes arranged along the back wall went for just as much. Not to mention the minuscule handbags that cost ten times as much as a good steak dinner.

"Come on, Gin," Finn wheedled, holding the pump out to me. "At least try it on."

I rolled my eyes, took the shoe from him, and hefted it in my hand. "Lightweight, nice enough color. Not the worst thing you've shown me today. And that skinny stiletto would make a decent weapon, if you took the time to snap it off the rest of the shoe and sharpen the end of it."

Finn sighed and took the pump away from me. "Have I ever told you how scary it is that you think of heels in terms of their possible shiv potential?"

I grinned at him. "Frequently. But my impeccable sense of improvised weaponry is one of the many things you love about me."

This time, Finn rolled his eyes and then started muttering under his breath about how he couldn't take me anywhere. My grin widened. I loved needling Finn as much as he enjoyed teasing me.

"Tell me again why I have to go to this shindig with you," I said when he finally wound down.

"It's not a mere *shindig*," he huffed. "It's the opening gala for an exhibit of art, jewelry, and other valuable objects from the estate of the late, not-so-great, and certainly unlamented Mab Monroe. Everyone who's anyone will be there, underworld and otherwise, and it's going to be *the* social event of the summer. Besides, aren't you the least bit curious to see what the old girl stashed away over the years? The things she collected? What she thought was beautiful or valuable or at least worth hoarding? She *was* your nemesis, after all."

Mab Monroe had been a little more than my nemesis—the Fire elemental had murdered my mother and my older sister when I was thirteen. She'd also tortured me. But I'd finally gotten my revenge when I shoved my knife through the bitch's black heart back in the winter. Killing Mab had been one of the most satisfying moments of my life. The fact that she was dead and I wasn't was the only thing that really mattered to me.

"Sorry," I said. "I have no desire to go gawk at all of Mab's shinies. They're not doing her any good now, are they? I'm quite happy simply knowing that she's rotting in her grave. And I still don't understand why you insisted on dragging me out to buy a dress. I have plenty of little black numbers in my closet at home, any one of which would be just fine for this event."

Finn snorted. "Sure, if you don't mind wearing something that's ripped, torn, and caked with dried blood."

I couldn't argue with that. Funny how killing people inevitably led to ruined clothes.

Finn sighed and shook his head at my lack of interest in Mab's many treasures. "I can't believe you won't go out of simple curiosity and unabashed greed. Those are certainly the reasons *I'm* going. And probably half the folks on the guest list. We've just covered why you need a new dress. As to why you have to go with me, well, naturally, I asked Bria first, but she has to work. I need *someone* to drink champagne with and make snide comments to about everyone else in attendance. You wouldn't deny me that pleasure, would you?"

"Perish the thought," I murmured. "But what about Roslyn? Or Jo-Jo? Why don't you take one of them instead?"

"Roslyn is already going with someone else, and Jo-Jo has a date with Cooper." Finn used his fingers to tick off our friends and family. "I even asked Sophia, but there's some classic Western film festival that she's planning to catch that night. Besides, she'd probably insist on wearing black lipstick, a silverstone collar, and the rest of her usual Goth clothes instead of an evening dress. Since I don't want to be responsible for any of the old guard having conniptions or coronary episodes, you're it."

"Lucky me."

"Besides, it's not like you have plans," he continued as though I hadn't said a word. "Other than sitting at home and brooding over lost love."

My eyes narrowed, and I gave Finn a look that would have made most men tremble in their wing tips. He just picked up a strappy canary-yellow sandal and admired it a moment before showing it to me.

"What do you think? Is yellow your color? Yeah, you're right. Not with your skin tone." He put the shoe back on the shelf and turned to face me.

"Look," Finn said, his expression serious. "I just thought it would be good for you to get out of the house for a night. You know, dress up, go out on the town, have a little fun. I know how hard this last month has been, with you and Owen on the outs."

On the outs was putting it mildly. I hadn't spoken to Owen Grayson, my lover, since the night he'd come to the Pork Pit a few weeks ago to tell me he needed some time to himself, some time away from me, from us.

But that's what happens when you kill your lover's ex-fiancée right in front of him. That sort of thing tended to make a person reassess his relationships—especially with the one who'd done the killing.

No matter how much I missed him, I couldn't blame Owen for wanting to take a break. A lot of bad stuff had gone down in the days leading up to me battling Salina Dubois, a lot of terrible secrets had been revealed, and he wasn't the only one who'd needed time to process and come to terms with everything. I might understand, but that didn't make it hurt any less.

Even assassins could have their hearts broken.

"Gin?" Finn asked in a soft voice, cutting into my thoughts.

I sighed. "I know you're just trying to help, but I'm fine, Finn. Really, I am. The important thing is that Salina is dead, and she can't hurt anyone else ever again. Owen and I . . . we'll eventually work things out."

"And if you don't?"

I sighed again. "Then we'll both move on with our lives."

I kept my face calm and smooth, although my heart squeezed at the thought. Finn had started to say something else when one of the saleswomen sidled up to him.

"Good afternoon, sir," the woman, a gorgeous red-head, practically purred. "What can I do for you today?"

We'd already been in the store for five minutes, and I was mildly surprised that it had taken someone this long to come over to us. In my boots, worn jeans, and grease-spattered black T-shirt, I didn't look like I had two nickels to rub together, but Finn was as impeccably dressed as ever in one of his Fiona Fine designer suits. The perfect fit showed off his strong, muscled body, while his walnut-colored hair was artfully styled. Add all that to his handsome features, and Finn looked just as polished as the jewelry he'd been admiring earlier.

The saleswoman's eyes trailed down his body and back up. After a moment, she smiled at him and then subconsciously licked her lips as though Finn were a hot fudge sundae that she wanted to gobble up. At the back of the store, a second saleswoman eyed her associate with anger. While Finn had been waxing poetic about bracelets and shoes, the two of them had been having a whispered argument about who got the privilege of waiting on him. Looked like Red here had won.

Finn, being Finn, noticed the woman's obvious interest and immediately turned up the wattage on his dazzling, slightly devious smile. "Why, hello there," he drawled. "Don't you look lovely today? That sky-blue color is *amazing* with your hair."

Red blushed and smoothed down her short skirt. Her gaze flicked to me for half a second before she focused on Finn again. "Do you and your . . . wife need some help?"

"Oh," he said. "She's not my wife. She's my sister."

The woman's dark eyes lit up at that bit of information, and Finn's smile widened. Despite the fact that he was involved with Detective Bria Coolidge, my sister, Finn still flirted with every woman who crossed his path, no matter how old or young or hot or not she was. Dwarf, vampire, giant, elemental, human. As long as you were breathing and female, you could count on being the recipient of all the considerable charm that Finnegan Lane had to offer.

"But my sister could definitely use your help, and so could I. What do you think about this color?" he asked, picking up the purple pump once again. "Don't you think it would look fabulous on her?"

"Fabulous," Red agreed, her eyes wide and dreamy.

I might be standing right next to Finn, but I was as invisible as the moon on a sunny day. I sighed again. It was going to be a long afternoon.

Twenty minutes later, after being dragged from one side of the store to the other, Red showed me to a fitting room in the back. Rightfully insisting that he knew more about fashion than I did, Finn had picked out several dresses for me to try on. Red placed the gowns on a hanger on the wall before brushing past me.

"I'm going to check on Mr. Lane and see if he needs anything," she said.

"Of course you are."

Red hightailed it over to the jewelry case, where the other saleswoman, a well-endowed blonde, was leaning over and showing Finn the diamond bracelet he'd been admiring earlier—along with all of her ample assets. Red stepped up next to Blondie and not so subtly elbowed her out of the way. Blondie retaliated by shoving her breasts forward even more. The two of them might as well have filled up a pit with mud and settled their differences that way. That would have been far more entertaining than the petty one-upmanship they were currently engaged in.

I rolled my eyes. Finn was the only man I knew who could inspire a catfight just by grinning. But it was a show that I'd seen many times before, so I stepped into the fitting room, closed the door behind me, and started trying on the dresses. The sooner I picked something, the sooner I could get back to the Pork Pit.

Too tight, too short, too slutty. None of the garments was quite right, not to mention the fact that Finn had chosen more than one strapless evening gown. My cleavage had never been all that impressive—certainly not on par with Blondie's—but of more importance was the fact that strapless gowns were not good for knife concealment. Then again, Finn didn't particularly care about such things. He didn't have to. He could always tuck a gun or two inside or under his jacket, which suited him just fine, as long as the weapons didn't mess up the smooth lines of the fabric.

I was just about to take off the latest fashion disaster—this one in that awful canary yellow that definitely wasn't my color—when I heard a soft electronic chime, signaling that someone else had come into the store. I wondered how long it would take Red and Blondie to tear themselves away from Finn to see to the new customer—

A surprised scream ripped through the air, along with a sharp smacking sound. The pain-filled moan that followed told me that someone had just gotten hit.

"Don't move, and don't even think of going for any of the alarm buttons," a low voice growled. "Or I'll put a couple of holes in you—all of you. Maybe I'll do that anyway, just for fun."

Well, now, that sort of threat implied that the person making it had a gun—maybe even more than one. I perked up at the thought, and a genuine smile creased my face for the first time today. For the first time in several days, actually.

I cracked open the fitting-room door so I could see what was going on. Sure enough, a man stood right in front of the jewelry case. He was a dwarf, a couple of inches shy of five feet tall, with a body that was thick with muscle. He wore jeans with holes at the knees and a faded blue T-shirt. A barbed-wire tattoo curled around his left bicep, which looked like it was made of concrete rather than flesh and bone. He held a revolver in his right hand, the kind of gun that could definitely put a large hole in someone, especially if you used it at close range.

Since it didn't look like the dwarf was immediately going to pull the trigger, my gaze went to the other people in the boutique. Blondie was the closest to the gunman. She had one hand pressed to her cheek, probably from where the dwarf had reached across the counter and slapped her, while her other hand was clamped over her mouth to hold back her screams. She wasn't entirely successful at that, though, and a series of high-pitched squeaks filled the air, almost like a dog whimpering.

Finn stood about ten feet away from the dwarf. He must have been talking to Red when the gunman entered the store, because he'd put himself in between her and the dwarf. Red had the same stunned, horrified expression on her face that Blondie did.

Finn had his hands up, although his eyes were narrowed, assessing the dwarf and the danger he presented, just like I was.

The first thing I did was look past the gunman and through the boutique windows, just in case he had a partner waiting outside, but I didn't see anyone loitering on the sidewalk or sitting in a getaway car by the curb. A solo job, then.

The second thing I did was study the dwarf to see if it looked like he was searching the store for someone else— me, Gin Blanco, the assassin known as the Spider.

By killing Mab, I'd inadvertently made myself a popular target in the underworld, and more than one of the crime bosses had put a bounty on my head, hoping to establish themselves as Ashland's new head honcho by taking me out. It wasn't out of the realm of possibility to think that the dwarf had followed Finn and me to the boutique on someone's orders.

But the only thing the dwarf was interested in was the jewelry. His eyes glinted, and his mouth curved up into a satisfied smile as he glanced down at all the expensive baubles. So this was nothing more than a simple robbery, then. Plenty of those in Ashland, even up here in the rarefied air of Northtown. Really, if the Posh owners were going to keep all those diamonds around, then they should have at least hired a giant or two to guard them.

"Move!" the dwarf barked, pointing his gun at Blondie. "Over there with the others. Now!"

Blondie, who'd been behind the counter, hurried around it and stopped next to Red, putting the other woman and Finn between her and the robber. Well, at least she had a good sense of self-preservation. Red knew it too; she gave her coworker a hostile glance over her shoulder.

I turned my attention back to the robber, wondering if he might have any magic to go along with his inherent dwarven strength and the hand cannon he was sporting. But the dwarf's eyes didn't glow, and I didn't sense anything emanating from him. No hot, invisible waves of Fire power, no cold, frosty blasts of Ice magic, and nothing else to indicate that he was an elemental. Good. That would make this easier.

"Give me the key!" the dwarf snapped at Blondie as he moved behind the counter. "Now!"

Blondie stepped around the others and over to the robber, pulling a set of keys out of her pants pocket and holding them out to him at arm's length, her hands shaking. The dwarf grabbed the keys and used one of them to open the lock on the jewelry case, instead of just smashing the glass and setting off the alarms. He threw the keys down on the floor and started shoving bracelets, rings, and necklaces into his jeans pockets.

I looked at the knives I'd piled on the bench inside the fitting room alongside my clothes. Normally, I carried five silverstone knives on me—one up either sleeve, one against the small of my back, and two in the sides of my boots—but I'd removed them when I'd started trying on the dresses. I couldn't exactly go outside with a knife in my hand, since that would ruin whatever element of surprise I had, and there was no time to change back into my regular clothes. Cursing Finn under my breath, I hiked up the long skirt of the dress I was wearing and opened the fitting-room door.

"Darling!" I squealed, rushing into the front of the store. "Isn't this dress just the most divine thing you've ever seen?"

I twirled around and managed to put myself in between Finn and the robber. With the yellow dress, I might as well have been a mother duck, watching over her little ones.

"'Darling'? I thought you said she was your sister!" Red hissed.

A dwarf had threatened to shoot her and was now robbing the store, and Red was still more worried about Finn's marital status than all that. Someone's priorities were a little skewed.

Finn winced and gave her an apologetic shrug, but he never took his eyes off the dwarf.

The robber's head snapped up at the sound of my voice, and the gun followed a second later. He stepped to the end of the counter and grabbed hold of my bare arm, his fingers digging into my skin as he pulled me next to him. His hot breath wafted up my nose, reeking of onions and garlic. I hoped he'd enjoyed whatever he'd had for lunch today, because he was going to be eating through a straw soon enough.

"Who the hell are you?" he growled, shoving the gun in my face. "Where did you come from?"

"I was . . . I was . . . I was in the back, trying on some evening gowns," I said in the breathiest, most terrified and helpless voice I could muster. "I don't want any trouble. Please, please, please, don't shoot me!"

The dwarf stared at me for several seconds before he lowered his gun and let go of my arm.

"Just so you know, that's the ugliest damn dress I've ever seen," he said. "You look like a daffodil."

He shook his head and reached inside the case to grab another handful of jewelry. The second his eyes dropped to the diamonds, I stepped forward, yanked the gun out of his hand, and drove my fist into the side of his face.

With his dense, dwarven musculature, it was like smashing my knuckles into a cement block. My punch didn't have much effect, except to make him stop looting the jewelry case and focus all his attention on me, but that was exactly what I wanted.

"Stupid bitch!" he growled, stretching his hands out to grab me. "I'll kill you for that—"

I pistol-whipped him across the face with the gun. My fist might not have had much of an impact, but the sharp edges and heavy, solid weight of the weapon did. His nose cracked from the force, and blood arced through the air, the warm, sticky drops spattering onto my skin.

The robber howled with pain, but he reached for me again. I tightened my grip on the gun and slammed it into his face once more. And I didn't stop there. Again and again, I hit him, smashing the weapon into his features as hard as I could. The dwarf fought back, wildly swinging his fists at me. Despite the blood running into his eyes, he was a decent fighter, so I grabbed hold of my Stone magic and pushed the cool power outward, hardening my skin into an impenetrable shell.

Good thing, since the dwarf's fist finally connected with my face.

Given his strength, the blow rocked me back, and I felt the force of it reverberate through my entire body, but it didn't break my jaw like it would have if I hadn't been using my magic to protect myself. Still, the dwarf took it as a sign of encouragement that he'd finally been able to hit me.

"Not so tough now, are you?" he snarled, advancing on me again.

"Tough enough to do this," I said.

I waited until he was back in range, blocked his next blow, and then used the gun to coldcock him in the temple. His eyes widened, taking on a glassy sheen, and then rolled up in the back of his head as he slumped to the floor.

"You know, Gin, you really should warm up before you tee off on somebody like that," Finn murmured, leaning across the counter and staring down at the dwarf. "Wouldn't want you to pull a muscle or anything."

"Oh, no," I sniped, letting go of my Stone magic so that my skin would revert back to its normal texture. "We wouldn't want that. Have I told you how much I hate shopping?"

Finn just grinned and pulled out his cell phone from his jacket pocket to call Bria and report the attempted robbery. I used the long skirt of the dress to wipe my prints off the gun and then put the weapon down on top of the jewelry case.

I'd just started to head to the fitting room to change back into my own clothes, when the two saleswomen blocked my path. They both looked at me with serious expressions. They were probably going to thank me for saving them—

"You know you have to pay for that," Red said.

"Oh, yeah," Blondie chimed in. "That's a ten-thousand-dollar dress you just got blood all over."

Blood? There hadn't been that much blood. It wasn't like I'd sliced the dwarf's throat open with one of my knives, which is what I usually did when bad folks crossed my path.

I had opened my mouth to respond, when I caught sight of my reflection in one of the mirrors on the wall. Dark brown hair, gray eyes, pale skin. I looked the same as always, except for the flowing yellow dress—and the blood that covered my hands, arms, and chest. Actually, being covered in blood pretty much *was* the same as always for me. But the robber had bled more than I'd thought, and the fancy gown now looked like it had come straight out of a horror movie where everyone dies at the big dance.

I started to push past the two women, but they crossed their arms over their chests and held their ground. Apparently, the sight of a ruined dress was more offensive than the fact that I had bludgeoned someone unconscious right in front of them.

"I saved your snotty little store from getting robbed, not to mention that I kept that dwarf from probably killing you both, and you actually think you're going to charge me for it?" I stepped forward. "Keep talking, and this dress won't be the only thing in here with blood on it, sugar."

Red paled. After a moment, she stepped aside. I turned my cold gaze to Blondie, who sucked in a breath and stepped aside too.

I stomped past them, went into the fitting room,

closed the door behind me, and peeled off the gown. I put it on its hanger and hung it on the back of the door. Now, instead of being canary yellow, the top of the dress had taken on a bright crimson color, and blood had also oozed down the full skirt, giving the whole garment a garish, tie-dye effect.

Still, as I stared at the disastrous dress, I couldn't help but smile.

Finn was right.

Yellow really wasn't my color—red was.

☼ 2 ☼

I grabbed some tissues out of a box in the fitting room and spent the next ten minutes scrubbing the dwarf's blood off my skin. After peering at my reflection in the mirror to make sure I'd gotten as much of it as I could, I put my own clothes back on, tucked my knives into their appropriate slots, and slipped on my boots.

That electronic chime sounded again, telling me that someone new had come into the store. So I stepped out of the fitting room and went into the front of the boutique.

Finn was once again standing in front of the jewelry case, but he'd been joined by my sister, Bria Coolidge. Bria wore her usual black boots and dark jeans, along with a light blue button-up shirt. A silverstone primrose rune rested in the hollow of her throat, and her gold badge was clipped to her black leather belt, along with her gun.

Red and Blondie stood against the wall behind the

case, arms crossed, eyes narrowed, glossy lips puckered with displeasure. They were none too happy about my sister's arrival. Even in her cop clothes, Bria was quite lovely, with her shaggy blond hair, rosy skin, and vivid blue eyes. Not to mention the adoring way Finn looked at her. He might flirt with every woman who crossed his path, but Bria was the one who made his eyes soften and his face brighten in that warm, special way. She was the one who had his heart, and Red and Blondie could see it just as easily as everyone else could.

But Bria hadn't come alone. A giant who was around seven feet tall reached down and hauled the dwarf to his feet before slapping a set of silverstone handcuffs on the robber. The giant's hair, skin, and eyes were all a rich shade of ebony, while his shaved head gleamed in the afternoon sunlight streaming in through the windows. Xavier, Bria's partner on the force, was another member of my make-shift extended family.

Xavier finished securing the cuffs, then put one hand on the robber's shoulder to keep the much shorter man from falling over. The dwarf's eyes were slightly unfocused, and blood still dripped from the cuts I'd opened up on his face when I'd pistol-whipped him. Still, he surged forward at the sight of me.

"You bitch!" he screamed. "I'll kill you for this!"

"Sure you will," I said in an easy voice. "Take a number and get in line."

Xavier tightened his grip on the dwarf's shoulder, holding him in place, and let out a deep, rumbling laugh. "I'll say this, Gin. There's never a dull moment when you're around."

I winked at him. "I do my best to keep y'all employed—and entertained."

Xavier laughed again and took the would-be robber outside, where a dark sedan with flashing blue and white lights waited by the curb.

I went over to the others. Finn leaned against the case, his elbows on the glass and his face propped up in his hands. He stared dreamily at Bria as she crouched down and examined some of the diamond jewelry scattered on the floor. Red and Blondie were still standing against the wall, although they'd now focused their laser-hot glares on Finn. Not that he noticed; Finn excelled at ignoring little unpleasantries like that.

I elbowed him in the side. "I think you've officially lost your fan club."

"Hmm?" Finn said, unabashedly admiring Bria's ass. "What did you say?"

I elbowed him a little harder and jerked my head at the two women. He finally deigned to glance in that direction.

"Oh, them? No worries," he murmured.

Finn straightened up, adjusted his tie, and plastered a smile on his face. Then he squared his shoulders and swaggered over to them with all the confidence in the world, even though anger still pinched their faces. But that was Finn for you—always ready, willing, and eager to tame the savage female beast. Or beasts, in this case.

"Ladies," he said. "Have I told you both how very brave you were? Why, it was just *amazing* the way you both kept your cool when that horrible *thug* stormed into the store . . ."

And he was off, telling the saleswomen just how much he admired their levelheaded gumption in the face of such terrible danger and other such nonsense. He only stopped talking long enough to draw in a necessary breath here and there, dazzling them with smile after toothy smile.

While Finn soothed their ruffled feathers and bruised egos, I stepped around the display case.

"Hey there, baby sister," I said.

Bria smiled and got to her feet. "Hey there yourself. You know, when Finn told me that he was taking you shopping this afternoon, I didn't imagine things would turn out quite like this."

My gaze dropped to the bloodstains on the thick gray carpet. "Me either."

"Still, you made my day a little easier," she continued.

"How so?"

She gestured at the store windows, through which I could see that Xavier had stuffed the dwarf into the backseat of the sedan and was now leaning against the side of the car. He had his sunglasses on and his head tilted back, enjoying the warm, early June sun.

"By catching the bad guy for me." Bria paused. "Or, rather, knocking him unconscious."

I grinned. "You know me and my methods."

"That I do."

She returned my grin before swiveling back around to the case. Bria picked up a necklace set with square diamonds that were the size of gumballs. She studied the flashing gems for a few seconds before putting the piece down on top of the glass.

"All these diamonds would have made for a nice haul if the guy had gotten away with them." She shook her head, making her blond hair shimmer. "The moon must be full or something. This is the second robbery I've been called out to today, and it's the fifth one this week."

"Well, that's not so unusual, is it?" I asked. "This is Ashland, after all. Somebody's always up to something in this town—usually something evil, dastardly, and violent."

She shrugged. "Maybe, but it seems like more bad guys than usual have come out of the woodwork these past few days. And the really weird thing? There's no one around to stop them."

Bria looked over at the saleswomen. "Excuse me, ladies. Does the store employ any security guards?"

Red actually glanced away from Finn long enough to answer her question. "We used to have a giant. But Anton called in yesterday and said that he'd gotten a better offer. So the owner hasn't had a chance to replace him yet."

Bria nodded, and Red turned her attention back to Finn.

"I've gotten that same explanation twice now," Bria said. "It's like all the giants who work as bodyguards have suddenly decided to move on up to bigger and better things. This is the third robbery I've seen this week where nobody's been guarding the goods, even with an obvious score to be had."

I frowned. That was strange. Vampires, dwarves, elementals, humans—lots of folks hired themselves out as security or bodyguards to banks, businesses, and wealthy individuals. Sure, it was a dangerous gig, especially in this town, but the money was good, and most positions came with excellent medical and dental. Some folks even offered their employees 401(k)s and profit-sharing plans. Not to mention the bonus hazard pay you could collect if you thwarted a robbery or an assassination attempt.

But given their tall, strong physiques, giants were the top choice when it came to keeping something or someone safe, especially among the underworld bosses. Practically every crime lord in Ashland had at least half a dozen giants—if not more—on his or her payroll. For the bosses, hiring them was a way to keep the rest of their underlings in line and hold on to their turf. For the giants, it was usually easy money for mostly standing around and looking tough. Win-win all the way around—unless you happened to cross somebody with a cadre of giants at his disposal. In addition to providing protection, giants were also very, very good at enforcing one person's unpleasant will on another—and beating you until you got the bloody message.

Bria shook her head. "Anyway, at least this case is cut-and-dried. All I need to do is get some witness statements from the saleswomen, and Xavier and I can take the perp over to the station—"

A soft, feminine laugh floated through the air, followed by a series of high-pitched giggles. Bria and I looked at each other, then over at Finn. Apparently, all had been forgiven, because the two saleswomen had practically draped themselves over him by this point. Red had her hand on one of his shoulders, while Blondie was cozied up on his other side, toying with his jacket sleeve. Finn's head swiveled back and forth between them, as though he was watching an intense tennis match. It was a wonder his neck didn't break from the speed.

"Good luck getting those statements," I murmured.

Bria smiled, showing a hint of teeth. "Oh, luck has nothing to do with it, big sister."

She strode over and planted herself in front of Finn and his adoring entourage.

"Bria!" he said. "I was just telling these two lovely ladies how brave they were when that terrible thug rushed into the store."

"Of course you were." Her voice was mild, although she raised her eyebrows at him.

Finn gave her a sheepish grin, but he immediately disentangled himself from the other two women and stepped forward. His sudden movement made the saleswomen teeter on their heels and almost crash into each other, but Finn didn't care. He leaned down and murmured something in Bria's ear that caused a fierce blush to bloom in her cheeks. Red and Blondie both frowned, but Bria just smiled at them. They all knew that she had Finn's full and undivided attention now.

He finally quit whispering to her and straightened up, a teasing grin on his handsome face. Bria stared back at him, her blue eyes warm and soft.

"I'm going to hold you to that," she murmured. "Tonight."

Finn's grin widened.

Bria blushed a little more, then cleared her throat, stepped past him, and addressed the other two women, back in full detective mode. "Ladies, I need to get some statements from you about what happened . . ."

I smiled at their antics, even though they made my heart twinge with pain. Seeing Finn, Bria, and their obvious happiness reminded me of how much I missed Owen. Not for the first time, I thought about pulling out my cell phone and calling him. The only problem was that I didn't know what to say. *I love you. I miss you. I killed your ex because it had to be done.* Not exactly sweet nothings.

Still, the urge to hear his voice was so strong that I went so far as to grab my phone out of my jeans pocket. My finger hovered over the button that would speed-dial Owen's number, but after a moment, I stuffed the phone back into my pocket. I sighed. I'd never considered myself a coward before, but when it came to Owen, I was as yellow-bellied as the dress I'd ruined.

But my conflicted feelings didn't change the fact that I needed to get back to the Pork Pit and help Sophia with the dinner rush. I'd just taken a step toward the front door when Finn blocked my path.

"Where do you think you're going?"

"Outside," I said. "To your car. So you can drive me back to the restaurant."

He shook his head. "Uh-uh. Nothing doing. No way. I told Sophia that you were taking the rest of the day off, and that's exactly what you're going to do. Besides, we are not leaving here until you get a new dress."

"You're kidding, right?"

Finn turned to the rack closest to him and grabbed a long dress that shimmered with red sequins. "What do you think about this one? Yeah, this is much too orange of a red for you. With all that pale skin, you need a blue-red, like this one."

He plucked another gown off the rack, held it out at arm's length, and examined it with a critical eye.

"Oh, yes," he said. "This would look *divine* with your complexion. And I think I saw some shoes earlier that would be absolutely *smashing* with this."

I just groaned.

After another hour of trying on dresses at the Posh boutique, Finn and I headed back to the Pork Pit to grab some dinner. The attempted robbery might have broken up some of the tediousness of dress shopping, but I still wanted some comfort food from my own restaurant. So I dished us both up some burgers, chili-cheese fries, and triple-chocolate milkshakes.

Later that evening, Finn finally dropped me off at Fletcher's house—my house now. Being a gentleman, he carried in the ridiculously expensive dress, shoes, and purse he'd picked out and insisted I buy. Then he headed out, saying that Bria was expecting him. Of course she was, given the heated promises he'd whispered to her in the boutique.

"Good luck with your seduction," I sniped, following him out onto the porch.

Finn waggled his eyebrows at me. "Luck? Finnegan Lane doesn't need luck, baby. Enough said."

His excessive confidence made me laugh, although a bit of bitterness tinged my chuckles. "Of course you don't."

Finn hesitated, picking up on my sour mood. "You know, I could always cancel with Bria, if you wanted some company tonight—"

"I'm fine," I said, cutting him off before I could see the

pity in his eyes. "In fact, I'm plumb tuckered out from all that shopping. I plan to take a shower, get in bed, and curl up with a good book."

Once again, he hesitated. "Well, if you're sure . . ."

I gave his shoulder a little push. "I'm sure. Now, go. Have fun with Bria."

Finn nodded, stepped off the porch, and got into his car. Cranking the engine, he waved at me before zooming down the driveway. I kept my arm up and my features fixed into a pleasant smile until he disappeared from sight. Then I let out a quiet sigh, and my fake, happy face melted like a scoop of rocky road on a hot summer day. I hadn't lied to Finn. I was tired—of pretending that I was okay. That I didn't miss Owen.

That my heart wasn't a bloody, pulpy mass of broken bits, splintered pieces, and sharp edges.

But standing outside and brooding into the evening sun wasn't going to help anything, so I shut and locked the front door, then went upstairs to my bedroom. I hung up the garment bag containing my new dress, stripped off my clothes, and took a long, hot shower to wash away the last lingering traces of the dwarf's blood. When that was done, I pulled on a pair of short, loose cotton pajamas patterned with blackberries and crawled into bed.

I glanced at the nightstand and the copy of *What's the Worst That Could Happen?* by Donald E. Westlake that I was reading for my latest literature class over at Ashland Community College. But I didn't feel like reading tonight, so I snapped off the light and snuggled under the soft, thin sheets, even though it was still early in the evening.

I tried to sleep, but the flickers began almost as soon as I closed my eyes. More nights than not, I didn't dream so much as I remembered old jobs, old dangers, and old enemies I'd faced . . .

The job had gone sideways.

It was supposed to be an easy hit. Fletcher Lane, my mentor and the assassin known as the Tin Man, had taken out drug lords like Peter Delov dozens of times before. Breach the perimeter, get close to the target, and twist the knife in until he was good and dead before slipping back into the shadows once more. Simple. Clean. Easy.

But it hadn't worked out that way at all.

I'd helped Fletcher gather intel on Delov for weeks, and I supposed him bringing me along tonight was my reward for all of that hard work. Plus, now that I was fifteen and two years into my training with him, Fletcher had said that it was finally time for me to see exactly what being an assassin really meant—and all the bloody violence that went along with it.

As if I didn't already know all about blood and violence from living on the streets—and watching the murders of my mother and my older sister.

But Fletcher had said that soon I'd be ready to start doing solo jobs and that these dry runs with him would help me prepare. I didn't really understand what he was talking about, though. On the few jobs I'd been on so far, all I'd done was stand in the shadows, watch him get close to the target, wait for him to deliver the killing blow, and then leave the scene of the crime with the old man. Not exactly the hands-on method I'd imagined.

But that had all changed tonight.

Fletcher had learned that Delov had sent his giant guards on down to his Miami mansion that afternoon, while his personal staff was at the airport, readying his private plane. Delov was leaving early in the morning to meet with his drug suppliers down in the Keys, and he was the sort who'd want everything picture-perfect for his trip.

Without the usual guards patrolling, it had been child's play for us to climb over the stone wall that ringed the estate, creep through the woods that surrounded the mansion, and then slip inside the structure. We hadn't seen a soul, not even Peaches, Delov's pet Pomeranian. Clear sailing all the way up to the third floor, where his bedroom was.

Only the drug lord hadn't been sound asleep like he was supposed to have been, given that it was one in the morning. Fletcher and I stood in the shadows that blackened Delov's bedroom, staring at the enormous, empty bed with its rumpled silk sheets.

"Where is he?" I whispered. "We've been watching him for two weeks now. He's always in bed by this time."

Fletcher shrugged, but I could see the tension in the tight muscles of his neck and shoulders.

"I don't know," he said. "But we have to find him and do this tonight. We won't be able to get this close to him again this easily."

Fletcher crept over and put his hand down in the center of the bed. "The mattress is still warm, which means that he's probably on this floor somewhere. Where do you think he went, Gin?"

The old man was always giving me little pop quizzes like this, always making me put myself in my target's shoes, always drilling into my head that it was better to think ahead, to plan, to act rather than to react, no matter what situation I was in.

I thought about all the things the old man had taught me and everything I'd learned about Delov while we'd been watching him. "The most common places for people to go in their own house late at night are the kitchen and the bathroom. So either he got up because he was hungry or he needed to take a leak. I'd vote for the kitchen, given his enormous appetite. He's always munching on something in all the surveillance photos I've taken."

Fletcher nodded, agreeing with me. "Okay. Now, stay close to me while we go see if you're right."

Together, we tiptoed over to the bedroom door and slipped out into the hallway. The third floor of the mansion was devoted to Delov's personal quarters, and each room was more opulently furnished than the one before it, all with slightly oversize chairs and tables, the better to accommodate the giant's tall frame. One by one, we peered into the rooms we passed, but they were all as empty as his bed had been.

Finally, we reached the last room on the floor—the kitchen. The double doors were thrown open, and light spilled out into the hallway. A soft *snick* sounded, like someone opening a refrigerator door, followed by the faint *rattle-rattle* of dishes. Fletcher grinned and gave me a thumbs-up.

Fletcher and I eased up on either side of the doorway, still keeping to the shadows as much as possible, and peered inside. The kitchen was just as large and spacious as the other rooms and featured two of everything, including twin refrigerators situated side by side along the left wall. The doors on both were wide open, and Peter Delov stood in between them, perusing all the items inside.

Delov was big, even for a giant, topping out at almost eight feet. His back was to us, but I knew from my surveillance that he had tan skin, brown eyes, bushy eyebrows, and dark brown hair that was always slicked back over his high forehead. Delov considered himself to be a handsome man, and given his massive drug empire, he treated himself to the very best of everything, from clothes to cars to women.

But his main passion was gourmet food, and both fridges were stocked with bottles of pricey champagne, tubs of expensive caviar, and wheels of exotic cheeses. I wrinkled my nose. Very smelly cheeses. Several packs of crackers were crowded onto the counter to the right, along with a tray of cold cuts and another one piled high with an elegant arrangement of chocolates, strawberries, and kiwi slices. Looked like Delov had developed a hankering for a late-night snack. I hoped he was enjoying it, because it would be the last meal he ever ate.

Maybe it was wrong, but I didn't feel bad about plotting Delov's death. Not bad at all. I knew exactly what kind of scum he was. The giant sold drugs, which was sleazy enough, but he specialized in getting kids hooked on the stuff. He had a whole network of dealers whose sole job was to push his product to the local middle and high schools. A few weeks ago, a thirteen-year-old girl had died after getting a bad batch of Delov's drugs, and her nine-year-old sister had also gotten sick and almost perished. The girls' parents had somehow reached out to Fletcher, and now here we were, about to get payback for the dead girl, her sick sister, and her grieving parents—permanently.

Fletcher gave me a hand signal. I nodded, understanding that I was to hold my position in the hallway and watch our backs, just in case there was anyone in the mansion who *wasn't supposed to be there. Fletcher palmed one of the silverstone knives he carried for jobs like these, slid into the kitchen, and crept closer to Delov.*

I was so busy studying Fletcher that the faint click-click-click *of toenails on the hardwood floor behind me didn't register for a few precious seconds. When it finally did, I froze for a moment, then slowly turned my head to the side and looked down.*

A fat, fluffy Pomeranian with golden fur sniffed my left boot like it was the most interesting thing in the world.

I bit back a curse. We hadn't seen Peaches while we'd been skulking through the mansion, and I'd thought he must have curled up on another floor and gone to sleep for the night. I liked dogs, really I did, but they'd screwed up more than a few jobs Fletcher had taken me on. Still, I couldn't kill the curious fluffball. Peaches was innocent, even if his owner wasn't. No pets, no kids—ever. That was the code Fletcher had taught me and I was determined to live by it.

I eased down to my knees and held out my hand, hoping that would distract the dog long enough for Fletcher to kill Delov. He was only about fifteen feet away from the giant now and closing fast. Ten more seconds, and he'd be in range. Five . . . four . . . three . . . two . . .

Peaches sniffed my fingers and gave them a tentative lick. And then he started barking—loud, yippy, there's-someone-new-new-new-in-the-house barks.

Oh, no.

Delov immediately whirled around at the sounds. Clutching the butcher's knife he'd been slicing cheese and cold cuts with, he slashed out at Fletcher with it. Fletcher managed to jump out of the way, but Delov came at him with the knife again. Back and forth, the two men fought through the kitchen, knocking over dishes, silverware, and plates of food. I winced at all the noise they made. Good thing the guards were away for the night, or we would have been well and truly screwed. Beside me, Peaches kept barking and barking, but he seemed smart enough to know he would get stepped on and squished if he darted into the kitchen right now.

I got to my feet, ready to charge in and help Fletcher, but there was nothing I could do. Since there was only one entrance to the kitchen, Delov would see me coming, so I couldn't even distract the giant by sneaking up on him from behind.

And then the worst thing of all happened. Delov's fist actually connected with Fletcher's chest.

Fletcher cursed and stumbled back. Delov surged forward, looking to press his advantage, but the old man grabbed a copper pot from a rack above his head and smashed it into Delov's face. The giant growled in pain. He staggered and slipped on some of the broken dishes that littered the floor, going down on one knee.

But instead of regaining his feet, Delov fumbled with one of the cabinet doors below the sink, yanked it open, and reached inside. A second later, the glint of a gun appeared in his hand.

"Run!" Fletcher yelled at me. "Run!"

The old man had taught me to obey his orders no matter what when we were out on a job, so he didn't have to tell me twice. I turned and ran, with him right behind me.

Crack! Crack! Crack!

Bullets chased us down the hallway, and the acrid stench of gunpowder burned through the air, overpowering the moldy cheeses. Fletcher and I darted into a sitting room, *raced through it and out into another hallway on the far side. We zigzagged through the third floor of the mansion, never taking the obvious, straight route but moving toward our escape point all the while.*

Delov must have stopped to reload or maybe grab another gun from somewhere, because we quickly outran him, and I didn't hear any sounds coming from behind us. But just before we got to the balcony and the stairs that would serve as our exit, Fletcher put a hand on my shoulder.

"Stop, Gin," he mumbled behind me. "Or at least slow down."

Slow down? We couldn't afford to slow down, not while we were still in the mansion. Delov having a gun was bad enough, but if the giant caught us, he could always beat us to death with his fists. They were almost as big as the wheels of cheese he'd been cutting into.

Still, it was an order from Fletcher, so I stopped and turned around—and that's when I realized he was bleeding. An ugly bullet hole had ruined his blue work shirt, close to where his left lung would be.

I gasped. "You're hurt!"

Fletcher tried to smile, but his green eyes crinkled with pain. "Looks that way."

For the first time, I heard the hoarse, raspy wheeze in his voice. It sounded like the bullet had done something to his lung, maybe even punctured or collapsed it, which meant I needed to get him to Jo-Jo—right now.

"Come on," I whispered, putting my arm under his shoulder and preparing myself to drag him the rest of the way out of the house, across the grounds, and into the woods. "I'm getting you out of here."

Fletcher shook his head. "No. Not before the job's done. We have to get Delov tonight. This is our best chance—our only chance. All of his guards are gone. It's just him and us. We have to end him now."

"But you're hurt," I pointed out. "And he has a gun. Maybe more than one by now. You always told me that it was okay to walk away from a botched job. And we both know that I messed this one up."

Fletcher shook his head again. "A dog barked. It happens, Gin, even to the best of us."

He bent over and started coughing. He put his hand to his mouth, but I still saw the blood trickle out between his fingers.

"Here, at least sit down," I said, helping him over to a nearby chair. "Rest for a few seconds, and then we'll get out of here."

"No," Fletcher said, his mouth settling into a thin, stubborn line. "I made a promise to the Kilroy family, and I intend to keep it. Besides, I'll be easy pickings for Delov now. We both know how fond he is of taking care of his dirty work himself."

In addition to his love of gourmet food, Delov also fancied himself something of a hunter, and more than one poor animal's head decorated the walls of his mansion. He even had a poaching trip planned for his time in the Keys. So I had no doubt that Delov would relish the challenge of tracking us down.

Fletcher couldn't kill the giant. Not now, not with that injury.

But I could.

"Give me your knife," I whispered.

He stared at me in surprise. "You don't have to do this, Gin. I can finish it. I can—"

Another coughing fit cut off his words, and more blood dribbled down the sides of his fingers, even though he tried to hide it from me.

Fletcher looked at me, his green eyes searching mine. "Can you do it, Gin? Are you ready for this?"

I stared at the knife still clutched in his hand. The silverstone gleamed like a sharp star in the semidarkness. I'd killed people before. Buried men in the falling stones of my childhood home. Stabbed a giant to death inside the Pork Pit. And I'd watched Fletcher kill a dozen more.

But this—this was different. Before, I'd lashed out at the others in the heat of the moment. Because they'd threatened me, hurt me, and I'd just been defending myself. But tonight I'd come here knowing that Delov would die. I just hadn't thought that I'd be the one to do it.

It was one thing to watch—it was another to twist the knife in coldly myself.

Maybe—maybe I wasn't as ready to be an assassin as I thought I was.

But there was nothing to be done about that paralyzing thought. No changing it, no fixing it, no time to think about it. Because it was him or us now, and I'd pick us every single time, no matter what it cost me in the end.

I hesitated a moment longer, then took the weapon from Fletcher. "I can do it."

"I know you can," he whispered back.

"Come on," I said, helping him to his feet. "I'll help you find someplace to hide. Then I'll go look for Delov."

Fletcher nodded, in too much pain to do anything else.

I put my arm under his shoulder again and led him deeper into the house, back toward Delov, ready to do what needed to be done . . .

My eyes fluttered open, and it took me a few seconds to remember where I was. That I was safe in bed in Fletcher's house and not being stalked by a giant with a gun and a grudge. I let out a breath, trying to calm my racing heart and banish the rest of the memories. Slowly, far too slowly, they finally faded away.

I didn't know what had triggered this specific memory of Fletcher and Delov. It certainly wasn't the worst one I had. In fact, it was pretty mild compared with some of the other things I'd seen, done, and been through over the years. But something about that night felt particularly important—and ominous, almost like it was a warning of things to come.

I wasn't an Air elemental, so I never got any glimpses of the future, not like Jo-Jo did. But I couldn't help but think that something was stirring all the same. Something dark, something dangerous, something that might finally be the death of me.

But then again, this was just a dream, just one of many terrible memories I'd collected over the years, and no doubt more were on the way.

"Paranoid much, Gin?" I said.

Of course, no one answered back. The house was empty. All the whispers of the stones told me so, but for once, the soft, familiar sounds didn't soothe me. I lay there and closed my eyes, but it was a long, long time before I was able to sleep once more.

* 3 *

Two nights later, Finn pulled his Aston Martin up to the back of a long line of cars.

"See?" he said. "This isn't so bad, is it? I've got a new car, you've got a new dress, and we're going to have a fabulous time lusting after all of Mab's loot. What could be better than that?"

"Oh, I don't know," I replied. "Sitting at home having a nice, quiet evening. Reading a book. Making some sort of sinfully rich and decadent dessert."

"Spoilsport," Finn huffed.

I sighed and crossed my arms over my chest. Despite the fact that I hadn't really wanted to come, I still found myself peering out the window. Curiosity. It was one emotion that always seemed to get the best of me, even tonight.

The exhibit of *Mab's loot*, as Finn had so eloquently dubbed it, was being held at Briartop, Ashland's largest, fanciest, and most highfalutin art museum, located in the uppity confines of Northtown. But what really made Briartop unique was its placement on a large island in the middle of the Aneirin River.

The island, also called Briartop, was like a miniature version of one of the Appalachian Mountains that ran around and through the city. The museum itself was perched on a wide plateau at the very top of the island. A series of stone walkways led out from each one of the three wings into the lush gardens and immaculate lawns that flanked the main building. The paths spiraled down the rocky hillsides before the landscape gave way to dense woods choked with briars and brambles. Back before the museum had been built, blackberry and other briars had covered the entire island in a thicket of thorns. Hence the name. Even now, the museum gardeners waged a constant battle to keep the briars from creeping up and overtaking the colorful flowerbeds and intricate copses of trees they'd worked so hard to cultivate over the years.

An old-fashioned, whitewashed, covered wooden bridge spanned the Aneirin River and led over to the island. The bridge was the only way to get to the museum, although it was only wide enough for cars to cross in single file, which is why Finn was waiting in line, along with a dozen limos and several luxury town cars.

Finally, it was our turn to cross. Finn's Aston Martin rattled over the heavy boards, then he steered the car up the winding road and pulled into one of the parking lots. We got out of the vehicle. Finn gallantly offered me his arm, and we headed toward the entrance.

Bria had been wondering where all the giant guards in Ashland had gone. Well, tonight they were at Briartop.

Giants were stationed at both ends of the covered bridge, communicating by walkie-talkies about when to let the next car cross. Others moved in and out of the parking lots, directing traffic, while several more milled around the museum's main entrance, checking invitations and enforcing the guest list.

I counted at least twenty giants before we even got close to the front door. Odd. Perhaps the Briartop board had hired extra security for the gala.

Finn and I waited our turn in the line that had formed by the entrance. I stared up at the museum while he fished his engraved invitation out of his jacket.

Briartop was a veritable castle, southern-style. The structure soared five stories into the air and boasted a series of fat, round, domed towers, each one topped with a gleaming weather vane. The gray marble shimmered like a silver star in the warm rays of the setting sun even as the sloping eaves of the coal-black slate roof melted into the gathering shadows. Four massive columns framed the main entrance, while thick crenellated balconies fronted all of the tall, narrow windows. Stone planters decorated each one of the balconies, the lush pink, purple, and white rhododendrons inside providing vivid splashes of color against the marble, almost like paint streaking across a clean canvas.

As if the structure itself wasn't impressive enough, a large fountain bubbled on the smooth front lawn, its jets of water arching through the air like streams of liquid diamonds. The constant churn of the water shrouded the area in a fine mist and spritzed the honeysuckle curling around and through a series of freestanding, whitewashed trellises that flanked the fountain. The rich, heady aroma of honeysuckle saturated the night air, carried along by a soft summer breeze.

The fountain, vines, and trellises made for a beautiful sight, but I looked away from them. I didn't much care for fountains. Not anymore. Not after Salina had used them and her water magic to murder people at her deadly dinner party—and tried to drown me in one.

Instead, I reached out with my magic and listened to the murmurs of the museum itself.

Actions, emotions, plots and schemes and hopes and dreams. People leave behind bits and pieces of themselves in the spots they frequent, in all of the buildings, offices, and houses where they spend their lives. All of those actions, feelings, and emotions—good, bad, and indifferent—sink especially well into stone. As a Stone elemental, I can sense and interpret all of those hidden vibrations as easily as if one of the museum tour guides were telling me all of the juicy gossip about every scandalous thing that had ever happened in and around the building. Tonight Briartop's silvery marble muttered with worry, mixed with sharp notes of tension and sly whispers of unease.

Curious—and troubling.

I'd been to Briartop many times before, both as the Spider trailing a target and as regular Gin Blanco. I'd even come here once or twice for some of the art classes I'd taken at Ashland Community College through the years. Every time I'd been here before, the marble had proudly murmured of the artistic beauty and treasures it housed, punctuated by light, trilling notes of vain pretentiousness and smug snobbery—nothing more.

But tonight the constant, worried mutters told me that someone here was up to something—probably more than one person, given all the tense murmurs and sharp, ringing *ping*s of unease.

Oh, the crowd looked innocent enough. Men and women dressed in fitted tuxedos and elegant evening gowns, expensive jewels and heavy watches flashing on their necks and wrists. But the stones never lied. They echoed the actions, emotions, and intentions of the people around them—nothing more, nothing less.

Once again, that vague, uneasy feeling I'd had ever since my dream a few nights ago crept back up to the surface of my mind. This time, I didn't try to push it away or ignore it. I'd stayed alive this long by being paranoid, and something just wasn't right here.

Finn and I stepped up to the giant working the door. She was dressed in a sleek black pantsuit that showed off her strong, toned curves, and I saw more than one person admiring her tall, lithe figure. Her auburn hair was pulled back into a sleek French braid, but the simple style only enhanced her hazel eyes and great cheekbones. A small gold nametag on her jacket read *Opal*.

Opal seemed to be one of the folks in charge, judging from the way the other giants deferred to her and how they raced up to whisper questions in her ear and draw her attention in this or that direction. Finally, she managed to look at Finn's invitation, hand it back to him, and check him off the guest list. She glanced at me, ready to mark me off as his plus-one, and froze.

Opal's eyes widened, her breath puffed out of her mouth, and her body completely stilled. While it only took her a second to recover, blink away her surprise, and plaster a bland smile on her face, her reaction ratcheted up my unease.

"Please proceed into the main exhibit area," she said in a low, smooth voice. "Everything's been set up in there."

"Thank you, Opal," Finn replied, and gave her one of his patented charming smiles.

She tipped her head at him and gave me a polite nod, although her sharp gaze lingered on my face a few seconds longer than it should have.

Finn pouted a little when he realized that he didn't have her full attention and that she wasn't going to fawn all over him like most women did, but he tucked his invitation back into his tuxedo jacket. I took his arm again, and we headed toward the entrance. All the while, though, I was aware of the giant at my back. I didn't like having people behind me, and my palms began to burn with the desire to reach for one of my knives, put it up against her throat, and demand to know what she was staring at.

Instead, I turned and smiled at Finn, as though he had said something amusing, allowing my eyes to slide past him to Opal.

"She's watching me," I murmured. "There's a line of people in front of her waiting to get inside, and she's watching me walk away instead of dealing with them."

Finn shrugged. "Maybe she likes women instead of men. You do look rather fetching tonight. Or maybe she recognized you as the mighty Spider. Infamy, thy name is Gin Blanco."

I grimaced at his flippant tone, but he had a point.

Opal wouldn't be the first person to freeze up upon realizing who I was. So I put her out of my mind and looked ahead once more.

Still, I couldn't quite ignore the itching sensation between my shoulders—like someone was going to bury a knife in my back before the night was through.

Finn and I walked up the shallow steps and entered the museum. High, vaulted ceilings, crystal vases full of roses, lilies, and other greenery perched here and there, stone planters bristling with bonsai trees tucked into the corners, slick marble floors and walls: Briartop was just as opulent inside as it was on the outside. Everywhere you turned there was another piece of art to look at, whether it was a series of soft, floral watercolors, a silver etching of a waterfall tumbling over a rocky ridge, or a woodcut of a bear ambling through a field of wildflowers.

We reached the main exhibit area and stood to one side of the entrance, scanning the scene. The enormous room was actually a rotunda topped by a high, domed ceiling inlaid with a starlike mosaic pattern made out of bright blue stained glass. The same pattern could be found on the floor directly below in alternating shades of gray, white, and blue marble. Small white lights had been wrapped around the columns ringing the round room, and the glowing strands stretched from the ground floor all the way up to the second-level balcony. Still more spotlights rose from the floor, dropped from the ceiling, or jutted from the walls, angled to highlight certain displays.

Finn had been right when he'd said that the exhibit

of Mab's loot would be the social event of the summer. I spotted several well-known, legitimate businessmen and businesswomen wading their way through the crowd, along with all of the big movers and shakers in the Ashland underworld. Folks like Beauregard Benson, Ron Donaldson, Lorelei Parker . . .

And Jonah McAllister.

McAllister had been Mab Monroe's lawyer for years, and his star hadn't fallen so much as been snuffed out completely since I'd killed the Fire elemental. Without Mab, Jonah was just another smarmy lawyer, desperately searching for a new crime boss to serve before he was chewed up and spit out by the rest of the underworld sharks. McAllister and I had plenty of history—and reasons to hate each other. I'd killed his son, Jake, last year for trying to rob the Pork Pit and then threatening me. For his part, the lawyer had tried to have me murdered more than once.

I eyed McAllister. Like all the other men, he was dressed in a tuxedo, although his was more impeccable than most, and his wing tips were as shiny as ink. His silvery mane of hair gleamed underneath the lights, and his face was smooth and unlined, despite his sixty-some years. Jonah kept his boyish complexion intact with the help of a strict regimen of Air elemental facials. A plastic doll would show more emotion than his tight, sand-blasted features.

"What's he doing here?" I asked Finn, jerking my head in the lawyer's direction.

"McAllister? He's one of the executors of Mab's estate, along with the museum director, and helped put the exhibit together," he replied. "The show was in the works even before Mab died. According to the rumors I've heard, Mab stipulated that her entire art collection be put on display here for at least one year before the museum can take ownership of it and do whatever they want to with it."

"That's sort of strange, don't you think?"

He shrugged. "It just sounds like Mab to me. She probably thought that if she put her collection on view, they'd rename the museum after her. Or one of the wings, at the very least. Although I doubt she realized just how soon she'd be requesting that honor."

I grinned. "I was more than happy to help her with that."

"I know you were." Finn returned my evil grin. "Either way, I still want to know what's going to happen to the rest of her estate. Mab had to leave all of her stuff to *somebody*, didn't she?"

It was a conversation we'd had more than once since Mab's death—wondering what was going to become of all of her earthly possessions. Oh, most of her business interests—especially the illegal ones—had already been snapped up by the other crime bosses. But her North-town mansion was just sitting there, with all of her things still inside it. I was mildly surprised that no one had gotten it into his or her head to loot the mansion yet, but I supposed the specter of Mab still loomed too large for that.

Mab didn't have any family that I was aware of, but that didn't mean much. For all I knew, there might be a cousin or two lurking around somewhere, maybe even another, closer relative. But so far, Finn hadn't been able to find out anything about what was going to become of her things.

"But we might not have to wait too much longer to learn who Mab left what to," Finn continued. "Rumor has it that the museum director is going to read a statement that Mab had written about the exhibit—along with her will."

"That's strange too, isn't it?" I asked. "Shouldn't McAllister have done whatever he needed to do with Mab's will by now? Why would she arrange it so the contents were announced here?"

He shrugged. "Maybe so she could have one last hurrah, even if she's not around to actually enjoy it."

"Or maybe she didn't fully trust McAllister to see that her wishes were carried out."

"Would you?"

"Good point."

"But enough about all that," Finn said, straightening his bow tie just a bit. "We're at a party, the night is young, and I look fabulous." He paused a moment. "And so do you."

"Good to know where I stand in your list of priorities. Although I don't know if *fabulous* is the word I would use," I muttered, and crossed my arms over my chest. "I told you that I at least wanted something with sleeves."

"And I told you that sometimes you just have to suffer for fashion."

I gave him a sour look, which he totally ignored.

Still, I had to admit he was right. I had cleaned up pretty well tonight, thanks to the dress Finn had picked out. The scarlet gown had a tight fitted top that emphasized the smooth skin of my arms and shoulders, while the front of the bodice swooped down to show off what assets I had there. Scarlet teardrop-shaped crystals decorated the seams that cinched in around my waist, adding some sparkle to the gown, before the fabric fell away into a long, flowing skirt, also dotted here and there with crystals. As I walked, the skirt swirled out around me, the slits in it showing teasing flashes of my legs. Finn had even insisted on my buying shoes the same color to match, although I'd held my ground and had picked a pair with a relatively low, two-inch heel instead of the sky-high pumps he'd tried to browbeat me into getting.

The gown was beautiful—certainly more beautiful than I was—but I couldn't help but feel exposed it in. The top left my arms bare, which meant that I couldn't carry knives up my sleeves like I usually did. Still, I hadn't come to the museum completely weaponless: two blades were strapped to my thighs underneath the long skirt, just in case. I would have preferred to be carrying my full five-point arsenal, so to speak, but two knives were usually enough to get the job done, especially when I was the one wielding them.

Still, I couldn't help but listen to the tense, worried mutters of the stone around me—mutters that had only gotten louder and sharper since we'd entered the rotunda.

And it wasn't just the stone's whispers that made me wary. There were increasingly more giants inside the museum than there had been outside, until it seemed like they were everywhere I turned in the rotunda. Most of the giants were dressed as waiters, but really, they were just glorified guards in black bow ties. They'd be ready to deal quickly, brutally, and efficiently with any problems that might arise. In fact, there were more giant waiters in the room than there were personal bodyguards. I supposed that some of the movers and shakers thought they'd be safe enough at such a public event and had left their muscle at home for the night.

Even so, the giants didn't bother me as much as the stares, snubs, and whispers. Opal wasn't the only person who recognized me, and more than one person turned in my direction to gawk. Apparently, an assassin attending such a high-society event was something of a shock. Please. I'd snuck into my share of their fancy parties over the years to get close to a target—and more than one person had died before the last bit of bubbly was drunk. Or perhaps they thought it was gauche of me to show my face at an event commemorating the woman I'd killed. As if they all hadn't wanted Mab dead for years.

Most folks limited themselves to whispering about me or turning their backs to me, but a few of the underworld figures had more interesting reactions. Ron Donaldson openly pouted at the fact that I was still breathing. I'd killed three of his men last month when they'd ambushed me outside the Pork Pit. Lorelei Parker was another petulant pouter. She'd sent two of her men after me just last week, and I had Sophia send them back to her in pieces.

Oh, yes. Tension rippled through the crowd with every move I made. But even beyond that, a nervous edge crackled in the air. I couldn't quite put my finger on the source of it, but I felt it all the same, buzzing around like lightning getting ready to streak down from the sky and fry someone to a crisp—me, most likely.

"Well, I think you look fabulous," Finn repeated. "Now, what do you say we get some champagne and have a look at Mab's loot?"

I snorted. "You're just trying to butter me up so you can get your way."

"Is it working?"

I sighed. "Doesn't it always?"

Finn grinned at me.

So I shut the stones' murmurs out of my mind and ignored the folks whispering about me, determined at least to try to have a good time.

We grabbed some champagne and spent the next few minutes wandering around the rotunda. Actually, Finn dragged me from one group of people to the next, cozying up to all of his clients, saying hello to everyone he knew, and introducing himself to the few folks who hadn't yet had the supreme pleasure of his acquaintance.

Finnegan Lane was one of the best investment bankers in Ashland, and he'd made a lot of people in this room a lot of money. We wouldn't take more than three steps before Finn would wave at someone he knew or a woman would sidle up and plant a coy, perfumed kiss on his cheek. Finally, after the fifth time that happened, I motioned at Finn that I was going on without him. He absently waved his hand at me and turned back to his apparently riveting conversation about tax shelters with a wizened dwarf wearing a dozen ropes of black pearls.

While Finn held court, I moved off into the crowd. I wandered from one display to the next, ignoring the awed whispers about my being the Spider and disappointed mutters about why I wasn't dead yet. Instead, I concentrated on all of the things Mab had collected over the years. Most of the items were exactly what I'd expected: pricey paintings, large sculptures, small, detailed carvings, even a few silk wall tapestries. Nothing too exciting or interesting. In fact, I was rather disappointed by the whole thing. Given how cruel and vicious Mab had been, I'd expected there to be *something* noteworthy on display, maybe a gun she'd used to kneecap someone, a knife she'd chopped off an enemy's fingers with, a bit of rope she'd wrapped around someone's throat and choked them into compliance with.

But I should have known that Mab wouldn't have had anything like that. She'd preferred using her Fire magic to hurt, torture, burn, and kill people. She hadn't needed anything else. No props, no weapons, no help from her giant guards. Just the mention of her name had been enough to inspire abject terror—and rightly so.

"What, exactly, are *you* doing here?" a low voice snapped.

I turned to find Jonah McAllister standing behind me, his fingers clenched around a champagne glass and his mouth pinched down with as much surprise and displeasure as his tight features would allow him to show.

"Why, hello, Jonah," I drawled. "Lovely to see you again too."

His cold brown eyes flicked up and down my body, carefully studying my gown as if he expected to find bloodstains on the expensive fabric. Maybe later. Like Finn had said, the night was still young.

"I told the guards to keep the riffraff out, but apparently, they didn't understand the meaning of the word," he said in a haughty, condescending tone.

I laughed in his face. McAllister had called me trash—and worse—on more than one occasion, but his insults didn't bother me in the slightest. In fact, I idly considered reaching out, grabbing the lawyer's lapels, and dragging him back into a dark corner so I could stab him to death with one of my knives. But alas, there were too many people, too many cameras, and too many giant guards posing as waiters in here for me to get away with murdering McAllister.

Still, the lawyer's days were numbered. I'd make sure of that.

An angry, mottled flush stained McAllister's cheeks at my light, happy, mocking laughter, and I could almost see the wheels furiously spinning in his mind as he thought about how he could get the better of me. He took another long, careful look at me, intently eyeing me from head to toe, then pivoted on his heel and strode away. I watched him for a few moments, but instead of going over to a couple of the giants and demanding that they escort me out, he pulled his cell phone out of his pants pocket and started texting on it. Maybe he was sending his demands to someone higher up the museum food chain than the guards.

Strange, even for McAllister. Usually, he had some sort of devious plan in mind when it came to me, one that involved my untimely demise. It wasn't like him just to walk away after merely one insult. I'd have to keep an eye on him—

"A fresh glass of champagne, ma'am?"

A silver tray appeared at my elbow, and I stared up at the person holding it, a giant about seven and a half feet tall. She looked to be in her mid-fifties, judging from the wrinkles fanning out from the corners of her eyes, the deep laugh lines grooving in and around her mouth, and the long crease slashing across her forehead.

She wore the same starched white shirt and matching black tuxedo vest, bow tie, and pants that all of the other waiters did, but her features were quite striking. Her shoulder-length auburn hair was a mass of tight, wild curls, while her hazel eyes were just a shade darker than her tan skin. Her understated makeup highlighted her full mouth, sharp nose, and high cheekbones, and even the waiter uniform couldn't disguise her generous breasts or how long her legs were. Put a gown on her, and she'd turn her fair share of heads in the room.

She also seemed vaguely familiar to me, like I'd seen her before, although I couldn't quite place when or where. I'd probably noticed her at some other event, serving as a waiter or maybe even as a bodyguard to one of the underworld bosses. As the Spider, I'd met a lot of giants in my time. Well, *killed* was more like it.

"Ma'am?" she repeated, moving the tray closer to my elbow. "More champagne?"

"No, thank you," I said, putting my still-full glass on her tray. "I seem to have lost my thirst for it."

"Men will do that to you, won't they?" she agreed.

Her voice was pure country twang, although the hard, knowing smile on her face told me that she was much smarter than the aw-shucks demeanor she radiated.

Before I could tell her that Jonah McAllister was in no way my sort of man, she moved on to the next person. I shook my head. First, the woman working the door had frozen up at my appearance, and now a waiter was giving me tips on my supposed love life with the smarmy lawyer. The night just kept getting weirder and weirder.

I'd just started to wade back into the crowd in search of Finn when a sly wink of silverstone caught my eye, and I noticed one more display tucked away in a recess in the back wall of the rotunda. Curious, I wandered over and finally found something noteworthy after all.

Two silverstone rune pendants lay on a bed of blue velvet behind a sheet of glass. One pendant was shaped like a snowflake, the symbol for icy calm. The other was a curling ivy vine, representing elegance.

I knew the symbols, knew exactly what they meant.

I'd once had a pendant just like them, one shaped like a small circle surrounded by eight thin rays. A spider rune, the symbol for patience.

The symbol that was branded into my palms to this day.

My hands balled into fists, my nails digging into the spider rune scars there.

Mab had put the marks there the night she'd tortured me, using her Fire magic to melt my silverstone pendant into my palms. It had been one of the most excruciating things I'd ever endured, but it was nothing compared with the utter shock I was feeling right now.

Because the snowflake was my mother Eira's rune. And the ivy vine had belonged to my older sister, Annabella.

❖ 4 ❖

I leaned forward, until my nose was almost pressed against the glass, and studied every single millimeter of the runes. The pendants weren't polished to a high gloss like everything else on view was. Rather, the chains they hung on were blackened, and what looked like streaks of soot and bits of ash clung to the surface of the silverstone runes, as though they'd once been in a fire and had never been properly cleaned.

They'd been in fire, all right—Mab's murderous elemental blaze.

Mab . . . Mab must have taken my mother and my sister's rune necklaces after she'd killed them that horrible night. I'd thought that the pendants had been buried in the rubble after I'd used my Ice and Stone magic to collapse the mansion on top of us all; or perhaps they had been pilfered by looters later on. But somehow Mab had gotten her grubby, greedy hands on them. She'd had the runes all these years, and now here they were, on display for everyone in Ashland to see, like a—like a damn *trophy* celebrating my family's murder.

I'd thought by killing Mab that I was finally free of her, that I was finally *done* with her, and that she couldn't shock, surprise, or hurt me anymore. I'd even gone to her funeral and said my piece to her ebony casket. But once again, the Fire elemental had managed to reach out from beyond the grave and mess with me.

Shock, anger, rage, hate. Those emotions surged through my body, matching the sudden, rapid, painful thump of my heart. For a moment, I considered using my magic to harden my fist so I could punch right through the thick glass. It would feel good, so fucking *good,* to smash the glass and grab the runes. Because they were *mine*—mine and Bria's—and I'd be damned if Mab or the museum was keeping them.

But I forced myself to slow my ragged breathing and calm my racing heart. No, I couldn't do that. There were too many security cameras in here for me to get away with such a crude smash-and-grab job. The guards would swarm me en masse, and I'd end up like the dwarf at the Posh boutique—bloody, beaten, handcuffed, and escorted off the premises by the esteemed members of the po-po.

No, this would require a different approach—a nice, quiet, after-hours visit to the museum. I wasn't leaving these last few precious pieces of my family behind.

I turned around to find Finn and tell him about the runes—and came face-to-face with Owen Grayson.

* * *

My breath caught in my throat.

Perhaps absence really did make the heart grow fonder, because I couldn't stop staring at my former lover. Black hair, intense violet eyes, a slightly crooked nose, a faint scar on his chin. I drank in the sight of his rugged features before my eyes traced over his broad shoulders and then down his muscled chest. The tuxedo he wore only made him look even more handsome and perfectly outlined the raw strength of his body.

Owen's eyes widened, and he almost lost his grip on his champagne flute before he clenched his fingers around it once more. He seemed as surprised to see me as I was to see him.

"Hi," he finally said in a soft, cautious voice.

"Hi yourself."

We stood there staring at each other for what seemed like forever, although I was ticking off the seconds in my head the way I always did. Ten . . . twenty . . . thirty . . .

Finally, at the forty-five-second mark, Owen cleared his throat. "I didn't expect to see you here tonight."

"Finn dragged me along. He said he wanted to come see all of Mab's treasures, but really, I think he just wanted to socialize with his clients. He's here somewhere, schmoozing the night away."

Owen smiled a little at that, and we fell silent again. The other guests swirled around us like dancers, talking, laughing, and drinking champagne, but the trill of their voices and the *clink-clink-clink* of glasses seemed distant and far away. All I was aware of was Owen. The way the soft white lights brought out the sheen of blue in his dark hair. The faint laugh lines at the corners of his eyes. The warmth of his body reaching out toward my own. Even his rich scent, the one that always made me think of metal. I noticed all that and more—so much more.

We hadn't spoken since that day at the Pork Pit when we'd agreed to take a break, and there were so many things I wanted to say to him, so many things I wanted to tell him. It wasn't only our romance we'd put on hold, but our friendship too. I loved Owen, but I also loved just talking to him—telling him about my day, hearing about his, sharing a laugh or a joke or a funny story one of us had heard. I'd lost not only my lover but also one of my best friends and confidants. I missed him, terribly.

"So . . . how have you been?" he asked. "Because you look—you look *amazing*."

His gaze trailed down my scarlet dress, and a bit of heat flashed in his eyes. I was suddenly very glad that Finn had dragged me out shopping and made me come here tonight.

"Thank you," I said. "You look good too. Better than good, actually. It's nice just to . . . see you."

Another smile flickered across his face, this one a little brighter. "Well, it's good to be seen, especially by you."

We fell silent once more, still staring at each other, both of us wondering what to say, wondering how to break through the polite chitchat and talk about the things that really mattered, the problems we had, and where we went from here—

"Owen!" a voice called out. "There you are!"

A woman emerged from the crowd and strode over to us. She shot Owen a dazzling smile, then smoothly threaded her arm through his like it was something she'd done a dozen times before. My heart clenched at the sight, but I forced myself to stay calm and study her. She wasn't as beautiful as some of the other women here tonight, but she knew how to play up her features. Smoke-black shadow rimmed her eyes, making them seem darker and larger than they really were, while the soft waves of her dark brown hair just tickled her shoulders, drawing attention to her toned arms and back.

"I thought I'd lost you. I've been looking everywhere for you." She smiled up at him again, then turned toward me. "Who are you talking to? You'll have to introduce me—"

Her words died on her red lips, and she did a double take, her eyes widening with surprise. It took me a second to realize that she wasn't reacting to how close I was standing to Owen or the tension simmering between us. Oh, no. There was a far more serious reason for her horrified expression.

I had on the exact same dress she did.

Fitted top, cinched waist, flowing skirt. Her scarlet gown was identical to mine, right down to the teardrop-shaped crystals that sparked and flashed beneath the white lights. My gaze dropped to her feet, which were peeking out from beneath the edge of her skirt. She even had on the same color shoes as I did, although she'd gone all out and opted for the four-inch stilettos.

"Owen?" the woman asked.

"Sorry," he said, finally glancing away from me. "I got . . . distracted and lost sight of you. I've been looking for you too."

Oh. So that's why he'd been behind me. Some small

part of me had thought—no, hoped—that Owen had seen me from across the room and had come over to me on his own. But he'd really been searching for another woman the whole time, and the dress had only fooled him. Well, that and the fact that the mystery woman and I were roughly the same height. I supposed we even looked a little alike from the back, since we both were wearing our dark hair down loose around our shoulders. A simple mistake, but it still made bitterness burn in my throat all the same.

She kept staring at me, and I at her, both of us sizing each other up the way women so often do.

Owen cleared his throat and made the introductions. "Gin, this is Jillian Delancey, a business associate of mine from Atlanta. Jillian, this is Gin Blanco—"

"An old friend," I interrupted him, and held out my hand to her.

I wasn't sure what Owen had been about to say about me, whether I was merely a friend or an ex or something else entirely, but I didn't want to find out. Not like this, anyway.

Still, the irony of the situation cut me like one of my own knives. The last time Owen had introduced me to a woman, it had been Salina, whom I'd had to kill. At the time, he'd failed to mention that she was his ex-fiancée. I wondered what sort of relationship he had with Jillian— if they'd been lovers in the past or if this was new.

Because it was obvious she wanted to start up something with him. I could tell by the way her hand tightened on his arm as she stepped even closer to him. Plus, the shoes were a dead giveaway. Women didn't wear heels like that because they were comfortable. They wore them because of the way they made their legs look long and lean—and made men salivate over them.

Was Owen—could he be—were they out on a *date*?

My stomach twisted at the thought of Owen with someone else. That he might have already moved on without even telling me. That our relationship might be well and truly dead. The idea hurt so much that I couldn't even *breathe* for a second.

But the shock of the moment passed, and the jagged, broken pieces of my heart kept right on beating just like they always did, even if every steady *thump-thump-thump* brought a fresh wave of pain along with it.

Despite my treacherous, unwanted, seesawing emotions, I decided to be gracious about things. Acting the bitch wouldn't help matters. Besides, Jo-Jo had taught me better manners than that.

Gin Blanco. The Spider. Notorious assassin. Polite to a fault.

"Love your dress," I joked.

Jillian smoothed down the fabric of her skirt. "Oh, yeah. Yours too."

We both laughed, but my voice sounded hard and brittle—just like my heart.

The three of us stood there, shifting on our feet, not sure what to say to each other to break the silence that was growing more strained and awkward by the second. I glanced around the rotunda, hoping Finn was nearby so I could excuse myself more easily. It took me several seconds, but I finally spotted my foster brother—and he wasn't alone.

Three other people stood with him. One was a tall, strong-looking man with blond hair that was slicked back into a ponytail. The other two were women, one young, only twenty, with dark hair and blue eyes, the other older but even more beautiful, with black hair and toffee-colored eyes and skin. Phillip Kincaid, Eva Grayson, and Roslyn Phillips. Familiar faces, since Phillip was Owen's best friend, Eva was his younger sister, and Roslyn was another member of my extended family.

Owen noticed me looking past him and turned to see what I was so interested in.

"Eva's here with me and Jillian," he explained, facing me once more. "We all rode over together with Phillip and Roslyn."

I nodded. Finn had told me that Roslyn was coming to the exhibit with someone else, since Xavier, her significant other, had to work tonight along with Bria. I just hadn't thought that someone else would be Phillip. Then again, Roslyn owned Northern Aggression, the city's most decadent nightclub. She knew everyone who was anyone in Ashland, including all of the underworld players like Kincaid.

Finn must have felt me staring at him, because he glanced in my direction. He started to look away but stopped and did a double take just as Jillian had. He stared at her a moment, then at me, his eyes flicking back and forth between our identical dresses.

Owen hesitated. "Actually, the reason Eva, Phillip, Jillian, and I are all here is that Finn gave me several extra tickets for the gala. He said that someone had given a bunch of them to him at his bank and he didn't want us to miss out on the exhibit. He also said to think of it as part of his apology to me for everything that . . . happened between us."

That *everything* had included Finn holding a gun on Owen while I cut Salina's throat. Needless to say, Owen had been plenty pissed about that, mostly at me, for asking Finn to do such a thing in the first place. Still, it didn't surprise me that he'd talked to my foster brother and had taken the tickets from him. Finnegan Lane could be exceptionally persuasive when he put his mind to it. Besides, what had happened that night had been my doing, no one else's. The responsibility, the burden of that, was mine to bear, and so was the guilt.

"Did he, now?" I murmured. "How considerate of him."

Finn had been so insistent that I come to the exhibit that I hadn't thought too much about exactly why he wanted me here in the first place. Oh, sure, he'd said that Bria was busy and that he wanted to get me out of the house and have some fun, but I was beginning to think he'd had an ulterior motive in mind. Getting me and Owen into the same space was exactly the sort of sneaky, underhanded thing Finn would do and then claim it was for my own good. I loved my foster brother, truly I did, but sometimes his cheerful meddling made me want to wring his neck.

This was one of those times.

"Well," I said, giving Owen and Jillian a bright smile. "Please excuse me. I really need to go see what Finn is up to. Jillian, it was nice to meet you."

"You too," she replied.

I looked at my lover, careful to keep my face blank. "Owen."

"Gin."

I nodded at him, and he returned the gesture.

And that was that. Nothing else was said, nothing else was done, and nothing had changed between us. I wondered if this was the extent of my relationship with Owen now—cool, distant, polite, impersonal. I wondered if this was all we would ever be now.

My heart clenched at the thought, but I forced myself to smile at the two of them a final time. My teeth ground together and my cheeks ached from the strain, but I managed to keep the expression fixed on my face until I stepped past them. Then I walked away, leaving them to their date.

I strode through the crowd, the sharp *snap-snap-snap* of my heels against the floor as loud as a series of firecrackers exploding, my wintry gray glare fixed on one man— Finnegan fucking Lane.

He saw me coming and edged behind Eva. Please. As if that would save him. Still, I stopped when I reached the group and addressed everyone in turn.

"Roslyn, you're looking as lovely as ever. You too, Eva. Phillip, nice to see you."

The three of them murmured polite greetings to me. I looked past Eva and stared at Finn, who was still keeping the younger woman between the two of us.

"Why, Finn," I drawled in a voice that was as sugary-sweet as the summer sun tea I made on Fletcher's front porch. "I didn't realize you'd asked some of our friends to come here tonight too. You are just *full* of surprises."

Finn eyed me over Eva's slender shoulder. "So," he replied in a voice that was just as easy and unconcerned as mine, "are you planning on killing me right here in the middle of the rotunda?"

I gave him a cool, murderous smile. "Sorry to disappoint, but I rather like the rotunda just the way it is, without your blood decorating the walls. It would be a shame to dirty up all this pretty gray marble, don't you think?"

"Absolutely," he agreed. "Personally, I like my blood right where it is, inside my body."

"Besides, it would be *so* much easier to stab you to death in the parking lot, stuff you into the trunk, stop your car at the entrance to the covered bridge, and heave your dead carcass into the Aneirin River. No muss, no fuss, and no evidence for the cops to find when they finally fish your bloated, rotting corpse out of the water."

He winced. "I take it things didn't go well with Owen?"

"No, things did not go well with Owen, unless you think stilted sentences and awkward pauses are the signs of a successful couple." I glared at Finn. "What were you thinking? I can't believe you didn't tell me Owen was coming tonight—and that you'd purposefully invited him."

Finn kept wincing, but he didn't answer me. Roslyn and Phillip exchanged a puzzled look, but it was Eva's reaction that caught my eye. She bit her lip and looked down at the floor, a guilty expression on her face if ever there was one. She glanced up, realized that I was staring at her, and let out a small sigh.

"Actually, it wasn't really Finn's idea," Eva admitted. "I was the one who suggested it."

"And *why* would you do that?"

She sighed again. "Because it's been almost a month since Salina's death, and you and Owen haven't seen each other in weeks. You haven't even spoken, as far as I know."

She was right about that, not that I told her so.

"I agree with Eva," Kincaid chimed in. "You and Owen need to at least start talking again."

"About what?" I asked, turning to face him. "How I slit Salina's throat right in front of him? Even though he asked me not to? Or maybe we should talk about how I told Finn to hold him back and how you helped with that? It's easy for you to tell me to start talking to Owen, especially since it seems like he's forgiven you, Finn, and everyone else for what happened—everyone except me, that is."

This time, Kincaid was the one who winced at my harsh words. Still, he didn't back down. "Salina's gone, Gin, and I say good riddance to her. But you and Owen are still here. The two of you care about each other, quite deeply, from what I've seen. If I were you, I'd be doing my best to fix things between the two of you."

I arched an eyebrow. "I don't really think you're in a position to be giving me relationship advice, *Philly*," I said, using Eva's childhood nickname for him. "Although I'm glad to see you're here tonight with someone who's age-appropriate. You *are* here with Roslyn, right? And not someone else?"

Anger simmered in Kincaid's blue eyes, and his jaw clenched, making his chiseled cheekbones stand out more. Not too long ago, I'd told Kincaid that I knew he was not-so-secretly in love with Eva. Phillip had helped Eva and Owen when the three of them had been living on the streets as kids, and he'd told me that Eva was the first person who'd ever cared about him. That was why he loved her, even though he was my age, thirty, and about ten years older than her.

Eva looked back and forth between me and Phillip, her brow furrowed, obviously wondering what I was talking about.

I sighed. Just because my love life was on the skids was no reason for me to take my anger and frustration out on everyone else, especially my friends.

"I'm sorry," I said. "It's just that seeing Owen took me by surprise. Especially since he's here with someone else tonight."

We all turned to look at the pair in question. Owen was staring blankly at a watercolor that depicted a snowstorm. Jillian stood by his side, murmuring something to him, her arm still threaded through his. I had to admit that she wore the scarlet gown a lot better than I did. They made a handsome couple, Owen dark and rugged in his tux, Jillian like a flash of fire next to him. Sadness filled me, but I tried to ignore the sensation.

"That was the other reason I asked Finn to get you to come tonight," Eva said. "Jillian."

"What's wrong with her?"

She hesitated. "Well, nothing, really. Except for the fact that she's not *you*."

I sighed again, then reached out and gave her arm a gentle squeeze. "I appreciate that, Eva, really, I do. But if Owen wants to move on and date other people, then that's his right."

No matter how much it hurts. I didn't have to say the words. They could all see the pain glinting in my eyes.

We fell silent for a few moments before Kincaid cleared his throat.

"Well, I don't know about you ladies, but I'm feeling a little parched. Can I get you anything to drink?"

Roslyn and I both politely declined, but Eva stepped over and smiled up at him, her face as bright, warm, and happy as a sunny day.

"I'll go with you, Philly," she said.

Eva had her back to me, so she didn't see me arch my eyebrow at Kincaid again. He noticed, though. A faint blush crept up his cheeks, but he still held out his arm to the younger woman.

"I would be delighted to be escorted by you, Eva," he said.

Eva giggled and took his arm, and Roslyn, Finn, and I watched them head toward the elemental Ice bar that had been set up on the opposite side of the rotunda.

"Well, I suppose I don't have to worry about Phillip hitting on me on the ride home tonight," Roslyn said. "He's crazy about that girl."

"I know. Problem is, she's still a *girl*."

Roslyn gave me a sidelong glance. "Not that much of one. Not the way she's looking at him."

I snorted. "Tell that to Owen when he finds out. Phillip might be his friend, but Eva's still his baby sister. He's not going to be happy with anyone she dates, especially not Kincaid, given all his underworld connections and business interests."

I looked at her.

"Why are you here tonight with Phillip, anyway? I didn't realize you knew him."

Roslyn shrugged. "We have business from time to time. Occasionally, he hires out some of my guys and girls for events on his riverboat. Xavier's also moonlighted for him as a guard at the casino on occasion."

She was talking about the *Delta Queen*, the luxe riverboat casino Kincaid owned. It was docked not too far away from Briartop Island. The *guys and girls* she was referring to were the hookers she employed at Northern Aggression. Roslyn had been a hooker herself, working the Southtown streets for years like so many vampires did, before she'd saved up enough money to open up her own gin joint.

"Sometimes I think you know more people than Finn does," I murmured.

"Impossible," Finn scoffed, grabbing another glass of champagne from a passing giant waiter. "I know everyone who's anyone, everyone who wants to be someone, and everyone who's not anyone too."

I snorted. Roslyn laughed, showing off her small pearl-white fangs.

While Finn grabbed some bite-size deep-fried macaroni and cheese hors d'oeuvres from another waiter, Roslyn put her hand on my arm.

"So how are you really holding up?" she asked, her dark eyes full of sympathy and concern.

I shrugged. "Just taking it day by day. Although coming here tonight and seeing Owen with someone else hasn't exactly done wonders for my confidence that we can work through our issues."

The vampire stared across the room, studying the couple. "Oh, she's definitely interested in him, all right. Anyone can see that from her body language, the way she's smiling at him, how close she's standing to him, the way she's keeping hold of his arm as they wander around the room. But I don't think Owen is into her at all."

"Why not?"

She turned back to me. "Because he keeps sneaking looks at you."

Hope surged through me at her words—bright, beautiful, shining hope. But then I heard Jillian laugh and Owen chuckling along with her, and the happy emotion was snuffed out like a candle flame being doused by a blizzard. Owen might be looking in my direction every once in a while, but he was still here with another woman.

"It'll be okay, Gin," Roslyn said, picking up on my darkening mood. "You'll see. You and Owen care about each other too much not to work things out eventually."

I let out a breath. "Even though I killed his first love?"

The vampire shrugged her slender shoulders. For all she knew about men and women, even she couldn't answer that.

And neither could I.

✲ 5 ✲

Roslyn gave my arm a sympathetic squeeze, then moved off to talk to a male vampire who was waving at her.

That left me standing alone with Finn. Somehow, while I'd been talking to Roslyn, he'd managed to snag a whole tray of hors d'oeuvres from one of the female waiters. In addition to the deep-fried macaroni, he was also scarfing down baked phyllo cups stuffed with creamy gourmet chicken-apple salad, pineapple boats piled high with a light, airy mixture of cream cheese and toasted slivered almonds, and mini fruit tarts topped with fresh blackberries, raspberries, and strawberries.

"You should make these mac-and-cheese things at the restaurant," Finn said, popping another one into his mouth. "Because they are absolutely *divine.*"

I grabbed one off the tray and bit into it. The crust was crispy, buttery, and golden brown, while the inside was the perfect temperature—not too hot to burn your tongue but warm enough that the sharp cheddar cheese still melted in your mouth.

"Not bad," I said after I'd finished it. "But they could use some more cheese and a bit of spicy kick in the filling. A dash or two of cayenne pepper or maybe even a sprinkle of cumin to give it some smoky heat."

Finn huffed. "Well, I think they're pretty good just the way they are. If you're going to criticize, then I'm eating the rest of them."

"Knock yourself out."

One by one, Finn devoured every single thing on the tray. When it was empty, he looked mournfully at the crumbs on the smooth silver surface, his mouth turning down into a pout. Then a waiter passed by with another tray of champagne, and Finn perked right back up. He bowed and gallantly handed the empty tray to the waiter in exchange for a glass of bubbly.

"Now, on to more important matters," Finn said, after his thirst had been quenched. He stabbed his finger in Owen's direction. "Sandy and Samantha are going to hear *all* about this little fashion faux pas."

I frowned. "What do you mean? Who are you talking about?"

"The two saleswomen at the Posh boutique. Sandy was the blonde, Samantha was the redhead," Finn said. "Don't you remember?"

I shook my head. I hadn't bothered to get their names. I figured saving them from the robber was good enough.

"Well, they *assured* me that your dress was an original, an absolute one-of-a-kind. In fact, they swore up one side and down the other that you were the only person to ever even try it on, so I happily let you pay their outrageous price for it."

"How noble of you."

Finn pretended not to hear my snide words and went right on with his rant. "But now here's some other sweet young thing wearing your dress at the biggest event of the summer. And not just any other woman but the one who came waltzing in on Owen's arm." He fumed for a moment. "Oh, yes, Sandy and Samantha are going to be getting a *very* harsh phone call from me Monday morning."

"It's just a dress. So another woman has on the same one. So what?"

His mouth dropped open, and he looked at me in horror. "Please tell me that those words did *not* just come out of your mouth. It is not just a dress—it is *your* dress. At least, I thought it was. Sandy and Samantha *assured* me that it was. They are going to be very, very sorry they misled me."

Finn went on a tear then, pacing back and forth, gesturing wildly with his champagne glass, and talking all about how he was going to take his fashion wrath out on the two saleswomen for daring to sell my dress to another woman.

I just sighed and listened to him rant. No matter how long I knew him, I didn't think that I would ever fully figure out or understand the inner workings of the mercurial mind of Finnegan Lane.

Finn eventually wound down, and the two of us strolled around the rotunda, but I couldn't concentrate on the showcase of Mab's loot. Two things were on my mind:

how I could come back later and steal my family's runes, and Owen and Jillian.

The first one wouldn't be too much of a problem. Other than the plethora of giant guards working tonight, security at the museum didn't seem all that tight. Oh, I was sure there were some lasers, alarms, and other hidden measures that would snap on when the lights went out, but there weren't nearly as many cameras as there should have been in the museum, and it would be easy enough for me to stroll through their blind spots. Nothing I couldn't handle.

As for Owen and Jillian, I kept watching the two of them out of the corners of my eyes. Laughing, talking, drinking champagne. They seemed to be having a good time together. But more than once, my eyes met Owen's, and it was all I could do to look away. But then, two minutes later, my gaze would find his again.

If I stayed in the rotunda, I'd just keep staring at Owen, so I decided to leave. Besides, several of the underworld bosses were still eyeing me with hostile intent, and I was tired of their murderous glances.

"I'll be back in a few minutes," I told Finn. "I need some air."

He was now talking to a petite vampire wearing an emerald choker and a matching tiara. He waved a distracted hand at me, telling me that he'd be fine on his own. Of course he would. Finn had never met a stranger.

I shook my head and left the exhibit room. I hadn't noticed before, but the crush of people inside the rotunda had raised the temperature in there by several degrees, and the cool, drafty air outside felt good against my flushed cheeks. I wandered from one hallway to the next, looking at all the objects on display. I hadn't taken an art class in a while, but I began to think that maybe I should mix it up and try painting or some sort of sculpture course next semester, instead of another literature class.

All of the art was housed on the first, main floor of the museum, and I roamed from one wing to the next and back again. The upper levels had all been closed off for the gala, but there wasn't much to see in them, anyway, just staff offices, spaces for artists to work, and rooms where paintings and more were being slowly, lovingly restored and authenticated.

The rotunda was in the front of the main wing of the museum, and it took me a while to make a full circuit through all of the hallways that curved around it. I passed a few more giants in my wanderings, but there weren't nearly as many guards out here as there had been in the rotunda. Eventually, I wound up back where I started, standing in the entrance that led to the exhibit of Mab's things. Since I wasn't ready to go in and look for Finn just yet, I headed for the bathroom.

Like everything else at Briartop, the bathroom was done on a grand, impressive scale. Several white crushed-velvet settees and matching overstuffed chairs had been arranged in the outer powder room, while the bathroom itself featured more gray marble, along with silver faucets and oval-shaped, silver gilded mirrors. A tangle of briars and brambles curving around a fancy letter *B*—the museum's rune—had been etched into the edges of the glass, adding to the mirrors' slick, glossy elegance.

I went into a stall, did my lady business, and came back

out. A couple of women finished washing their hands and left, leaving me alone. I washed my hands, then leaned forward and peered at my reflection.

On the outside, I looked as calm as ever—distant, remote, cold even. I wondered if I was the only one who could see the purple smudges under my eyes, the ones the makeup couldn't quite hide. I wondered if I was the only one who noticed the faint slump in my shoulders or the way my mouth always seemed to turn down with a hint of sadness these days.

Because the truth was that Owen wasn't the only one haunted by Salina's death—I was too.

More than once, I'd dreamed of the night I'd killed her. The sharp, curved thorns of her water magic ripping into my skin, trying to tear me apart. My desperate struggle to release enough magic to overcome hers. My elemental Ice glittering all around us like a field of cold crystal. The way Salina's blood had spilled down her neck in a cascade of crimson teardrops.

Killing Salina had been a necessity. She'd told me herself that she'd never quit, not until she'd taken her revenge on everyone she thought had wronged her. And that she'd never stop loving Owen or trying to win him back by any means necessary—including murdering me.

Yes, killing her was something that just had to be done, but it didn't make the memories any easier to bear.

Because there was a second twisted truth to this situation, one that kept me up late brooding into the dark of the night: the fact that I was more like Salina than I cared to admit. Cold, brutal, ruthless. And I'd done some of the same things she had over the years, like killing people for revenge, or money, or because letting them live just didn't fit into my plans.

Maybe Owen was right to keep his distance from me. Maybe it would be better for both of us if I went ahead and ended our relationship for good. That way, at least maybe he could move on, even if I couldn't—

The door erupted open with such force that it almost banged against the marble wall before a hand reached out and stopped it at the last second. My head snapped to the right. Thoughts of Salina still filled my mind, and for a crazy moment, I thought the water elemental was coming after me again, or at least her ghost was.

But it wasn't Salina who stepped into the bathroom— it was the giant waiter who'd spoken to me earlier. Curly auburn hair, hazel eyes, nice features. The same waiter who'd been hovering nearby while McAllister and I had been insulting each other.

The giant realized that I was watching her. Maybe it was the hard, flat stare I gave her, but she hesitated a moment before stepping into the bathroom and letting the door swing shut behind her.

"Sorry about the door," she said, a slightly sheepish tone in her twangy voice. "It got away from me."

I didn't respond. All giants were strong, but she'd practically ripped the door out of its frame in her haste to get in here. And she'd pulled at least one of the hinges loose, since the door didn't quite line up with the wall anymore.

Given her seeming urgency, I expected the giant to scurry into a stall, but instead, she meandered over to one of the sinks and turned on the faucet. For a moment, the only sound was the steady hiss of water streaming over her hands.

"Lovely night, isn't it?" she said.

"Just gorgeous," I muttered.

The giant quickly washed her hands and dried them, before throwing her used paper towel into the silver trash container. I'd thought she'd go back out to the party, but instead, she turned to look at me again. She stared at me for another second before smiling and leaving the bathroom. The door shut behind her, once again not quite closing the way it should.

Well, that had certainly been odd. But since the giant hadn't pulled a gun out of her pants pocket, come at me with clenched fists, or otherwise tried to end my existence, I put her out of my mind and turned back to the mirror.

I was staring at my reflection and brooding once more when the door opened again a few seconds later. Only this time, it wasn't the giant who stepped through—it was Jillian Delancey. Of course. Because that was just my kind of luck.

Jillian stopped when she saw me standing in front of the mirrors. I wondered if she was as offended by the fact that we were both wearing the same dress as Finn was, but I decided not to be rude and ask.

"Oh," she said. "Hello again . . ."

"Gin," I said, when it became apparent that she didn't remember my name. "Like the liquor."

"Gin. Right."

Jillian walked over and put her small black beaded clutch down on the counter. Even though Finn had made me buy a purse to match my dress, I hadn't bothered bringing it inside the museum. I had my knives. That was all I needed.

Jillian opened up her clutch and pulled out a tube of scarlet lipstick, along with a small compact so she could touch up her face.

I washed my hands again, just to have something to do, and I took my sweet time drying them off. Finally, Jillian finished with her makeup. She put everything back into her bag, snapped the top shut, and headed toward the door. But just before she reached it, she turned around and faced me.

"So," she said. "Do I need to be worried about you and Owen?"

"Me and Owen?"

She hesitated. "When I came over to the two of you earlier, it looked like you were both . . . involved in something."

I didn't know that we were *involved*, so much as feeling awkward with each other, but I could imagine how we must have looked to her, each one of us staring at the other, pain and tension glinting in our eyes.

"No," I said. "We weren't involved in anything except a nice little chat. Owen and I are old friends."

That's what I'd introduced myself as to her before, and that's what I was going with now, since it was far less complicated than the truth. I'd hoped that would be enough to satisfy her, but Jillian kept staring at me, her brown eyes dark and thoughtful.

"So I'm not encroaching on your territory, then?" she asked in a blunt tone. "Because I'm not the kind of woman who goes around trying to poach men who are already involved with someone else. And I especially don't like being anybody's rebound fling."

I arched an eyebrow. "Well, that's a colorful way of putting things."

She shrugged, but she lifted her chin and kept her eyes steady on mine. I admired her for that—I admired her a lot for that. It took moxy to confront your date's ex, or whatever I was these days, and ask her point-blank what was going on. So I decided to be polite about things.

"Owen's a big boy," I said. "His actions are his own— and so are mine."

Jillian frowned, clearly not understanding my words, but I didn't feel like explaining them to her. I wasn't quite sure what I meant myself. But if she wanted to make a play for Owen and he decided to move on with her, I wasn't going to stand in their way. I owed Owen that much—her too. No matter how much it hurt.

"What I'm trying to say is that I hope you have a nice night," I said. "With or without Owen."

She nodded, accepting my words. What she really thought about them and me, I couldn't tell, but they seemed to ease her mind.

"Well, I guess I should be getting back to the party," she said. "I believe Mr. McAllister is about to start his speech."

"Oh," I drawled. "You certainly wouldn't want to miss *that*."

Finn had told me that sometime during the evening McAllister and a few of the muckety-mucks who were on the Briartop board were going to talk about what a wonderful benefactor of the arts Mab had been, how much she'd supported the museum throughout the years, and how generous it was of her to endow Briartop with her art collection postmortem. Lies, lies, and more lies, all the way around. The only things Mab had ever generously dished out had been pain, misery, and suffering, courtesy of her Fire magic.

If that was what was next on the agenda, I'd be quite happy staying in the bathroom until all the pretty speeches were over with. I'd rather scrub my hands until they were red, raw, cracked, and bleeding than listen to people prattle on about how damn *noble* the Fire elemental had supposedly been. And I certainly wasn't going to raise a glass of champagne and toast Mab with it. Especially not now, when I'd discovered that she'd had my mother's and Annabella's rune necklaces all these years—

"Anyway, it was nice seeing you again, Gin," Jillian said, cutting into my dark thoughts. "You have excellent taste in clothes. And men."

She was trying to make a joke and lighten the mood, so I forced myself to laugh, hoping she wouldn't notice how tight and hollow the sound really was. "You too."

Jillian smiled at me a final time, then opened the bathroom door and headed out into the powder room. But the door didn't quite shut behind her, and I watched her through the wide gap. Jillian walked through the powder room, opened the exterior door, and stepped through to the other side. That door was just swinging shut behind her when she jerked and let out a small, startled gasp, then—

Pfft! Pfft! Pfft!

The sounds were soft, no more than harsh whispers, but they made me reach for one of my knives all the same.

Because unless I was mistaken, someone had just been shot with a silenced gun.

❖ 6 ❖

The first thing I did was toe off my shoes so the heels wouldn't clack against the marble floor. At the same time, I reached through a slit in my skirt. I'd just stepped out of my second shoe when my hand closed around one of the two knives I had strapped to my thighs. I slid the weapon free and pulled open the interior door just wide enough for me to slip into the powder room. Then I tiptoed over to the exterior door. I stood there, head cocked toward the heavy wood, but I didn't hear anything else.

But there was a pane of glass that served as a vent in the top of the door, so I picked up one of the white velvet chairs, carried it over to the door, and climbed up onto the seat so I could see through the glass.

Jillian Delancey lay on the floor right outside the bathroom door—dead.

At least, I assumed it was Jillian. It was kind of hard to tell, since most of her face had been blown off.

But she wasn't alone. A giant stood over her body. He was on the small side, a few inches short of seven feet tall, but he made up for it by having a ripped, chiseled figure that would have put any bodybuilder to shame. His biceps bulged so big I doubted that he could rest his arms down against his sides. His skin was exceptionally tan, bordering on orange, the sort of fake, unnatural color you got out of a bottle. Everything else about him was pale, though: his hazel eyes, his curly blond hair, even the wispy soul patch that clung to his chin like puffed-up peach fuzz.

But the most interesting thing about him was the fact that he was wearing the dark blue uniform of one of the museum's security guards—one that didn't quite fit. The pants legs stopped an inch short of his black socks, and the chest and sleeves of the shirt threatened to split open with every breath he took. It almost looked like he was playing dress-up in someone else's clothes.

He clutched a silenced gun in his right hand, the weapon trained on Jillian as if he thought she was suddenly going to come back to life with that much of her face missing. Not even Mab could have survived something like that.

For a moment, sorrow washed over me. I hadn't known a thing about Jillian Delancey, other than that she'd come here with Owen and had been interested in him, but she hadn't deserved to die like that.

But the real question was, why had the giant killed her? Why here? Why now? All around me, the marble whispered as Jillian's blood oozed across it and the giant's ugly, violent actions soaked into it. I'd thought the stones had sounded upset before, but now they practically hummed with tension and whined with worry. Whatever was going down, it was happening now.

Lucky for me, there was a guy standing right outside the door who could tell me exactly what that was—and how I could stop it before anyone else got hurt.

I started to get down from the chair so I could yank open the door and confront the giant when another sound caught my ear—*clack-clack-clack-clack*. Footsteps, hurrying this way. The giant's head snapped up, and he moved away from Jillian's body so the new arrival could see his gruesome handiwork.

The giant waiter who'd entered the bathroom earlier stepped into view. Dropping to one knee beside Jillian, she was careful not to get too close to the blood spreading across the floor. She looked at Jillian—or what was left of her—and shook her head, making her tight curls bounce every which way before they settled back into place.

"What a fucking mess," she said. "Why the hell did you shoot her in the face so many times?"

"Are you kidding me?" the second giant asked. His high, whiny voice reminded me of a mosquito buzzing around. "With her reputation? I wasn't taking any chances. Not with this bitch. And see? It worked."

Her reputation? My stomach clenched, and I started to get a bad, bad feeling.

"Yeah, it worked because you blew half her skull off." The female giant shook her head again. "I told you to kill her, Dixon. Not splatter her brains everywhere."

"Well, who cares as long as she's dead?" Dixon, the male giant, said. "Come on, Clementine. You know I'm right about this."

Clementine? That wasn't a very common name, and it rang a bell in the back of my mind. I studied the giant, but once again, I couldn't quite place who she was or where I might have seen her before tonight. I was going to find out, though—real soon.

"We're the ones taking all the risks," Dixon said, his voice taking on a pleading, petulant note. "I say we do whatever we want, as long as we get the job done in the end. This is the score of a lifetime. I don't want anything to screw it up. Do you? So three in the head, and the Spider's dead."

The Spider. That sick, sick feeling ballooned up in my stomach, choking me from the inside out, burning as cruelly as the hottest elemental Fire. They thought that they'd killed the Spider; they thought that they'd murdered *me*. But it was Jillian lying there on the cold marble—or what was left of her.

Finn had been so upset when he'd realized that Jillian had on the same dress as I did. He'd never dreamed it would get her killed, and neither had I. Scarlet dress, dark brown hair, strong, slender build. Owen had mistaken me for Jillian earlier, and Dixon had made the same error in reverse.

The cold, cruel irony twisted into my gut, adding to my agonizing guilt, and my own scarlet gown seemed to cinch tightly around my waist, like a corset compressing my lungs and slowly suffocating me. I could feel each and every one of the delicate crystals around the waist digging into my stomach like tiny daggers. For a moment, I was seized by the unbearable urge to tear off the gown and rip it to shreds with my knife. I wanted to scream and shout and beat my fists against the marble walls about how fucking *unfair* it was that an innocent woman had died because of me.

But that wouldn't calm my raging emotions.

Nothing would—except killing the giants.

Clementine studied Jillian's body. After a moment, she nodded. "You're right. Dead is dead, and dead is good in her case. Besides, it's not like you can put her face back where it used to be."

Dixon let out the breath he'd been holding. He smiled at the other giant, but it was a nervous expression, punctuated by a faint twitching of his left eye, and it took him a moment to relax the tight, white-knuckled grip he'd had on his gun. He'd known that Clementine wouldn't be happy with what he'd done, and he'd been afraid of what she might do to him.

Whoever Clementine was, she was definitely in charge, and Dixon was scared of her. He had shot an unarmed woman in the face, but he was still taking pains to tiptoe around the other giant. That told me a few things about Clementine, namely that she was even more dangerous and ruthless than Dixon was.

Clementine got to her feet and glanced at her watch. I didn't get a good look at it, but I could still see the flash of diamonds and the gleam of silverstone around her wrist. An expensive piece, one far too pricey for a simple waiter. Then again, Clementine wasn't what she seemed to be, any more than I was.

Didn't much matter. She was getting dead in another minute, two tops.

I'd wait until they left Jillian's body behind, creep

through the shadows after them, then ram my knife into Clementine's back. Once she was dead, I'd find a quiet, secluded corner in the museum where I could question Dixon—a place where no one would hear him scream out the answers. Depending on what he told me, I'd either wipe his blood off my knives and go back to the exhibit, or I'd find Finn and tell him that we had a situation to deal with—

"Is everyone else in position?" Clementine asked.

Dixon reached down and grabbed a walkie-talkie that was clipped to the black leather belt around his waist. "Team one?"

A staticky crackle sounded, along with a male voice. "In position."

"Team two?" he asked.

Another crackle, another voice, this one female. "In position."

He repeated the procedure, checking in with three other teams. I didn't know how many folks were on each team, but I was willing to bet that it was several. This was what the stones had been murmuring about all evening. Whatever was happening, I was going to stop it—and the giants.

Clementine nodded, satisfied. "All right. Grab her, and let's get out of here."

"Aw, do I have to?" Dixon whined again. "Why don't *you* do it?"

"Because you're the idiot who shot her in the face. You made the mess, so you can carry her. Do you have a problem with that?" Her voice was calm, polite even, but her hazel eyes were cold, flat, and empty.

"No, no, no, that's okay," Dixon said. "I can get her. No problem, boss."

This time, Clementine smiled. The expression reminded me of a fox baring its teeth at a fat hen. "Good. Then let's get the show started. We wouldn't want to keep our guests waiting."

Turning her back on her underling, Clementine set off down the hallway.

Dixon stared at Jillian's body for a moment, his lips curled with disgust. Finally, sighing, he holstered his gun and attached the walkie-talkie to his belt again. He reached down, grabbed Jillian's leg, and hurried after his boss. His inherent giant strength and the smooth marble floor made it easy for him to drag the body, like a kid pulling a wagon behind him. In seconds, the two of them had rounded a corner and disappeared from sight.

I got out of the chair, went back into the bathroom, and grabbed my shoes. Then, knife still in my hand, I opened the exterior door and eased out into the hallway, looking left and right. Not seeing anyone else or hearing any footsteps clattering in my direction, I hurried down the hallway after them, my shoes clutched in one hand and my knife in the other. The marble floor felt as cold and slick as an ice rink against my bare feet, but I didn't dare take the time to stop and put my heels back on. They'd make too much noise cracking against the floor, anyway.

Guilt surged through me once more. I should have realized something was wrong the second Clementine had sidled up to me in the rotunda, and especially when she'd done the same thing again in the bathroom. Clementine had been making sure I was inside so Dixon could shoot me. But somehow, while they'd been off plotting my demise, the two of them had missed Jillian entering the bathroom. And since he'd shot Jillian so many times in the face, destroying her features, they both assumed he'd killed the right woman in the red dress.

I didn't know anything about Jillian Delancey. Didn't know if she was good or bad, kind or indifferent, sweet or cynical. If she had a family, if she was a loner, if she had a couple of cats at home. If she gave money to charity, if she saved every penny, if she was a ruthless businesswoman who crushed everyone who stood in her way. All I did know was that Jillian had been in the wrong place at the wrong time—and wearing the wrong damn dress.

The giants were going to pay for that—in blood.

The determination to end Clementine and Dixon burned through me, but I made myself rein in my anger and focus on the pertinent questions.

As for why the giants might want me dead, it could be any number of reasons. But I kept wondering. Why would the giants consider me such a threat? There were lots of bad people here tonight. So why target me and not someone else?

This had the feel of a hasty hit, something arranged and executed on the spur of the moment. If all they'd wanted to do was murder me, then Clementine and Dixon had already succeeded—or at least thought they had. With their mission accomplished, they should be hightailing it out of Briartop and off the island, not dragging Jillian's body off to parts unknown. Even more telling was the fact that they hadn't bothered to hide or clean up the mess they'd left behind. Jillian's blood was sprayed all over the bathroom door and the floor in front of it for all the world to see. Then there were the other teams they'd checked in with—and why they needed so many other people in the first place. No, something else was going on here besides killing me. That alone made me curious enough to figure out what Clementine and her pals were up to and do whatever it took to derail their scheme.

I reached the end of the hallway. I eased up the corner and peered around it, expecting to see the two giants heading toward the doors that led outside at the far end of the corridor.

But the hallway was empty, completely empty.

I looked behind me, then up ahead again, but no one else appeared. This particular hallway branched off in two directions. If Clementine and Dixon hadn't gone for the exit, that left only one other destination: the rotunda.

I frowned. Why would they go back there? Especially since Dixon was dragging Jillian's body around like a rag doll. What good would that do—

Crack! Crack! Crack! Crack!

The harsh, stinging retort of gunfire exploded in the museum, followed by the even louder, sharper sounds of people screaming. Crashes, bangs, breaking glass—all that and more reverberated through the hallways, echoing back on one another until it sounded like someone had detonated a series of bombs inside the marble walls. Maybe they had.

I cursed. I should have taken care of Clementine and

Dixon outside the bathroom, not let them get so far ahead of me that they'd been able to put their plan into action . . . whatever it was. I'd wanted to be quiet and cautious about things, and now it was coming back to bite me in the ass.

Even as I hurried down the hallway toward the rotunda, I realized that I was already too late. An iron gate barred my way, stretching from wall to wall and floor to ceiling, just like a portcullis in a real castle. I reached out and rattled the metal—or at least tried to—but it was no use. There was a lock on the other side of the gate, and even if I'd managed to open it with a couple of elemental Ice picks, I simply wasn't strong enough to lift the heavy sheet of metal.

Crack! Crack! Crack! Crack!

More gunshots and more screams rang out as the violence continued inside the exhibit space—where my friends, my family, were.

I cursed again and backtracked, hurrying down hallway after hallway around the rotunda, but all of the entrances were similarly blocked by gates. That must have been what at least some of Clementine's teams had been standing by for, her signal to lower the gates and trap all the partygoers like fish in a barrel.

Well, if I couldn't go through or around the gates, I'd go up instead. I backtracked yet again until I reached a set of stairs to the second-floor balcony overlooking the rotunda. Unlike the ones that led to the museum's upper levels, the stairs here hadn't been blocked off for the gala, I supposed so folks could get a bird's-eye view of the exhibit if they were so inclined.

I crept up the staircase and paused at the top. A gate was hanging up here too, but it hadn't been lowered like the ones on the first floor. Sloppy, sloppy, sloppy of the giants not to have secured *all* the entrances to their little show. Then again, most folks didn't think about protecting more than the ground floor of any structure, and Clementine hadn't counted on any stragglers being outside the rotunda when she sprang her trap.

I put my shoes down on the top step, then dropped to my stomach. Knife still in hand, I slithered across the floor and peered over the edge of the balcony at the scene below.

When I'd been in the rotunda earlier, folks had been snacking on hors d'oeuvres, sipping champagne, and admiring Mab's many treasures beneath the glow of the soft white lights strung up all around them. But now all of that beauty had been destroyed. Glass cases full of miniature carvings had been smashed and overturned, stone sculptures had toppled over and broken into chunks, paintings had fallen off the walls and been trampled. Black scorch marks marred some of the columns where bullets had bounced off them, while bits of marble littered the floor where the flying projectiles had chipped away at the stone.

Then there were the bodies.

Three men and two women sprawled across the floor, their arms and legs bent at impossible angles, their eyes dull and sightless, their expensive clothes red and mottled with blood. The bodies were clustered right in front of the main entrance to the rotunda. It looked like the bad guys had come in with guns blazing, not caring who they mowed down with that first initial blast. The people in front never even knew what hit them.

But everyone else did.

All of the surviving guests had been herded into the center of the room so that they were standing on the enormous mosaic star embedded in the floor. Giants holding guns surrounded them on all sides. Some in the crowd were crying, a few were clutching the wounds they'd gotten from the bullets flying around, but most were staring at the giants, their eyes wide, wondering what was going to happen next.

My gaze went from one face to another, looking for my friends, my family—Finn, Eva, Phillip, Roslyn, and Owen.

Finally, I found them, huddled together near the back of the crowd of hostages. I carefully examined each one of them in turn, but they all looked fine, if a little shaken up. Owen had his arm wrapped around Eva, while Roslyn stood on her other side. Meanwhile, Finn and Phillip were staring at the giants with narrowed eyes, obviously hoping for an opening so they could try to take them out. I would have told them not to bother. Even if they could get past a few of the guards and make a break for one of the exits, there was no way they could raise one of the lowered gates before they were shot to pieces.

The five of them weren't too far away from where my mother's and sister's pendants were, and I caught a glint from the silverstone runes from my position on the balcony, winking at me like mocking eyes. So close yet so far away. Just like my friends. I wondered if Finn or one of the others had spotted the necklaces and realized what they were, but I quickly pushed the thought away. All that mattered right now was that my friends were safe—and figuring out how to keep them that way.

So I looked down again, but this time, I concentrated on the bad guys. About three dozen men and women, all giants and all holding at least one gun, had arranged themselves around the rotunda, their weapons pointed in at the hostages. Waiters, guards, the parking staff. Every single one of the giants was wearing some sort of uniform. I'd thought there had been more security on the scene tonight than usual. Now I knew why.

. . . it seems like more bad guys than usual have come out of the woodwork these past few days. And the really weird thing? There's no one around to stop them . . . It's like all the giants who work as bodyguards have suddenly decided to move on up to bigger and better things . . .

Bria had said those words to me a few days ago at the Posh boutique. I wondered if the giants' presence with Clementine was the reason there had been so many robberies lately. It would make sense. Why spend your time working at some lowly security job when you could be in on a sting like this? Just the jewelry off everyone in the rotunda would be enough to set this crew up for life. Add Mab's trinkets on top of that—at least, the ones that hadn't been damaged in the initial attack—and the dollar figure climbed even higher.

Bigger and better things, indeed.

The more I stared down at the giants and the frightened crowd, the more I felt a sinking sense of déjà vu. The scene was eerily similar to what had happened a few weeks ago at the Dubois estate. Salina had hired some giants to hold folks hostage so she could use her water magic and a series of fountains to try to drown all the people she had blamed for her father's murder. I wondered if Clementine's plans would involve as much death.

My gaze moved to Clementine, who was standing in the rotunda entrance, talking to Dixon. Opal, the giant who'd taken Finn's invitation, was also standing with them. The three of them must be running the show.

Well, now I knew why Opal had been so taken aback by my appearance outside. She'd recognized me just like Finn had thought and had realized that I could be a threat to their plans. She'd probably alerted the others as soon as I'd gone into the museum so that Clementine and Dixon could be on the lookout for me and start planning my murder. Still, why not just trap me in the rotunda with everyone else? Why take on the added risk of killing me?

My gaze went from one face to another. Hazel eyes, square jaws, strong cheekbones, long, sharp noses. For the first time, I noticed the familial resemblance among the three of them. Opal had to be Clementine's daughter, given that she was practically a twenty-something carbon copy of the middle-aged woman. Dixon looked to be roughly the same age as Opal. He didn't resemble the two women quite as strongly, but it was obvious he was somehow related to them. Maybe a nephew or a cousin.

Dixon nodded at something Clementine said and left the rotunda. A few seconds later, I heard a faint *rattle-rattle*, along with the *screech-screech-screech* of metal. Dixon must be lifting one of the gates and creating an opening so the giants could come and go as they pleased, now that they'd cornered everyone else in here.

Clementine smoothed down her black tuxedo vest, then strode to the center of the room to stand directly in front of the hostages. Opal took up a position on her right.

Clutching a gun in her right hand, Clementine put her left hand on her hip, cocking it to one side. She gazed out over the crowd, almost like a circus ringmaster getting a feel for the audience before a big performance. Slowly, the hostages quieted down, realizing that she was the one in charge of everything—including whether they lived or died.

"Good evening, ladies and gentlemen," she said, a broad smile creasing her face. "My name is Clementine Barker, and this here is a holdup."

❖ 7 ❖

Clementine looked out over the crowd again, then threw back her head and laughed. Her loud, booming guffaws echoed off the thick walls just like the screams and gunshots had a few minutes earlier. Somehow, though, her dark chuckles seemed far more sinister. Or maybe that was because I'd seen how casually she'd reacted to Dixon shooting Jillian and knew that she'd do the same thing to anyone who got in her way.

"Forgive me," she said, her laughter finally dying down. "I always wanted to say that."

Everyone stared at the giant, but no one said anything. No one dared to.

I put her theatrics out of my mind and focused on something else: her name. *Clementine Barker.* Again, it sounded familiar, like someone I'd heard Bria or maybe even Finn talk about. A glimmer of a conversation came back to me, something Finn had said in passing recently about some up-and-coming security firm started by a giant. The woman running it had approached Finn's bank about taking over the security there, but the higher-ups had turned her down.

She had an unusual name, Finn's voice whispered in my mind. *Clementine. It made me want an orange.*

I wondered if Clementine had plied her services to other Ashland businesses, if maybe the folks on the Briartop board had hired Clem and her men for tonight's event, to help out as waiters, to direct traffic in the parking lots, maybe even to beef up the museum's security staff. That would have been one way to get so many of her men onto the island without raising suspicions. Then all they would have had to do was wait until the moment was right to overpower the regular guards, and the museum—the whole island—would be theirs. Just like it was now.

"But it is true," Clementine said, continuing her one-sided conversation with the crowd. "This is a robbery. So why don't we start moving things along? If you will all be so kind as to remove any jewelry, watches, cuff links, and other valuables you have on, some of my boys will go around and collect them. And to save them the effort of patting you down, go ahead and put your phones into the bags too. Now, we've already set up a series of cell-phone jammers inside the museum and cut the landlines to the island, so no calls are coming in or out. But let's just go ahead and remove all temptation to try calling for help anyway. This is a private party, and I'd like to keep it that way."

Three of the giants reached into their pants pockets,

drew out black plastic garbage bags, and snapped them open. But before they could step up and repeat their demand that folks take off their jewelry, or else, one of the hostages pushed his way to the front of the crowd.

Jonah McAllister.

The lawyer pinned his cold brown gaze on Clementine. His hands were balled into fists by his sides, while anger stained his unnaturally smooth cheeks a bright beet red.

"You won't get away with this," McAllister said in a furious voice, stabbing his finger at the giant. "None of you will get off this island alive. I have no doubt the police will be here any minute to round you up and throw you in prison where you belong—"

Crack!

Clementine didn't even wait for McAllister to finish sputtering before she stepped forward and backhanded him across the face. The sharp, stinging blow threw the lawyer five feet to his right and slammed him into a pedestal topped by a glass case housing a dainty tea set. The pedestal seesawed back and forth, making the dishes rattle, before McAllister managed to grab it. He hung on to the stand and slowly used it to push himself upright. Then he turned to face the giant again. I had to give McAllister credit. He didn't cringe—much.

Instead, eyes wide, he blinked like an owl for several seconds before slowly raising a hand to his face, which was bleeding. Clem had opened up a cut low on his left cheek, probably with the sharp edge of her watch. That was no way to treat such an expensive timepiece.

"You were saying?" Clementine asked.

McAllister blanched at the blood on his hand and slowly stepped back. It took him a few seconds, but he didn't stop backpedaling until he was on the opposite side of the room, as far away from her as he could get and still be standing with the other hostages. Clementine smirked at him for a moment before turning her attention to the crowd again.

"Now, in addition to all those pretty little rings and watches you folks have on, my boys and I are also going to load up Mab's treasures in the rotunda to take with us. In fact, we plan to clean out the whole museum while we're here," she said. "Since this is a once-in-a-lifetime opportunity. So to speak."

She chuckled at her own bad joke, but I was thinking about her words. Loot the entire Briartop museum? Countless millions in art decorated the hallways, galleries, and other exhibit spaces. I'd counted around twenty giants outside earlier, and there were more than thirty in here right now. No wonder she'd brought so many men. She'd need them all to haul so much loot away with her. Clementine definitely didn't think small. I wondered how long she'd been planning her heist—and what I could do to stop her.

"So while my boys and I go about our business, you're all going to be spending some quality time here in this beautiful rotunda," she continued. "As long as you sit still, be quiet, and behave, you will all come out of this just fine. My boys and I are only interested in what the museum has to offer. We don't want any more blood dirtying up things. Lowers the resale value."

She let out another hearty chuckle, but once again, no

one joined in her laughter. Couldn't imagine why. She should have brought a giant with a set of drums along with her. That way, he could *ba-dum-dum* in time to every one of the corny jokes she was cracking.

"But know this," Clementine said. "We won't hesitate to fill your guts full of lead if you so much as twitch funny."

Her smile stayed soft and pleasant, her voice as warm and welcoming as apple pie, but her eyes took on a chillingly empty look. She stared at first one hostage, then another, making sure they all realized how serious she was. Everyone got the message loud and clear.

"Now," Clementine continued, "there's actually another reason why my boys and I are here tonight, other than the obvious payday we're getting. And that reason is that we're tired—tired of all of *you*."

The hostages glanced at one another, wondering what she getting at. So did I.

"We're giants," Clementine said. "We're tough, we're strong, and we're damn near unstoppable, but for years— for *years*—we've been relegated to hiring ourselves out to protect you. We've put ourselves in the line of fire over and over again, serving you, saving your miserable hides. And for what? Some measly paycheck? Some small hope of advancement? Well, not anymore. No, starting tonight, my boys and I are going to take what we want—take what we're *due*—and to hell with anybody who tries to stand in our way. This is the dawn of a new era in Ashland, when *we're* in charge. The way it should have been all along."

All around the rotunda, the other giants nodded their heads in eager agreement. They were totally buying what

Clementine was selling and seemed completely committed to her uprising.

She gestured with her gun at the bodies lying on the floor in front of her. "Now, I think that my boys and I have already proven our mettle, but just in case you need some more convincing, I have one more example to show you. Bring her in!"

Dixon stepped back into the rotunda—with Jillian. He might not have had any problems shooting someone in the face, but it seemed as if the giant didn't like actually getting his hands dirty, judging by the stiff way he held Jillian out in front of him like she was a piece of smelly trash he needed to rid himself of as soon as possible.

Clementine handed Opal her gun, then moved over and took the faceless Jillian from Dixon with quick, easy movements. I thought she might approach the hostages with the body, but instead, she turned and threw it into the middle of the crowd.

Jillian Delancey had been a fit woman, but her body still weighed more than a hundred thirty pounds, every single ounce now dead, floppy, and awkward. But Clementine hefted the body through the air like it was nothing more than a football. All giants were strong, but this—this was an impressive display of sheer, raw power. The only other giant I'd seen with that kind of muscle had been Elliot Slater, Mab's henchman. Clementine looked to be just as strong as Slater had been, maybe even stronger.

People screamed and scattered when they realized what Clementine was doing, and Jillian's body slid to a stop on the mosaic star embedded in the floor. Horrified gasps rippled through the crowd like a tree full of crows all cawing at once. More than a few folks turned away from the body, hands clamped over their mouths to try to smother their screams or choke down the bile rising in their throats. Even in Ashland, where violence was so common, someone missing most of her face wasn't an everyday sight—and it certainly wasn't a pretty one.

"I want everyone to gather 'round and take a good, long look," Clementine said. "My nephew, Dixon, did that a few minutes ago. Put enough bullets in this woman's face that even her own mama wouldn't recognize her. And he and the rest of my boys will do the exact same thing to you at the slightest whisper of trouble."

The giants waved their guns, and everyone shuffled forward, although most of them tried very hard not to actually look at Jillian, or what was left of her. Couldn't blame them for that. It even turned my stomach a little. Or perhaps that was just the guilt I felt, gnawing away at my insides.

"Now, I know she's not the nicest thing to stare at, but there's one more thing that's important about this woman," Clementine said. "One more thing that everyone here needs to know: her real identity. Because that's not just some tarted-up trophy wife or debutante doll lying there getting blood all over the floor. Oh, no. *That*, ladies and gentlemen, is none other than Gin Blanco. The Spider herself. Ashland's most infamous assassin. Deader than a fencepost."

More shocked gasps rippled through the crowd. I closed my eyes, the guilt rising in my throat and choking me from the inside out.

"Come one, come all. Don't be shy. Step right up and

get a good long look at her. And think about this: me and my boys took out the Spider tonight. The toughest bitch in all of Ashland. Just like that." She snapped her fingers. "Now, if we can do that, why, just imagine what we could do to all of *you*."

While the crowd chattered and whispered at the giant's revelation, I forced myself to open my eyes and study Jillian. Made myself commit to memory every gruesome detail of her blown-off face and slack figure. The smooth skin of her shoulders compared with the ragged edges of her ruined face. The pretty, shimmering, constant twinkle of crystals on her skirt next to the absolute stillness of her leg. The blood still oozing out of her horrible wounds, the color a perfect match to the glossy polish gleaming on her manicured nails.

I stared at Jillian until the sight of her was burned into my brain, an image I would never, ever forget. And then I shifted the image, the memory, to the heavy load of guilt that was already yoked across my shoulders.

I couldn't bring Jillian back, but I could avenge her.

I could make Clementine realize what a stupid, sloppy, fatal mistake she'd made.

I was so wrapped up in my dark thoughts of guilt, rage, and revenge that it took me a moment to realize that my friends had forced their way to the front of the crowd.

Eva was the first to react, letting out a weak, strangled gasp and clamping her hands over her mouth. The rest of my friends wore similar stunned expressions as they stared down at the body.

I knew what the horrified looks meant: they all thought I was dead.

❈ 8 ❈

Eva. Finn. Phillip. Roslyn. Owen. The realization hit all
of them at about the same time. One second, they were
trying not to look at the body like everyone else. The
next, they couldn't stop staring at it, mouths open, eyes
wide, features tight with shock and sorrow.

Roslyn immediately put her arms around Eva and
turned the younger woman away from the horrible sight.
Eva's shoulders shook, and a loud sob broke free from her
lips before she could swallow it. Phillip turned away too,
his lips curled in anger and disgust.

Owen kept staring at the body, his face blank and
completely closed off. His eyes were empty, his gaze dull
and far away, as if he was so shocked, so stunned, that
he wasn't even really seeing what was in front of him. I
couldn't tell what he was thinking. I couldn't tell what he
was feeling. If he was absolutely horrified or just relieved
that I was gone. I hoped—I hoped—that he at least *cared*,

that he at least felt *something*, but I just couldn't tell what it might be, one way or the other.

And then there was Finn.

He had an entirely different reaction. Instead of shying away from the body, he moved even closer to it, stepping in front of Owen. Finn's green eyes narrowed, and he slowly, carefully, quietly examined the body from head to toe. His gaze lingered on Jillian's shoes, which peeked out from beneath the edge of her skirt, before going up to her hands. Finn leaned down, staring at one of Jillian's palms as though it held all the secrets of the universe.

I knew exactly what he was looking for: my spider rune scar.

When I was younger, the scars had been red, raw, and puckered, but over the years, they had slowly smoothed out and faded to a pale silver, given that they were really silverstone that had been melted into my palms. Everyone in the underworld might think that I was the Spider. They might recognize my rune and the fact that I took my assassin name from it, but none of them knew that the symbol was actually branded into my palms. Only my closest friends and family knew that story, and only they had ever seen the scars. Oh, I didn't try to hide the marks, not even when I was working at the Pork Pit, but unless you knew they were there, you wouldn't notice them. Besides, who ever bothered to look at the palms of someone else's hands?

After a moment, Finn's shoulders sagged, his face relaxed, and his jaw unclenched. He knew that it wasn't me lying there—that it was Jillian instead. I waited for my foster brother to turn and whisper the news to the others, but he didn't.

"See something you like?" Dixon called out, noticing Finn's interest in Jillian. "You one of those freaks who likes to get down and dirty with bodies?"

Finn slowly straightened up and looked at the giant. "Hardly," he drawled. "Although it's interesting that was the first thing *you* thought about me doing. Maybe that says something about *your* sexual preferences. Why, I bet that *you're* the one who likes to get his freak on with corpses. Who knows what you did with her before you so gallantly carried her in here?"

Dixon charged forward, his hand already dropping to the gun holstered on his belt. At the last second, Clementine held out her hand, stopping him. He looked at her, a clear plea in his eyes, but she slowly shook her head. It took him a moment, but Dixon swallowed his anger. She might be his aunt, but he didn't want to cross her.

Clementine gestured for one of her men to come over to her and whispered something in his ear. Dixon glared at Finn and slowly drew his finger across his throat in threat.

Finn, being Finn, puckered his lips and blew the giant a big, fat, sloppy kiss.

More anger stained Dixon's cheeks, breaking through his orange fake bake, but he didn't draw his gun. Instead, he just stared at Finn with murder in his eyes. After a few seconds, Clementine finished her conversation with the other giant and crooked her finger at her nephew. Dixon stepped closer to her. I let out a breath. If Finn didn't play nice, he was going to get himself shot before I could rescue him and the others.

Too bad I had no idea how I was going to do that.

I couldn't just leap over the balcony and start taking on

giants. Not with only two knives. There were too many of them and too much of a chance of people getting hurt in the confusion and crossfire. Plus, I had no doubt that Clementine would have no qualms about killing as many of the hostages as it took in order to take me out.

I was mildly surprised that she hadn't let Dixon go ahead and shoot Finn for mouthing off, but at this point, she probably wanted to keep everyone calm for as long as possible. As long as folks thought they had a chance of going free, they'd behave like good little boys and girls and play by her rules.

Oh, I could see some of the underworld figures staring at the giants, trying to figure out how to overpower them. Beauregard Benson coldly eyed a giant's throat like he wanted to rip it open with his bare hands. But nobody wanted to be the first—or only—person to make a move against the guards. Even though they all knew that everyone here was most likely marked for death.

If this had just been a simple sting, Clementine and her crew would have all been wearing masks, not walking around with their faces exposed for everyone to see. There were a lot of heavy hitters at the gala, a lot of folks with a lot of money and power who wouldn't take too kindly to being robbed. The sort of folks who would expend a lot of time, energy, effort, and resources tracking down every single one of the robbers and horrifically executing them.

Clementine was smart and sly, which meant that she knew the score as well as I did. But she'd boldly announced herself and her intentions to all of the hostages. There were only a couple of reasons I could think of for her to do that.

The first, and most obvious, was that she wasn't planning on leaving any survivors around to identify her after the fact. A bloody option but effective in the end.

The second was that she really thought that she and her squad of giants could handle any repercussions or reprisals from tonight. That she could take control of the underworld. That her little uprising would actually take. A pie-in-the-sky hope, at best.

And the third was that she'd already made arrangements to leave Ashland far, far behind and that, despite her talk of running the town, she'd already set herself up somewhere she thought no one would ever find her. But that was still a big risk to take. Nobody could hold a grudge like the folks in Ashland—nobody. The Hatfields and McCoys had nothing on us.

Still, it didn't much matter what Clementine Barker had planned—because I was going to make sure that she didn't live through the night.

"Now," Clementine said, after everyone had taken a good, long look at my supposed corpse and the whispers had died down once more, "I suggest that everyone sit down and start taking off their valuables. The sooner we rob you, the sooner we can leave."

She let out another loud howl of laughter, one that had all the hostages hurrying to plant themselves on the marble floor just as quickly as they could.

I stayed in my position on the balcony and watched as the three giants with the trash bags moved through the crowd, collecting everyone's rings, watches, necklaces, and cell phones. Once everything was gathered up, the giants handed the bags off to Opal, then rejoined the other guards ringing the hostages. Clementine stepped forward once more, a bright smile on her face.

"Now, that wasn't so bad, was it?" she said in that same deceptively friendly voice. "And don't worry. We'll keep the jewels, but y'all can have your cell phones back after we're done. We wouldn't want to put y'all out any more than we already have by making you get new phones."

Clementine chuckled, turned, and murmured something to Opal. The younger giant put the trash bags down on the floor and started sorting through all of the items inside. Opal carefully set all of the jewelry and watches off to one side while tossing the cell phones into a haphazard pile. Meanwhile, several other giants started moving through the rotunda, some roughly plucking the paintings off the walls while the others carefully took them out of their frames, rolled them up, and slipped them into long, slender tubes. More than a dozen additional giants holstered their guns and trooped out of the rotunda, probably to start looting the other rooms. Plenty of guards remained behind to watch the hostages.

"And now I'm afraid that I have to leave y'all for a little while," Clementine said. "Things to do and all that. But don't you worry. My girl, Opal, and the rest of my boys will take good care of y'all while I'm gone."

She laughed yet again, and the dark sound made more than a few folks shiver.

"Actually, I need one of you to come with me," Clementine continued. "And help me with a very special art project."

I frowned. Special project? What was she talking about? As far as I knew, all of Mab's art was in here, making it the most valuable room in the whole museum. Sure, there were plenty of other pricey paintings and sculptures throughout Briartop, but most of them were just wired to the walls or housed under glass. Nothing a giant's strength and a few well-placed punches couldn't take care of. Since I hadn't heard any alarms blaring, Clementine and her crew must have already taken care of the real guards and the security system; they wouldn't be worried about clipping wires or smashing through any glass case they wanted. So what else could they be after? What could they possibly need help with?

The partygoers looked around, wondering what she was talking about. Suspicion filled their faces as they eyed one another. They were thinking the same thing I was—that someone here was working with Clementine and her crew.

"You see, there's a particular bit of metal that I need help dealing with," Clementine said. "And there's someone here with just the right kind of magic to help me and my boys handle it."

As soon as she said the word *metal*, my heart clenched in my chest. I knew exactly what kind of magic she was talking about—and exactly who had it.

"Owen Grayson," Clementine called out in a booming voice. "Come on down."

❊ 9 ❊

For a moment, I closed my eyes again. The night just kept getting better and better. First, Jillian had been murdered, then Clementine and her crew had taken everyone hostage, and now this.

Murmurs rippled through the crowd, and folks turned to stare at Owen, who was just as shocked by the giant's announcement as everyone else. But Owen's surprise quickly turned to wariness. He glanced at Phillip and Finn, but the other two men shrugged, their own faces tight with concern. They didn't know what Clementine wanted with him any more than I did, but we all knew it couldn't be anything good.

"Ah, come on, now, Mr. Grayson," Clementine said. "I see you over there. Don't be shy. Get to your feet and step up on here."

She grinned and pointed her gun at the woman sitting closest to her. "Or I'll shoot this pretty lady in the face."

The woman gasped and ducked her head, as if that would somehow help her magically melt into the floor and get away from the giant and her gun.

"Right now, if you please, Mr. Grayson," Clementine continued. "Or a lot of people are going to get covered in a whole lot of blood. Blowback is a bitch, especially at close range like this. Not to mention the damage the bullets themselves will do. Why, this lady's head will probably explode like a ripe watermelon dropped on a rock—*splat*. And who knows where the bullets will go from there? Why, they could clip two or three more folks before they finally stop."

There was nothing Owen could do, no way he could possibly stop the giant from pulling the trigger except by obeying her. Like Clementine had said before, she and her boys had already taken out the Spider. So what was to stop them from murdering everyone else?

Owen climbed to his feet and slowly shuffled toward the front of the room, picking his way through the seated hostages. The faint *tap-tap-tap* of his wing tips on the floor sounded like nails being driving into a coffin. Clementine might want him alive right now, but she'd kill him the second she didn't need him anymore.

Owen finally stopped in front of Clementine, his violet eyes practically glowing with anger.

"I don't know what you're planning or what you think I can help you with, but I'm not going to do it." He spat out the words. "You can kill me if you want, but I'm not going to help you. Not after what you've done."

His gaze dropped to Jillian's body, and his mouth twisted with anger, regret, and sorrow. I wondered if it was for me—or her.

Clementine smiled. "Sure you will. Because if you don't, I'll have my boys shoot people until you change your mind. And just to speed things along, they'll start with that pretty little sister of yours."

She jerked her head, and Dixon waded into the crowd, grabbed Eva's arm, and hauled her upright. Phillip, Roslyn, and Finn surged to their feet as well, but Phillip was the quickest. He yanked Eva out of the giant's grasp and put himself in front of her before stepping forward and slamming his fist into Dixon's face. I heard the sharp, satisfying *snap* of the blow all the way up on the balcony. Dixon staggered back, blood pouring out of his broken nose and leaving garish streaks on his orange skin.

"You bastard!" Dixon screamed, blood spewing out of his mouth too. "I'll kill you for that!"

Phillip growled and lunged forward, his fingers curved into claws like he wanted to rip out the giant's throat with his bare hands. That made two of us. But another giant came in on Phillip's blind side and pistol-whipped him across the face before he could get his hands on Dixon. But Phillip was strong, thanks to his mysterious giant and dwarven parentage, and the blow only rocked him back instead of knocking him into next week. He shook it off and started forward again—

Click.

The distinctive sound made Phillip draw up short of tackling the giant who'd hit him. He whirled around and realized the same thing I did, that Clementine now had her gun leveled at Owen's head.

"Stop," she commanded. "Or I might just decide that I don't need Mr. Grayson after all."

A hard knot of fear clogged my throat, choking me, but I immediately reached for my Ice magic, ready to blast Clementine with it. The giant was about fifty feet away from me, with Owen standing in front of her, but I wasn't about to let her shoot him. I'd find some way to stop her with my magic or my knives or something, any-thing—*anything*—to save Owen.

But I didn't have to. Phillip cursed, but he slowly low-ered his hands to his sides and stepped away from the giant.

"Good boy," Clementine said, and dropped her gun from Owen's face.

But one person wasn't satisfied that Phillip had quit fighting. Dixon spat out a mouthful of blood. His aim was spot-on, and the mess splattered onto Phillip's shoe and pants leg. Phillip stiffened, but he didn't move. Dixon studied him a moment, then pulled his gun out of the holster on his belt and shot him.

Phillip grunted and crumpled to the ground.

"Philly!" Eva screamed and dropped to her knees be-side him.

Finn and Roslyn rushed forward too. I couldn't tell exactly where he had been shot, what side the wound was on, or how close to his heart and lungs it was, but I could see the bright splash of blood on his white shirt—a whole lot of blood. Finn ripped off his tuxedo jacket and im-mediately pressed it to the wound, trying to stanch the blood flow.

For a moment, Dixon's features twisted with satisfac-tion. Then he glanced over his shoulder at Clementine, who gave him a sharp, murderous glare. Dixon swallowed. Looked like he wasn't supposed to shoot any more hostages, at least not yet.

Still, Clementine didn't let the rest of the crowd see the slight dissension in the ranks. Instead, she tilted her head to the side and studied Finn and Roslyn as they tried to help Phillip. For a moment, the rotunda was completely silent except for Phillip's hoarse rasps of pain.

"Well, now, that looks like a nasty wound," she said. "Painful but not fatal. Not immediately, anyway."

I let out the breath I'd been holding.

"Why, if you come with me right now, Mr. Grayson, you might return in time to get your friend to an Air elemental and get him all healed up," Clementine drawled. "It's your choice, but I suggest you be quick about it."

Owen stared over his shoulder at Finn and Roslyn, and they all exchanged grim looks. Finn shook his head. There was nothing they could do. Not without all of them and a whole lot of other people getting hurt in the process.

Owen turned back to her. "Fine," he growled. "You've made your point. I'll help you."

"Good," Clementine replied. "I'm glad you've decided to be reasonable. Now, follow me."

She strolled out of the rotunda. Dixon stepped over, shoved his gun into Owen's back, and forced him to follow her. Opal gathered up the jewelry she'd been sorting through, put it into a silverstone case lined with black velvet, and went with them, as did two other giants.

Owen managed one more tight, worried look over his shoulder at the rest of our friends before he disappeared from sight.

✹ 10 ✹

I remained in my position, lying flat on the balcony floor, and considered my options. There were really only two: stay here and keep an eye on the hostages, or follow Owen and see what Clementine wanted with him.

No choice, really. I hated leaving them behind, but Finn and the others were safe enough for now. The other hostages had been properly cowed, and I doubted anyone else would be stupid enough to try anything. Yes, Phillip was seriously injured, but Finn and Roslyn would slow the bleeding and help him as much as they could. Given his above-human strength and muscled body, the bullet probably hadn't gone quite as deep and done quite as much damage as it would have to a normal person. That probably meant he had at least a few hours left.

On the upside, Clementine had just split up some of her men, which meant that she'd also split her attention, energy, and resources. She couldn't be everywhere at once, and she'd already done the dividing for me. All I had to do now was conquer, or, rather, kill. One on one, I had a chance against the giants.

More than a chance as the Spider.

I scooted back across the floor toward the doorway. When I was sure I was out of sight of everyone below, I stood up, grabbed my shoes, and eased down the stairs to the first level. The chill of the marble had sunk into my skin from lying on the floor for so long, and it felt good to move, even though I could still hear the worried whispers of the stones and the sharp stings from the gunfire that had already seeped into them. I pushed these things from my mind.

A soft, familiar mechanical whirring sounded. I looked up and realized that a security camera was mounted above the staircase entrance. I hadn't paid any attention to the cameras when I'd rushed out of the bathroom earlier. Clearly, nobody had spotted me running toward the rotunda on the feed because nobody had come charging onto the balcony after me. Besides, the crew had been focused on the hostages then, not the possibility that one lone woman had somehow escaped their sticky web. But now that Clementine and her giants had taken control of things, I didn't want to give myself away by barreling down the hallways in plain view of all the cameras.

The camera moved in a slow, steady arc, so it was easy enough for me to dart past just outside of its line of sight when the lens turned in the opposite direction. I stared down the hallway at the next camera mounted on the wall, but it likewise moved in the same slow half-circular pattern and was just as simple to dodge.

Repeating the maneuver, I slid from shadow to shadow, hallway to hallway, all the while keeping my eyes and ears open for any sign of anyone else lurking in Briartop. But the only ones moving through the museum were the group Clementine was leading. Wherever her other men were, they were all busy with the tasks they'd been given. I stayed one hallway behind Clementine and the others, close enough that I could hear her voice as she barked out orders to her men and the faint crackles of the walkie-talkies as they reported back to her.

"Team one, status?"

"Starting on Exhibit Hall A."

"Good. Keep to the schedule."

"Roger that. We'll load everything up and move on to Exhibit Hall B when we're done in here."

And so on and so on. Clementine and her crew really were looting the whole museum, stripping it bare like locusts chewing through a field of sweet summer clover. Good for them, for thinking big.

Too bad she'd singled out Owen to help with her heist. She was going to die for that, for threatening my friends, for Dixon shooting Phillip, for ordering Jillian's murder—for all of it.

It was one thing to want to kill me. I expected it as the Spider. I'd practically signed on for it, taking out Mab the way I had, then being foolish enough to let all the underworld bosses live through Salina's ambush. But nobody preyed on my friends and family, nobody scared or hurt or used them as pawns. *Nobody*.

My heart pumped with cold, steady rage, and I reveled in the blackness, embraced it like the old, familiar friend it was, let it seep into every part of my being until there was nothing left but me, my knives, and my sharp, bloody will to use them on every enemy who crossed my path tonight.

Finally, the soft scuffles of shoes and crackles of conversation stopped. I eased up to the end of the hallway I'd been creeping down, made sure I was in the cameras' blind spots, and looked around the corner.

Clementine had led Owen deep into the museum, past a dozen exhibits and gallery after gallery, until they were in the center of the main wing in the very heart of Briartop. She approached two giants standing in front of a large metal door marked *Museum Personnel Only— Special Clearance Needed.* The museum's rune—that tangle of briars and brambles—curled around the words on the sign.

The two men both wore security-guard uniforms. Well, that confirmed my suspicion that Clementine had gotten some of her men hired on as guards for tonight's event and had taken out the rest. With them out of the way, she and her crew could rob the museum at their leisure, without worrying about setting off any alarms or someone calling the police.

Even if someone did manage to summon help, Clementine had a whole rotunda full of hostages to use as leverage, and there were enough important people here tonight to make the cops think twice about simply storming the museum. None of the underworld bosses would appreciate being collateral damage, especially since so many of them paid the po-po to look the other way when it came to all of their illegal activities.

No, Clementine had been smart about things—just not quite smart enough, since I was still alive and eager to mess up her plans.

One of the men standing by the door opened it. Dixon pushed Owen through the opening, and the two guards went inside behind him. Clementine turned to the two giants who'd followed her here from the rotunda.

"Tanner, you go inside with the others and help them get set up. Gary, you go over to the security center and see if Rose needs any help monitoring the camera feeds. We've got the museum locked down tight, but I want some extra eyes on the hostages in the rotunda, just in case any of them get any dumb ideas about playing hero."

The giants nodded and did as she commanded, heading down the hallway and leaving her alone with her family. When the others were out of earshot, she turned to Opal and Dixon.

"How did we make out with the jewelry?" she asked.

Opal lovingly patted the silverstone case she was carrying. "At least five million in this case and another five to ten million easy in the garbage bags. Maybe more."

Clementine nodded. "Good. Go back and deal with the jewelry. I want it out of the rotunda and secured as soon as possible. Dixon, you know what to do with that case."

"Sure thing, Aunt Clem."

Dixon expectantly stretched his hand out to his cousin. Opal's fingers clenched around the handle of the case for a moment before she finally passed it over to him. Dixon smirked at her, his swollen nose and the dribbles of blood on his face making his orange skin look even more cartoonish. Opal coldly eyed him like she wanted to rip the case out of his hand and make him eat it. Definitely no love lost there.

Clementine checked her fancy watch. "If everything goes according to plan, it shouldn't take Grayson more than an hour to work his magic. Most of the art should be loaded into the trucks by then. Then the rest."

Opal and Dixon both smiled at her words, their faces creasing with dark delight.

The rest? What else did they have planned? And what did they need Owen for? I also wondered why Clementine was so concerned about making sure she had all of the hostages' jewels, when her men were busy robbing the entire museum. But I shrugged the questions away. I'd find out the answers soon enough—body by bloody, bloody body.

"All right," Clementine said. "I'm going to go motivate Mr. Grayson. You two know what to do, so go do it."

"Yes, Mama," Opal said.

Dixon also murmured his agreement, and Clementine went through the door and closed it behind her.

For a moment, the two cousins stared at each other, before Opal stepped up to Dixon.

"You'd better take good care of that case," she said in a low, ugly voice. "Or I'll pull your insides out through your nose—while it's still broken."

Dixon winced, and his hand crept up to his swollen face. "Geez. Relax, Opal. Everything's going just fine so far. Even I couldn't screw up this job. It's easy money, just like Aunt Clem said it would be. And the best part is that we don't have to share."

I frowned. *Don't have to share?* What about all the other

giants? I doubted they were working for free, so what was Dixon talking about?

Opal cocked an eyebrow. "That remains to be seen. But know this—if you do screw up, it'll be for the last time. I'll make sure of that. This is a dangerous job. Plenty of chances for . . . accidents to happen."

She smiled then, her face soft, pretty, and pleasant, despite the shimmer of violence in her hazel eyes.

Well, well, well. It looked like Opal had the same ruthless streak her mama did. It was certainly enough to scare dear cousin Dixon, who winced again.

"And go clean up and wipe that blood off your face," Opal snapped. "You look like a pig gorging on a trough full of tomatoes."

Dixon nodded vehemently. "Sure, I'll go do that. Just as soon as I take care of the jewelry."

He clutched the case to his chest and backed away several steps before turning and scurrying down the hallway as fast as he could without actually running.

"Idiot," Opal muttered before walking in the opposite direction.

I waited until they were both out of sight and the cameras had pivoted away before slipping around the corner and hurrying over to the door. I tried the handle, but it was secured from the inside. Frustration surged through me; it was a sturdy, high-end lock, not the sort of thing I could finesse open with a couple of elemental Ice picks. Finn could have managed it, but I wasn't as good with locks as he was. Plus, an electronic card reader was attached to the wall to the right side of the door, something else I couldn't easily bypass.

Well, just because I couldn't open the door didn't mean that I couldn't see what was going on inside—and exactly what Clementine was making Owen do.

I hurried down the hallway, heading in the same direction as Gary, the giant who'd left for the security center. With cameras covering the entire museum, there had to be at least one that would let me see what was happening behind that door with Owen.

Despite my desperate need to make sure he was okay, I still made myself be cautious and quiet about things. Looking, listening, and creeping from one pool of darkness to the next. It was frustrating, especially since I had to keep dodging the security cameras, but I wouldn't be able to help anyone if Clementine and her crew spotted me before I was ready for them to.

Finally, I reached the end of a hallway next to the security center. I stopped in another blind spot, drew in a breath, and peered around the corner.

Gary stood in front of a steel door with a sign that read *Security Center—Authorized Personnel Only*.

"Come on, come on," he muttered, patting down the pockets on his uniform.

At first, I wondered what he was doing, but then I realized another electronic card reader was mounted on the wall beside the door. He must be looking for some sort of key card to slide through the device. He should have found it already, because his lapse was going to cost him his life.

All I had to do was figure out a way to kill the giant—on camera—and get away with it.

Yet another security camera was mounted in the hall,

high up on the wall across from the door. I studied its slow movement, which was an arc pattern just like the others. I could sneak up and kill the giant while the camera was turned the other way, but there was no way I could get rid of his body before it swiveled back around.

I cocked my head to one side. Unless it *didn't* swivel back around.

I thought about my idea for a moment, but it seemed solid enough. Besides, the giant would find his key card any second now, and I didn't have time to think of anything else. So I tucked my knife back into its holster, laid my hand on the marble wall, and reached for my Ice magic.

A bit of cold silver light leaked out from underneath my palm; it only took a second for small crystals to spread out from underneath my palm, run up to the top of the marble wall, and snake down the hallway toward the camera. I alternated looking at the camera and at the giant, but he wasn't an elemental, so he didn't sense me using my magic.

I waited until the camera was turned away from the giant before I pushed even more of my power outward. A second later, an inch of elemental Ice encased the camera, freezing it in its tracks, so to speak.

As soon as the camera was Iced over, I grabbed my knife and headed for the giant. I let the cold, black rage rise in me once more, even as I crept up behind him, my bare feet as soft and quiet as silk skimming across the marble floor, since I was still carrying my heels in my other hand. The giant had a gun in a holster on his leather belt, along with his own fists and whatever other weapons he might have.

It really wasn't fair—to him.

"Where is the stupid thing?" he muttered, still digging in his pockets.

He was so distracted that he didn't hear the faint rustle of my skirt or see my shadow sliding up the wall next to him like a murky movie monster about to gobble him up. I stopped about five feet behind him. Then I stood there and waited—just waited for the right moment.

"Finally! There it is—"

I dropped my shoes on the floor.

The giant whirled around at the sharp *crack-crack-crack-crack* of the heels hitting the marble, a plastic key card clutched in his long fingers. "What the—"

I stepped up and buried my knife in his throat before he could utter another word.

As I ripped the weapon out of his windpipe, blood gushed through the air, spraying onto the gray floor and walls and soaking into my scarlet dress. The giant gurgled and clawed at the fatal wound, frantically pressing the plastic card against his neck as if the small rectangle could keep all the important fluid inside his body. Card or not, there wasn't enough pressure in the world for that.

His hand slipped off his bloody neck, and the card dropped from his fingers and clattered onto the floor. The giant staggered back and hit the wall. His legs buckled, and he slowly slid down the marble until he came to rest on the floor, like a puppet whose strings had been severed. The sightless glaze of death already coated his dark eyes.

I paused, looking left and right, but I didn't see anyone, and no heavy footsteps thumped in this direction. I padded over to the door and pressed my ear against it, but I didn't hear any movement on the other side. The metal was too thick for that. Good. That meant that whoever was inside the security center probably hadn't heard us either.

Too bad I had no idea how many more of Clementine's men might be inside. One, two, a dozen. I had no way of knowing, but it was a chance I had to take. I needed to make sure Owen was okay, and I needed to see exactly what Clementine was making him do that was so important. Both of those things would help me plan my next move.

I dropped to a knee beside the dead giant and started patting him down—another calculated risk, but I was hoping that it would be at least a couple of minutes before someone decided to investigate why the frozen camera wasn't working. There were at least fifty giants in the museum, and I needed some more weapons to kill them with.

But there wasn't much to find. He didn't have any ID on him, and the only thing of real value or interest was the leather utility belt he wore. In addition to the gun I'd noticed earlier, the belt also contained an extra clip of ammo, a metal baton, a small bottle of pepper spray, and, most important, a walkie-talkie. The device was turned on, but currently no squawks or cracks of static echoed from the black plastic.

I unbuckled the belt and tugged it out from underneath the giant's body. I stood and cinched it around my waist, looping it as tight as it would go. Even then, it sagged and rode low on my hips. Good enough.

Then I did something that would have made Finn wince with agony and shriek with despair: I chopped up my dress.

Using my bloody knife, I sliced off the bottom half of the skirt, so that the fabric ended just above my knees. I also made several more slits in the skirt, making it easier for me to reach through them and get to the second knife I had strapped to my thigh. Finn would no doubt bitch and moan when he saw what a hack job I'd done on the beautiful gown, but the long skirt just wasn't practical for fighting. Besides, the giant's blood had already ruined it, and I imagined I'd get the garment quite a bit more messy before the night was through. More like before the next two minutes were up.

I also used my knife to cut the extra fabric into long strips, threading a couple of them through the straps on my heels and tying them to the left side of the utility belt. I couldn't risk wearing the shoes, but I didn't want to wander around barefoot all night either. I stuffed the rest of the fabric strips into a pouch on the belt.

As a final measure, I checked the giant's gun, making sure the safety was off and that there was a round in the chamber. I also practiced drawing it out of the holster a few times until I could do it quickly and smoothly. I didn't much care for guns, but I'd use them if the situation called for it—and it certainly did tonight.

When I was ready, I leaned over and grabbed the key card from where it had landed next to the giant's body, using the edge of my shortened skirt to wipe the blood off the plastic. Then I turned toward the door and drew in a breath.

I wasn't sure what I would find behind the metal, but I was as ready as I could be to face it—and to kill whatever danger might be coming my way.

✻ 11 ✻

I slid the card through the reader. A light on the top
flashed a bright green, and the door *snick*ed open. I
stuffed the card into a pouch on the utility belt and tightened my grip on my knife.

I rushed through the opening, my knife up and ready
to slice into whoever was standing inside. But instead of
cutting down another giant or two, I found myself in an
empty hallway.

Actually, it was more like an antechamber, a wide stub
of a room. A wooden coat rack stood in the corner, its
empty arms making it look like a scalped tree. A series of
metal lockers lined the left wall, fronted by a long metal
bench.

My gaze snapped to the second, interior door ahead
of me, and I waited, just waited, for someone to open it.

But no one did.

No one came to investigate. No one poked a head out

of the interior room to ask a question of a fellow robber. No one ambled over to the snack machine that hummed against the right wall, its fluorescent bulbs flickering like a bug zapper.

Well, if they weren't going to come out to me, I had no problems going in to them.

Still moving as quietly as possible, I pulled the exterior door shut behind me and headed for the one at the far end of the chamber. This door was made of wood instead of metal, and I could hear music playing, some twangy country song about a woman getting revenge on a man who done her wrong. Even worse, whoever was on the other side was singing along in a very loud, very screechy, very off-key voice. I winced. Somebody needed some singing lessons. A chorus of dogs howling and cats hissing would have sounded better. But the caterwauling told me that there was only one person inside. No one else would have put up with the country-western karaoke act.

I shut the awful screeching out of my mind, reached forward, and tried the knob. It turned easily, and I opened the door just a crack. The actual security center wasn't much bigger than the antechamber, and a series of monitors took up the back wall, along with several keyboards, joysticks, and a control panel, all arranged on a long table. Another table stood at a right angle to the first one. It too was covered with monitors, although all of those screens were fuzzy with snow.

No wonder, since they were peppered with bullet holes. I eyed the monitors and the blue and white sparks flickering inside them. Judging from the blood spatters on the broken glass, someone had been shot in front of the monitors. Maybe even more than one person, given the amount of blood.

A couple of chairs squatted in front of the screens that were still working, but only one was occupied. The offending singer was another giant, one who was tossing her long black hair from side to side as she rocked back and forth in her chair to the music like she was some kind of country diva. An iPod blared on the table. I eyed the device. That was going to be the second thing in here that I killed.

I held my position, waiting to see if the giant would sense me watching her, but she was too engrossed in her song, so my gaze moved past her to the bank of monitors. A few of the screens were dark, but almost all of the cameras that were on were focused on the rotunda, showing the hostages from several different angles. One screen on the top row of monitors was fuzzy, as though there was a thick film covering the lens. That must be the camera in the hallway that I'd Iced over. I also spotted Clementine and Owen on one of the monitors in the far bottom left corner, although I couldn't tell what they were doing from this distance.

The song on the iPod finally came to an end, and, mercifully, so did the giant's singing. She leaned forward and grabbed the device, as though she was going to cue up another song. While she was distracted, I tucked my knife back into its slot and grabbed the gun out of the holster on my belt. I used the nozzle of the gun to push the door open slowly the rest of the way. *Three in the head, dead, dead, dead,* just like Dixon had said—

The door creaked.

The giant's eyes immediately flicked to one of the blank monitors, and I knew she could see my reflection there. I raised the gun, but it was already too late.

More quickly than I would have imagined, she whirled around and chucked her iPod at me. I ducked the sailing bit of plastic, stepped forward, and raised the gun again, but the giant kicked out with her foot, causing me to jump to the side. My hip slammed into the corner of the second table off to the right, causing a hiss of pain to escape my lips. The table rocked back and forth, causing more sparks to shoot out from the broken monitors.

Before I could raise the gun a third time, the giant barreled out of her chair and chopped her hand down, smacking the weapon out of my fingers. She charged at me again, spreading her arms out wide and trying to catch me in a bear hug and squeeze the life out of me. She probably expected me to retreat, but instead I stepped forward and leaped up, head-butting her in the chin. She growled and staggered back, but she didn't quit. Once more, she surged at me.

This time, I let her come.

Just before the giant put her hands on me, I sidestepped her and hooked my right foot around hers, making her stumble. Grabbing her utility belt, I played off of her own momentum and shoved her into the still-sparking monitors. Her head slammed through one of the glass screens, and a shower of white and blue sparks erupted. Hisses, cracks, and pops sounded, and the giant screamed as her body started convulsing. I took a few steps back, making sure that I was clear of the electricity surge. She screamed a second time, the sound as high, sharp, and whiny as a power saw. I winced again, as if that would somehow protect my eardrums. At this point, I'd kill her just to get her to stop making that awful noise.

But I didn't have to. After a few moments, the giant quit screaming, her body quit convulsing, and she slumped down onto the table, her head still stuck inside the monitor. The sizzle and stench of charred flesh told me that she was dead.

"Hurrah for the sound of silence," I murmured.

With the giant dead, I grabbed the gun from where it had fallen on the floor and slid it back into its holster on my belt. I also took a moment to pull out one of my knives and set it down on the table within easy reach, just in case one of her pals came into the security center before I was ready to leave.

Careful to keep away from the giant, I turned my attention to the bank of monitors on the back wall, the ones that hadn't been shot up and were still working. I did a quick scan of the cameras showing the scene in the rotunda, but things were the same as before. Hostages sitting on the floor, giants surrounding them, Opal transferring the jewelry from the garbage bags to two more silverstone briefcases.

Once again, I wondered what Clementine thought was so important about the jewelry when she had so much art to loot, but I didn't have time to puzzle it out.

I scanned the monitors until I found an angle that showed my friends. Eva, Finn, and Roslyn were still clustered around Phillip. His eyes were open, and he was gazing up at Eva. He didn't look to be any worse, but I couldn't really tell without seeing him in person. One thing was for sure, he wasn't going to get any better just lying there.

That mental clock in my head started ticking a little louder and a whole lot faster. Because every minute, every second, that passed was one that might mean the difference between Phillip living or dying. As the Spider, I'd done jobs on specific timetables, but a friend's life hung in the balance tonight. There was nothing I could do about the time that had already passed, but I could control how I took down Clementine and her crew—the sooner, the better.

So I turned my attention to the last monitor, the one in the bottom left corner that showed Clementine and Owen. I squinted at the screen. The two of them seemed to be standing in front of a very large door, with three of her men waiting behind them. The angle sucked, and I couldn't hear what they were saying, so I started pushing buttons, sliding controls, and toggling the joysticks back and forth. It took me a few seconds, but I was finally able to zoom in on the two of them. I hit another button, and the sound of the giant's country drawl flooded the security center.

"Isn't it a beauty?" Clementine said. "Why, it's almost a work of art itself."

She paced back and forth, walking in and out of the view of the camera. For the first time, I noticed a lock on the door, along with a large round wheel, and I realized exactly where Clementine had taken Owen: the museum's vault.

"The vault walls are marble, just like the rest of the museum, but the door itself is reinforced silverstone, more than six inches thick," Clementine said. "That's the tricky part, and that's where you come in, Mr. Grayson."

Reinforced silverstone? Well, the Briartop directors had certainly gone all out. Silverstone was one of the strongest metals around, with an insanely high melting point. It wasn't something you could just blast through with a couple of sticks of dynamite or a brick of C-4. No, you needed real power to get through any kind of door with silverstone in it—elemental power. Even then, you'd need to find someone with a whole lot of juice, since the metal could absorb all forms of magic. Or you could do what Clementine had done and find someone with an elemental talent for metal to help you.

Someone like Owen.

"Really?" he asked. "Why is that?"

She looked at him and smiled. "Because you're going to open it for me."

For a moment, everything was silent, except for the soft hum of the camera feed and the faint, tinny flicker of the black-and-white monitor in front of me. On the screen, Owen stared at Clementine a moment, then threw back his head and laughed.

"You think I can crack that vault?" He let out another series of chuckles. "Lady, you are out of your mind."

Instead of being insulted, her smile widened. "Not at all."

Owen realized that she was serious, and his laughter abruptly cut off, the last notes dying on his lips. He looked at the vault door again, really studying it.

"What's in there that you want so badly?"

"Funny you should ask. You see, art isn't the only thing that Mab Monroe left behind," Clementine said. "In addition to all those baubles on display in the rotunda, the Fire elemental also had a vast personal fortune. But the most interesting thing is that she didn't keep it stashed away in some bank or even just lying around as cash. No, it seems that Ms. Monroe preferred a more tangible, old-fashioned currency: gold."

Owen frowned, his black eyebrows drawing together in thought. "You're telling me that Mab Monroe kept her personal fortune all in gold, and all of it . . . here?"

"Almost like a dragon out of some fairy tale, if you think about it," Clementine said. "Except, of course, that Mab was much more dangerous than any old dragon out of any old story. But now that she's gone, well, we don't have to worry about someone breathing elemental Fire on us, now, do we?"

She slapped a hand to her side and guffawed. It was good that she amused herself, because I didn't find one thing about this funny, and neither did Owen, judging from his grim, worried expression.

When she was done congratulating herself on being so clever, Clementine started pacing again. "But to answer your questions, yes. I have it on good authority that a big chunk of Mab's gold is stashed right here in this very vault. Apparently, Mab had a thing about not trusting banks, and she thought it would be less obvious storing her gold here rather than at one of the downtown banks. Plus, I believe the museum director was into her for a substantial gambling debt, so she took it out in trade for this."

Owen shook his head. "Well, that's a nice story, but it still doesn't explain how you think I can help you get into the vault."

"I've done my research, Mr. Grayson. I've learned quite a bit about silverstone these last few months. How tough it is, how durable, and how you need elemental magic to get around or even through it. And I think that you're just the man for the job."

"Why?" Owen shot back at her. "Just because I have an elemental talent for metal?"

Clementine waved a hand at him, dismissing his concerns. "Oh, I know all about your power, Mr. Grayson, especially the sculptures and weapons you make in your spare time. In fact, I bought one of your knives at a charity auction just last month. Exquisite craftsmanship."

My gaze dropped from the screen to the knife I'd set down on the table. The blood from the giant I'd killed in the hallway outside outlined the spider rune stamped into the hilt. Owen had made this knife and four others for me as Christmas presents, and they were indeed exquisite weapons, just as Clementine had said about her own blade. Light, strong, durable, razor-sharp. I'd used the knives more than once on my enemies, and they'd never failed me.

Owen shook his head. "You've got it all wrong. Yes, I have an elemental talent for metal. Yes, I can craft all sorts of things out of it. But that vault door? Six inches of reinforced silverstone? That is well beyond my magic."

"I thought you might say that, and you just might be right. But believe me when I tell you that I've planned ahead. I don't expect you to do it all by yourself."

Clementine snapped her fingers. One of the giants stepped forward, a duffel bag swinging from his hand. He put the bag on the floor, unzipped it, and reached inside it. A moment later, he came out with a welder's torch. Another giant with another bag stepped forward and pulled out a similar torch.

The third giant stepped forward, but instead of reaching into yet another bag, like I expected, he simply held out his hand. A moment later, elemental Fire crackled to life in his palm, the flames flowing from one of his fingers to the next and back again.

Owen eyed the torches and the Fire, but he didn't say anything.

"Now, taken as one piece, the vault door is pretty much impregnable, just like you said," Clementine said. "There's no way to blast through it. But I don't need to get through the door, just around it. So you and my boys are going to use the torches to superheat the silverstone locking mechanism, along with the help of Oscar's elemental Fire. When it gets hot enough, you'll use your magic to gut the lock so that it's useless. Once that's done, you'll go to work on the hinges, popping those off, and then I'll just move that big slab of a door right out of the way."

It was a good plan—a smart plan. I'd thought that Clementine was all about brute strength, raw force, sheer power, given what had happened in the rotunda earlier, but she was also clever. The more I learned about her, the more I admired her, sort of like appreciating a copperhead's coiled beauty on the green forest floor, knowing that it would bite you the second you were in range of its curved, venomous fangs.

Owen shook his head again. "I'm telling you that I can't do it. I don't have enough magic for that sort of thing."

"This isn't about strength, Mr. Grayson, it's about finesse. A small, controlled, precise manipulation of metal and magic. Something you do exceptionally well, judging from what I've seen of your work. You can shape, mold, and work with silverstone like nobody else I've ever seen."

Owen didn't respond.

"Believe me, I know that you're not the strongest elemental out there," Clementine said. "Now that Mab's dead, I imagine that title would go to your girlfriend. If Ms. Blanco were still alive, that is."

Owen stared at her—just stared and stared at her. His face pinched, his body stiff and straight, his hands clenched into fists. The giant noticed his shock, distress, and anger. She smirked at him, her pretty features twisting into an arrogant sneer. All at once, Owen let out a wild, angry roar, put his head down, and charged at Clementine.

He barreled into the giant, throwing her back against the vault door. Clementine snapped her fist forward, but Owen caught her hand in his. Owen didn't have her giant strength, but he was no lightweight. Working all those long hours and years in his forge had made him strong. More than that, though, he was a smart fighter. While their hands seesawed back and forth, Owen brought his other fist up and punched her in the face with it.

The solid, heavy *smack* of his hand cracking against her skin made me smile.

Clementine grunted with surprise and annoyance, but

Owen wasn't done. He managed to hit her in the face three more times before two of her men stepped forward, grabbed his arms, and dragged him away from her. Even then, Owen fought back, kicking, bucking, and trying to break loose. But the giants tightened their holds until he realized he couldn't get free. Slowly, his struggles ceased, although I could hear his quick, ragged breathing through the camera feed.

Clementine straightened up and pushed away from the vault door. She pressed a hand to her face, pulled it away, and stared at the smear of blood on her fingers. Owen had split her lower lip open with his last punch.

"I'll give you that one," she said. "Although the next time you lay a hand on me, you'll wish that you hadn't."

One of the giants holding Owen shivered at her words, but he raised his chin in defiance.

"Now, enough talk," Clementine said. "It's time for you to get to work."

"And if I can't do it?" he asked in a low, angry voice. "Or refuse to?"

She shrugged. "Then I'll let Dixon and the rest of my men take turns with your pretty little sister out there. She'll die screaming, along with the rest of your friends. So I'd figure it out if I were you, Mr. Grayson."

Owen sucked in another angry breath, but he forced himself to let it out and slowly unclench his fists. "Fine," he muttered. "You win."

He would do anything to protect Eva, even help the giants break into the vault.

Clementine let out a delighted laugh. "Of course I win. I *always* win. Now, get started. Time's a-wasting."

Once again, Owen didn't respond.

Clementine went over to one of her men. "I'm going to go check in with the others," she said. "You three get started. And don't stop until the door is ready to be moved. You understand me?"

The giant nodded.

Clementine moved to the back of the room, out of sight of the camera, and a few seconds later, I heard a door shut, telling me that she'd left the vault.

One of the giants drew several pairs of safety goggles out of his duffel bag. He handed a pair to Owen, which he reluctantly slipped on, along with some heavy work gloves. He stood by while all three of the giants put on their own goggles. Then one of the men handed Owen a torch and carefully fired it up. Another giant fired up the second torch and turned toward the vault door while the last one reached for his Fire magic, making flames dance across his fingertips once more.

Owen hesitated, staring first at the lit torch in his hand, then at the giants. I knew he was thinking about using the torch to toast the three men. I would have been.

But I wasn't surprised when he finally faced the vault door, stepped forward, and used the torch to start heating up the silverstone lock. Because I would have done the same thing then too. I would have played along nicely until I was sure the others were safe, then I would have laid into Clementine and her crew for all I was worth, even if I knew that I wouldn't survive the fight. But the giant had her hand clutched around Eva's and the others' throats, and she and Owen both knew it. He had no choice but to go along with her scheme—for now.

I studied the monitor for a few more seconds. I didn't have Owen's elemental talent for metal, so I didn't know how long it would take him to get through the silverstone. Forty-five minutes, maybe an hour, given what I'd heard Clementine tell Opal and Dixon earlier. It depended on how slowly he decided to work, and he would probably drag things out as long as possible, in hopes of figuring out some way to turn the tables on Clementine and her men.

But Owen didn't have to worry about that—because I was going to do it for him.

Clementine might claim that Mab's gold was stored inside the Briartop vault, but I didn't necessarily believe her. Maybe it was gold, maybe it was diamonds, maybe it was something else entirely. But whatever it was, Clementine wanted it.

And I was going to take it from her.

Clementine would just as soon kill me as look at me. She'd proven that already tonight. She wouldn't be threatened, scared, or intimidated in the slightest by me. And if she realized that I was still alive—that the Spider was still alive—sneaking through the museum and killing her men, she'd grab Finn or one of my other friends and hold a gun to their heads until I agreed to surrender. Once I did that, she'd put a couple of bullets in my skull, and that would be the end things for me and everyone else in the rotunda.

No, whatever was in that vault was the only bit of leverage I would be able to get here. If I swiped it first, Clementine would have no choice but to deal with me to get what she wanted, and I'd force her to trade my friends and the rest of the hostages for the treasure in the vault. Of course, Clementine would no doubt try to double-cross and murder me, but that was nothing new.

Still, to steal whatever was in the vault and rescue Owen, I needed supplies, and I needed help—and I knew exactly where I could get them both.

I turned away from the monitors and went over and looked at the giant I'd killed earlier, still careful not to touch her. She seemed to have the same gear that the first guard had: leather belt, gun, ammo, baton, pepper spray. I wouldn't have minded another gun and some more ammo, but I didn't want to electrocute myself to get them.

So I pulled out the metal baton I already had and used it to smash the rest of the security camera monitors. I'd seen what I'd needed to, and I didn't want Clementine and her crew using them to try to find me when I finally made my presence known.

When that was done, I went out into the antechamber where the lockers were. It was easy enough for me to use my Ice magic to freeze and then shatter their flimsy metal locks. I sorted through the items inside, but I didn't find anything useful or interesting, except for the fact that one of the guards kept a stash of porn in the bottom of his locker. Of course he did. Why stare at priceless works of art for hours on end when you could look at fake, inflated boobies?

I also came across a small red cooler, which I opened. Someone had brought his lunch along tonight. A tuna fish sandwich, from the rancid smell of it. I wrinkled my nose. Ugh. I shut the lid and put the cooler back where I found it.

I had turned away from the lockers and started to go over to the exit when I noticed a door next to the vending machine, one I hadn't spotted before. A sign on the front read *Broom Closet*, but I was more interested in the blood smears on and around the handle. Senses alert and knife in hand, I carefully opened the door—and immediately stepped back as bodies tumbled out of the dark space.

Five poor souls had been killed and stood up and crammed into the closet, and they pitched forward and thumped to the floor like dominoes. Three men and two women, all giants, all with multiple bullet holes in them. Well, now I knew what had happened to the museum's real guards. They'd been shot, probably while they'd been looking at the monitors in the other room. There was nothing I could do for them, so I left them on the floor, although I did take a moment to close their eyes.

My search complete, I headed over to the exterior door. I listened a moment, but I couldn't hear any more through it than I had before, so I cracked it open and gazed out into the hallway.

The dead giant lay in the same position as before, although more blood had pooled under and around his body. Sharp, shocked whispers reverberated through the gray marble, but I shut those sounds out of my mind and listened for any other notes of warning, danger, or unease that might be rippling through the stone. But there was nothing. Now that Clementine and her crew had taken control of the museum, the stones had settled down a bit, their tension lessened—at least, until I killed someone else within the marble walls.

I considered moving the giant's body inside the antechamber but discarded the idea. He was far too heavy for me to carry. Sure, I could drag him, but it would take some effort on my part, and I needed my energy for more important things. I couldn't have cleaned up all that blood, anyway, not without Sophia and her Air elemental magic to help me. Sooner or later, one of Clementine's men was sure to stumble across the dead giant, but I just had to hope that luck, that capricious bitch, would let it be later. I doubted my chances on that, but there was nothing else I could do.

I shut the security-center door, stepped over the giant's body, and went on my merry, murderous way.

I moved through the museum halls as quickly and quietly as possible. Since the evening's festivities had been centered in the rotunda area, most of the other lights had been turned down low, casting many of the hallways in darkness. Fine by me. The lack of light gave me more shadows to skulk through.

Three times I passed rooms that Clementine's men were busy looting, the exhibit halls I'd heard her mention before on her walkie-talkie. The giants had switched the lights on in those areas, the better with which to see the art they were stealing. I repeatedly thought about storming inside and taking out the giants, but there were six men in each room, which was about four too many for me to kill with anything resembling quiet. Besides, I needed to get out of the museum before the bodies were discovered, so I tiptoed across the open doorways when the robbers' backs were turned and hurried on.

Finally, I reached a door that led outside. It was locked, but my stolen key card changed that. In the hushed quiet of the museum, the metallic *snick* the door made seemed to reverberate from one hallway to the next, like a locator beacon *ping*ing and giving away my position. The giants were probably too busy rolling up paintings and hefting sculptures around to notice the noise, but I still needed to move. So, knife in hand, I slipped outside and pulled the door shut behind me, wincing once more at the unwanted sound it made.

A series of rhododendron bushes had been planted on either side of the entrance, and I wormed my way in between them and the marble wall of the museum, ignoring the tickles and faint scratches of leaves and stems along my bare arms and the soft, loose soil working its way between my toes. Crouching down, I stared out into the night.

I was on the left side of the museum, facing west toward the river. A series of lush gardens rolled across the landscape in front of me. A gray stone path zoomed from the door straight to the gardens before splitting into three separate branches that plunged even deeper into the dark foliage, like a pitchfork stabbing into the shadows. Whitewashed benches and gazebos stood here and there among the manicured beds of roses and pansies, while weeping willows towered over them all, their tendrils kissing the soft petals below. Magnolia and mimosa trees had also been planted in the gardens, right next to sunflowers that drooped under the heavy weight of their own seed-laden heads. Old-fashioned iron streetlights placed along the paths provided a soft golden glow, filtered by the wash of bugs dancing around the globes. Once again, the aroma of honeysuckle saturated the air, although now the scent seemed sickly sweet, as though it were the funeral-home stench of perfumed, floral death.

I didn't see or hear anyone, but I stayed low, hugged the marble wall, and followed the path of the rhododendrons all the way around to the front corner of the building. It was just as quiet here as it had been in the back, and only the annoying hum of the mosquitoes broke the silence. I started to ease across one of the side lawns so I could slip into the parking lot when a small beep sounded, and a door hissed open to my left. I hunkered back down into the bushes.

Two giants carrying a couple of cardboard boxes each stepped out into the night air, along with Dixon, who was speaking into his walkie-talkie. I'd turned the volume down on the one I'd swiped from the first giant I'd killed so it wouldn't crackle and give me away at the wrong time, but Dixon wasn't even trying to be quiet, so I was able to hear his words loud and clear.

"We're outside. I'm going with Leroy and Keith to load up one of the trucks, then checking on Hannah and Anton down by the bridge."

"Good." Clementine's voice sounded through his walkie-talkie. "Tell Hannah and Anton to make sure the job is done right. I don't want any mistakes. If the bridge goes too soon, we're screwed."

The bridge? What were they doing at the bridge?

"Understood." Dixon clipped the walkie-talkie back onto his belt, then gestured at the giants. "Well, you heard her. Let's get going."

Dixon led the two giants toward the museum's main entrance. I stayed behind the bushes and followed them. Four large moving trucks were now parked in front of the building. The back of one truck was open, revealing long, skinny tubes and odd shapes covered with thick sheets of bubble wrap—all the art the giants had grabbed so far.

"All right, let's get what's in these boxes loaded up," Dixon said.

The other two giants climbed up into the back of the truck and started unloading the contents of the boxes they'd been carrying, carefully stacking up more tubes and rearranging the padded sculptures so they could have as much room as possible inside for their stolen loot.

Dixon stayed on the ground and watched the other men work. While they were distracted, he casually bent down as though he was going to tie his boot. Instead, he slipped a small cell phone out of his pants pocket and hit a button on it. A faint beep sounded. Dixon nodded to himself and slid the phone into his pocket again before smoothly getting back to his feet.

My eyes narrowed. What was Dixon up to? And why didn't he want his comrades to know about it?

The giants finished unloading their latest haul and

hopped out of the back of the truck with their now-empty boxes. Dixon waved them toward the museum.

"You two go back inside and get the next load," he said. "I'm going down to the bridge to check on the others."

The giants nodded, walked up the main steps, and disappeared into the museum. Dixon set off in the other direction, heading away from the truck and the museum. Curious, I crept after him.

Dixon followed the main road down the sloping hill to the covered bridge. Luckily, the gardens ran alongside the pavement, so I was able to slide from tree to tree and bush to bush and move parallel to him. My bare feet didn't make a sound on the soft, dew-covered grass, but Dixon didn't even think to look around and see if someone might be following him. He thought everyone was secure inside the museum.

He'd realize how wrong he was soon enough—when I killed him.

Finally, Dixon reached the bridge. I stopped in the gardens and hunkered down behind a holly bush, about twenty feet from him. Two of the old-fashioned iron streetlights were planted in the pavement on either side of the bridge, although their golden glow did little to dissipate the shadows spilling out from the mouth of the structure.

Two other giants—a man and a woman—were crouched right inside the bridge entrance. The woman was shining a flashlight at the wooden boards while the man rummaged through a duffel bag on the ground next to him. I thought he might have another welder's torch stuffed inside, like the men in the vault had, but instead, the giant drew out a crowbar and a roll of duct tape.

Along with a bomb.

I squinted and leaned forward, wondering if I was imagining things, but the giant held the device up in the flashlight's beam, and I got an even better look at it. A flowery blossom of colored wires and a cell phone taped and plugged into a small, foil-wrapped brick. Yep, that was a bomb all right. My eyebrows shot up in my face. What the hell were they going to do with that?

"How's it going, Anton?" Dixon asked.

"Good," the male giant replied. "We're just getting ready to put everything into place."

Anton set the bomb and the duct tape aside, picked up the crowbar, and used it to pry up one of the bridge boards. The old, weathered wood groaned in protest, but it was no match for his strength. When the board was free, Anton taped the bomb to the underside of the wood before slowly, carefully fitting the board back into its original position.

"You're up, Hannah," Dixon said, looking at the female giant, the one with the flashlight.

Hannah got down on her knees and held out her hand. A moment later, a bit of elemental Fire sparked to life on her index finger, and her eyes began to glow a dull orange from her power, like two matches burning in her face. Her magic pricked at my skin like tiny, invisible needles, making me grind my teeth together. Hannah didn't have nearly as much juice as Mab had. In fact, she was quite weak in her magic, but she still had enough power to lean down and trace something into the top of the board: a rune.

In addition to using them as their personal, familial,

and business symbols, elementals could also imbue runes with magic and get them to perform specific functions. No doubt Hannah was scorching some sort of Fire symbol into the wood.

Hannah finished creating the symbol and leaned back on her heels. She let go of her power, and the elemental Fire was snuffed out on her fingers, causing a bit of smoke to waft up into the night sky. The uncomfortable feel of her magic vanished a moment later.

"Good job," Dixon said, clapping her on the shoulder. "Your rune and that explosive will be more than enough to blow the bridge."

So that's *what* they were planning, to toast the bridge. The *when* was easy enough to figure out: after they'd sacked up all of the art and were on the mainland once more. But why destroy the bridge at all? All of the hostages would already be dead, so it wasn't like there would be anyone left to follow them or sound an alarm . . . unless . . . unless the giants didn't plan to kill the hostages after all.

I tapped my fingers against the hilt of my knife as I tried to figure things out.

Obliterating the bridge was one way of trapping all of the hostages on the island and avoiding chase. But why even leave the hostages alive in the first place? It wasn't like Clementine had any qualms about killing people. So why let anyone live who could identify or come after her after the fact? It didn't make sense that she would, especially if she wanted her giants to take over the underworld from all the crime bosses being held in the rotunda.

And it wouldn't solve the problem of the cops that

would be hot on her trail just as soon as someone sounded the alarm. By the time the giants got done in the museum, they'd have four big, heavy trucks full of art—too much for a quick getaway, especially given the twisting, curving two-lane road that led from the museum back down into the city. Clementine had to have realized that. So what else did she have up her sleeve? How was she planning to evade the po-po? That I didn't know worried me.

"Pack it up and get back to the museum," Dixon said. "We've still got more rooms to go through."

Hannah grinned. "Sure thing. We wouldn't want all that art to just hang there, now, would we?"

All three giants laughed. Bad jokes seemed to be the calling card of this crew.

Dixon left the bridge and headed back up the hill, leaving the other two giants behind to collect the gear they'd stowed a few feet away from the bridge entrance. Dixon started whistling, and the cheerful sound made the black, murderous rage beat in my heart once more. I would have liked nothing more than to follow the bastard and knife him in the back for what he'd done to Jillian, but he wasn't important right now—the bomb was.

Hannah turned off her flashlight and put it down on the pavement while Anton shoved his crowbar back into his duffel bag. Dixon was already out of sight—and, more important, earshot, since I couldn't hear him whistling anymore.

Knife in hand, I straightened up and headed toward the edge of the garden. Unfortunately, the foliage stopped short of the bridge, leaving about ten feet of dead space and plenty of chance for the giants to see my approach.

I thought about using my Stone magic to harden my skin in case they were able to get to their guns quicker than I was able to get to them. But in the end, I decided not to. I wanted to conserve my magic as much as possible, since I didn't know how many more giants I might have to fight before the night was through.

So I grabbed my second knife from its holster, drew in a breath, and stepped forward—

A twig cracked under my bare foot.

It wasn't a loud sound, but it seemed to boom as big as a clap of thunder in the hushed night air. I cursed my own sloppiness and bad luck. First the creaky door, now this. I just couldn't catch a break tonight—or at least be quiet enough to sneak up on someone.

For a moment, the two giants froze, staring at each other. Then Anton fumbled for his gun while Hannah turned toward where I was, more elemental Fire flaring to life in the palm of her hand.

I stepped up and threw my first knife at Hannah, but my aim was off, and the knife only sank into her shoulder. Still, it was enough to break her hold on her magic, and the Fire was snuffed out in her hand. She screamed, clutched at the blade in her body, and staggered back against the wooden railing that ran along the outside of the bridge.

Even as she fell back, I raced forward, this time focusing my attention on Anton. He managed to yank the gun from the holster on his belt and take aim at me. I threw myself forward, rolling, rolling, rolling, the pavement digging into my sides, stomach, and shoulders.

Pfft! Pfft! Pfft!

Anton's gun had a silencer, just like Dixon's, so the bullets didn't make too much noise as they flew through the air over my head and raced away into the darkness. Well, that was one small favor, although Hannah's scream had already been far too loud for my liking. But there was nothing to do now but finish my enemies and hope that no one would hear the commotion.

I came to a stop right in front of Anton, and I surged up onto my knees and sliced my knife across his thigh. The wound wasn't deep enough to sever his femoral artery like I'd wanted, but it was still a serious cut, and blood spattered across my neck, chest, and hand.

Anton screamed and went down on his ass. He kicked his legs out and crab-walked backward across the pavement, scurrying away from me and heading toward the bridge opening—and the bomb.

I didn't know if he was deliberately moving toward the explosive or just trying to get away from me no matter what, but I could *not* let him touch that Fire rune. Depending on how it was rigged, the rune could ignite at the slightest touch and trigger the bomb, which could blow us all sky-high.

A gleam of metal caught my eye, and I saw his crowbar sticking out of the top of his duffel bag. Scrambling to my feet, I grabbed the weapon and lashed out with it.

I cracked the crowbar against the giant's knee, stopping his backward progress. He moaned and started to curl into a ball to protect himself, but it was too late. I raised the crowbar and brought it down again, this time on his head. The curved end stuck in the giant's skull, and when I ripped it out, blood spurted up like a geyser, coating the pavement, and Anton's eyes took on a glassy sheen. He'd be dead in another minute, two tops—

The crackle of magic filled the air, and I ducked to one side. A ball of elemental Fire streaked by my head and exploded against a nearby maple, sending smoke and sparks whooshing up into the sky. I whirled around to find Hannah standing behind me, the knife that should have been in her shoulder lying on the pavement at her feet.

"I'm going to burn you alive!" she hissed, another ball of elemental Fire flickering to life in her hand.

"Oh, I doubt that," I drawled, twirling the crowbar in my hand.

She reared back her hand to throw her magic at me, but I didn't give her the chance. I closed the gap between us, raised the crowbar high, and cracked her across the skull with it, just like her partner. Hannah staggered back, a dazed look on her face, but I went after her again and again, hitting her across the skull, neck, and chest as hard as I could, driving her back toward the wooden railing that ringed the edge of the island.

When I got close enough, I dropped the crowbar and buried a knife in her heart.

She sucked in a breath to scream, but I ripped the blade free, pivoted, and lashed out with my left foot, kicking her in the gut. Hannah grunted and stumbled back, the weight of her body causing the weathered wood railing to creak and groan. I pivoted once more, kicking her again. This time, the railing didn't hold, making the same sharp, snapping sound that the twig had made earlier under my foot. Hannah's arms windmilled, and she fell backward into the darkness. A few seconds later, I heard the splash of her body hitting the river far, far below.

I stood there in the middle of the road, bathed in the golden glow of one of the garden lights, my weapon clenched in my hand. I looked and listened, but the only sounds were my soft, quick breaths and the faint *plop-plop-plop* of blood dripping off the end of my knife. No shouts of alarm rattled through the air, no footsteps smacked in my direction, no bullets came my way. No one had heard the fight, although the pieces of pavement underfoot had already started to mutter about their sudden, violent deaths.

I grabbed my fallen knife, put both of my weapons back into their holsters, then stooped down and searched Anton. He didn't have anything particularly noteworthy, although I did trade my gun for his silenced one and reloaded the weapon with the spare ammo I found in his duffel bag. I also picked the crowbar back up and grabbed Hannah's flashlight. Once that was done, I got to my feet and stared at the bridge. Thinking.

After a moment, I grinned. If Clementine wanted to blow something up, I'd be more than happy to oblige her.

❊ 13 ❊

I decided to leave Anton where he lay on the pavement in front of the bridge. I didn't care if anyone found him. If things went according to my plan, everyone would know about me in a few more minutes anyway.

I stepped over the giant's body, walked through the bridge entrance, and dropped to my knees in front of the board I'd seen them messing with earlier. I clicked on the flashlight and moved the beam back and forth over the area. A symbol had been scorched into the top of the wood: a small circle surrounded by several wavy rays.

A sunburst. The symbol for fire. Mab's personal rune.

Well, I supposed that using that particular rune was rather appropriate, since the giants intended to steal all of the Fire elemental's treasures. I wondered if Clementine was as big a fan of irony as I was. Probably not.

The symbol glowed with a faint orange light, as though it were still hot and smoking from being burned into the wood. Usually, some action was required to trigger a rune like this. If it had been traced into a door, whoever was unlucky enough to open it would get a face full of elemental Fire for his or her trouble. In this case, it seemed like the giants planned to detonate the bomb underneath to get the rune to flare to life and add to the fire, heat, and damage from the explosive itself.

Well, not if I could help it.

I set the flashlight down, then put my hand on the adjoining board, careful not to touch and jostle the other piece of wood—or the rune on top of it—in any way. I had no desire to blow myself to kingdom come. At least, not before I'd saved my friends.

I flattened my hand on the wood, feeling a splinter stab into my thumb, then reached for my Ice magic. Once again, a cold silver light flickered, centered on the spider rune scar in my palm. It only took a moment for me to bring my magic to bear. Elemental Ice crystals quickly spread out from my palm, across the wood, and onto the adjoining board with the rune on it. I concentrated, forcing the crystals to flow all around the sunburst rune without actually touching it. Then, when the entire board was coated with an inch of my Ice, I let the crystals creep inward toward the rune.

The sunburst hissed and flashed with the elemental Fire it contained, threatening to erupt, engulf me in its deadly heat, and trigger the bomb below. But I slowly, carefully forced my Ice on top of the symbol, choking the Fire with the cold crystals of its opposing element.

Sweat beaded on my temples and gathered in the hollow of my throat, my head ached from concentrating so hard, and my flattened hand trembled and threatened to cramp with every passing second. Releasing a sudden burst of raw, unfocused magic was one thing. Even the weakest elemental could do that with relative ease, and it was the most popular form of attack during the desperate moments of an elemental duel. But small, controlled, precise bits of magic like this were difficult, tricky, and draining.

Still, it was something I'd been working on lately with Jo-Jo. I was strong in my magic, but I wanted to be smart with it too. Part of that meant going beyond raw, brutal force and learning how to better focus my power and use it to control, manipulate, and manage my elements and their impact on the environment around me. Simply put, I wanted to develop more of the finesse that Clementine had mentioned to Owen earlier.

And now here I was, doing the same thing to the sunburst rune that Owen was doing to the silverstone vault door. I wondered if he was having as difficult a time with it as I was. Probably not, since he used his magic like this all the time in his forge, crafting some new sculpture or weapon. He didn't have the sheer power that I did, but he definitely had the finesse aspect of his magic down pat.

Thinking about Owen motivated me to focus even more. I forced another layer of Ice over the sunburst rune, and the last bit of elemental Fire was finally snuffed out, choked to death by the cold power of my magic. I let out a breath that frosted in the air, despite the sticky summer humidity.

The rune neutralized, I was still careful as I used the crowbar to pry up the board and remove the bomb that had been taped to the underside. I put down the crowbar, picked up the flashlight, and focused the beam on the device. I was no expert in explosives, but Finn liked to make the occasional bomb in his spare time, and he'd taught me something about them. This one was pretty standard. A brick of what looked like C-4 with an attached cell phone that could be used either as a remote trigger or as a timer methodically ticking down until the bomb went *boom*.

I clicked off the flashlight, put it through a loop on my belt, and got to my feet. Since Clementine and her men weren't ready to leave the museum just yet, I felt safe enough carrying the bomb in my bare hand. Besides, I planned on using it soon enough.

So, bomb in hand, I turned, slid into the shadow-filled gardens once more, and headed back toward the museum.

The main doors to the museum now stood wide open to make it easier for the giants to haul their ill-gotten goods outside, I supposed. But no one was loading the trucks at the moment, so I was able to slide back into my spot between the museum wall and the greenery that ringed the building. There were a couple of other things I wanted to check before I put the next part of my plan into action. I set the bomb down next to a patch of briars that had sprung up in the middle of the rhododendrons and wiggled my way through the bushes. A few branches tugged at my hair, while twigs and leaves added more faint scratches to my arms, but I broke free to the other side. After that, it was simply a matter of crouching low, running over to the moving truck the giants had been loading up earlier, dropping to my stomach, and scooting underneath the large vehicle.

The caustic scents of gas, exhaust, and motor oil assaulted my nose, but I held back a cough and slithered forward, the pavement digging into my hips and stomach. Dixon had been messing around next to the truck for a reason, and I wanted to know what it was. When I reached the rear bumper of the truck, I rolled over so that I was on my back, slid the flashlight out of my belt, turned it on, and focused the beam up at the underside of the truck.

Nothing. I saw nothing out of the ordinary.

Just the wheels, pipes, and axles that made up any large vehicle. I moved the light this way and that, but I didn't see anything suspicious. In fact, the vehicle looked exceptionally well cared for, and all the parts practically gleamed, including the muffler and the box that was attached to it—

Wait a second. I was no mechanic, but mufflers didn't have boxes on their sides, as far as I knew. I wiggled up a little more so I could get a better look, and I realized that there was a hole in the box. I reached up and hooked my finger in the slot. To my surprise, the metal slid back easily, revealing what was inside the box.

Another bomb.

I froze, wondering if I might have somehow armed the device just by opening the box, but as the seconds passed and I didn't get blown into next week, I relaxed.

A little.

I let out a tense breath and slowly moved the light over the device. This bomb was just like the one I'd pried off the bridge board, a brick of explosive with a cell-phone trigger. It wasn't an enormous bomb, but it probably had enough juice to torch the truck and everything in it. That must have been what Dixon was checking with his phone earlier—to make sure that he could blow the device when the time was right.

I frowned, even more puzzled than before. Why would Dixon rig the moving truck to blow? Especially since there was already several millions of dollars' worth of art on it, with more on the way. Blowing the bridge was one thing. Clementine needed that to help with her escape. But this—this made no sense. Why destroy the things you had come here to steal in the first place?

I lay there under the truck a moment longer, thinking. Then I turned off my flashlight and wormed my way out from underneath the vehicle. I got to my feet, crept to the front of the truck, and looked inside the cab, but it was empty except for a set of keys hanging in the ignition.

I quickly scurried around to the other three trucks and looked into their cabs as well, but they too were all empty except for their respective keys. Since they giants hadn't started loading them up yet, the backs of them were all still shut and locked.

I paused a moment, thinking. Not seeing or hearing any giants headed my way, I decided to risk checking on one more thing.

I climbed into the back of the truck that was open, the one that I'd seen the giants stuffing with art earlier.

It was almost full, with only a narrow path leading from the front to the back, and I imagined the giants would fill in the rest of the available space soon enough. I snapped my flashlight back on, moving it over everything inside. Rolled-up tubes, bubble-wrapped statues, empty frames made of gold and silver. The giants had certainly been thorough in their looting.

But there was one thing that was missing: the silver-stone case that I'd seen Dixon carrying earlier.

I moved the flashlight over everything again, but the case wasn't here, which meant that the jewelry wasn't in the truck. But Dixon hadn't been carrying the case when he'd come out here with the giants before. So where had he taken the jewelry? And why not store it in here with everything else?

I snapped off the light and stood in the darkness, thinking some more. Then I shook my head, slid the flashlight back through the loop on my belt, and crept toward the open end of the truck.

Once I made sure that the coast was clear and no giants were coming my way, I hopped out of the back of the truck and slipped into the shadows again. I thought about prying the bomb off the undercarriage, but I decided to leave the device where it was. I already had one explosive, and, really, that was all that I needed.

Because now it was time to spin my own web of death and destruction—and for Clementine to finally feel the Spider's sting.

My next destination wasn't nearly as picturesque as the covered bridge.

I stopped long enough to retrieve the first bomb from where I'd left it behind the bushes. Then I hurried down into the parking lot and scurried through the rows of cars until I reached Finn's Aston Martin.

I checked to make sure there weren't any giants lurking

around, but the area was deserted. Once I was satisfied that I was alone, I scooted around to the front of the car and the tag there—FINNSTOY. I shook my head at his vanity, then reached around behind the tag until I felt something small, hard, and metal. I gave it a good yank, and a car key slid into my hand.

Given the shady life we led and all the people Finn, Fletcher, and I had killed over the years, the extra key was a little safety precaution we took. Finn had them stashed on all his vehicles, just like I had one on my car. Just in case one of us wanted to get into the other's ride without making a lot of noise or needed to make a quick, clean getaway.

I used the key to pop the trunk, which contained a couple of black duffel bags. Finn always kept extra gear in his various cars, just as I had some stashed in the back of the Pork Pit, at Jo-Jo's salon, and other places that I frequented. In case of emergencies. I'd say tonight definitely qualified as one of those.

I unzipped one of the duffel bags. Pistols, silencers, ammunition, cleaning oil. Most of the items inside were gun-related, since those were Finn's weapons of choice. I dumped the gun I'd taken off the giant and grabbed one of Finn's instead, along with a silencer and several clips of ammo. Guns jammed too much for my liking, but my foster brother was obsessive about keeping his in tip-top shape, so I knew they would be far more reliable than the giant's.

Finn also had an extra suit, shirt, tie, and socks and a pair of glossy wing tips stowed in a small suitcase in the trunk, along with an iron. Not helpful, unless I wanted to steam and starch someone to death. I shook my head again, this time at his obsessiveness when it came to his appearance.

Finally, I unzipped the final bag—my bag.

Finn kept some of his things in my car, and I reciprocated in his. After the gun, the next items I grabbed were two extra knives and their holsters. I buckled the bands of leather around my thighs and slid the weapons into the appropriate slots. Now I had four blades instead of just two. Good for me, bad for everyone else.

Last, I pulled a pair of black boots out of my bag.

The scarlet heels I'd worn earlier were still tied to the leather belt around my waist. After dropping them in the trunk, I grabbed a pair of socks out of the bag and sat on the rim of the open trunk. I used some of the cut-off fabric from my dress to wipe as much of the dirt, dew, and grass off my feet as I could before sliding the cotton socks and boots onto my feet.

The black socks and boots didn't exactly go with my dress. Or maybe they did, given how tattered, torn, and bloodstained the scarlet gown was now. Either way, now I wouldn't have to watch where I was walking or worry about cutting up my feet. Besides, I felt better in the boots—stronger and more grounded. Steel toes tend to bolster a girl's confidence in her ability to kick some serious ass.

When I was properly attired, I walked around the car, opened the passenger door, and grabbed my purse off the seat. I didn't carry a purse all the time, and I hadn't wanted to keep up with one tonight, which is why I'd left it in the car. But there was one final item in the tiny bag that I needed—a cell phone.

Clementine had mentioned that she had set up jammers inside the museum to stop people from calling the cops, but I was hoping that she hadn't thought to put them outside too, especially way down here in the parking lot. I powered up the device and was pleased to see that I had a signal.

I checked the time. Ten-oh-three. Forty minutes had passed since I'd stepped outside the museum. Owen should almost be through the vault door by now, if Clementine's calculations had been correct. Add the twenty minutes I'd spent roaming around inside the museum, and Phillip had been shot roughly an hour ago. That meant he probably had another hour left. Maybe two if we were both lucky.

Tick, tick, tick. Time to get on with things.

I touched a contact on my cell phone. It rang three times before she picked it up.

"Detective Coolidge." My sister's warm, confident voice flooded the line.

"Hey there, baby sister," I drawled. "Have I got a story to tell you."

✳ 14 ✳

"Are you joking?" Bria asked three minutes later when I'd finished explaining everything. "Please, please, *please* tell me that you're joking."

"Unfortunately not."

"You're telling me that a group of giants is holding everyone at the Briartop museum hostage? And robbing the place while they're at it?"

"You got it," I replied. "I'm out here in the parking lot, taking a halftime break before I head back in and let Clementine know that things aren't sewn up quite as neatly as she thinks they are."

"What are you going to do, Gin?"

The suspicion in her voice might as well have been code for *How many people are you planning to kill?* Always a valid question when it came to the Spider.

"Well, right now, I'm going to take the bomb I got off the bridge, go back into the museum, and blow something up. I haven't decided what, exactly. Any suggestions?"

Bria was silent for a moment. Then she let out a rueful laugh. "Well, I'd suggest the abstract wing. I never understood what all the fuss was about with that. Art should look like art, trees and flowers and people, not weird shapes and splotches of color all smeared together."

I grinned, even though she couldn't see me. "A woman after my own heart."

Through the phone, I heard Bria typing on her keyboard. She was at the police station, and as soon as I'd told her Clementine's name and description, she'd started searching for information on the giant.

"Here she is. Clementine Barker. Fifty-eight. Lives on Bear Hollow Road. Head of Barker Industries. Private security firm offering personal and corporate protection. I'm looking at the company website right now . . ." Bria let out a low whistle. "Wow. It looks like she's hired at least fifty, sixty giants in the last few weeks, judging from all the announcements on their press page."

"She actually put all her new hires on her website?"

"Yep," Bria said. "She's got up photos and bios listing all of the giants' credentials."

"Well, that would certainly fit in with the *rah-rah-giants* speech she gave in the rotunda earlier."

I told Bria what Clementine had said about getting her crew together so the giants could finally take what should have been theirs all along from the museum and everyone at the gala. When I finished, Bria hit some more buttons on her computer.

"No arrests on record for Clementine or her daughter,

Opal," Bria continued. "But it looks like her nephew has had more than a few brushes with the law. Dixon Barker: bar fights, drunk and disorderlies, even an assault charge he managed to skate on a few months ago."

"Oh, yes," I said. "I've seen Dixon. He's a real Prince Charming."

"As for Clementine, it looks like she's kept her nose clean, although there have been several complaints filed against her, her company, and her employees for assault, intimidation, things like that. She's also been questioned in a couple of murders. Seems like a few folks that Clementine was providing protection to died under mysterious, violent circumstances on her watch."

"You mean that she helped them along herself. Or got a better offer from someone else to eliminate her clients."

Bria snorted. "I'd say that's a distinct possibility from the autopsy photos I'm looking at right now. Most of the victims were beaten to death. No weapons were ever recovered, so I'd say Clementine used her fists on them. Nothing's stuck, though. Seems like Clementine has enough money and clout to get herself out of most scrapes. That, or she's paid off enough of the right people in the police department to make some of the more serious unpleasantness simply go away."

I nodded. That sounded exactly like something Clementine would do, given what I'd seen here tonight.

"So what do you need me to do?" Bria asked.

"Grab Xavier and get out here," I said. "Just you two. I don't want a whole bunch of cops showing up, sirens blaring, and spooking the robbers before I'm ready. Also, track down Jo-Jo. Finn had said that she was on a date with Cooper tonight. I couldn't tell how badly Phillip was injured, but at the very least, he's lost a lot of blood, and I want her to be able to heal him just as soon as it's safe."

"I'm waving Xavier over here right now. I'll call Jo-Jo and tell her to get out there as soon as she can. I'll text you when Xavier and I are on the island."

"Good," I said. "I've disarmed the rune trap on the bridge, but I'd still leave your car on the mainland side and cross on foot. After the two of you are on the island, stay in the gardens and move through them. That should keep you and Xavier away from any giants who might be patrolling the museum perimeter. I'm going inside right now to get Owen away from Clementine and her men. Once I have him, we'll head to the gardens on the west side of the island. Clementine's set up some cell-phone jammers inside the museum, so if I miss your text or don't respond, you and Xavier work your way through the gardens to that part of the island. That's where we'll meet."

"See you there." Bria hesitated again. "And, Gin?"

"Yeah?"

"Watch your back."

The concern in her voice warmed my heart. It always amazed me how far our relationship had come in the months since Bria had returned to Ashland. How we'd gone from suspicion, anger, and mistrust to understanding, acceptance, and respect.

"Don't worry, baby sister. I always do."

I hung up with Bria, silenced my phone and clipped it to my belt, and closed the trunk on the Aston Martin.

Then I grabbed the bomb and carefully set it on top of the smooth metal lid so I could study the cluster of wires and figure out which buttons to push to turn the attached cell phone into a timer that would trigger the device.

While I worked, I also turned up the volume on my stolen walkie-talkie. Clementine had trained her crew well, because there was no unnecessary chatter clogging up the airwaves. Just brief bursts of conversation about the giants moving from one room to the next, stripping all of the art from the floors and walls, and loading it up.

"The first truck is full," Dixon said at one point. "We'll have to open the second one now."

"Roger that," Opal responded. "I've got the rest of the jewelry loaded into the other two cases and ready for transport."

Once again, I wondered where exactly the giants were stashing the jewelry, but it didn't really matter. I didn't care about the gems and what became of them—only what happened to my friends and the rest of the hostages.

After that . . . silence, as the giants continued with their various tasks. I'd just found the command to program the cell-phone timer when the walkie-talkie crackled again.

"Anton?" Clementine's voice filled the air. "You and Hannah back inside the museum yet?"

I hesitated, debating whether or not to answer her. Anton had been one of the giants I'd killed at the bridge, so it wasn't like he was going to chime in. I didn't want to say the wrong thing and tip off Clementine that someone was running around the museum murdering her men, but I still needed a few more minutes of anonymity before I made my presence known.

"Anton?" Clementine asked again, her voice sharper and more demanding than before.

From the conversations I'd heard, it didn't sound like the crew was using complicated code words, so I decided to risk it.

"Done," I said, making my voice as deep and manly as possible. "Heading back now."

"Good," she responded. "Grayson is almost through the last of the hinges on the vault. Shouldn't take him more than another five minutes. So get your ass back up here, help the others load up the rest of the art, and get ready to move out."

"Roger that," I rumbled again.

I waited a few seconds, but Clementine didn't respond, and I didn't hear any other chatter either. It seemed like she'd bought my act, so I turned the volume back down, grabbed the bomb, and left the parking lot.

I snuck through the bushes until I was flush against the museum once more. I hugged the wall and hurried all the way around the building to the same side door I'd first snuck out of. Looking inside through the glass, I saw that the area was still dark. No giants moved in the hallway or adjoining rooms, so I used my stolen key card to open the door and slipped inside. Once again, the small *snick* sounded as loud as a gong banging in the mausoleum quiet of the museum, but there was nothing I could do to muffle the noise.

Now it was decision time. Where to plant the bomb? I needed a spot close enough to the vault to get Clementine's attention but far enough away to give me a chance to grab Owen, figure out what she was after in the vault, and get out before she realized that the blast was just a diversion.

Near the rotunda, I decided. The giants might have raised one gate so they could come and go from the area, but the hostages had zero chance of escaping with all of the other exits blocked. The bomb should have more than enough power to blow through one of the gates and create an opening.

I headed in that direction, once again tiptoeing across open doorways where Clementine's giants were still looting various parts of the museum. Judging from all the tubes, boxes, and crates clustered in the rooms, she'd trained her crew to be quick and efficient. She had tens of millions packed up already, more than enough to fund the most lavish criminal syndicate—or retirement—imaginable. So what was in the vault that was so important that she'd risk sticking around to get it? What score was bigger than what she already had?

I was going to find out—just as soon as I set off the bomb.

I made it all the way back to the main hallway that led into the rotunda. It was easy enough to hurry over to one of the side entrances, attach the bomb to the center of the metal gate there, and set the timer on the cell phone for ninety seconds.

90. I stared at the numbers on the phone, drew in a breath, and then let it out, preparing myself for the bloody battle to come. I was going to do this—I *had* to do this for Owen, Phillip, Roslyn, Eva, Finn, and everyone else the giants had trapped inside the rotunda. And for everyone Clementine and her men had already hurt and killed tonight—including Jillian.

Especially Jillian.

That black, murderous rage rose in me again, coating every part of my heart and soul, freezing my softer emotions, and making me cold, hard, and strong enough to do what was necessary. I leaned forward and hit the Send button on the cell phone. As soon as the timer started, I turned and ran in the opposite direction, not caring who saw or heard me.

Because there was no stopping the bomb now.

Or the Spider.

* 15 *

As I raced toward my destination, I counted off the seconds in my head.

Ten . . . Reach the end of the rotunda section . . .

Twenty . . . Start sprinting toward the vault . . .

Thirty . . . Reach the hallway that leads to the vault . . .

Forty-five . . . Slow my steps, quick, quick, quiet, quiet now . . .

Sixty . . . Look for a place to hide out of sight of the vault entrance . . .

Seventy . . . There, behind that doorway will do, giants have already looted this room . . .

Eighty . . . Knife in my hand, the spider rune stamped into the hilt pressing against the larger scar on my palm, familiar, comforting . . .

Ninety . . . Take a breath . . . get ready . . .

BOOM!

For a moment, there was just—noise. I couldn't see the

explosion, but I heard it, this great, thunderous roar, like a dragon belching fire, which rocked the whole museum. All around me, the stones screamed as the bomb blasted through the gate and into them, scorching the marble with heat and smoke and force and fire. I winced and shut the anguished wails out of my mind. I didn't like destroying stone, especially something as beautiful as the museum's gray marble, but it was a necessary evil—just like all the other horrible things I planned to do before the night was through.

More like before the next three minutes were through.

As soon as the last rumble from the blast faded away, I started counting off the seconds in my head once again.

Ten . . . twenty . . . thirty . . . forty-five . . .

The door that led toward the vault area flew open, banging into the wall so hard that it cracked the stone there. Clementine raced out, a gun in one hand and her walkie-talkie in the other. Dixon rushed along behind her, his gun also drawn. Given what I'd seen on the security camera earlier, that meant that there were at least three men still in the vault with Owen, maybe more.

"What the hell was that?!" Clementine screamed into her walkie-talkie as she ran.

Crackles and hisses burped back to her, but I couldn't make out the sounds or what the other giants were saying. It was all just background noise anyway. The only thing that mattered right now was reaching Owen and getting him to safety.

I waited until the two giants had disappeared down the hallway, then grabbed a second knife and sprinted for the open door. It led into a short hallway that opened up into an enormous chamber, with the vault sitting at the very back of that room. I raced forward, not even bothering to be quiet or cautious. The time for that was long over, along with hiding in the shadows.

Too bad the giants were waiting for me.

There were three of them in the chamber, just as I'd seen earlier through the security-camera feed. All three had their guns drawn and were facing the door, forming a solid line of mass, muscle, and malice. For a moment, my gaze flicked past the giants to Owen, but I couldn't see him clearly, so all I got was the sense that he was standing behind them, nothing more. One of the giants stood at more of an angle to the door than the others, his weapon trained on Owen instead of me. Still, the sight lifted my heart, because if Owen was still standing, then he was still breathing, still alive—which meant that I still had a chance to save him.

As soon as they saw me running toward them, two of the giants lifted their guns and fired. Not able to avoid getting hit, I reached for my Stone magic and used it to harden my skin.

Crack! Crack! Crack! Crack!

Bullets zipped through the air all around me, and the stench of gunpowder mixed with the haze of smoke and fumes from the elemental Fire and the welders' torches that had been used on the vault. A couple of the bullets hit my chest and bounced off, adding more holes to my already ruined dress, not to mention ugly black spider-web cracks to the walls.

I threw myself forward onto the giant on the far right, since he was holding a gun in one hand and a ball of elemental Fire in the other.

My knives punched into his chest in a quick one-two combination. The giant screamed, rammed his gun against my chest, and pulled the trigger, but the bullet hit my hardened skin and bounced off like all the others had. With his other hand, he shoved the ball of Fire into my chest, but I stepped forward and plastered my body to his, smothering the flames before they could do much more than singe my dress.

I stepped to one side so that the giant was between me and his friends, pulled my knives free, and then plunged them back into his chest once more in that same brutal one-two combo, like a boxer working his opponent on the ropes. Only instead of going in for another quick jab, I yanked the knives out a second time and sliced one of the blades across his throat.

I'd just repositioned the knives in my hands when the giant in the middle cursed and shoved his dying comrade out of the way. He dropped his gun, realizing that it wouldn't do him any good, and slammed into me, driving me across the chamber and into the far wall, right next to a table filled with art supplies. The force of the blow ripped my knives out of my hands and forced the air from my lungs with an evil hiss. My head snapped back against the marble, and I blinked and blinked, trying to fight off the sudden daze. My hold on my magic slipped, and my skin reverted to its normal soft texture. The giant noticed and grinned, drawing his fist back for a killing blow.

Desperate, I reached down, searching for something, anything, that I could use to fend off the giant. My hand closed around a handle on a small bucket of paint. I brought it up and slammed it into the side of the giant's face. Scarlet paint erupted out of the bucket and splattered all over him. The giant grunted and shook his head, trying to clear the fog from his mind and the paint out of his eyes.

I tossed the bucket aside and reached down again. This time, my hand closed around a paintbrush with a thick handle. I snapped the brush down at an angle on the edge of the table, causing the wood to crack on a diagonal and giving me a sharp point to work with instead of just a blunt block of wood.

The giant reached for me again, and I buried the daggerlike tip of the paintbrush in his throat. The wood wasn't nearly as sharp as one of my knives, but I kept sawing it in deeper and deeper, and the giant quickly started backing away from me instead of surging forward.

I didn't let him.

I held on to the end of the paintbrush and followed him, still twisting the wooden point into his body. When his legs finally started to buckle, I ripped the wood out of his throat and drove the point through his right eye, causing him to topple to one side.

He was dead before he hit the floor, but I was already moving, moving, moving toward the third and final man.

"You bitch!" he growled.

The last man had a gun too, which he immediately turned in my direction. But the giant had forgotten that Owen was also still in the vault—and holding a burning welder's torch. Owen reached up, grabbed the giant's shoulder, and shoved the concentrated flame into the back of the giant's head. His hair went up in a *whoosh* of smoke, and the acrid smell of charred flesh flooded the vault. The giant forgot all about shooting me. Instead, he screamed and batted at Owen, trying to push him away. I grabbed my knives from the floor, and a blade to the giant's heart ended his struggles and misery.

I stood there, a knife in either hand, breathing hard and trying to suck down as much oxygen as I could and push away the dull, pulsing pain of the fight. Owen slowly lowered the torch and turned it off.

We stared at each other, blood everywhere, three dead giants at our feet, the air hot, thick, and caustic with the stench of melted metal, burnt hair, and singed skin. Not exactly a romantic reunion, but I'd take what I could get, especially since we'd both survived the fight.

"Gin?" Owen whispered, his face white and tight with shock. "Is that really you?"

I grinned. "Isn't all the blood a dead giveaway?"

"But I thought . . . in the rotunda . . . the body . . ." His voice trailed off, as if the words choked him.

I shook my head.

He looked at my ruined dress, and understanding flashed in his violet eyes. I kept staring at him, wondering what he was thinking, what he was feeling now that he knew I was still alive.

Without a word, Owen stepped forward, dragged me into his arms, bloody knives and all, and crushed his mouth to mine.

❄ 16 ❄

I sighed, welcoming the sensation, welcoming the embrace, welcoming *him*.

For a moment, our bodies melded together, even as our tongues dueled back and forth in a hot, furious kiss. His fingers pressed into my back, and I stepped even closer to him, desperate for more, aching for every single part of me to be touching him. Owen's mouth slid off mine, and he buried his lips in my hair, his arms tightening around me even more, even as we both trembled and tried to catch our breath.

I closed my eyes, brought my hands up to his muscled back, and returned his hug, careful not to cut him with my knives. Then I just enjoyed the moment—the solid strength of his arms circling me again, the warmth of his skin pressing into mine, the hot whisper of his breath in my hair. I drank it all in, imprinting it on my mind, holding it close to my heart, and savoring every last second of it.

Then I dropped my arms and slowly pulled away from him, because we weren't safe yet, and the danger was far from over.

"How are you?" I asked. "Did they hurt you?"

Owen shook his head. "No. They just wanted me to open the vault, which I finally managed to do, right before that explosion ripped through the air. Your handiwork?"

I grinned again. "Of course."

Owen grinned back at me. Once again I savored the moment, then headed over to the vault door. Except for the wheel and hinges, which both had a smushed, melted look to them, the once-sturdy door was still intact—it just wasn't standing in front of the vault anymore. The door had been moved to one side, creating a five-foot-wide opening into the vault.

Owen noticed me staring at the door. "Once the giants and I got through the lock and hinges, Clementine picked up the door and lifted it out of the way all by herself. It was impressive. I had no idea she was that strong."

He was right. It *was* impressive—and worrisome. Because Clementine being that strong meant that I'd have to be even stronger to kill her. And I simply wasn't. Not now.

Oh, I was a powerful elemental, but I'd already used up part of my magic fighting her crew. I had some power stored in the spider rune ring on my index finger and the knives I was carrying, but I didn't know if it would be enough. Now I was starting to wonder if the power, magic, and energy I'd already expended would mean the difference between Clementine dying—or me.

Owen sighed and slumped against the side of the vault. For the first time, I noticed the sweat and soot on his face, the tired slant of his mouth, the slight sag of his shoulders. Sparks from the torches had landed on his tuxedo, leaving holes in his jacket, shirt, and pants, and his black hair was plastered to his forehead. Still, I thought he'd never looked more handsome or appealing.

"Are you okay?" I asked.

He nodded and straightened up. "Yeah, just tired. Using my magic on the door was hard—one of the hardest things I've ever done." He jerked his head at the opening. "But it worked just like Clementine said it would."

"Well, then," I said. "Let's finish the job for her and see what's inside."

The inside of the vault resembled something you'd see in a bank rather than a museum. A series of metal boxes lined one of the walls, while sturdy metal shelves took up two others. Three long tables cut through the center of the area, although their surfaces were clean and empty, I supposed so that the museum staff could open the metal boxes and sort through their contents there.

"Well, I certainly don't see any piles of gold," I said. "Do you?"

Owen shook his head.

Oh, there were valuables in the vault, and not just the expected paintings and sculptures. A pale jade elephant adorned with gold and emeralds peeped out from one of the shelves, right next to a small onyx statue of a mythological Nemean prowler, its ruby eyes flashing with some evil inner fire. A small antique violin gleamed inside an open case, while a diamond choker perched on a blue velvet stand, the gemstones proudly singing about their own exquisite clarity. The cluster of stones in the middle and the long, swooping lines of the necklace almost made it look like a spider spinning a web of diamonds.

It looked like Mab wasn't the only power player in Ashland who had stashed her shinies at Briartop. But there was no hoard of gold and nothing that looked like it was remotely worth the risk Clementine and her giants had taken in breaking in here, versus the art they had already swiped from the rest of the museum.

"If it wasn't gold, then what is Clementine really after?" Owen asked, voicing my thoughts.

I shook my head. "I don't know, but start looking. Whatever it is, we need to find it and get out of here before Clementine and her men come back."

Owen started looking at the white labels on the metal boxes along the left wall, while I took the opposite side of the vault, scanning first one shelf, then another. All the while, I was counting off the seconds in my head. It wouldn't be too long before Clementine realized that she'd been tricked and headed back this way. We needed to be out of the vault by then, or we were dead. But we also needed to find whatever she was after. Otherwise, we'd have no leverage to use to free the hostages.

A minute passed, then two. But all I saw were paintings, jewelry, more small statues, and a couture dress made of crimson feathers and adorned with rubies that was draped over a mannequin in the back corner. Well, Finn certainly would have considered that valuable enough to store inside the vault. And it was even in my color. Heh.

"Anything?" I asked.

Owen shook his head. "Nothing that jumps out at me. You?"

"Same."

Owen turned toward the wall of boxes again, but I took a step back and examined the vault. We could look for an hour and not find what Clementine had been after, and the giant and her men would return any second. As my gaze flicked from one shelf to another, I realized something important, something I should have remembered before now: that the inside of the vault was made of marble, just like the rest of the museum. An idea popped into my head of a way that I could at least narrow down our search area. I leaned forward, laid my hand on the wall closest to me, and reached out with my magic, concentrating on all the whispers of the stone.

The stone walls hummed with various emotions, mostly lofty pride and haughty arrogance at all the precious things they had housed and kept safe over the years. But those feelings were also mixed with notes of sweet relief, as the museum staff had been glad when certain items had been moved elsewhere so they wouldn't be held responsible for them anymore. I reached for more of my magic and let myself sink even deeper into the stone, straining to hear every single thing I could from the marbles walls, every harsh note, every soft whisper, every sly murmur.

And I finally found something—a suspicious mutter that was just a little louder and just a little sharper than all the others. I trailed my fingers over the smooth stone, following the echo of that mutter like notes on a roll of sheet music. The sound led me all the way over to a shelf in the back of the vault. To my surprise, there was only one item on this shelf: a tube made out of ebony.

Small, thin, lightweight. There was nothing extraordinary about the tube, except for the design inlaid in the center of the black wood, a thumbnail-size ruby surrounded by several wavy golden rays.

A sunburst. The symbol for fire. Mab Monroe's personal rune.

"I found it," I said.

"Are you sure?" Owen asked, coming around one of the tables to where I was.

My fingers closed over the tube, and that mutter in the marble took on an even uglier, darker, harsher note. "I'm sure."

"What do you think it is?" he asked. "A portrait? Maybe some sort of small painting?"

I shrugged and stuffed the tube into one of the pouches on my stolen utility belt. I also took a moment to snag the diamond necklace I'd noticed earlier and dropped that inside the pouch too. "Don't know. We can look at it later. Right now, we need to move."

❊ 17 ❊

Owen followed me out of the vault. I stopped in the exterior chamber long enough to do a quick pat-down of the three dead giants. Key cards, a couple of metal batons, pepper spray, walkie-talkies. Same old, same old. Owen picked up two of the men's guns, while I handed him all the extra ammo I found stuffed in their pockets. He reloaded both weapons before tucking one against the small of his back and keeping the other one in his hand at the ready. He nodded at me, and together we crept up to the exterior door and peeked outside.

I didn't see anyone in the hallway, but I heard something just as worrisome—the steady *thud-thud-thud* of footsteps, growing louder and louder as they pounded in this direction.

"Let's go," I whispered. "They're headed this way."

Owen nodded again and followed me into the hallway. I headed right, away from the sound of the footsteps, and we ran in that direction. What followed was a desperate series of zigzags as we tried to avoid the giants. Clementine's men were everywhere we turned, walkie-talkies screeching as they yelled instructions at each other and searched for whoever or whatever had caused the explosion. Three times we started down a hallway only to pull up short and backtrack when we caught a glimpse of a couple of giants lurking at the far end, guns up and ready to fire at the slightest movement. Oh, yes. Everyone knew that I was here now.

There was no way we could break through the perimeter they'd set up without making a whole lot of noise and bringing them all down on top of us, so Owen and I ended up crouching behind a doorway in a room down the hall from the vault entrance. It was far too close to the vault and the main force of giants in the rotunda for my liking, but all the other exits from this part of the museum had been cut off. We'd just have to hunker down and see what happened.

We didn't have long to wait. We'd just slid into the shadows when Clementine ran down the hallway, with Opal and Dixon following her. The three giants rushed through the open door that led into the vault area.

"Dammit!" Clementine's scream erupted out of the chamber a minute later.

I grinned. Such a satisfying sound. Always nice when you could make your enemies bellow with anger. Across from me, Owen gave me a sly wink.

A moment later, Clementine stormed out of the vault entrance and back into the hallway. Opal and Dixon followed her, although the two younger giants were careful to keep out of arm's reach of her. A good idea, on their part.

Clementine raised her walkie-talkie to her lips. "Somebody go out front and see if the cops are here. Right *now*."

"It's not the cops," one giant answered her a few seconds later. "I'm out by the moving trucks, and there's no one here. No police cars, no cops, nobody. All of the art is still inside the truck, and it doesn't look like anything's been stolen. Er . . . re-stolen."

"Roger that. Stand by for further instructions." Clementine clicked off her walkie-talkie and stuck it back onto her belt.

She paced back and forth for a few seconds before whirling around and facing Opal and Dixon again. Her features, which I'd thought so attractive before, were twisted and mottled with purple rage. Lips flat, nostrils flared, eyes narrowed to slits.

Opal and Dixon glanced at each other and took another step back. Dixon swallowed, and Opal wiped a bit of nervous sweat off her forehead.

"How the hell could this happen?" Clementine finally barked at them.

"Now, Mama, just calm down," Opal said, holding her hands palms up in a placating gesture. "I'm sure we'll get this all figured out. Whoever set off that bomb couldn't have gotten far. It's not the cops, so that's a good thing. We'll take care of whoever it is."

Clementine cocked her head to one side, and she advanced on Opal, who immediately sucked in a breath and plastered herself against the wall. Dixon scooted out of the way. Opal glanced at her cousin for help, but he smirked at her. Opal sighed and turned her head back in her mama's direction.

Clementine coldly eyed her daughter. After a moment, she drew back her fist. Opal shuddered, waiting for the blow—but it never came.

Instead, Clementine slammed her hand into the wall beside Opal's head. The sharp, stinging *crack* reverberated down the hallway, seeming almost as loud as the bomb blast. But the giant didn't stop with just one punch. Again and again, Clementine rammed her fist into the marble inches away from her daughter's head. Opal stood there and watched her. Mouth open, nostrils flared, eyes wide. Her expression a far more terrified version of her mother's murderous one.

Finally, Clementine stopped her assault on the wall and glared at her daughter once more.

"I don't care about the damn *bomb*," Clementine said, every word as sharp and clipped as the punches she'd just plowed into the wall. "What I *do* care about is the fact that someone used it to lure us away from Grayson and the vault. Something that is *your* fault, my darling girl, since you assured me that *everyone* was corralled inside the rotunda."

"Yeah, Opal." Dixon sneered, sidling up to Clementine's side. "That was *your* job. Looks like you're the screw-up tonight. How does it feel, cuz?"

Clementine immediately turned on her nephew, grabbed him by the throat, and lifted him off the ground. She slammed him back into the wall and kept him there.

I eyed Dixon's feet, which were dangling six inches above the floor. Dixon was no lightweight, but Clementine was holding him up with one hand like he didn't weigh any more than a wet kitten. My gaze flicked to the basketball-size dent she'd punched into the marble wall. Impressive, indeed.

"And you, you little weasel," Clementine growled. "You can't do anything without half-assing it or fucking it up completely. Where do you think our surprise guest got the bomb from? My guess is the bridge or one of the moving trucks. Which means that whoever it is has probably been following you around for who knows how long, watching you check the charges with your phone, and you were too stupid to even notice."

Dixon's mouth opened and closed, and opened and closed again, but the only sound that came out was a faint, pitiful squeak, the kind a rabbit might make before a wolf snapped its jaws around the rabbit's throat. Clementine shook him once, then dropped her hand and stepped back. Dixon landed in a heap on the floor, a perfect red handprint ringing his throat like a rash.

"We'll fix it, Mama," Opal said, her voice a little higher and more desperate than before. "We'll find whoever's responsible for this and make them pay."

"You'd better hope so," Clementine growled. "You'd both damn well better hope so."

Opal vigorously nodded, trembling as badly as a bobblehead doll someone had set to bouncing.

More footsteps sounded, saving Opal and Dixon from any more of Clementine's wrath—at least for the moment. The giant smoothed out her features and turned to face the two men who were running down the hallway toward her.

"Anything?" she asked when they finally stopped in front of her.

They both shook their heads. Like Opal and Dixon, the giants took obvious care to stay out of reach of her long arms. Smart move, given the murderous rage that still glinted in her hazel eyes.

Clementine raised her walkie-talkie to her lips. "All teams, report in."

"Team one, here."

"Team two, here."

And on and on it went, with the giants reporting back to Clementine—all except the ones I'd killed.

When Clementine realized that she couldn't raise her people in the security center or the two who'd been down by the bridge, she let out another loud curse. She lowered her walkie-talkie and stabbed her finger at the men standing in front of her.

"You two, come with me," she growled before glaring at Opal and Dixon. "You two, stay here and start organizing a search. I want to know who was in the vault, how many of them there are, everything they took, and where they and Grayson are now. So move! Now!"

Opal and Dixon scurried back into the vault area to do her bidding. Clementine marched off down the hallway with the other two giants, heading away from Owen and me. I waited until I was sure she wasn't coming back, then looked at Owen.

"Come on," I whispered. "Let's get while the getting's good."

The giants had started their search from the vault and the rotunda, spreading out toward the exits. They didn't bother checking behind them, so Owen and I were able to trail along in their wake, weapons in hand, eyes open in case any of them doubled back on their search pattern.

"We need to get outside," I told Owen. "Bria and Xavier should be here soon. Jo-Jo too. She can heal Phillip after we take out the guards in the rotunda."

"If he's even still alive," Owen said, his forehead creasing with worry.

I shrugged. Another twenty minutes had passed since I'd first gone into the vault after Owen, but there was nothing I could do about the time that just kept *tick-tick-tick*ing away. First, I had to get Owen to safety. Then I'd worry about rescuing Phillip and the others.

Finn would realize that I was planning something, though. Knowing that I was still alive, he would have figured that I was up to my usual tricks as soon as I set off that bomb. He'd help Eva, Roslyn, and Phillip until we could free them. Finn might be selfish, flighty, and infuriating and have an inflated sense of his own self-worth, but if there was one thing I could always count on, it was for him to be there when the chips were down—and they were certainly down tonight.

Finally, a pair of guards we'd been following reached a set of exit doors and checked them to make sure they were locked. Owen and I slipped into one of the rooms that branched off from the hallway and looked out the doorway at the giants, keeping an eye on them.

"West exit secure," one of the guards said into his radio. "We haven't seen anyone. Haven't found any more bombs either."

After a moment, Clementine's voice crackled back. "Well, retrace your steps and keep searching. They have to be in the museum somewhere. Go back through and look again. Check every room—I want them found. *Now*. Got it?"

"Understood," the giant said, and clipped the device back onto his belt. He jerked his head at the other man. "Come on. You heard her. She wants us to keep searching."

Damn and double damn. I'd hoped that Clementine would order the giants to start sweeping the grounds. That way, Owen and I would have been able to follow them outside, kill them, and slip into the gardens before anyone was the wiser. Instead, the two men turned and headed back in our direction, which meant there was nowhere for us to go.

"Gin?" Owen whispered, raising his gun. "What do you want to do?"

We couldn't backtrack deeper into the museum without risking running into more giants, and I didn't want to try to take out the two men in front of us—not now, when they were on high alert, guns drawn and ready to shoot at the first hint of trouble. Oh, we could kill the giants, but I doubted we could do it quickly or quietly enough to make it outside before the others heard the commotion and came running. If Clementine and her men surrounded us, we were done—simple as that.

My eyes flicked around the room we were in. The lights were turned down in here, casting everything in soft shadows. The giants hadn't looted this area yet, so paintings still covered the walls, and several statues squatted out in the middle of the open floor. But none of them was big enough for us to hide behind, not even for the few seconds it would take to spring a surprise attack. I'd thought we might have to stand our ground by the doorway and risk going at the giants head-on after all, when I spotted a larger statue in the very back of the room.

"Over there." I grabbed Owen's arm and tugged him in that direction.

The statue was a life-size scene, some twenty feet wide, and featured a boy in a thatched hat and overalls sitting down and holding a pole as though he were fishing in the pond of white rock in front of him. Next to him, a girl wearing a gingham dress sat on a rope swing, her feet pulled back and her bare toes digging into the ground as if she were about to launch herself up into the air. A maple tree arched over the two of them, its branches stretching up and down, almost like it was reaching out to hug the boy and the girl, before the limbs ran together and formed the back of the piece. Well, it definitely wasn't abstract art; Bria would approve.

I sprinted to the right. The statue was set flush with the wall, so we couldn't hide behind it. I'd just turned back to Owen to tell him to get ready to fight after all, when I noticed a shadow on the statue that looked a little deeper and darker than the others. I stepped up onto the carved stone and peered around the girl on her swing. Sure enough, there was a slight gap between the tree trunk and the rock wall that formed the back of the statue. Not exactly the best or most creative hiding place, but it would have to do.

"Up here!" I hissed at Owen. "Hurry!"

He climbed up onto the statue, and we managed to

squeeze in behind the tree. The space was small, barely big enough for one person, much less the two of us wedged in behind it. Owen had his back to the tree, while mine was pressed against the rock wall. I wasn't completely hidden by the trunk like Owen was, and I just had to hope the giants wouldn't notice half of my head, arm, and shoulder sticking out from behind the tree.

I shifted, trying to squirm even farther into the shadows, but the rocks snagged on my dress, and I couldn't move without ripping the garment down the back and making even more noise.

"Here," Owen whispered. "Let me."

He drew me away from the rock wall and into his arms, then shifted to his left, dragging me behind the tree and sculpting his body to mine so we could better blend into the shadows together. My concern about the giants spotting us quickly melted away as I realized just what an intimate position Owen and I were in.

Our bodies pressed together, chests to hips to thighs, and all the hard and soft spots in between. His arms around me, my leg between both of his, our faces level, given the bit of rock I had climbed up on. Our breaths mixed and mingled in a hot rush of air, our lips a heart-breaking inch apart. His eyes stayed steady on mine, and we stood there in the darkness, staring at each other. Heat flashed and shimmered in Owen's violet gaze, the same heat that was scorching through my veins. His scent washed over me, that rich, metallic aroma, and I breathed in, drawing it deep into my lungs.

Whatever our problems were, the attraction was still there, and he seemed to feel it just as much as I did. It gave me hope that we could work through the rest of our problems—if we managed to live through the next three minutes.

Owen had a gun in his hand, and I had a bloody knife in mine, but we moved even closer together in the darkness, careful with our respective weapons. Owen's lips brushed my cheek before sliding into my hair. I pressed my cheek against his, then slowly turned my head, burying my face in his neck—

Something clicked, and light flooded the room, shattering the moment.

"Come on," one of the giants said. "Let's sweep this area and go on to the next room."

They didn't say anything else, and for several long seconds, the only sounds were Owen's raspy breath in my ear and the staccato slap of the giants' shoes on the floor. The steady *tap-tap-tap*s echoed all around the room, so I couldn't tell where the giants were. By the door, in the middle of the room, in front of the statue, guns up and ready to plug us full of bullets.

Tap-tap-tap.

Tap-tap-tap.

Tap-tap-tap.

Owen's muscles clenched, and his body swelled with tension with every passing second. I slowly, carefully, quietly raised my hand to his and squeezed his fingers. Owen exhaled, and I felt some of the worry leave him.

"Come on," one of the giants finally said. "They're not in here. Let's go."

More *tap-tap-tap*s sounded. Ten seconds later, the footsteps faded away, and the room was quiet once more.

Owen and I stayed where we were. Bodies flush, lips close together, eyes locked on each other.

I would have liked nothing more than to have stayed with Owen in the shadows, but after thirty more seconds had passed and I was reasonably sure the giants weren't coming back, I made myself step out of his arms and slide away from him.

Because this wasn't the time for such things. What was important right now was making sure that we lived to have a later—and so did our friends.

"Come on," I whispered. "We should be able to make it outside now."

Owen nodded.

I let myself remember the heat of his body against mine for a moment longer before I turned, hopped off the statue, and headed for the door.

I'd just started to peer out the opening when one of the giants stepped back into the room.

✳ 18 ✳

"Wait a second," the giant called out to his buddy, look-ing back over his shoulder. "I left the lights on in here, and the boss lady said to turn them off when—"

There was no time to run, nowhere to hide, and no way to keep things quiet. The giant turned to face me. He gasped and stopped short in surprise, but I was already rushing toward him, slashing my knife through the air.

The giant managed to throw himself back so that my blade only sliced across his chest instead of tearing open his throat. Still, the shallow, stinging cut made him bel-low with pain and surprise.

"Paul?" the other man asked, stepping into the room. "What's wrong—" His eyes widened as he realized what was going on, and he immediately raised his walkie-talkie to his lips. "I've got them! I've got them! Near the west exit!"

The giant in front of me started to raise his gun, but

I sliced my knife across his wrist, making him drop the weapon and howl with pain.

"You take the other guy!" I yelled at Owen. "Clear a path!"

Owen stepped up beside me, already drawing a bead on the second giant, who was backpedaling.

Crack! Crack!

Two bullets slammed into the doorway right next to the giant, making him curse and duck back out into the hallway. Owen hurried over to the door, stuck his arm out, and fired two more shots.

Crack! Crack!

A high-pitched yelp sounded out in the hallway.

"I winged him, but there are already more of them at the end of the hallway and heading this way!" Owen called out. "We need to go, Gin! Now!"

I shoved the injured giant out of my way and drew my own gun. I peered around the doorframe. Owen must have hit the giant in the leg, because he was hobbling into another room that branched off the hallway. But what worried me more were the four giants at the far end of the corridor. They spotted us and started shooting even as they raced in our direction. Bullets *ping-ping-ping*ed off the walls, and the marble started to wail from this fresh assault on it.

There was only one thing left to do now: run.

I jerked my head at the exit door thirty feet to our left and handed Owen the key card to open it. "Stay behind me!" I screamed at him. "I'll cover you!"

Owen nodded, realizing what I had in mind. I reached for my Stone magic, used it to harden my skin, and stepped out into the hallway, with Owen right behind me. While he ran for the door, I turned around, raised my gun, took aim at the giants, and pulled the trigger.

Crack!

Crack! Crack!

Crack!

My hail of gunfire slowed the giants down and made them duck for cover, but it didn't stop them from returning my bullets with several shots of their own. One of the projectiles punched square into my chest, making me stumble back. The bullet would have bored right through my heart if I hadn't been using my magic to protect myself. I kept backing up, heading toward the exit, and firing away until my clip was empty.

"Gin!" Owen shouted behind me, holding the door open. "Come on!"

I turned and raced toward him.

Crack!

Another shot rang out. In front of me, Owen grunted and staggered outside, leaving behind a smear of blood on the glass door.

"Owen? Owen!" I made it through the opening, let the door close behind me, and ran over to him.

He clutched his left shoulder. "I'm okay. I think they just winged me—"

Bullets slammed into the door behind us, cracking the glass and making us duck down.

I put my arm under Owen's shoulder, and together we staggered down the stairs and headed for the shadows and sanctuary of the gardens.

* * *

I led Owen to the far western edge of the gardens, where the lush flowers gave way to the creeping briars. Despite the giants' shouts behind us, I risked turning my flashlight on for a few seconds and swept it back and forth in front of a hedge of four-foot-tall briars. Finally, I found what looked like a small animal trail through the thorns. I clicked the flashlight off and turned to Owen.

"Can you go on a little farther?" I whispered.

He nodded, although he was still clutching his shoulder.

"Okay," I whispered back. "Follow my lead, and just take it easy. Don't fight the briars. Go where they let you. We don't want to leave a trail of broken branches behind us that will tell the giants exactly where we went."

Owen nodded. I went first, worming my way deeper and deeper into the branches. The briars clutched at my tattered dress, but I went slowly, carefully moving branches out of my way. Owen followed along behind me, his breath rasping against the back of my neck.

Ten feet in, a copse of weeping willows soared up out of the briars, and I slid into a small open space between two of the trees that was free from the thorns. Fifteen feet beyond the back side of the bramble patch, the island sheared off in a straight drop down to the Aneirin River two hundred feet below.

It was as good a spot as any to hide from the giants, so I gestured at Owen to stop. He sat down on the ground and put his back against one of the weeping willows, the long tendrils brushing against his shoulders like a masseuse's fingers. I sank down on my knees beside him.

"Let me see your arm," I whispered.

He nodded, and I helped him shrug out of his tuxedo jacket. I used one of my knives to slice open his white shirt. Two neat holes blackened his left bicep, blood trickling out of each one of them. It was an ugly wound, one that would hurt, ache, and burn with every move, but relief pulsed through me that it wasn't worse.

"It looks like a through-and-through," I said in a soft voice.

"Just help me bandage it up. It stings, but it's not that bad." Owen grimaced. "Not nearly as bad as what Dixon did to Phillip."

I ripped his jacket up and used it to make a tight bandage. Owen grimaced, and sweat beaded on his forehead, but he swallowed down most of the pain.

Once that was done, I crouched down a few feet away, with my back to the river and my gaze on the faint path we'd made through the thorns. I didn't think the giants would venture this far from the museum, but I wanted to be ready in case they did.

And then we waited.

In the distance, I could hear the giants' shouts as they searched for us. I just hoped they would focus on this side of the island and not the front, where Bria and Xavier would be coming in any minute now. I pulled my cell phone off my belt, intending to text my sister about the new danger, but the moonlight filtering down through the trees revealed a bullet hole in the middle of the device. I bit back a curse and clipped the phone to my belt once more, even though it was useless now. Bria and Xavier were on their own—just like Owen and me.

A minute passed. Then two. Then five.

All the while, the giants swarmed through the gardens, yelling back and forth to one another.

"Where are they?"

"Do you see them?"

"Where did they go?"

Every once in a while, the bright beam of a flashlight would cut across the foliage above our heads, making Owen and me duck down further in the shadows. But the briars made the giants keep their distance, and they didn't find us.

Eventually, the sounds of their shouts died away altogether, along with the beams of light, and I relaxed. The danger had passed us by—for now.

Finally, Owen spoke, his voice a hard, flat note against the cheery chirp of the crickets in the underbrush. "Jillian's dead."

"Yes," I said. "She is."

Still keeping watch for the giants, I told him about Clementine sidling up to me first in the rotunda and then later on in the bathroom. I also told him how she had left and Jillian had come in, although I didn't mention that we'd talked about him.

"Jillian never had a chance," I said. "Dixon was waiting for her as soon as she stepped out of the bathroom. I don't know if I would have had a chance to react either."

Owen's gaze dropped to my dress. The designer gown was a tattered, ruined, ragged mess, stained with blood, soaked with sweat, and scorched with black bullet holes. His mouth tightened, and he rubbed his forehead. No doubt he was thinking about Jillian and the fact that she was dead because of me.

I wondered if he was still thinking about Salina and how she was also dead because of me—by my own hand, no less.

"I'm sorry," I said in a quiet voice. "About Jillian. She didn't deserve to die like that."

Owen looked away from me. "Me too. She was a friend."

I wanted to ask if that was all she had been, but I kept my mouth shut. I wasn't sure I wanted to know the answer. I dropped my gaze from Owen, and both of us concentrated on the thorns around us instead of staring at each other. We were both silent until he finally cleared his throat.

"So now what?" he asked. "We might be out here away from the giants, but Eva, Phillip, and the others are still inside."

"Now we see what kind of leverage we have."

I pulled the small ebony tube out of the pouch on my utility belt. Mab's sunburst rune glimmered in the moonlight, deadly and beautiful, just like the Fire elemental herself had been. I reached for my Stone magic, used it to harden my skin, and traced my finger over the sunburst, wondering if the rune might hold some sort of booby-trap. But the symbol didn't flare to life or spew explosive, elemental Fire in my face.

Still, the problem was that I didn't see a way to *open* the tube. Flat discs of silverstone covered both ends of the wood, but I couldn't pry them off with either my nails or the tip of my knife. I handed the tube to Owen, who ran his fingers up and down it, but he couldn't figure out how to get inside it either. It had to open, because there was something inside, something that rustled back and forth whenever I shook the tube. I needed to know what that something was so I could deal with Clementine accordingly.

Of course Mab wouldn't make it *easy* to loot whatever was inside the tube, especially when I was under pressure and pressed for time. I imagined the Fire elemental was laughing at me even now from wherever she was in the great beyond.

"Laugh your ass off, Mab," I muttered. "You've certainly earned it tonight."

I held up the tube, wondering if there was something I was missing. Once again, my eyes focused on the sunburst rune. The wavy golden rays took on a muted silver tinge in the moonlight, while the ruby smoldered like a dull, banked ember in the middle of the design. Maybe it was the mocking way the rune seemed to wink at me, but an idea popped into my mind. I put my thumb on the ruby and pressed in on it.

A soft *click* sounded, and one of the silverstone discs on the end of the tube popped up.

"Here goes nothing," I murmured.

I hinged the silverstone to one side and tipped the contents of the tube into my hand. I'd been expecting jewels, a fistful of rubies or something like that, something that would have been in keeping with Mab's bold, flashy, fiery nature.

Instead, a single piece of rolled-up paper slid out of the hollowed-out wood.

"That's it?" Owen asked. "That's all that's in there?"

I shook the wood, but nothing else came out. "Yep, that's it. So let's see what's so important about it."

I carefully unrolled the paper. It was hard to make out

everything, since the print was so small and the night was so dark, despite the golden glow from the garden lights in the distance, but I managed to skim through it.

"It looks like some sort of legal document. I think . . . I think this is Mab's will."

Owen frowned. "Why would Clementine go to so much trouble to steal Mab's will?"

"I don't know," I murmured. "But apparently, she wanted it bad enough to arrange the heist and everything else tonight. But you're right. The question is why."

"Well, what does it say?" he asked. "Who did Mab leave what to?"

I squinted and read a few more paragraphs. "A bunch of legal mumbo jumbo, and . . . it looks like . . . she left everything to one person. Someone whose last name is also Monroe—M. M. Monroe."

I stared at the paper. It seemed innocent enough, but I couldn't help but feel like the earth had just opened up at my feet and I was about to tumble into an abyss.

"M. M. Monroe?" Owen asked. "Did I hear you right?"

All I could do was nod.

Finn had mentioned there was a rumor that the contents of Mab's will were going to be revealed at the gala tonight. Now that I'd read the document myself, I could easily imagine Mab arranging for things to go down like that. Like Finn had said, it would have been one last hurrah for her—an opportunity to remind everyone how powerful she had been, and a chance to announce her successor in the most dramatic way possible.

Because Mab hadn't left anything to Jonah McAllister, her other business associates, or even charity. No, she'd given everything to this M. M. Monroe.

I wondered if this mysterious relative had the same devastating Fire magic Mab had wielded.

I wondered if this person knew about the massive fortune he or she had inherited.

I wondered if this Monroe would decide to come to Ashland to oversee Mab's empire in person—and how much trouble he or she might cause for me if so.

My mother and Mab had been enemies for years before Mab had murdered her and my older sister. Their parents had been enemies before them, and their parents before them. At least, that's how it had been according to Mab. So it wasn't too much of a stretch to think that the family feud would continue on into another generation, if that's what this was. It already had with me and Mab, really.

Once again, I'd thought that I'd taken care of everything when I'd killed the Fire elemental, that I'd finally set myself *free* from her, but she just kept screwing with me, even from six feet under.

"It doesn't really matter who Mab left her fortune to," I finally said, rolling up the paper and sliding it back into the tube. "Just that we have the will and Clementine wants it. We can use it for leverage."

Owen shook his head. "She's not going to let the hostages go, if that's what you're thinking. You know that as well as I do. Not now, when everyone's seen her face and knows exactly who she is. She can't afford to let any of them live."

"That's what I thought at first too. But I think good ole Clem has a slightly different plan in mind."

I told Owen about the bombs I'd found on the bridge and under the bumper of the moving truck.

He frowned. "Okay, I understand about the destroying the bridge to help with their escape, but why would Clementine want to blow up the moving trucks?"

I shrugged. "I haven't quite figured that out yet. But it doesn't really matter, because the only way she's leaving this island is in a body bag."

Owen studied me in the moonlight. "Because of what she and Dixon did to Jillian?"

I didn't say anything, but he could see the answer in my cold, angry eyes—along with the guilt.

"That wasn't your fault, Gin," he said. "It was a mistake, her having on the same dress as you. Just a stupid, simple, cruel twist of fate." He hesitated. "She was a friend, but you don't have to avenge her for me, if that's what you're thinking. I wouldn't ask you to do that."

No, he wouldn't. Owen preferred to handle such things himself, just like I did. It was one of the many things I admired about him.

"I know you wouldn't ask me that," I said. "But I need to avenge Jillian for *me*. Because it should have been my face that got blown off, not hers."

"I'm not blaming you for Jillian's death, if that's what you're thinking."

"No," I replied, weariness creeping into my voice. "You just blame me for Salina."

His ex-fiancée's name hung in the air between us, writhing around and around like a poisonous snake. But

I'd said the words, and there was no taking them back. Despite the danger we were in, the danger we were *all* in, Eva, Phillip, and the others were right: Owen and I needed to start talking, to start figuring out where we stood and what kind of future we might have together. If I was going to die tonight, if we both might die tonight, well, I wanted to clear the air between us—about this, anyway.

Owen grimaced. He reached out and touched one of the brown briars wrapped around the weeping willow, sliding his thumb over one of the thorns. It was several seconds before he finally spoke.

"I don't blame you for Salina's death. You did what you thought needed to be done."

"But you didn't agree with it then," I said. "And you still don't now."

He sighed, looking as sad and tired as I felt. "Like I told you before, everything's all mixed-up inside me right now. You, Salina, how I feel about her death and your part in it. I keep going over it again and again in my head, wondering if I could have done something different, if I could have changed things. But I can't see how I could have, other than waking up and realizing what Salina was really like when we were young. But I didn't see the real her, and now she's dead. I can't change any of that, and I haven't sorted any of it out. Not really."

It was a shortened version of the same speech Owen had given me at the Pork Pit a few weeks ago, when he'd told me that he needed some time to himself. I'd hoped that tonight's events, that the danger and emotions we'd shared, had meant that he'd come to terms with at least some of his issues. But he hadn't, and I didn't know if he ever would.

"Jillian was a friend," he continued. "But I wasn't one to her. Not really. Because I didn't even realize that she wasn't in the rotunda with the rest of us. When Clementine threw that body down, and I thought it was you . . . I couldn't think about anything else but you being dead. I always seem to let down the people I care about. Eva, Phillip, Cooper, you. I let you all down because of Salina. And tonight, I didn't even notice that Jillian was missing. Some friend that makes me, huh?"

Owen barked out a harsh laugh, his face twisting with guilt and misery.

"And that kiss you laid on me in the vault?" I asked.

He didn't look at me. Instead, he pressed his thumb into the thorn, drawing a bit of blood, pain etching lines in his sweaty, rugged, soot-streaked face. "I was just so glad that you were alive, Gin. I will *always* be glad for that, no matter what."

Despite the fact that I'd killed Salina. That's what it seemed like he really meant. But I couldn't blame him for his feelings. He'd loved her once, and I'd cut her throat even though he'd asked me not to. It wasn't exactly the kind of thing you got over easily, if ever.

Still, I'd hoped—I'd hoped that by saving Owen, I could save us too. Hope. Such a stupid, foolish emotion. One that could lift your heart to the heavens and then grind it into the ground in the very next instant. My emotions felt as tangled and twisted as the briars around us. And every move I made, everything I did to try to make things better, just stabbed another sharp, brittle thorn deep into the desolate wasteland of my heart.

"Gin?" Owen asked again, all sorts of questions in the soft, single syllable of my name.

Before I could answer him, bullets zipped in our direction.

❊ 19 ❊

Crack! Crack! Crack!

Bullets zinged through the air. I started to throw myself forward onto Owen, but he shook his head and held up his finger, pointing at the tree branches above us, and I realized what he was getting at. Those shots had been far too high for someone to have seen us. So why was someone shooting? Why waste their ammunition like that?

Crack! Crack! Crack!

"Come out, come out, wherever you are," a mocking voice called out.

Owen and I looked at each other and reached for our weapons. I didn't know how many giants were waiting, but we'd fight our way through them just like we had all the others tonight—

A loud sigh sounded. "Quit messing around, Dave," a second voice, this one female, said. "We're supposed to be searching for the thieves. Do you want somebody to hear the noise and shoot us by mistake?"

"Please," Dave, the first giant, said. "Whoever set off that bomb is long gone. So I say we have a little fun before we go back inside. Besides, we're the only ones still out this far. Everyone else has headed back to the museum already, from what I've heard on the radio."

A knife in my hand, I crawled over to the weeping willow at the other end of the hedge of briars and slowly got to my feet. Owen took cover behind another tree. Using the long, fluttering tendrils as a screen to hide me from sight, I peered around the tree trunk.

I spotted two giants in the semidarkness, both holding guns and standing about twenty feet away from us beyond the row of thorns. The male was tall and extremely skinny, with a shaved head that looked like a cue ball in the moonlight, while the woman was a bit shorter, with a plump body.

"Come on, Dave," the woman said again. "We need to get back so we can help load up the rest of the art."

"Sure, Cindy. We'll go back—in a minute."

Crack! Crack! Crack!

Dave laughed as he fired off a few more random shots.

"Will you stop that?" Cindy hissed. "It's creepy enough out here already without you acting like a jackass—"

A sharp crackle of static filled the air, and a second later, Opal's voice sounded. "Team one, what's your position? I thought I heard shots in the trees near the west exit."

Cindy raised her walkie-talkie to her lips. "It's nothing, Opal. Dave thought he saw something and fired off a few rounds, but it was just a rabbit. We're coming back inside now."

"Roger that," Opal replied.

Cindy clipped her walkie-talkie back to her belt and shot Dave another hot glare.

I put my finger to my lips, then made a circle and a slashing gesture with my knife at Owen. He nodded and held up his gun, telling me that he was ready to help.

Despite everything that had happened between us, Owen knew that we were in this together. Once we got off the island, well, we'd have to see where we stood. But for right now, we were together, and I was going to enjoy the solidarity while I could, even if I knew it was a result of circumstances, rather than of choice.

The tangle of briars wasn't quite so thick around this tree, so I was able to maneuver around the far side of the trunk past the row of thorns and circle around so that I was parallel with the two giants.

"Come on, Dave," Cindy said, a little more heat in her tone this time. "Let's go back."

"Fine," Dave muttered, holstering his gun. "I'm out of ammo anyway."

Out of ammo? What a shame. I smiled and headed toward my enemies. Maybe something was finally going to go right—

Cindy turned her head at exactly the right moment to see me step out from behind the trees.

"Dave!" she yelped. "Watch out!"

As always, I cursed fickle, fickle luck for messing with me yet again, but there was nothing I could do but follow through with my strike.

Thanks to Cindy's warning, Dave was able to sidestep my initial attack. The giant was quicker than I expected, and he grabbed hold of my arm and shoved me into the closest tree before stepping up and driving his fist into my kidneys.

I hissed from the impact, but I returned the favor by snapping my elbow back into his ribs as hard as I could. Dave took several steps back, which put him right in Owen's path. Owen crashed through the middle of the briars, raised his gun high, and smashed the weapon into the side of Dave's head. The giant grunted, reached out, and tackled Owen. The two of them fell to the ground, rolling back and forth in front of the thorns.

I whirled to face the other giant, but Cindy must have started moving away the second she saw me, because she was already fifteen feet away from my position. Cindy kept right on moving, even as she fumbled for her walkie-talkie. I started after her, but I'd only taken three steps when my boot snagged on one of the briars, making me pull up short. Even as I tried to yank free, I knew that I wouldn't be able to get to the giant in time. Helpless, I watched as Cindy raised the radio to her lips—

Pfft!

The walkie-talkie shattered into a dozen pieces.

Pfft! Pfft!

Two holes suddenly appeared in Cindy's throat. Her eyes widened in pain and surprise, but she dropped to the ground without making another sound.

Dave managed to throw Owen off him and scramble to his feet. He turned to shout or maybe run—

Pfft! Pfft!

Two holes appeared in his forehead, and he went down as well.

I finally pulled myself free from the branch and darted behind the closest tree, wondering what this new danger might be, but there was no need.

A second later, Bria stepped into sight, Xavier right behind her, each holding a gun at the ready. I let out a tense breath and walked out where she could see me.

"Hey there, baby sister," I drawled. "It's about time you got here."

We all stood there, listening, but the only sounds outside the museum were the wind rustling through the garden and Owen's raspy breathing. Wherever they were, the other giants hadn't heard the fight, which meant that we were safe for at least a few minutes.

Bria stalked over and hugged me tight. I returned her embrace, feeling a little bit of the worry ease from my body. Two against Clementine and the rest of her crew wasn't great odds. Four against all those giants wasn't much better, but it leveled the playing field a bit, especially given what I had in mind.

"Are you okay?" Bria whispered in my ear. "I was worried about you."

I pulled back. "I'm fine. Just a little bruised and bloody, but that's pretty much par for the course for me, isn't it?"

Bria's gaze swept over my body, taking in the tattered dress, the long, thin scratches on my hands, arms, and legs from crawling through the briars and bushes, the blood that coated me like some sort of macabre body art. She grimaced and shook her head, telling me exactly how battered and beat-up I looked. And that didn't even take into account all of the dull, throbbing aches in my body from where the giants had hit me tonight. But I was still alive, breathing, and upright, at least.

My eyes dropped to the gun in Bria's hand. "When did you get a silencer?"

"This?" she said, holding it up so I could see it better. "It was a present from Finn for our three-month anniversary."

"How romantic."

She grinned. "Well, at least it's useful, and it does last longer than flowers or a box of candy. I thought it might come in handy tonight. I know how you love to keep things quiet."

"That I do," I said, moving past her.

I went over to Owen and touched his arm, the one that wasn't injured. "Are you okay?"

He nodded, then winced as he gingerly probed a bruise that was already forming on his right cheek from where he'd been grappling with the giant. "I've been better, but I'll live."

I turned back to Bria. "Where's Jo-Jo?"

"She's on her way," Bria said. "She and Cooper were having dinner at Underwood's. She said it would take a while for them to get over here. She told me to come on, that you'd need me and Xavier before she could get here."

I nodded. Jo-Jo had a bit of precognition. Most Air elementals did, since the currents and emotions on the wind whispered to them of all the actions people might take. I didn't know what Jo-Jo might have gotten a glimpse of, but if she'd sent Bria on ahead, that meant that things were going to get a whole lot worse before they got better—if we all didn't get dead in the meantime.

"Tell me about the giants."

Bria shook her head. "We'd just made it across the bridge and slipped into the gardens when we heard them coming our way. One minute, Xavier and I were alone. The next, there were giants everywhere. In the parking lots, on the bridge, in the gardens. All yelling back and forth and looking for something—or someone. So we found a place to hide and waited them out. It took a while, but eventually, they all headed back up to the museum. The last we saw of them, they were clustered around some moving trucks by the entrance. That's when we headed in this direction."

"Yeah," Xavier chimed in. "We were wondering where you and Owen might be, but then we heard someone shooting. So we just followed the sound of the gunshots. And look, they led us straight to you, Gin."

He grinned at me, and I returned the gesture.

"Gunshots are a pretty good indicator that I'm lurking around," I said.

"So what's the situation on this end?" Xavier asked.

I quickly filled them in on all my wanderings, killings, and stealings in the museum, including how I'd gotten Owen out of the vault and swiped Mab's will.

Bria frowned. "Okay, robbing the partygoers and the museum I understand. But why would Clementine want to steal Mab's will?"

I shrugged. "I don't know, but she must want it something fierce to go to all this trouble—"

The walkie-talkie on my belt crackled. I'd turned the

volume down while Owen and I had been hiding, al-though I'd made sure it was loud enough for me still to hear the giants' squawks to one another as they searched for us. But this voice sounded louder and far more force-ful than the others, the cadence of the words different, so I adjusted the volume so that we could all hear what was being said. I didn't catch all the words, but I didn't have to, since she apparently decided to repeat herself.

Clementine's voice came through loud and clear. "I'll say it again. This message is for whoever's been going around killing my boys. We need to talk."

I raised my eyebrows, mildly surprised it had taken her this long to reach out to me. I grabbed the walkie-talkie, brought the speaker up to my mouth, and hit the button on the side.

"Why, hello, Clementine," I drawled. "I was wonder-ing when you might call."

❋ 20 ❋

"Who the hell are you?" Clementine demanded.

Well, she was blunt, I'd give her that.

"I'm the person who took what you were after in the vault. That's all you need to know."

Clementine had heard my voice before in the rotunda and bathroom, so I made my tone low, throaty, and raspy, as though I'd spent my life chain-smoking and chugging down mountain moonshine—sort of like Sophia's voice.

"Who are you?" she asked again. "Some sort of thief?"

Tension eased out of my shoulders. I'd thought she might put two and two together and realize that Gin Blanco, the Spider, was alive and well, especially given that I'd used my knives to kill some of her men. But apparently, she was still under the impression that Dixon had murdered me outside the bathroom. Good. That was good. Because if she didn't realize who I really was, then she also wouldn't realize that she had all the leverage she needed—Finn, Roslyn, Eva, and Phillip—to get me to do exactly what she wanted.

"Something like that," I replied. "You didn't think you were the only one who had the bright idea of hitting the big gala, now, did you? All that art on display here tonight, all those jewels, all the publicity surrounding the event. Why, the Briartop staff practically *begged* me to show up and take something."

"You bitch," she snarled. "You piggybacked onto my heist."

"You stung the museum, so I decided to sting you instead," I corrected. "Honor among thieves is highly overrated. And why should I do all the hard, dirty work of getting into the vault when you and your crew were so eager to do it for me? I was prepared to crack it myself, but what happens when I finally go for it? Why, I find you in there ahead of me. So I decided to wait for the perfect moment to get what I came for—or, rather, to create the perfect moment."

"The explosion."

"The explosion," I agreed. "You really shouldn't leave bombs lying around where just anyone can find them."

"And what was it *exactly* that you came for?" Clementine asked.

I plucked the diamond necklace I'd swiped from the vault earlier out of a pouch on my belt. I held it up, admiring the sparkle of the jewels for a moment, before tossing it over to Bria. "A lovely little necklace. Exquisite diamonds. All nice and shiny and ready to be fenced. That ebony tube you were after just happened to be a bonus."

Silence. I could almost hear Clementine thinking, trying to figure out whether to admit that the tube was what she'd broken into the vault for. In the end, she decided to come clean. She didn't have another play here, and we both knew it.

"And how did you even know that tube was what I was after?"

"Oh," I said, "I have my ways. You wouldn't want a girl to reveal all her trade secrets, now, would you?"

More silence.

"What's your name?" Clementine asked.

"Well, I could give you a name, but I think we both know it wouldn't be my real one," I said. "So why bother?"

"Fine, Ms. No-Name. Here's how this will go down. You either give me back what you stole, or I start killing people," Clementine said, her voice just as polite and pleasant as mine. "Starting with Eva Grayson. I'm sure you saw her earlier tonight. Such a pretty girl. It would be a shame to have to put three bullets in her face."

Owen stiffened, and his violet eyes blazed with anger. He started to open his mouth, but I shook my head and held my finger up to my lips.

I thought she might say something like that, and I was ready for her threat. I chuckled, making the sound light, carefree, and just a tad mocking. "You go right ahead. I don't care in the slightest whether some poor little rich girl lives or dies."

"Well, Mr. Grayson might care," Clementine said, changing tactics. "Why don't you put him on so I can ask him?"

Owen looked at me, but once again I shook my head.

"Grayson's dead," I rasped. "He took a couple of bullets helping me get out of the museum. Bled out quick after that."

"I don't believe you," Clementine replied. "You went to a lot of trouble to get him out of the vault."

"Wrong. I went to a lot of trouble to get my diamond necklace and your mystery tube out of the vault. Grayson was just there. I took him along as a human shield, in case I ran into any of your giants, which, of course, I did. He served his purpose, then outlived his usefulness."

I stared at Owen. He frowned at me, doubt filling his eyes—doubt about me and my words. He was wondering what I was playing at. The fact that he couldn't just trust me after everything we'd been through hurt, another briar burrowing into my heart. But I wasn't surprised by his lack of trust. That was another thing I'd sliced in two when I'd cut Salina's throat.

"Well, if Grayson's dead, then why haven't one of my men found his body yet?" Clementine asked.

"Because your men aren't nearly as good at this game as I am. I hope you got them at a discount rate. I haven't been impressed so far. I've killed, what, eight, nine of them now? And I haven't got a scratch on me."

Not true, of course, but she didn't need to know about all my aches and pains, or my dwindling reserves of magic.

Clementine was quiet for a moment. Thinking. "Why haven't you left the island yet?"

"Well, let's just say that I didn't count on you bringing along quite as many giants as you did. They've made things a bit more difficult than I expected."

"You won't get off Briartop alive," she vowed, anger coloring her voice.

"If you want to lose more men, that's fine by me. I don't have any plans for the rest of the night, and I've got plenty of guns and ammo, thanks to all the weapons I've taken off your men. Rest assured that I have ten million little reasons to motivate me to live—and to kill whoever gets in my way."

More silence.

I let Clementine stew a few seconds before speaking again. "However, all that doesn't mean that we can't come to some sort of agreement. Things don't need to get any bloodier and more unpleasant than they are already. Besides, if there's one thing I'm always interested in, it's increasing my profit margin. I'm rather lazy that way."

I was totally channeling Finn and his never-ending greed, but I figured it was an emotion the giant would understand well.

"What do you want?" Clementine asked.

Ah, the money question. Now she was finally getting down to business—and so was I.

"Now you're talking, sugar. I consider myself a reasonable person. I'm willing to trade you the tube and its contents."

"In exchange for what?"

"Two things. First, and most important, safe passage off the island."

"And the second?"

I drew in a breath. "Second, you let all the hostages live."

It was a calculated risk, but it was one I had to take.

"And why do you care so much about those folks?" Clementine asked. "Considering that just a minute ago, you were telling me to put a couple of bullets into Eva Grayson?"

"Well, let's just say that this isn't exactly a solo job. As I'm sure you know, you can't pull a heist like this without greasing a few palms. Well, more than a few. This is Ashland, after all. Anyway, I have a connection or two in the rotunda whom I'd like to see live through the night. Connections that will make it far easier for me to cash in on all my lovely, lovely diamonds."

"Well, if you care so much about your supposed friends, I could just start shooting people until you decide to turn that tube over to me," she threatened.

"You could," I agreed. "Although there are, what, two hundred and some people in the rotunda? The odds aren't good that you'll kill my connections. At least, not immediately. Besides, you start shooting folks, and the others will rise up and try to stop you. Self-preservation has a nasty habit of kicking in like that. And while you're busy fighting off a mob, I'll be slipping off the island. I'll find some way off this rock. Trust me on that. The second I'm back on the mainland, I'm a ghost, gone, and whatever's in this fancy tube along with me. Do you really want to take that chance, sugar?"

She fell silent again. All around me, the others shifted on their feet. The hums of crickets and the bellows of bullfrogs filled in the quiet. In the distance, I could hear the faint sloshing of the Aneirin River as it flowed around the island.

"Fine," Clementine finally snarled. "I want what's in that tube more than I want to kill the hostages."

Well, that, and she had been planning to let them live all along. But I'd take what I could get.

"Excellent," I drawled. "I thought you might see things my way."

"Meet me at the boathouse on the back side of the island," Clementine said. "That's where we'll make the exchange. You don't show, and I tell my men to start shooting."

It took me a moment to figure out that she was talking about the dock. In the summer, the museum let visitors rent out small plastic paddleboats and steer them through a series of canals that had been carved into and around the island. All the paddleboats were launched from the large dock at the back tip of the island.

I frowned. Why would Clementine want to meet way out there? Why not in the rotunda? Or out by the moving trucks? At least, that way, if things went badly, she could always order her giants to kill me or hop into one of the trucks and make good on her getaway—

Getaway.

The word, the thought, the idea, echoed through my mind, along with everything I'd seen and heard this evening. Clementine boldly announcing herself to the hostages. Opal taking such care sorting through the jewelry. Dixon saying they wouldn't have to share their loot. The bomb under the moving truck.

Clementine's getaway plan—that's what this was all about.

I'd wondered before why the giant and her crew hadn't worn masks. I'd thought it had been because they were going to kill all of the hostages. But now I knew the real reason: Clementine planned to fake her own death. She was going to blow up the first moving truck, and no doubt all the other ones too, with all of the art and all of the giants inside them . . . probably right as the vehicles were crossing the covered bridge. The wooden structure would collapse from the force of the blasts, plunging the trucks and everything and everyone inside them into the Aneirin River. The currents ran deep, swift, and sure around Briartop Island. They'd carry the blasted remains of the art and the robbers downstream and muddy the waters of the subsequent investigation, so to speak.

That's why the jewelry was so important. It was the only thing Clementine planned on taking with her. Well, that and the tube that held Mab's will. I still didn't know exactly what she wanted with that, but it didn't much matter at the moment.

What did matter was the fact that Clementine was going to sacrifice her own men and millions in art so that she, Opal, and Dixon could get away clean. No one would come looking for them after the fact, because everyone would think that they were as dead as the other giants. And by the time the bodies were sorted out and folks realized what had happened, well, Clementine would be ensconced on some tropical island far, far away from Ashland.

And to do all this, Clementine had to have a boat stashed at the dock. That's why she wanted to meet down there.

No doubt, the giant thought she could go kill me, take the tube, and drift on down the river with Opal, Dixon, and all the jewels they'd stolen before any of the other giants realized that she'd left them behind. Not a bad idea, considering how much I'd already screwed up her original plans. She could definitely improvise in a pinch—but so could I.

"Are you still there?" Clementine asked. "It's the boathouse or nothing. I want you as far away from my men and our art as possible. You've already done enough damage to both this evening."

Of course she did, but not for the reasons she was saying.

"Don't you worry, sugar. I'll be there. When you tell your men to release the hostages, I'll hand over the tube. Then we can both go our separate ways."

"Fine," Clementine snapped. "You have thirty minutes. Be there, or I tell my boys to start shooting—and not to stop until every single person in the rotunda is dead."

Static hissed through the walkie-talkie, indicating that the giant was done talking. Good. So was I. Now it was time to act. I turned down the volume on the device and looked at the others.

"You know she's going to double-cross you," Bria said. "Just as soon as she gets the chance. She's probably already ordering her giants to get into position all around the boathouse to take you down."

I shook my head. "No. She'll order some of her men to guard the hostages in the rotunda, and the others will be out by the moving trucks, protecting the art. The only ones who will be at the boathouse will be Clementine, Opal, and Dixon. They're the only ones in on the real plan."

"What plan?" Owen asked.

I told them what I thought Clementine was really up to.

Xavier let out a low whistle. "She's going to blow up all that art and all her men just to make sure that she escapes. She's certainly determined. So what are we going to do about it?"

"Well, while I meet Clementine at the boathouse, you, Bria, and Owen will get into position on the second-floor balcony above the rotunda," I said. "That'll give you the high ground and the chance to take out the giants by sniping at them from above. It's not ideal, since the hostages will still be in danger, but it's the best chance we have to rescue those folks with minimal loss of life to them or us. The only chance, really."

Bria shook her head, the moonlight making her blond hair glimmer like spun silver. "No," she said. "I'm not leaving you to face Clementine alone. It's too risky. Especially since she'll have Opal and Dixon for backup."

"It's a risk we have to take," I said in a quiet voice. "If we have any chance of saving Phillip and everyone else. It's been more than ninety minutes since he was shot. Phillip doesn't have much time left. We need to take out the giants in the rotunda now, or he dies."

I gave her a crooked grin.

"Besides, I don't plan on meeting Clementine so much as leaping out of the shadows, driving my knife into her back, and cutting her throat."

I didn't mention that such a sneak attack was probably the only way I could kill the giant now, given her incredible strength and all the licks I'd already taken tonight.

Bria looked at me, her mouth pinched with frustration. After a moment, she let out a tense breath. My sister didn't like it, but she knew I was right. "At least, promise me that you'll be careful."

I slung my arm around her shoulder and hugged her tight. "Don't worry, baby sister. I can take care of myself. You know that."

Bria nodded, but her face remained grim. We all knew what I was up against—what we were all up against.

Finally, Owen spoke. "You don't have to risk yourself for everyone else, Gin. Not for any reason."

I knew he was talking about Jillian and the guilt I felt over her death, but I just shook my head. "That's where you're wrong. I have to do this. You know I do."

Jillian was dead because of me. It was stupid and cruel and random, just like Owen had said, and there was no way I could go back and fix things, no way for me to bring her back. But I could make sure her murderers paid the same price they'd forced upon her. It wouldn't make up for what Jillian had suffered, and it wouldn't lessen my guilt. But it needed to be done, and I was the only one capable of doing it.

Instead of arguing, Owen just looked at me, his gaze slowly going over me from top to bottom, just like Bria's had a few minutes before. Ruined dress. Black boots. Blood on all the spaces in between.

It wasn't a pretty picture, I knew it wasn't, and I waited for Owen to turn away from me. He was still struggling with his feelings about Salina's death, including the conflicting ones he had for me, and I knew that how I looked right now wouldn't help my cause any. It would only reinforce what I did as the Spider—and what I'd done to Salina.

Owen kept staring at me, his violet eyes on my gray ones. I wondered what he saw there and what he thought about it all.

Bria and Xavier glanced back and forth between us, but they remained quiet. All around us, the hums of the crickets continued, punctuated every now and then by the haunting hoot of an owl hidden in one of the trees.

"Yes," Owen finally said. "I suppose you do."

Instead of the uncertainty and disgust I'd expected, his gaze softened with understanding—and respect. It was the first time he'd looked at me like that in weeks. It was the first time he'd looked at me without pain in his eyes since Salina's death.

"But you're not going alone," he continued. "I'm coming with you."

"But you're hurt. Your arm—"

He shook his head. "Doesn't matter right now. You do. You said that Clementine would have Opal and Dixon for backup. Well, you need somebody too. You don't know what tricks the giants might pull. Bria and Xavier can handle things in the rotunda. They're both better shots than I am. Besides, I have my own score to settle with Clementine and Dixon. I know you understand that."

He smiled at me, and I found myself grinning back. Once again, a tiny bit of hope sparked to life in the cold, black ashes of my heart, hope that maybe Owen and I could get through this after all. That we could eventually move past this, together.

I embraced that hope for a moment, grabbed onto it with both hands, and held it close like the rare treasure it was. Then I let go of it, let it float away like a butterfly on a bright day, because the darkest part of the night was yet to come, and there was no place for it here.

❊ 21 ❊

Bria, Xavier, Owen, and I left the gardens and went back to the museum. We didn't see or hear anyone as we scurried from the edge of the flowerbeds over to the side entrance I'd used before. I gestured for the others to stay hidden behind the bushes, while I sidled up to the door and peered through the cracked glass.

Once again, the hallway was dark and empty. I hadn't heard Clementine issue any more orders over the radio, but I was sure she'd told all of her remaining giants to either hightail it back to the rotunda or go outside and guard the trucks. Only one way to find out. The giants had busted the lock in their haste to chase after Owen and me, so I didn't have to use my stolen key card to open the door this time.

I winced as a bit of glass fell out of one of the doorframes and plinked against the stone, but the noise didn't keep me from ducking inside. I stood by the entrance, a knife in hand, looking and listening, but I didn't see or hear any guards. I turned and waved for the others to come on in.

We headed toward the rotunda. During my earlier wanderings, bumps and thumps and shouts had echoed from one room to the next as the robbers had looted all the art. But now everything was still and quiet, and the only sounds were my friends moving beside me and the tense mutters of the marble. The stone could sense all of my dark intentions. It knew that the violence was far from over.

We made it back to the stairs I'd used before without incident. We climbed up them to the second floor, then got down on our bellies and slid over to the edge of the balcony, staring down.

The scene hadn't changed much since I was here last. The hostages were all sitting together in the middle of the rotunda, surrounded by giants with guns. Good. They didn't realize it, but the giants had made themselves easy targets by standing over the hostages. Bria and Xavier could easily pick off the guards without worrying about a hostage getting in the line of fire. Once the shooting started, I imagined everyone on the ground would duck farther down for cover anyway.

Another thing working in our favor was the fact that there were only about a dozen giants left standing guard in the rotunda. All the others must be out by the moving trucks. They probably thought protecting the art was their number one priority now. Poor fools. They didn't realize that Clementine planned to blow them sky-high just as soon as she could.

It took me a few seconds, but I finally spotted my friends in the crowd. Roslyn and Finn were hovering over Phillip, still applying pressure to his gunshot wound. Roslyn would press down on his chest for a minute before Finn moved forward to relieve her. Then, after another minute had passed, they'd switch places again. Eva cradled Phillip's head in her lap, stroking his golden hair and whispering to him, even though he was unconscious. Phillip's skin looked pale and sweaty, but his chest moved up and down with a slow, steady rhythm.

I let out a quiet sigh. He was still breathing, which meant that we still had a chance. Jo-Jo and Cooper would be here any minute. As soon as the giants were dead, Bria and the others could carry Phillip out of the rotunda and find Jo-Jo when she arrived so that she could heal him with her Air elemental magic.

Owen realized that Phillip was still alive and also let out a relieved breath. After a moment, he reached over and squeezed my hand. I squeezed back, telling him that I understood his fear and worry and that I was going to do my best to make sure that we all lived through this.

Footsteps sounded, rattling into the rotunda, and we all tensed. A moment later, Clementine appeared at the main entrance, followed by Opal and Dixon. She whispered something to one of the giants standing guard, then stared at the hostages. She plastered a pleasant smile on her face, stepped forward, and addressed the crowd once more.

"I thought it was about time to come and give you ladies and gentlemen an update," she said. "My boys and I are almost through loading up all of our lovely new art, so we'll be out of your hair soon enough. I'm sure that will come as a relief to all of you."

Most of those in the rotunda let out a collective sigh, although they still regarded her with cold, wary suspicion. This was Ashland, after all, the city where double-, triple-, and even quadruple-crosses were a daily occurrence. The hostages knew that they wouldn't be truly safe until Clementine and her crew were either gone or dead.

"But before we wrap up our last bit of business here, I need to call upon the services of one more person," Clementine said. "Eva Grayson."

Eva gasped, as startled by the request as everyone else was.

If it wouldn't have given away our position, I would have opened my mouth and let loose with all the loud, blistering curses that burned on the end of my tongue. Damn and double damn—and then some. I'd hoped my bluff about Owen being dead would have persuaded Clementine to leave my friends alone, but it seemed like she hadn't bought my story after all. I wondered if she'd finally figured out that she'd killed the wrong woman— that the Spider was still alive.

Either way, there would be no sneaking up on her in the boathouse and stabbing her in the back. No, now that she had Eva, I had to play the game Clementine's way and approach her head-on, even if it would most likely get me killed in the end.

Clementine gestured at Opal and Dixon, who waded into the crowd of hostages. Dixon grabbed Eva's arm, hauled her upright, and handed her over to Opal. Finn surged to his feet and lunged for Dixon's gun, but the giant was ready for him. Dixon slapped his hand away, yanked the gun from its holster, and smashed the weapon into Finn's face.

Crack.

Finn fell on his ass, a dazed expression on his face and blood gushing from a cut on his forehead.

"Not so mouthy now, are you, pretty boy?" Dixon sneered.

"Do me a favor," Finn said, shaking off his daze and wincing as he touched his cut. "Hit me with the gun again instead of your hand. It's probably cleaner."

Dixon's orange skin reddened with anger, and he drew back the weapon for another blow. Finn just grinned at the giant, his green eyes as cold and hard as ice in his blood-covered face.

"Enough!" Clementine said, her voice booming like thunder through the rotunda. "We need to get moving. *Now*, Dixon. Don't make me tell you again."

The clear threat in her voice was enough to cut through Dixon's anger. He gave Finn another venomous glare, then turned and stomped back through the crowd. Opal tightened her grip on Eva's arm, dragged the girl over to where Clementine was standing, and then shoved her forward. Eva stumbled, lost her balance, and almost plowed into Clementine before she was able to right herself.

The giant gestured with her gun toward the hallway. "Move, girl. Before I decide to shoot you where you stand."

Eva swallowed and glanced back at Finn. He nodded, telling her to go ahead—as if she had a choice. She bit her lip and stepped out into the hallway. Clementine followed her, along with Opal and Dixon, and the four of them vanished from sight.

I watched a minute longer, but the crowd settled down once again, and it didn't look like anyone was going to try anything stupid, like charging at the giants. Good. Everyone needed to stay put. We were the only heroes here tonight.

I gestured at the others, and we slithered back out of sight on the balcony and crouched together at the top of the stairs. I didn't bother to ask Owen if he was still coming with me. Now that Clementine had taken Eva, there was no way I could have persuaded him to stay behind. I would have done the same thing if Bria had been the one in danger, and I wasn't about to deny Owen the chance to save his sister.

I looked at Xavier and Bria. "Can you two handle things here?"

They both nodded and checked their weapons.

"Okay," I said. "Give me and Owen ten minutes to get into position, then start shooting."

"What are you going to do about the giants now that they have Eva?" Bria asked.

I shrugged. "There's nothing I can do but walk right into Clementine's trap and try to distract them long enough for Owen to sneak up and steal Eva away from them."

Bria's face tightened with worry, but after a moment, she nodded. So did Xavier and Owen. We all knew this was how it had to be now.

Owen got to his feet and headed down the stairs. I

started to follow him but turned and grabbed Bria's hand instead.

"And if I don't come back," I whispered, "there are a couple of things in the back of the rotunda that belong to us. Some things I noticed among Mab's treasures. Make sure you get them."

Bria frowned. "What? What are you talking about?"

I thought about telling her about our mother's and sister's runes, but I clamped my lips shut at the last second. It wouldn't do any good to tell her about them. Not now. She'd just be distracted thinking about them, as I had been earlier.

Maybe if I hadn't been brooding about the runes, I would have realized what Clementine was up to. Maybe then I would have been able to save Jillian. Maybe . . . maybe I had too many damn *maybe*s cluttering up my mind.

Instead of answering her question, I shook my head. "You'll know them when you see them. Trust me."

Bria gave me a quizzical look, obviously wondering what I was babbling on about at a time like this, but she finally nodded. She squeezed my hand again before she moved over to Xavier. The two of them slid into position at the edge of the balcony and slowly, carefully, quietly trained their guns on the guards below.

I hurried down the stairs. Owen was waiting for me at the bottom. He fell into step beside me as we walked down the hallway. We didn't speak as we moved through the museum. We didn't have to. After everything we'd been through these past few weeks, the companionable quiet felt nice, comfortable, and soothing, even if I was probably marching toward my own death. Well, at least he was here with me for the end. Owen would get Eva to safety, and I'd take care of the bad guys, the way I always did.

We made it back to the side door and stepped outside. After that, it was just a matter of following the stone path down the hill to the bottom of the island. The sweet perfume of the ever-present honeysuckle seemed to have gathered strength while we'd been inside, hanging over everything like a thick, humid cloud. This side of the island wasn't as manicured and cultivated as the front, and the farther down the slope we went, the more the landscape darkened with thick tangles of briars and brambles. I didn't mind the change in scenery, though. The briars were beautiful in their own right, sharp and curved, rough and prickly, hardy enough to survive on the island, resilient enough to flourish here despite all the many concentrated attempts to kill them off. Just like me. At least, that was my hope tonight.

We stopped at a curve in the path just out of sight of the boathouse. Time to split up.

"How do you want to do this?" Owen asked.

"I'll go at Clementine straight on and try to keep her focused on me as long as possible," I said. "Do you think you can get in the water and wade around to the back of the boathouse? That way, we can attack from two sides at once. I think that's our best chance of saving Eva."

He nodded and rolled his shoulders. He winced a little, but I knew that he wouldn't let the pain of his gunshot wound stop him. "I can do it. You ready?"

I held up my knife so that it caught the moonlight and reflected it back. "Always."

"Be careful," he said.

"You too."

Owen hesitated like he wanted to say something else, but in the end he just nodded.

I nodded back, not trusting myself to speak. Despite the situation, I'd wanted—no, *hoped*—for something here. Some small sign that things were getting better between us. Some small sign that things were going to be okay. But Owen didn't give it to me. Instead, he just looked at me a moment longer before disappearing into the briars.

So I drew in another breath, let it out, and started down the path again.

⁂22⁂

I rounded the bend and was reminded of something else that Briartop was known for: its statues.

A dozen stone statues lined either side of the path, all shaped like Civil War soldiers, all with their rifles held high, as if they were about to pull the triggers and give me a twenty-one-gun salute. Well, twenty-four, in this case. From what I remembered, one row of statues was Union soldiers, while the others represented the Confederacy. Even more soldier statues perched behind the front lines, the figures all forming a sort of stone battle-field in the middle of the lush greenery. Supposedly, back during the war, some battle had been fought for control of Briartop. And here I was, fighting Clementine for it tonight.

I slowed my steps, staring at each one of the figures, wondering if perhaps Clementine, Opal, or Dixon was hiding somewhere among all the stone arms and legs, preparing an ambush like I'd wanted to. But it seemed the giants were nowhere in sight.

I'd started to move past the statues, when the moon slid out from behind a cloud, highlighting the soldier closest to me. Maybe it was the way the light reflected off that particular statue, but it made me think of another place, another time, another enemy . . .

I crept through Peter Delov's mansion as quiet as the pro- verbial mouse, searching for the giant.

I'd left Fletcher in a library on the third floor five min- utes ago. I'd helped the old man hide underneath a desk, then grabbed a tin of Jo-Jo's healing from my vest. I'd ripped Fletcher's shirt open and spread it over his wound. The bullet hole in his chest wasn't immediately fatal, and Jo-Jo's salve would help stop the bleeding, but that was all. Fletcher was in no shape to do anything more strenuous than breathe right now. So it was up to me to find and kill Delov as quickly as I could—before he found us.

I tiptoed through the hallways, eased up to the doorways, and looked in every room I passed, repeating the evaluation process Fletcher and I had used to find the giant in the first place. But Delov was nowhere to be seen. Had he somehow gotten past me already? Or was he watching me right now from some dark corner, getting ready to strike? I didn't know, and every second that passed ratcheted up my tension—

Scrape-scrape. Scrape-scrape.

The sound came from around the corner. I froze, my cold fingers tightening around the knife in my hand.

Scrape-scrape. Scrape-scrape.

The sound came again, moving faster now, heading right toward me. I sucked in a breath and got ready to fight. As soon as Delov stepped into view, I was going to leap forward and plunge Fletcher's knife into his chest. It wasn't much of a plan, but it would have to do, even if I knew deep down inside that there was no way I could kill the giant face-to-face, not given how big and strong he was. But I had to try, if only to protect Fletcher—

Peaches, the Pomeranian, rounded the corner, looking all bright-eyed and bushy-tailed, and I sagged against the wall in surprised, sweaty relief. The dog. It was just the dog.

I drew in a breath and pushed away from the wall, determined to keep searching for Delov, even if I didn't really believe I could take him out like I was supposed to, like Fletcher needed *me* to.

But Peaches had other ideas. The dog fell into step beside me as I moved down the hallway, his nails click-click-clicking and sounding as loud as trumpets on the polished hardwood floor. I might as well have raised a bullhorn to my lips and shouted my position to Delov. That's how much noise it seemed like the dog was making.

"Go away!" I hissed, and made a shooing motion with my hand.

But Peaches only gave me a goofy grin and kept right on following me like we were playing the best game ever. Finally, I stopped, leaned down and petted the dog's head, hoping that might appease him. But the Pomeranian just perked up more and started dancing in circles around my feet, apparently deciding that I was his new best friend.

Click-click-click. Click-click-click.

Again and again, Peaches' nails scraped against the floor, the sound seeming to intensify with every happy wag of the dog's bushy tail. I stood there, a wave of frustration washing over me. There was no way I could hope to sneak up on Delov, not with my pesky little shadow skipping along beside me, and I couldn't kill the dog to make him be quiet—I just couldn't.

I supposed I could lock Peaches in a room or a closet somewhere, but that would probably just make him start barking and reveal my location before I could scurry away. Delov would hear the noise and come running, ready to beat me to death with his massive fists—

Click-click-click. Click-click-click.

Peaches circled me again, wondering why I'd stopped petting him. I shook my head in frustration. I had to find a way to get the dog to stop making so much noise—

Noise.

My eyes narrowed in thought. Peaches wasn't going to be quiet—it wasn't in his nature. But maybe I didn't need the dog to be quiet. Maybe I needed him to make as much noise as possible.

As fast as I could, I crept back to the kitchen, where Fletcher and Delov had had their earlier fight. I stepped inside, my gaze sweeping over the appliances and other furnishings until I found what I wanted: a glass container of gourmet dog biscuits on one of the counters.

I went over, opened the container, and pulled out several of the biscuits. Peaches' black nose quivered with anticipation. I had his complete attention now.

"You want one of these, boy?" I whispered to the fluffball.

The Pomeranian pranced around, letting out hopeful, squeaky yips. I winced at the noise and quickly fed the dog one of the biscuits to quiet him down. I might not need him to be dead silent, but I needed to get the critter and myself in place before Peaches started yapping again.

*I held out another dog biscuit, waving it over Peaches'
fluffy head. "Come on, boy," I whispered again. "Follow me
for your treat."*

*Keeping an eye out for Delov, I hurried back toward the
library, where I'd left Fletcher. I stopped outside the entrance
and took a moment to crumble the dog biscuits into small,
bite-size pieces. I scattered some of the biscuits around the library entrance, then tossed a few more deeper into the room.
They didn't make a sound as they tumbled over the thick
Persian rugs.*

*Peaches hesitated a moment, not sure whether he wanted
to stay with me or sniff out the food I'd promised him. After
a second, the dog decided on the treats and moved toward
the library. I slid back into the shadows and crouched down
beside a table on the opposite side of the hall about fifteen feet
away from the library entrance.*

*The Pomeranian quickly gobbled up all the biscuits
around the door, then ventured into the library and lapped
up those treats too. But instead of coming back to me for more
food, the dog caught a new scent and headed even deeper into
the library—toward Fletcher.*

Just like I'd wanted him to.

*Peaches discovered Fletcher's hiding place underneath the
desk and let out a loud, delighted bark, as if he'd just found
some secret treasure. I could hear the old man trying to shush
the dog, but that only made Peaches bark louder, until it
seemed like the high-pitched yip-yip-yips echoed through the
entire floor.*

Just like I'd wanted them to.

*Maybe it was wrong of me to use Fletcher like this, but I
couldn't think of another way that I could kill Delov. Going*

toe-to-toe with the giant was out of the question. He'd take my knife away and then beat me to death at his leisure—or worse.

I needed something to distract the giant, so that's why I'd sicced the dog on Fletcher. I was hoping Delov would focus on the two of them instead of wondering where I might be lurking. This way, at least I had a fighting chance of sneaking up on the giant and taking him down.

Of course, if I didn't kill Delov, not only would I be dead, but so would Fletcher, since I'd just signed the old man's death warrant by leading the giant straight to him—

A mourning dove *coo-coo-coo*ed out a sad wail somewhere in the gardens, and I shook away the rest of the memory. Maybe I'd taken too many blows to the head tonight, because this was not the time to be lollygagging around, thinking about some old job. No, right now, I needed to focus on Clementine and how I could save Eva and kill the giant. Nothing else.

So I tightened my grip on my knife, gave the soldiers a respectful nod, and hurried on my way.

This part of the island curved to a sharp tip, almost like the end of a hook, and the boathouse perched on this last bit of land, as though it were a fish that had been caught. The boathouse was made out of the same gray marble and built on the same grand scale as the rest of the museum. Instead of a simple shack, it was as big as any Northtown mansion. Tall, slender columns supported the domed roof, giving the structure an elegant, open-air design.

The Aneirin River rippled by on either side of the wide path, the water constantly churning back and forth and sucking at the cattails on the muddy banks. Water lilies bobbed up and down on the surface of the river, the strong currents spinning them around and around in endless circles and ultimately taking them nowhere.

The good thing about meeting Clementine down here was that there was no way she could ambush me, since there weren't any trees for her to hide behind. No thickets of brambles for her to crouch down in. No high spots for her to snipe at me from. Just the stone path, the boathouse, and water, water everywhere.

The bad thing was that I was out in the open for everyone to see. No cover for Clementine meant there was no place for me to retreat to either when things went to hell, as they most surely would.

By this point, I was fifty feet away from the boathouse. My gaze locked onto the entrance, but I didn't spot Clementine, Opal, Dixon, or, more important, Eva. All I could see ahead of me were darkness and shadows—a metaphor for my life if ever there was one. But this was the path I'd chosen, in more ways than one, and there was nothing to do now but see it through to the end.

So I stepped forward and went to meet my enemy.

❋23❋

As I neared the boathouse, I thought about reaching for my Stone magic and using it to harden my skin. If I was Clementine, I would have ordered Opal and Dixon to shoot first and search my body later.

But in the end, I decided not to use my magic. I'd already depleted some of my power fighting the other giants, and I had a sneaking suspicion that I'd need every scrap of magic I had left to take out Clementine. Besides, with any luck, she would want to make sure that I actually had Mab's will on me first before she killed me.

I hoped so, since I was betting my life on it.

I walked slowly down the path, scanning the shadows in front of me for any hint of movement, any sign that one of the giants was going to pop out and start shooting at me. The closer I got to the boathouse, the more I felt like there was a target on my chest. Then again, this was nothing new. There was always a target on me these days, a big red bull's-eye I'd put there myself just by kill-ing Mab, just by being the Spider.

But like I'd told Owen before, I had to do this. And not just because my friends were being held hostage in-side the museum or the fact that Eva was in danger out here now. An innocent woman was dead when I should have been instead, and Clementine had to pay for her mistake, simple as that.

I kept walking until I reached the front of the boat-house. I waited a moment, but Clementine didn't call out to me, so I stepped inside.

Moonlight sliced in through the gaps between the col-umns, painting the inside of the boathouse a soft silver and letting me see that it was like a museum unto it-self. No paintings decorated the interior, but each of the marble columns had been carved with intricate designs of fish, birds, and flowers, all of which peeped out at me from among the curling clutches of the museum's briar rune. Several statues also stood inside, although I could clearly see only the one closest to me. An old man with his pants rolled up to his knees, hefting a spear as if he were about to lean forward, toss it into the river, and stab a fish.

Maybe it was the sly grin on the fisherman's face, but the statue reminded me of Fletcher.

Thinking about my mentor calmed me, and once again, I let the cold, black rage well up out of the deep-est part of my soul and seep through me, until there was nothing left but my dark desire to kill Clementine.

I looked away from the statue and took another step forward.

"That's far enough," Clementine called out.

A second later, a soft *click* sounded. I tensed, expecting a burst of orange gunfire to erupt from the shadows, but lights blazed on instead. I squinted and blinked rapidly, trying to get my vision to adjust to the sudden brightness.

Just like the rotunda, the boathouse was shaped like a giant circle. Alternating columns and statues ringed the path that ran all the way around the outer rim. Two more walkways cut through the interior, one going from left to right and the other running front to back, creating a capital T in the middle of the circle. Water ran between each one of the two main paths, forming three large pools, while metal gates set into the walkways could be hoisted up to let the boats move from one pool to another and then out into the river itself. Short metal poles had been pounded into the marble paths at intervals, and red, white, and blue paddleboats bobbed silently up and down on the river. The currents made the boats' fiberglass hulls bump into the stone docking stations, causing the ropes that secured them to creak faintly, almost like there were crickets nesting inside them.

I was standing on the main path, with Clementine about twenty feet in front of me. The other two giants were about twenty feet behind her in the very center of the boathouse, where the two walkways met. Opal was on the far right, having flipped a light switch on one of the columns, while Dixon hovered off to the left, one hand clenched around Eva's arm. All of the giants had guns.

My eyes met Eva's, and she drew in a surprised gasp. Shock filled her pale face. For a moment, I wondered why, and then I remembered—she thought I was dead.

Eva wasn't the only one who was stunned by my appearance. Clementine blinked and blinked, as if she didn't believe what she was seeing. No doubt, she'd expected someone clad in black from head to toe, someone suave and confident, someone who looked more like a cat burglar, rather than the victim of some bloody, horrific accident, like I did right now. Her eyes widened as she realized exactly who and what I was.

"You!" she hissed.

"Hello, Clementine," I drawled.

"You're supposed to be dead!" she hissed again, then turned and fixed her cold, angry glare on Dixon.

He stared at me in horrified shock for a moment before his gaze snapped over to Clementine. I hadn't thought it possible, given how much self-tanner had soaked into his skin, but his orange face actually paled and took on a sickly, sallow tint. He swallowed once, his Adam's apple bobbing up and down like a fishing lure that was stuck in his throat.

"But—but you saw her!" he sputtered. "I killed her! I killed the Spider! I blew her face off!"

"No," I snapped. "You killed a woman who had on the same dress as I did. Nothing more. Her name was Jillian, and she didn't deserve to die like that."

Eva sucked in another breath at the revelation of Jillian's fate. Apparently, so much had been going on in the rotunda that Eva hadn't realized that Jillian wasn't there, just like Owen hadn't.

"She was in the wrong place at the wrong time," I said, for Eva's benefit. Then I stared at Clementine. "Your nephew there was just too dumb to realize that he'd killed the wrong woman. Maybe if he hadn't shot her in the face so many times, he would've seen his mistake before now—and you would have too."

Anger stained Clementine's cheeks, her hazel eyes narrowed, and even her hair seemed to curl tighter with wrath, but she didn't respond to my taunts. Instead, she stared at me for the better part of a minute, her sharp gaze taking in my hacked-off ball gown, the belt around my hips, the black boots on my feet, the blood spattered all over me.

"You look like you've been rode hard and put up wet," she said. "Not what I expected from the mighty Spider."

I shrugged. "Well, I do aim to please, but as you know, my plans for this evening were interrupted. I'll give you this, you don't do anything halfway. Robbing the entire Briartop museum and holding Ashland's finest at gunpoint at the same time is no small feat. You should give yourself a pat on the back. You've earned it."

Clementine grinned. "My mama always said, why steal one million, when you can steal two. Or a hundred, in this case."

I snorted. "Give it a rest. You're not stealing a hundred million."

She cocked an eyebrow. "Oh, why is that?"

"Because you're planning to blow all of that pretty art to smithereens."

Dixon blinked. "How do you know that?"

I stared at him. "Because in addition to the one I stole from the bridge, I also found a bomb hidden underneath one of the moving trucks. My guess is that the three of you were going to load all of that art and all of the other giants onto those trucks, then blow them all sky-high when they crossed the bridge. That way, all your men would be dead, and everyone would think that the three of you were too."

Clementine kept staring at me, but Opal and Dixon shared a nervous glance behind her back, confirming that I was right.

"No, the only things the three of you ever planned on leaving here with were that tube from the vault and all of the jewelry you took off the hostages," I said. "Pry the gems out of their settings, and they're a lot easier to fence than well-known pieces of art. Since the jewelry wasn't in the moving trucks, I'm willing to bet that it's down here somewhere."

Opal's head snapped to the right. I followed her gaze and realized that there was something else tied up to one of the slips in the very back: a small speedboat. I could just see the glint of a silverstone case that had been propped up in one of the seats.

"I'll take that as a yes."

Nobody said anything, and the only sound was the steady rush of the river flowing around us. Finally, Clementine barked out a laugh.

"Well, maybe I was wrong to be so hasty in my previous judgment about you being so disappointing," she said. "Because you certainly are clever."

"I do try."

Yeah, I was preening a little bit, but only so I could give Owen as much time as possible to get into position to rescue Eva. I didn't want the giants to remember that he was out here somewhere and realize that all my blustering was just a ploy to distract them from his rescue attempt.

Clementine's face hardened. "Enough talk. Why don't you hand over the tube before I tell Dixon to blow the girl's head off?"

Dixon grinned and waggled his gun at me. I looked at him a moment longer, not giving any hint about the waterlogged figure I saw climb up one of the ladders at the very back of the boathouse, sneak over to the outer circular path, and head in his direction.

Since I had a knife in my right hand, I reached down with my left and slowly slid the ebony tube out of the pouch on my belt. I held the tube up high and then slowly turned it around, making sure that Clementine saw the flash of Mab's sunburst rune on the smooth wood.

Her eyes narrowed, and she studied me a moment longer.

"Put it on the ground, and roll it over here," she said. "Real easy-like. Or the girl dies."

I slowly bent down and did as she asked. The tube hopped and skipped across the stone, heading toward her. Clementine raised her foot, then brought her boot down gently on top of the tube, stopping it. Still keeping her eyes and her gun on me, she bent down and picked up the tube.

"Opal, you keep your gun on her," Clementine said. "You too, Dixon. I want to make sure that Ms. Blanco gave us what she promised she would."

I gave her a bright, carefree smile. "Why, Clementine, would I lie?"

"Certainly," she replied. "I would."

Apparently, Clementine was more familiar with the tube than I was. Instead of taking a moment to figure out how to open it, she immediately pressed on the ruby in the middle of the sunburst rune. Interesting, that she would know to do that.

Clementine slid the paper out of the hollow tube, unrolled it, and read the sheet. Opal and Dixon kept their guns trained on me, and I stayed perfectly still, not wanting to give them any reason to shoot me or, worse, Eva.

Clementine scanned the sheet for the better part of two minutes before she was satisfied. I kept my eyes on Dixon—and the shadow that was creeping closer and closer to him. Another minute, two tops, and Owen would be ready to make his move, as would Bria and Xavier in the rotunda.

When she finished reading, Clementine rolled the paper up, slid it back into the tube, and stuffed the whole thing into her pants pocket. Then she looked at me again.

"You know, I'm rather surprised that you gave it back to me just like that."

I shrugged. "It's just Mab's will. What do I care about that? It's not like she left me anything. Although I am curious about why you want it so badly. Care to share? After all, you're just going to kill me anyway."

"You'd better fucking believe it," Clementine agreed. "But I'm not dumb enough to tell you anything, especially while you've got that radio clipped to your belt. Why, who knows who might be listening in?"

Well, it had been worth a shot. More important, though, Owen had crept closer to Dixon. He was now standing on the outer circular path behind the column nearest and parallel to the giant. He couldn't move any closer for fear that Dixon or Opal would spot him, but he was well within striking distance. All I had to do now was distract the giants until the right moment.

"You know, you and I are a lot alike, Gin," Clementine said.

"Really? How so?"

She stared at me. "We both do whatever we have to in order to survive. In fact, I rather admire you. Why, to hear the rumors, you're the most heartless, ruthless bitch this town has ever seen."

"My, my, my," I drawled. "What a lovely compliment. Especially coming from someone like you."

"I mean it," she continued in a genuine voice. "The things you've managed to do as the Spider, the folks you've taken down these past several months. I've heard about them, you know. Tobias Dawson. Elliot Slater. Elektra LaFleur. And then of course the biggie, Mab Monroe herself."

I shrugged. "What can I say? I don't like bullies. That's what all of them were—just like you."

Her eyes glittered in her face, but her voice was calm, friendly even, when she spoke again. "Actually, you killing Mab has made life better for a lot of folks, including me. My boys and I have had a lot of fun with that Fire elemental bitch out of the picture. My protection business has been booming. Of course, what the idiots who hire me don't realize is that there's no one around anymore to keep me from taking whatever I want, whenever I want it, especially from them."

"Well, I'm happy that I could help a small business succeed."

"But the problem is that a lot of other people have had the exact same idea," she continued, as if I hadn't spoken. "In some ways, things are even worse than before. At least, with Mab around, you knew where you stood: below her. Now everybody's fighting everybody else. It makes things . . . messy for us all. It's one of the reasons I've been thinking about getting out of town for a while now. Too much damn drama going on these days."

"Pardon me if I don't shed any tears for the trials and tribulations of Ashland's criminal element," I said. "I've got my own problems with them, in case you haven't heard."

Clementine grinned. "Oh, I've heard, all right. Did you know there's a huge betting pool about who will kill you and when they'll do it? Last time I'd heard, the pot was more than a million bucks."

I didn't respond, but the news didn't surprise me. There was already some fool supposedly selling T-shirts with some cheesy slogan about eating at the Pork Pit and living through the experience. I didn't know whether to be flattered or annoyed that people were cashing in on my notoriety. Finn would have been annoyed, especially since he wasn't getting a cut of the action.

"Really?" I asked. "Well, who am I to stand in the way of commerce? Although I pity the folks who try to collect on that particular wager. It's a deadly gamble."

Her grin widened. "I thought you might say something like that. That's another way we're alike. You make sure that your enemies don't live too long, just like I do."

"Well, I'd say that you've failed pretty miserably at that

so far tonight, since I'm still breathing. Then again, you should never trust a minion to do something important, especially one who doesn't know when to quit with the self-tanner." I looked at Dixon. "You do realize that you look like a pumpkin on steroids, right?"

"Hey!" Dixon shouted, his features turning petulant and sullen. "I'll have you know that this was a spray tan. The best spray tan money can buy."

Opal rolled her eyes. So did Clementine.

"And my point is made. If you want something done right . . ." I let my voice trail off.

"Oh, don't you worry, Ms. Blanco," Clementine said, flexing her free hand into a fist and taking a menacing step forward. "I plan to give you my personal attention this time around—"

A sharp, high-pitched squawk sounded through the walkie-talkie on Clementine's belt, followed by several more distinctive sounds.

Crack! Crack! Crack!

Gunshots burped through the device. Looked like Bria and Xavier had finally pulled their triggers on the giants in the rotunda, so to speak.

"Clementine! Clementine!" a voice screamed through the walkie-talkie. "We're taking fire! We're taking—"

The voice abruptly cut off with a loud gurgle, although other screams and more *crack-crack-crack*s of gunfire continued to sound through the walkie-talkie. Clementine stared down at the device, then her head snapped up to me.

"What the hell did you do, you meddlesome bitch?" she demanded.

"You have your crew, and I have mine," I said. "Right now, they're killing your giants in the rotunda. And when they're done up there, they'll come down here and help me finish off you and the rest of your sick, twisted family—"

Clementine didn't bother responding to my taunts. Instead, she raised her gun and fired at me.

❋24❋

The second Clementine started to raise her gun, I ran to my right, ducking behind the fisherman statue.

Crack! Crack! Crack!

The three bullets she'd just shot at me slammed into the statue. One of them punched through the brim of the old man's hat, causing the marble to wail.

Dixon also raised his gun to fire at me—just as Owen stepped out from the shadows.

"Eva!" Owen screamed. "Get down!"

Eva twisted out of Dixon's grasp and immediately dropped to the ground. Dixon whipped around, searching for this new danger even as he brought his weapon up. Owen didn't give him a chance to react. He raised his gun and shot the bastard in the face.

Crack! Crack! Crack!

With each shot, Owen stepped forward. He knew as well as I did that it took a lot of bullets to put down most giants, so he emptied the whole clip into Dixon, catching him in the face, throat, and chest. Owen might not have been as good a shot as Bria and Xavier, but Dixon was a big target and hard to miss, especially with Owen closing the distance between them.

The giant screamed and jerked as the bullets tore through his tan flesh. Shock and surprise filled his face—what was left of it, anyway. Owen had blown off a chunk of Dixon's chin and peppered his throat with bullets. Good. It was time the giant got a taste of his own medicine.

Click.

The gun was empty, so Owen tossed it aside and grabbed another one from against the small of his back. He didn't have to use it, though.

Dixon opened his mouth and tried to mumble something, but apparently, it's hard to talk when the bottom half of your face is missing. He staggered back, tripped over Eva, who was huddled into a tight ball on the stone behind him, and did a header into the water.

"Dixon!" Clementine screamed. "Dixon!"

But it was too late for her nephew, and we all knew it. Owen raced forward and helped Eva to her feet. He shoved his sister behind him and started backing up, moving his gun back and forth between Opal and Clementine, ready to shoot them if they made a move toward him and Eva.

Across the distance, Owen's eyes met mine. He hesitated, and I saw the worry and concern in his gaze as he debated whether to step away from Eva and try to help me. But I made the choice for him.

"Go!" I screamed at him. "Go! Go! Go!"

Owen hesitated a moment more before nodding, grabbing Eva's hand, and heading toward the front of the boathouse, keeping to the outer circular path and darting from column to column and statue to statue for cover. I sprinted from the statue over to a column on the far right side of the boathouse so the giants couldn't shoot all of us at once.

Clementine didn't hesitate. She leveled her gun at me once more and squeezed off several rounds. Like Owen, she wasn't going to stop with just a couple. But I kept behind the columns and statues as I moved, and all of her bullets just bounced off the marble and rattled every which way through the boathouse, ricocheting into other columns, the statues, even the ceiling high overhead.

Click.

This time, Clementine's gun was the one that was empty. She screamed and tossed the weapon at me in frustration, but it landed in one of the pools of water with a loud *plop*. She whirled around to face Opal, who was staring at Dixon's body, which was bobbing up and down in the river right next to a couple of white water lilies.

"Opal!" Clementine bellowed. "What are you just standing there for? Shoot her! Now!"

Opal shook off her shock and did as her mother asked.

Crack! Crack! Crack!

More bullets whistled through the air, but I grabbed a second knife from my thigh holsters and kept moving deeper into the boathouse, hiding behind the columns and statues again and letting Opal empty her whole clip at me.

Crack! Crack! Crack!

The rest of Opal's shots went wide, although I heard the marble scream as more and more bullets slammed into the columns, causing stone chips to zip through the air like shrapnel.

Click.

As soon as I heard that Opal was out of ammo, I rushed out from behind the columns, stepped onto the path that ran left to right through the boathouse, forming the top part of the T, and headed toward her.

Clementine finally realized what I was up to and why I was running toward Opal instead of away from her.

"Opal!" she screamed, waving her hand at her daughter. "Move! Get away from her! Now!"

But it was too late. Opal started backpedaling, trying to get back to regroup with her mother, but she didn't look where she was going, and her foot caught in a rope that secured one of the paddleboats to its slip. She grunted and yanked her foot free, but those few precious seconds of delay were all I needed to catch her.

My knives arched up, the blades flashing underneath the lights as I slammed them into Opal's chest. She threw back her head and shrieked with pain. Her gun flew out of her fingers, and her hands flapped around as though I were a bothersome mosquito she was trying to shoo away. I was hungry for blood, all right, and I yanked my knives out and stabbed her again. This time, I managed to slide one of the blades between her ribs and into the soft, sweet spot of her heart.

Opal's shrieks abruptly faded into hoarse, rapid, pain-filled rasps. I pulled my knives out of her a second time.

She lashed out with her fist, catching me in the jaw. The force of the blow spun me around and made me stagger back five feet, but the damage to her was already done.

Opal stared down in disbelief at her chest and all of the blood pumping out of her wounds. She put first one hand and then the other over her heart, then held them out, as if she couldn't believe that there was so much blood on them. Finally, she looked over at Clementine, her light eyes already starting to dim with death.

"Mama?" Opal whispered.

Then she pitched forward, her body landing with a dull *thump* on the walkway. The current had dragged Dixon's body over to where Opal was, and her hand slid forward into the water and landed on his broad back, almost as if she were reaching down to try to fish him out of the river.

Silence.

Clementine stood in the middle of the main walkway, slowly swaying from side to side. After a moment, she shuffled forward until she was standing over the bodies of her daughter and her nephew.

"Opal . . . Dixon . . ." she whispered.

While Clementine was caught up in her grief, I eased back the way I'd come, circling all the way around until I was standing in the front of the boathouse right next to the statue of the old man fishing. I didn't want the giant to make a sudden move, charge past me, go after Owen and Eva, and try to get her revenge that way. No, this ended right here, right now. I watched her the whole time, just watched and waited for the rage that was sure to come.

To my surprise, a welling of tears cascaded down

Clementine's face, and she looked every one of her fifty-eight years as she stared down at the bodies.

"Opal . . . Dixon . . ." she said again, her voice dull and small. "They were the only family I had left."

I hadn't thought she would be so emotional, given how I'd seen her threaten, bully, and intimidate Opal and Dixon earlier tonight, but apparently, she'd cared about them more than I'd realized.

"You killed them. You killed them both," she murmured.

Clementine raised her eyes to mine. Hate brightened her hazel gaze, and her mass of curls bristled around her head, giving her a wild, crazed look, like a rabid animal with its fur up, one that was about to attack. And I knew that there was only one thing that would satisfy her now: my blood.

Good. Because I felt the same way about her.

"Looks like it's just you and me now," I said, taunting her. "Let's hope you have more fight in you than Opal there did. Why, I didn't even break a sweat cutting her down."

Clementine's lips flattened out, her nostrils flared, and her eyes narrowed to slits. It was the same murderous expression I'd noticed earlier, when she'd been browbeating Opal and Dixon outside the vault. The mottled flush of her skin and her low, breathy snarls told me just how fully enraged she was, like a bull about to charge at a matador waving a red cape—or rather me in my ruined red dress.

"Come on," I taunted her again. "Come on, already. What are you waiting for? Let's dance, bitch."

"You wanna dance?" Clementine asked, her hands closing into fists as she slowly advanced on me. "By the time I get done with you, there won't even be any bones left to feed the fish."

"Come over here and say that again, sugar."

She let out a loud roar and charged forward.

❖ 25 ❖

I raised my blades and let her come to me. I also reached
for my Stone magic and used it to harden my skin. Despite my mockery of her, Clementine was a dangerous
enemy, made even more so by the grief, rage, and adrena-
line pumping through her veins right now. I needed to
put her down as quickly as possible, or I'd be in a world
of hurt.

When she was in range, I stepped forward and slashed
out with my knives, determined to end her with that first
strike. But Clementine anticipated my plan and sidestepped me at the last second, so my weapons only sliced
through empty air. I whirled around for another strike,
but Clementine was already moving, moving, moving.
Her fist slammed into my jaw, spinning me around and
making a few stars wink on and off before my eyes. I
stumbled back, but I managed to stay upright and keep
my grip on my Stone magic.

Clementine came at me again, her fists raised in a classic boxer's stance. For the better part of a minute, we bobbed and weaved back and forth, each one of us trying to end the other. Clementine wanted to plant her fist in my chin again, while I wanted to slice her from guts to gullet with my knives. But we both dodged this way and that, trading shallow, glancing blows and never giving each other a clear opening.

The longer we bobbed and weaved, the more I felt the dreaded exhaustion creeping up on me. My breaths grew hoarse and raspy, sweat trickled down my face, neck, and back, and my legs twitched with the effort of staying upright. It had been a long night already, and now here I was, locked in another fight to the death. Sometimes it just didn't pay to leave the house.

Not for the Spider, anyway.

Back and forth and around and around, we do-si-doed in the front of the boathouse, neither one of us able to break through the other's defenses.

At least, not until my boot slipped.

I didn't know where the puddle came from. Maybe a paddleboat bumping into a docking station and spraying water everywhere, maybe a freakishly large wave arching up and spilling over onto the stone, maybe even a fish jumping in the river and doing a cannonball. But water had pooled on the marble walkway, making it as wet and slick as glass. I blocked the giant's latest blow and stepped forward to deliver one of my own—and slipped. Even as I windmilled my arms and tried to stay upright, I lowered my guard, just for a second, and Clementine took the opening.

She slammed her fist into my face.

Since I was still holding on to my Stone magic, the blow didn't crush my cheekbone, but it knocked me back all the same. Clementine immediately pressed her advantage. She slapped one of my knives away, then the other one. The weapons skidded along the stone walkway, the blades throwing up bright silver sparks as they tumbled end over end. Before I could reach for my other pair of knives, the giant was on top of me.

"You think you can kill my girl—my *Opal*—and get away with it? I'll show you," Clementine snarled. "I'll show you."

She grabbed my arms, lifted me into the air, and then slammed me into the ground with all the force she could muster. She would have splintered every bone in my back if I hadn't had my magic to protect me. Even with my Stone power, I still felt like I'd plummeted out of a high window and hit the ground at warp speed—*splat*. Before I could even think about moving, much less fighting back, Clementine was straddling me.

Thwack. Thwack. Thwack.

She pounded her fists into my body over and over again. Each punch seemed to add fuel to her rage, and every blow was harder and sharper than the one before it. Any one of them would have been enough to do major damage. The only thing saving me right now was my Stone magic and the hard shell of my skin, but that wouldn't last long under a beating like this.

It was always a concern when fighting dwarves or giants, letting them get their hands on you. Because once they did that, it was just a matter of them wearing you down. Power was still power, whether it was a giant's strength or an elemental's magic. One always succumbed to the other in the end, and the loser died.

This time, the loser was going to be me.

Clementine kept hitting me and hitting me. She showed no signs of tiring. Or stopping.

But she quickly realized that something was wrong, since I wasn't screaming with pain and gushing blood from every available surface. She snarled with disgust when she realized that her blows weren't having the desired effect, and she finally noticed the magic glinting in my gray gaze.

"Stone magic," she muttered. "I should have remembered that you have that. I fucking *hate* Stone magic. But don't you worry. You'll run out of that long before I get tired of hitting you."

She stopped her assault and pulled back just long enough for me to throw my hand to the side, reach for my Ice magic, and use it to form a sharp, cold knife. I raised the weapon and drove it into her chest, but since I was flat on my back, I couldn't put enough muscle behind the thrust to make it do any real damage.

Clementine stared down at the Ice knife sticking out of her chest a couple of inches above her heart. "Really? That old tired trick? Does that ever actually work for you?"

Her distraction let me reach down and fumble for the other weapons on my utility belt. I didn't have much to work with. I'd emptied my gun during the firefight with the giants earlier in the museum hallway, and the metal baton was too long for me to slide it out of its loop. So was the flashlight that was tucked through another loop. But there was one other small tube hooked onto the belt: the pepper spray I'd taken off the first giant I'd killed.

Clementine pulled the knife out of her chest and crushed the Ice with one hand before flinging the melting bits off her fingers. "Is that the best you can do?" she mocked. "Why, that didn't hurt any more than a little ole bee sting—"

I pulled out the tube, flipped the nozzle, and gave her a face full of pepper spray, even though the close proximity made my own eyes water and nose burn. Clementine cursed and slapped the spray out of my hand. It too disappeared into one of the pools of water. The giant looked at me, her whole face red, puffy, and soaked with tears.

She drew in a breath, and I thought she might start screaming with pain.

Instead, she laughed, leaned forward, and started hitting me again.

Thwack. Thwack. Thwack.

I was flat on my back on the stone walkway, with Clementine on top of me, her knees squeezing in on my ribs. The irony was that I'd done this same thing more than once, used the weight of my body to slowly drive the air out of someone's lungs. I usually ended things rather quickly with a knife to the heart, but Clementine seemed content to keep beating me until her fists punched all the way through my body and out the other side.

Thwack. Thwack. Thwack.

She kept hitting me, her blows even, steady, and achingly hard as she got into the rhythm of the fight. And all I could do was lie there and take it. I couldn't reach the knives strapped to my thighs with her on top of me, and she'd already shown me how useless an Ice knife was. Even the pepper spray hadn't bothered her all that much. I was out of weapons. Right now, it was all I could do to concentrate on my Stone magic to keep her from pummeling me into a bloody smear. Soon that would be gone too.

Finally, though, Clementine grew tired of using me as her own personal punching bag.

"Fine," she growled. "Your skin might be as hard as a rock, but let's see how you do without any air, bitch."

Still kneeling on me, she wrapped one hand around my neck and used the other to cover my nose and mouth. She might not be able to punch her way through my skin, but Clementine had a death grip on my throat and was slowly pushing her fingers into my windpipe with all her might. I clawed and clawed at her, drawing her blood with my short nails, but she was in the position of power here, not to mention how much stronger she was than me. I didn't have a chance, and we both knew it.

It was inevitable. All the fights I'd been through tonight, all the nicks and cuts and lumps and bumps I'd gotten. None of them debilitating or life-threatening, but they'd all chipped away at my strength, at my magic, until I had nothing left in the tank. And now the giant was cutting off my air supply. I'd be dead in another minute, two tops, unless I could figure out some way to get her off me long enough for me to regroup and grab one of my knives. Even then, I didn't know if I'd have strength enough to kill her with one of the blades—

Strength.

The word rattled around in my mind, bouncing from one side of my skull to the other, and I remembered what Clementine had said to Owen earlier tonight in the vault.

This isn't about strength, Mr. Grayson, it's about finesse.

And I realized that's what this fight really came down to—my strength versus Clementine's. Physically, I wasn't a match for the giant, especially not now, since she was using the weight of her body to pin me down. But maybe I didn't need brute strength, raw force, sheer power, to beat her. Maybe all I needed was a little of that finesse she'd talked about earlier.

Or maybe the lack of air was already making me hallucinate, because I just couldn't think of a way to stop her.

Still, I kept fighting—clawing, slapping, and punching with all my might. Clementine continued to laugh. Apparently, my weak, pitiful struggles amused her. She let go of my throat long enough to slap my hand away from hers, the blow so hard that it caused my knuckles to crack into the marble walkway—

Wait a second.

Marble—I was lying on a solid sheet of marble. In fact, the whole boathouse was made out of stone. I'd once collapsed an entire coal mine, so I knew that I could use my magic to do the same thing to the boathouse. But as satisfying as that might be, dropping a couple of tons of rock on top of Clementine's head wouldn't help me. The rocks would either crush us outright or shatter the walkway and drag us both down to the bottom of the river. I didn't want to drown, especially not if Clementine was going to be trapped on top of me for all eternity.

Still, there had to be some way to use my magic against her without killing myself in the process. Oh, I'd sacrifice myself if it meant murdering her too, but I wasn't ready to give up yet. Not until my air was almost completely gone and I had no other chance of stopping her.

I moved my head left and right, my gaze shooting every which way, but there wasn't much to see. Just the marble ceiling over my head, the columns on either side of the boathouse, and the statue of the old fisherman to the left of Clementine—

The statue.

My gaze locked on it, but it wasn't the figure of the old man I was interested in—it was the spear clutched in his hand. I hadn't made a dent in the giant with my silverstone blades or Ice knife, but that spear looked to be at least six feet long and three inches thick. That spear would take down anyone, even a giant as tough and strong as Clementine Barker.

All I had to do was find a way to finesse it right into the bitch.

I quit fighting the giant, quit clawing at her hands, quit kicking and punching and trying to buck her off me. I even quit using my Stone magic to harden my skin. Instead, I gathered and gathered the power inside me, combining it with all the Ice magic I had left, added to what was stored in the spider rune ring on my right index finger.

Clementine noticed that my skin had reverted back to its normal texture. She paused and drew her hand away from my nose and mouth. I sucked down breath after breath, but all the while, I kept reaching and reaching for my magic, getting ready to make one final strike with it.

She grinned. "Out of magic already, Gin? How disappointing. I thought that the legendary Spider would be tougher to beat than this. Why, I haven't been hitting you more than three minutes now. Going to let me beat you to death after all? Pathetic. But I have to thank you. This will be so much more fun than simply smothering you."

She drew back her fist and drove it into my chest.

Thwack.

One of my ribs cracked.

Thwack.

Another rib splintered.

Thwack.

She went for my shoulder that third time, and pain exploded in the socket and reverberated along my collarbone and down into my arm. Fuck. I *hated* having a broken collarbone.

The pain almost overwhelmed me, but I forced it to the back of my mind and concentrated on the cold, raw fury of my magic, drawing it up from the deepest, darkest, blackest part of me. I let the Ice power flood my body first, numbing me from head to toe, until I couldn't feel the sharp, pulsing pain in my ribs or the fact that my collarbone felt like broken bits of confetti barely clinging together. I reached for more and more of my Ice magic until all I felt was cold—and the determination to end this bitch once and for all.

Clementine stopped hitting me long enough to throw back her head and laugh again. She didn't notice me stretch my arms out to either side of my body and press my palms flat on the stone walkway. Looking past Clementine, I stared at the statue of the old man, my gaze narrowing in on the spear in his hand.

Finally, she quit laughing. "But as much as I'd love to break every single bone in your body, you were right before, Gin," Clementine said. "I have a boat to catch and a fortune to spend. It's a crying shame that Opal and Dixon won't be around to help me use all that money, but I'll toast to them—and your death—with the finest champagne. Good-bye, oh, great and not-so-mighty Spider."

Clementine drew back her fist for the final, killing blow. Instead of trying to fight her off, I reached out with my Stone magic, pushing it toward the statue. The giant finally noticed that I wasn't paying attention to her anymore. She hesitated, wondering what I was doing.

"You know what, Clem?" I mumbled through a mouthful of blood, my eyes still on the statue.

"What?"

"Don't count your diamonds before they're fenced," I snarled.

And that's when I finally unleashed my power.

❖ 26 ❖

I pushed my magic out through the marble. The force of it made the walkway ripple like the surface of the river below us, but I focused, aiming the power across the floor and then forcing it up into the statue. The figure of the old man seemed to shudder as my magic raced up his legs, then spread into his chest and out into his arms.

Clementine felt the walkway rise and fall beneath us. She glanced at me a moment, then turned her head to look over her shoulder, trying to figure out what I was doing with my magic. "What the—"

I focused even more and pushed more of my magic into the statue, putting everything I had into the marble—all of my Stone magic, all of my Ice power, every single drop of magic that I had left, along with what was stored in my spider rune ring. And then I grabbed hold of all that magic, all that power, and I made the statue *move*.

It was difficult—so damn *difficult*. It was one thing to

fling around raw magic. Any elemental could do that, just like any giant could throw a couple of punches. But this was a finesse job, a surgical strike, just like what Owen had done earlier tonight in the vault and how I had disarmed the rune trap on the covered bridge.

Just like my fight with Peter Delov all those years ago. Back then, I'd made the giant go where I wanted him to, and now I was going to do the same exact thing to Clementine.

I wanted to unleash my magic more than anything, wanted to send it racing out through the marble in all directions until it pulverized the statue and every other rock it came into contact with.

That wouldn't save me, but maybe this would.

For a heartbeat, nothing happened. Then the old man shuddered again. Bits of marble chipped off his arms and legs, but his stone chest slowly swiveled in my direction, and so did the spear in his right hand.

Sweat poured down my body, mixing with my blood, but the only things I was aware of were that spear and the growing mutters of the marble as I forced it to go exactly where I commanded it to.

Clementine finally realized that I was up to something, because she leaned forward and clamped her hands over my nose and mouth once more. "Oh, no you don't—"

I'd gotten the statue into position. Now it was time to do the same thing to the giant. I sent out a burst of magic, forcing a bit of my Ice and Stone power into a small crack I'd sensed in the side of the statue.

The old man's left arm shattered with a roar.

Clementine's head snapped around just in time to see

the explosion of stone. Instinct took over, and she lurched to one side, trying to get out the way of the falling bits of rock. But I reached out, dug my hand into the back of her tuxedo vest, and held on tight, keeping one eye on the statue all the while. My deadweight took Clementine by surprise and made her pull up short. She grunted and lunged forward again, causing her vest to rip down the back. So I lashed out, driving my foot into the back of her knee and making her land on her ass on the walkway.

She sat right in front of the old man and his spear.

Clementine started to crab-walk backward to get out of the way of the falling stone, but she put her elbow down in the same puddle of water that I had earlier, causing her arm to slip out from under her.

Before she could even think about moving again, I focused on the statue once more, forcing my power down into the old man's remaining arm. His fingers twitched, and the spear wobbled back and forth, causing more bits of stone to break off the figure.

Come on, old man, I thought, still staring at the statue. *Come on!*

I sent out one last, final burst of magic, putting everything I had into the statue, bending it to my will.

The old man's right arm snapped down and forward, ramming the stone spear straight through Clementine's chest.

The weight of the blow threw her back and pinned her to the ground right next to me, even as the rest of my magic ripped through the statue unchecked.

For a moment, there was just—noise.

Crash after crash after crash as the rest of the statue

toppled over, broke off into chunks, and went flying through the boathouse. One of the old man's legs sailed through the air and disappeared with a *plop* into the river. His head spun around and around in a circle on the floor, rattling this way and that like a child's top that was out of control. Dust choked the air, and it seemed as though the entire boathouse bucked and heaved for several seconds before the statue finally stopped breaking apart and the marble settled into place once more.

I rolled over onto my side and lay there, panting against the pain that flooded my ribs and collarbone. I was all out of magic, and the numbing effect of my Ice power was rapidly wearing off. But I didn't mind the pain—it told me that I was still alive.

And so was Clementine.

She was flat on her back, the spear sticking up out of her stomach, the old man's arm still attached to the top of the weapon. She arched up, as if she could somehow wiggle out from under the stone tip, even though it had driven all the way through her body and punched into the walkway underneath. Clementine was pinned as securely as a butterfly in a glass case.

The giant realized that I was staring at her. She snarled and stretched out, her hand curving into a claw as she aimed it at my throat—

And came up two inches short.

Clementine flailed and flailed at me, snarling and grunting and cursing all the while, but she just couldn't move those last two precious inches in order to throttle me. Her fist slammed into the stone walkway between us over and over again in frustration, her movements getting weaker and slower with every glancing blow. After about thirty seconds of that, the last of her strength left her, and her hand dropped to the floor and stayed there.

Still, she glared at me, her eyes bright with pain, fury, and the cold, cold death that was creeping up on her breath by breath.

"Bet you really hate my Stone magic now, don't you?" I said.

Clementine opened her mouth, but no words came out, only a spurt of blood. After a moment, even that slowed and slopped. Her whole body shuddered once, her eyes dimmed, and then she was still.

❊ 27 ❊

I lay where I was and watched Clementine Barker die.

When I was sure she was gone, I put a hand on the walkway and tried to push myself upright. But I moved too quickly, and the pain in my ribs and shoulder was too great. My arm slid out from under me, and I slumped back down onto the cold stone.

I knew that I needed to move, to get up and go see how the others had fared in the rotunda, but I just couldn't make myself do it. My vision narrowed, as though I were standing in a train tunnel, and the light at the end began to fade. Even though I tried to fight it, I felt myself sliding into that sweet blackness where there was no pain, no worry, only the dreams, the memories . . .

I was hiding behind a table, waiting for a giant to come and kill me.

At least, I was pretty sure that's how it would go. But I'd set my trap for Delov anyway, knowing it was the best chance

I had to kill him—the only chance, really. Now all that was left to do was see if he fell for it—

A floorboard creaked farther down the hallway.

I drew in a breath, trying to slow my racing heart, and peeked around the edge of the table.

Delov stood at the end of the hall. A patch of moonlight sliding in through the lace curtains illuminated him, making him seem even larger and more dangerous than before. He squinted into the shadows, looking left and right and back again. I froze, not even daring to try to curl into a tighter, smaller ball. After a moment, the giant eased forward, heading toward the library, where Fletcher was still trying to get the yip-yappy Pomeranian to shut up.

Game time.

I waited until Delov had stepped into the library, then got to my feet and tiptoed across the hall, easing up against the wall. The giant snapped on a light, and its harsh golden glare filled the library like the rays of a noontime sun. Peaches started barking even louder. The dog scuttled out from underneath the desk, skipped over to Delov, and wound his way through the giant's feet before prancing back over to the desk. The giant frowned, looking at the dog and watching his happy, excited movements. After a moment, his mouth tightened, and he raised his gun.

"Come on out from behind that desk," Delov growled. "I'd hate to ruin all that antique wood by plugging it full of holes, but I will."

Silence.

Then the leather chair rolled away from the desk, and Fletcher slowly crawled out from his hiding place and got to his feet. He faced Delov and raised his hands. Despite the *healing salve he'd used, even more blood covered Fletcher's blue shirt than before, along with the palms of his hands where he'd used them to keep pressure on the wound.*

"You thought you could come into my house *and murder me?" Delov snarled. "Who do you think you are?"*

Fletcher just grinned at him, which only infuriated the giant even more. Delov stepped forward and leveled his gun at Fletcher's head, ready to put a few more bullets into the old man.

And that's when I made my move.

I slid into the library as quiet as a shadow. Delov was so focused on Fletcher that he never thought to look behind him, so he never saw me coming. Instead of going for the giant's back, I aimed low, slicing my knife across his right hamstring as brutally as I could, hoping to put him down on my level, so to speak. Delov let out an angry, pain-filled bellow, even as his leg buckled and slid out from under him. The gun went off, shattering one of the glass windows to Fletcher's right and not the old man's skull.

But Delov wasn't done. He rolled over onto his back, bringing his gun up and around and searching for the person who'd attacked him.

I didn't give him a chance to fire a second shot. I surged forward and slashed down with the knife, cutting into his right wrist. The silverstone blade skittered off the thick bones there. Delov howled with pain again, and the gun slid from his hand. I kicked it away, then threw myself on top of him—knife-first. I sank the blade deep into Delov's chest, scraping against his ribs. The giant screamed and dug his left hand into my hair, yanking me back and off him. I kept hold of the knife, though, and as soon as the blade slid free of his chest, I twisted around and stabbed his arm with it. When he let go of my hair, I brought the knife back down into his chest again—and again and again, until his screams faded away and he finally quit fighting me.

When it was over and Delov was dead, I got to my feet and turned to face Fletcher, who was leaning against the desk for support. The old man looked down at Delov, then Peaches, who was sniffing his master's body.

"I was wondering why that dog suddenly decided to come in here," Fletcher said, lifting his green gaze to mine. "You led him and Delov straight to me, didn't you?"

I nodded.

"You used me, Gin," he said, a note of accusation creeping into his voice. "You used me as bait for Delov. As a stalking horse."

I winced and nodded again. "I couldn't think of another way to take him down. I couldn't kill him myself, not face-to-face, anyway, and I thought I'd have a better chance with a sneak attack."

Fletcher didn't say anything. He just kept staring at me with a thoughtful expression, as though I were some curious creature he'd never seen before.

"Are you angry with me?" I whispered, my heart twisting at the thought.

He gave me a rueful grin. "Well, I won't deny that you gave me a scare there for a minute. But I'll get over it. You did what you had to in order to save us both, Gin. Don't ever apologize for that. Especially not to me. I've done far worse than you tonight. Used people, manipulated them, lied to them time and time again in order to accomplish my goal. Using folks, deceiving them, putting them in certain situations—it's all part of being an assassin. If you live long enough, you'll do worse yourself, even to folks you consider friends, maybe even to those you love. You'll hurt them, whether by choice, chance, accident, or design."

I shook my head. "No, I would never do something like that."

"Sure you would. You just did. Here, tonight."

I looked down at Delov. The answer was in the giant's blood slowly soaking into the colorful rug underneath his body.

A sad smile curved Fletcher's lips. "I don't blame you, Gin, and you shouldn't blame yourself either. It's just the nature of what we do—of what you do now. But no matter what, remember this: all that really matters in the end is protecting the people you care about, even if they don't like how you do it, even if they hate you for it. Because I'd rather have somebody alive and hating me than dead and buried, with me knowing that I failed them."

I nodded, listening to his words, even if I didn't really believe that I could ever do anything horrible enough to somebody I cared about to make him hate me for it.

"But that's enough philosophical talk for one night," Fletcher said. "Delov is dead, and we aren't. So what do you say you drive me over to Jo-Jo's so the old girl can patch me up?"

I nodded and pointed at the Pomeranian. "And what about Peaches? We can't just leave him here. There's no one to take care of him."

Fletcher regarded the fluffball. "No, I suppose not. Maybe we'll give him to the Kilroy girl, the one who lived. Might help take her mind off her sister's death. Besides, every girl should have a dog. So grab him, and let's go."

While Fletcher hobbled down the hall toward our exit

point, I slid the bloody knife up my sleeve and picked up the Pomeranian, staring into his soft, liquid brown eyes.

"You're just lucky you're so cute," I muttered to the dog.

Peaches barked and licked my cheek, and I let out a relieved laugh—

Something wet splattered onto my face, snapping me out of my memories.

I punched my hands in the air, thinking that maybe Clementine wasn't as dead as I thought she was. The motion made my ribs and collarbone ache worse, and I groaned with pain. A moment later, more wet drops hit my skin, and I realized that it was just the river sloshing up onto the walkway where I was lying.

I sighed and blinked away the last fragments of my dream. I was in the same position as before, sprawled next to Clementine's body in the boathouse. Everything was still and quiet, except for the soft, constant rush of the river and the macabre mutters of the marble as it soaked up the violence I'd committed here tonight.

I stared at the giant. Blood was still oozing out of the wound in her chest; I hadn't been out that long. Five minutes, maybe ten. Either way, it was time to find the others and let them know I'd survived.

I sucked in a breath and slowly started to move, inch by inch, foot by foot, surfing each fresh wave of pain until it died down to a more manageable level. It took me a while to push myself up into a sitting position, then longer still to reach out, grab hold of the spear in Clementine's chest, and use it to help me climb to my feet.

I clutched the spear so I wouldn't fall back down while I assessed my injuries. Broken ribs, broken collarbone, a body full of aches and pains. The Saturday night special for the Spider. But my ribs hadn't punctured my lungs, my breath came easily enough, and my heart beat with a strong, steady rhythm. I'd be all right until Jo-Jo could work her healing magic on me.

The same couldn't be said for the giants, though. Dixon was still facedown in the river, and I could see the silver flash of curious fish drawn to the scent of his blood in the water. Opal lay on the walkway next to him, eyes open and mouth slack in surprise, a swarm of mosquitoes hovering over her like a dark thundercloud. And finally, there was Clementine, flat on her back, the spear stuck through her chest like it was the center of a bull's-eye.

For the final time that night, I leaned down over a dead giant. I searched through Clementine's pockets for the one thing I wanted: Mab's will. I tucked the ebony tube into one of the holsters under my skirt so it would be out of sight from any prying eyes.

I took a moment to lift Clementine's hand and examine the fancy watch on her wrist that I'd noticed earlier. Mother-of-pearl face, diamonds all around, silverstone band. It was a nice bit of bling. Once I had memorized what it looked like, I let go of her hand. Then I grabbed my knives from where they had landed on the walkway and put them back into their appropriate slots.

When I was finished, I turned and grinned at what was left of the Barker crew. "The family that steals together dies together. Couldn't have happened to a nicer bunch of folks."

The only sound was the ripple of the river as I shuffled out of the boathouse to go find my friends.

❉ 28 ❉

Not only did my entire body ache, but I was also bone-weary from using up all of my magic in my fight against Clementine, so it took me the better part of five minutes to hobble my way back up the hill to the museum.

I'd almost reached the side entrance when a gust of magic swept through the air.

In my experience, sudden bursts of unknown magic were almost never good, so I immediately stepped off the path and plunged into the shadows of the gardens. I stopped a moment to look and listen, but I didn't hear any footsteps hurrying my way. No leaves rustling, no branches snapping, nothing that would indicate that someone was headed in my direction. Well, if they weren't going to come to me, I'd just have to sneak up on them, broken ribs and all.

I tiptoed through the gardens, careful not to rustle the honeysuckle vines that seemed to wind over, through, and around everything, along with the briars. It wasn't hard, given how slowly I was moving, but I gritted my teeth, pushed the pain away, and kept going. Finally, I reached a spot in the garden where I could see the side entrance. I crouched down, even though it caused my ribs to ache even more, and peered around a cluster of bonsai trees.

A middle-aged dwarf sat on the top step at the side entrance, her back as tall and straight as if she were a queen perching on a throne. She wore a very nice suit jacket in a soft, cotton-candy pink, and her matching skirt stopped just past her knees. Her legs were bare, and dainty white sandals encased her feet, although I could see the shimmer of hot-pink polish on her toes through the slits in the shoes. A string of pearls hung around her neck. The moonlight made the stones gleam the same color as her white-blond hair.

Even sitting outside a crime scene, Jolene "Jo-Jo" Deveraux managed to look every inch the elegant southern lady she was. My worry vanished, and I sighed with relief—especially since Jo-Jo had Phillip with her.

He was lying flat on the stone step. Eva was there too, holding his hand and sitting on the other side of him. Jo-Jo murmured something to Eva that I couldn't hear, then reached for her power. Once again, the feel of her Air magic danced along the night breeze, pricking my skin like hundreds of tiny, invisible needles. The sensation made me wince, but I kept quiet and stayed where I was, not wanting to break the dwarf's concentration.

Jo-Jo's eyes glowed milky white in the semidarkness, and the same light coated the palm of her hand. She leaned over Phillip and went to work. Up and down, back and forth. Jo-Jo moved her hand over Phillip's chest again and again. A few seconds later, I heard something *plink* onto the stone step; Jo-Jo had grabbed hold of the oxygen in the air and had used it to fish the bullet out of his body. Now she'd be circulating even more oxygen through the wound and using all of those molecules to pull the rough edges of his skin back together. I knew, because she'd done the exact same thing to me more times than I could remember.

Five more minutes passed before Jo-Jo dropped her hand, and the pale glow finally faded from her eyes.

"All better now," Jo-Jo said, reaching over to pat Eva's hand. "He should wake up in a few minutes."

Then she turned and looked in my direction as though she could see right through the trees I was still crouched behind. "You can come on out now, darling," she said. "I believe it's your turn now, anyway."

"Jo-Jo?" Eva asked. "Who are you talking to?"

"You'll see."

I straightened up and trudged out from behind the bonsai trees. It took me a minute to walk over to the elemental and another one still to ease up the steps, but I managed it.

"I hate that I can never sneak up on you," I teased. "You always took all the fun out of playing hide-and-seek when I was a kid."

Jo-Jo smiled, the lines on her face grooving even deeper into her skin and adding to the welcoming warmth in her clear, colorless eyes. "Well, it's nice to know that my Air magic is good for something besides patching up folks. Besides, I like keeping an eye on you. Someone has to."

A gasp sounded, and I looked at Eva, who was staring at me with wide eyes.

"Gin?" she asked.

I grinned at her. "Back from the dead. Again."

"Gin!"

She got to her feet, threw her arms around me, and hugged me tight. I winced as more pain exploded in my ribs, but I managed to choke down my discomfort enough to return her hug.

Eva drew back and looked me over. "But . . . but *how*?"

"I'll tell you all about it later," I said. "Right now, I'd like to let Jo-Jo patch me up, if it's okay with you. Clementine got a few good licks in on me before I managed to take her out."

Eva helped me sit down on the step next to the dwarf. Jo-Jo eyed me, taking in my ruined dress, my cuts and bruises, and the dried blood that flaked off my skin with every move I made.

"I would ask if you had a rough night," she murmured. "But I think that's pretty self-evident."

I laughed, even though it made my ribs clench with pain once more.

I wasn't as bad off as Phillip had been, so it only took Jo-Jo a couple of minutes to heal me. When she finished, I drew in a breath, but the pain from Clementine's punches had vanished like it had never even been there to start with. I still felt tired, though, and I knew I would for the next several hours. That's how long it would take my brain to catch up with my body and realize that I was whole and well once more.

"Good as new, once again," Jo-Jo said. "Sorry I can't do anything about the blood, darling. Or your dress."

I stared down at the ruined fabric. "Don't worry about the dress. In a weird way, it saved my life tonight."

Jo-Jo frowned, obviously wondering what I was talking about, but before she could ask what I meant, Phillip let out a small sigh and slowly opened his eyes. His blue gaze was tired and cloudy with confusion.

"Eva?" he rasped.

She smoothed back his golden hair. "I'm right here, Philly. Jo-Jo healed you up, and everything's just fine now. So go on back to sleep. You need your rest."

"Okay." He nodded, closed his eyes, and drifted off once more.

Eva kept stroking his hair, although she stopped long enough to brush a few tears out of the corners of her eyes.

I turned to Jo-Jo. "Are the others still inside?"

She nodded. "Yep. In the rotunda, cleaning up the mess. They wanted to go check on you, but I told them that you'd be along in a few minutes."

I left her to watch over Eva and Phillip and went inside. At first, everything was as quiet as ever, but the closer I got to the rotunda, the louder it got. Finally, I reached the entrance and stopped, staring at the scene before me.

Giants, giants everywhere. The bodies of Clementine's crew littered the floor in a circular pattern—the same pattern they'd been standing in while they'd been guarding the hostages. From what I could see, most of them had been put down with headshots where they stood. I scanned the rotunda, but it didn't look like any more of the guests had been killed. All the hostages were still here, clustered together on the right side of the room next to the elemental Ice bar. Everyone was talking at once, hence the noise.

I spotted Xavier holding hands with Roslyn, so I headed in that direction. The second Roslyn saw me, she opened her arms, came forward, and enveloped me in a tight hug.

"I'm so glad you're okay," she whispered in my ear.

"Me too," I murmured back. "Me too."

I stepped back, cleared my throat, and gestured at the closest giant. "Looks like our plan worked."

Xavier nodded. "That it did. Bria and I sniped at the giants from the balcony. Most of them never knew what hit them, and without Clementine around to keep them in line, the rest just panicked. A few bolted out of the entrance, but the others raised their guns and returned fire. But since we had the high ground, we took them out pretty easily. We'd gotten all of them but one, and he waded into the crowd and grabbed a woman to use as a human shield. But Finn grabbed a gun from one of the other giants we'd already killed and took him out."

An arm circled my shoulders, and I turned to find Finn grinning at me.

"In other words, all's well that ends well," he said.

I slipped my arm around his waist, rested my head on his shoulder, and just enjoyed the moment. My friends were all safe and sound, and I'd survived another night, another battle, another enemy intent on killing me.

As we stood there, it slowly dawned on me that I was once again the center of attention. Now that the initial shock of being rescued had worn off, everyone was looking around, seeing who'd survived and who hadn't. The fact that I was still among the living caused more than a few folks to do a double take, their eyes darting from me to Jillian's body and back again. Not to mention my ruined dress and how horrible I looked. The murmurs and speculation quickly spread, until it seemed like the only sound in the rotunda was the whisper of my name: *Gin . . . Gin . . . Gin . . .*

"I hate to say this, but not everyone seems happy that you're still alive," Finn said, picking up on the glares coming my way.

"You can't please everyone," I drawled. "And you know how much I hate to disappoint our dear friends in the underworld."

He snorted.

One of Finn's clients came up to talk to him about what had happened, and Xavier and Roslyn drifted a few feet away, having their own private conversation.

I stayed where I was and kept scanning the room. It took me two minutes to find the person I was searching for: Owen. He stood near the back of the rotunda not too far away from where my family's runes were. Owen was talking to a dwarf with an unruly head of salt-and-pepper hair. The reddish plaid of the dwarf's suit jacket matched the rusty color of his eyes. Cooper Stills, the Air elemental blacksmith who was Owen's mentor and Jo-Jo's date for the evening.

Cooper noticed me watching him. He grinned and waved, and I returned the gesture. Owen looked to see who the dwarf was waving at, and his eyes widened as he realized that it was me. Maybe it was my imagination, but after a moment, Owen seemed to relax, as though he'd been worried about me. He hesitated, then lifted his hand and waved at me too. Once again, I returned the gesture. We stood there, staring at each other across the room. I didn't know whether to go over to him or stay where I was. I didn't know if he would welcome me or turn away.

In the end, I didn't have to decide. A hand touched my shoulder, and Bria stepped in front of me, blocking my view of Owen, perhaps for the best.

"Are you okay?" she asked. "Owen told us about the fight in the boathouse. That you were facing down Clementine and Opal alone. What happened?"

I shrugged. "Nothing much. I took out Opal easily enough. Clementine almost beat me to death, but I got her instead."

Bria nodded, then glanced across the rotunda at Owen, who was still speaking to Cooper. "And what about Owen?"

"What about Owen?"

"You two were together an awful lot tonight. Surely, you talked about a few things."

"You mean before or after we killed all those giants?"

She looked at me.

Finally, I sighed. "No, we didn't really get a chance to talk about anything. There was just blood, dead giants, and a lot of awkward pauses."

"Well, you should know that he brought Eva here into the rotunda after we secured the area. The second he knew that she and the others were safe, he helped Xavier carry Phillip outside, then immediately started to head down to the boathouse to help you," Bria said. "He would have too if Jo-Jo hadn't showed up and told him that you were fine and on your way back up to the museum. He still cares about you, Gin, and I know you care about him."

"I do care about him," I admitted. "But I don't know that it's enough—for either one of us."

"What do you mean by that?"

I didn't know how to tell her that Salina's death was still an issue between me and Owen. That I just didn't know if he could ever forgive me for what I'd done to the woman he'd once loved. And that his forgiveness wasn't the only thing I wanted from Owen—that I needed his acceptance too. Of what I'd done in the past and all the bad things I'd do in the future.

"Gin?" Bria asked.

"Nothing," I said. "It's been a long night, and I'm not thinking straight right now."

"Well, maybe after this is over, you and Owen can finally talk."

"Yeah. Maybe."

"Either way, I'm glad that you're all right."

Bria hugged me, her care and concern even warmer and stronger than her arms wrapped around me. After so many years of thinking her dead, it always surprised me to realize that she was alive and here with me—and that she loved me just like I loved her. I wondered if I'd ever stop feeling that way. Maybe it wouldn't be a bad thing if I didn't. Because I never, ever wanted to take her for granted—or any of my other loved ones.

Bria pulled back. The motion made the primrose rune around her throat wink, and the sly flash of silverstone reminded me that there was one more thing I needed to do tonight—for both of us.

I held my hand out to Bria. "Come with me. I have something to show you."

She frowned in puzzlement, but she wrapped her fingers around my bloody ones. I led her over to the back of the rotunda and the recess where our mother's and sister's rune necklaces had been on display.

"Remember when I told you before that there were some things in here that belonged to us?" I asked.

"Yeah?"

"Well, here they are."

I stopped in front of the wall and held my hand out—

But the recess was empty.

The glass had been smashed, and I immediately began scanning the floor around the recess, but all I saw were splinters of glass and chips of marble. I stalked back and forth along the wall, searching all around me.

Nothing—absolutely nothing.

The robbers must have looted this spot along with everything else. There was no sign of my mother's and sister's necklaces and no telling where they were. Maybe they were mixed in with the pile of cell phones in the front of the rotunda. Maybe they were outside in one of the moving trucks or in one of the cases I'd seen on the getaway boat. Maybe they'd even disappeared into someone's pocket when everyone was looking the other way. There was just no way of knowing. I could search the museum for days and never find them.

They'd been right *here*, close enough to touch, and now they were gone again, vanished once more like they'd never existed to start with. Pain stabbed through me at the loss of these last two pieces of my mother and my sister.

"Gin? What is it?" Bria asked. "What's wrong?"

I just shook my head. I didn't have the heart to tell her what I'd seen—and what we'd both lost.

Again.

29

After that, things followed a predictable pattern. The po-po arrived, and all the fine boys in blue started taking witness statements and collecting evidence.

I didn't know why they were bothering. Clementine, Opal, and Dixon were dead. So were a good portion of the giants they'd conned into helping them. The ones who'd left the rotunda when the shooting had started or had been outside guarding the moving trucks were being rounded up right now, and the few who'd piled into the trucks and raced the vehicles across the bridge and over onto the mainland shouldn't be too hard to track down, thanks to all those photos and bios Clementine had posted on her website.

The only person who'd gotten away clean was Clementine's boss, whoever that was.

Oh, she had certainly acted like she was in charge, and she'd had all of her crew fooled into thinking that this was just the beginning of the giant uprising she had planned for Ashland. But too many things about tonight didn't quite add up. Namely, the fact was that there was no reason for Clementine to break into the museum vault just to steal Mab's will—unless someone else had hired her to do the job in the first place.

My eyes roamed over the crowd of folks still in the rotunda. Unless I missed my guess, Clementine's boss was here tonight, hidden among the rest of what passed for high society in Ashland. I wondered if he was studying me right now, wondering how much Clementine had told me before she'd died. He would have been pleased to know that she hadn't said a word about him, but that didn't mean he'd never be discovered. In fact, I had some ideas about exactly who had orchestrated the heist and why. I just needed to get Finn to check into a few things for me.

But that could wait until tomorrow. Best to let Clementine's employer think that he'd gotten away with it, at least for a few days. Let him relax his guard and go about his business. Let him think that he was in the free and clear and that no one was coming after him.

Let him think that no one would ever figure out what he'd done—because that's when I'd finally strike.

I stood off to the left side of the rotunda. The familiar *creak-creak-creak* of wheels sounded, and a few seconds later, the coroner pushed a metal cart inside the round room, followed by some assistants with several other carts. All the evidence had been gathered, and now it was time for the cleanup to start.

The coroner and his assistants all gave me solemn, respectful nods when they passed. Well, that was something new and different. Although I suppose they had a vested interest in my activities. The more people I killed, the more overtime they clocked.

Gin Blanco, the Spider, Ashland's newest cottage industry. Yeah, that was me, all right.

Finn wandered over to me. He stood beside me, and we watched the coroner work, although Finn's gaze kept sliding over to Bria. I'd told my sister about Clementine's getaway boat, and she and Xavier had retrieved the three silverstone cases full of jewelry from the vessel. The two of them were busy trying to give everyone back their belongings. Not surprisingly, it was a slow process, especially since some folks saw this as an opportunity to leave with someone else's jewels.

"Well, I promised that you'd have a good time," Finn finally said in a cheery tone. "I *totally* delivered on that one."

I gave him a flat look.

"What?" he asked. "Don't tell me that you're blaming *me* for this fiasco?"

I kept staring at him.

"Okay, okay," he said. "I know that you didn't want to come here tonight in the first place. But how was I supposed to know that Clementine and her crew would try to rob the museum?"

"Because you're Finnegan Lane," I said. "And you're supposed to know everything that goes on in this town."

Finn straightened up and adjusted his black silk bow tie. "True," he said. "But I hadn't heard a whiff about tonight. And none of my sources has either. While you were getting patched up by Jo-Jo, I was getting patched in. Clementine kept her entire scheme under wraps, which is surprising, given how many giants were involved."

"Not Clementine," I said. "Her boss."

Finn blinked. "Boss? What boss? Did Clementine say that she had a boss before you dispatched her into the great beyond?"

I thought of how she had immediately known how to open the tube that held Mab's will and all the other things she'd said and done tonight, all the information she'd had about me and my loved ones.

"Not in so many words."

This time, Finn arched his eyebrow. "Well, what did she say, exactly? Or have you branched out into voodoo and decided to start reading blood spatters and weird stuff like that? Because she's certainly not going to tell you anything now."

"Interesting idea," I said. "And one that I should probably look into, given all the people I've killed tonight. I wouldn't mind some peeks into the future and getting a heads-up on all the trouble that's headed my way. But no, I didn't deduce anything from Clementine's blood—only that she was dead and I wasn't."

"So how are you going to figure out who orchestrated this?" Finn asked. "Because as skilled as you are, even you can't make the dead speak."

"Oh, the dead tell us plenty of things," I said. "And so do people when they're alive. Clementine gave me more than enough information to track down her boss, even if she didn't realize it."

Finn eyed me. "Have I mentioned how much I hate it when you're cryptic?"

I just laughed.

Finn went over to Bria to see if he could swipe a necklace or two for himself, but I stayed where I was and watched the coroner work. He'd finally gotten around to Jillian. In the chaos and confusion, her body had been rolled over to one side of the rotunda like it was a wad of dirt that needed to be swept up, instead of a beautiful, vibrant woman who'd been alive only a few short hours ago.

My heart ached with sadness, and I couldn't take my eyes off Jillian's dress—our dress. The scarlet fabric wrapped around her body like a bloody shroud. That's what it was now. She'd been killed because of it, because she'd been in the wrong place at the wrong time and wearing the wrong damn dress.

And it was all my fault.

Oh, I knew that it was just bad timing, just bad, dumb, stupid luck that Jillian had stepped out of the bathroom before I had. Maybe if it had been me instead, I would have been able to avoid Dixon and the bullets he'd wanted to put in my skull. Maybe I would have been able to use my Stone magic to harden my skin before he pulled the trigger. Maybe I would have been able to kill Dixon and Clementine before they hurt anyone else.

Or maybe I would have been just as dead as Jillian was.

Either way, I'd never know, and an innocent woman had paid the price instead of me.

Owen walked over to me. We stood there and watched while the coroner and one of his assistants carefully loaded Jillian into a body bag.

After a moment, he sighed. "A couple of hours ago, I was talking to her, laughing with her. And now she's gone. It doesn't seem possible. It doesn't seem *real.*"

"I know," I said. "I'm sorry. We talked a little in the bathroom before . . . it happened. She seemed . . . nice."

"She *was* nice," Owen said. "But I never should have brought her here tonight. And not just because of Clementine and everything that happened."

"What do you mean?"

He turned to face me. "I mean that Jillian was just a friend. She was in town so we could work out the details of a new business arrangement, and I mentioned the gala in passing to her. She asked if she could come along with me and Eva, and I said yes. She made it clear tonight that she wanted to be more than just friends and business associates, but I didn't. It didn't . . . feel right."

I nodded, accepting his explanation about why he'd been here with Jillian. "And that kiss you gave me in the vault? Have you thought any more about that? Because that definitely wasn't just a friendly kiss."

He hesitated, and pain seeped into his rugged features once more. "That doesn't feel right either. Or maybe it feels too right. I don't know anymore, Gin. I just don't know."

"It's okay," I said, my heart breaking once again. "I understand."

And I did understand. I had plenty of things in my life that haunted me—memories of the people I'd killed, the torture I'd endured, the horrible things I'd done just to survive. It was hard to be happy when I always had so much weighing me down, hard to think that I deserved any kind of peace, light, or love in my life. Now Owen was struggling with the same feelings, the same emotions, when it came to Salina. He didn't feel like he had a right to move on yet.

Just like I couldn't move on from Jillian's death.

Sure, I'd killed Dixon, Opal, and Clementine, the masterminds behind her murder, but it wasn't going to bring her back. I'd avenged Jillian the only way I knew how, and it still wasn't enough. It would *never* be enough, and it was one more thing that I was just going to have to live with.

Owen stayed right beside me until the coroner zipped up the black body bag, hiding Jillian's ruined face from sight, and started pushing the cart out of the rotunda.

"I should go," he finally said. "See how Phillip and Eva are doing. And try to find out if Jillian has any family that I need to contact."

I nodded, not sure what to say.

Owen reached out and touched my hand. Once again, that treacherous hope flared to life in my chest, even as he let go.

"Are you okay?" he asked. "I should have come over and asked you before, but I was . . . thinking about things."

I smiled, but it wasn't a pleasant expression. "You know me, Owen. I always find a way to survive."

"Yes," he said, his voice catching on that one word. "You do."

He stared at me, and I looked back at him. All the care, concern, worry, and pain of the night had left its mark, etching deep, harsh lines into his face, but I thought he was more handsome than ever. On impulse, I reached up and cupped his cheek with my hand. Owen turned his head, caught my hand in his, and pressed a kiss to my palm, right in the center of my spider rune scar, despite the blood, sweat, and grime that still covered us both.

His violet eyes flared as bright as a star, and he opened his mouth as if he wanted to say something. Then his face shuttered, the light dimmed, and he dropped my hand.

"Owen?"

He tried to smile, but he couldn't quite make himself do it. "Take care of yourself, Gin. We'll talk soon, okay?"

All I could do was nod and watch as he turned and walked away from me.

❊ 30 ❊

The Briartop heist dominated the airwaves and newspapers for the next few days. Story after story was written and broadcast about what had happened, about Clementine Barker and her plans, and how a few brave folks had banded together to eventually take down the robbers.

I let Bria and Xavier take all the credit for thwarting the giant and her crew. It was more or less the truth. After all, they were the ones who had saved the hostages. Besides, I had enough enemies already without getting my name splashed all over the newspaper or having some nosy reporter come barging into the Pork Pit trying to get an interview with me. Still, the rumors got out the way they always did, and I heard more than a few whispers about how deadly the Spider's sting had been to Clementine.

Finn also told me about all the reports he'd heard from his sources, each one more outlandish and ridiculous than the last. So far, my favorite story was the one that claimed

I had chopped the giant into little pieces, had stuffed her into a cooler, and was using her remains as bait for fishing in the Aneirin River. Heh. If that didn't increase the pot in the betting pool on my mortal demise, nothing would.

I didn't care what people thought or said about me as long as they left me alone, but I knew that I'd just created even more trouble for myself by taking matters into my own hands at the museum. Because in addition to killing Clementine, rumors abounded that I'd also gotten away with a chunk of the art and jewels she'd been trying to steal. It wasn't true, of course, but that wouldn't stop some folks from thinking it was. It wouldn't be long before some idiot decided to try to steal stolen art that I didn't even have.

The truth was that I had only two things left from that night: my memories and the ebony tube that contained Mab Monroe's last will and testament.

In fact, the tube was standing on the porch railing in front of me right now. The evening sun hit the sunburst rune on the side, making the gold gleam and the ruby burn with an inner fire.

"Disgusting," Finn said, snapping down the newspaper he was reading. "Absolutely disgusting. The reporter didn't even mention me at all. Not one word about me, the giant that I killed, the hostage that I saved."

It was a week after the heist, and we were sitting on the front porch of Fletcher's house. Dishes clustered around our feet, covered with the sticky remains of the blackberry cobbler and heaping scoops of vanilla bean ice cream we'd just devoured. I'd made the dessert in honor of all those blackberry briars I'd crawled through at Briartop. I could still taste the scoops of ice cream, which had provided a soft, cool contrast to the cobbler's warm, sugary berries and golden, buttery crust. I took a swig of my milk, reached for my magic, and added a few more Ice crystals to the glass to chill the liquid some more.

The sticky, humid heat of the day had finally broken, and the critters in the woods were out and about, skittering through the leaves, climbing up the trees, and generally getting a little livelier and more active as the sun set over the ridge. Just like me. I always did my best work in the dark, and tonight was going to be no exception.

"Why are you so upset the reporter didn't mention you?" I asked. "Fletcher always told us that it was better to blend in with the shadows than to stand out in the crowd."

"Did you not *see* how smashing I looked in my tuxedo? I was hoping the museum photographer gave at least one good picture of me to the press. But no."

He sniffed, but his snit was far from over. "The newspaper has run a photo of practically every single person who was there that night *except* me. They even had a photo of Jo-Jo sitting on the steps with Eva and Phillip, and she wasn't even at the gala. Not really. And what do they put on the front page today? Yet another story all about the stolen art and how long it's going to take to get everything sorted out, cleaned up, repaired, and put back on display. Please. As if people actually *care* about that sort of thing."

Finnegan Lane, art lover extraordinaire—or not.

Finn put down his newspaper and rocked back and forth in his chair for a few moments. Brooding. Then he turned his green gaze to the railing.

"And then there is *that*." He stabbed his finger at the ebony tube sitting there. "I still can't believe that you plan to turn Mab's will over to Bria so she can get it into the right hands and make sure that it's properly executed. It's crazy, I tell you. Just flat-out insane. Like you're doing Mab a fucking *favor*."

"Yes," I murmured. "You've made it quite clear what you think about my plan for Mab's will."

Finn had ranted up one side and down the other when I told him that I wanted Bria to make the will public. Shouting. Cajoling. Pleading. But he didn't change my mind. And in the end, he had to agree with me that it was the only way we could make sure that Clementine's boss got what he so richly deserved.

Finn shook his head. "I'm telling you again, you should just burn that piece of paper inside and pretend like you never read it. No good can come from it."

I shrugged. "But that wouldn't stop anything. Not really. It would only delay the inevitable. Mab had to have left behind more than one copy of her will. Sooner or later, somebody's going to come forward with it. Or a fake version they try to pass off as the real thing."

"Maybe," he said. "Maybe not. You'd be surprised how many folks put stuff like that off, especially people as powerful as Mab. People with magic *always* think that they're going to live forever. Either way, do you really want some long-lost relative of Mab's coming to Ashland? We don't even know who this person is, much less what he or she might be like."

Despite all of his many connections, Finn had been unable to track down the mysterious M. M. Monroe whom Mab had left all of her earthly possessions to. He'd spent the past week scouring land deeds, bank accounts, birth certificates, family histories, and more, but whoever M. M. Monroe was, he or she didn't have much of a paper trail in Ashland or beyond. And given how many Monroes there were out there in the world, it wasn't like Finn had a narrow pool of suspects to start with. He was still working on it, but it would take weeks, if not months, before he might happen upon the right Monroe—if that person was even still alive.

"If this person is anything like Mab, well, it's going to mean nothing but trouble for all of us, especially you," Finn said. "You killed Mab. You shouldn't have to take out the rest of her family too."

I grinned. "Ah, but you know us Southerners. We love us some family feuds. Mab had one with my mom that carried over into my generation. You might say that I'm keeping the tradition alive by inviting Mab's relative to come to town and visit for a spell."

"Well, I still think it's a mistake," he grumbled.

I didn't say anything. Maybe I was making a mistake by not destroying the will, but it had roused my curiosity more than anything else. I wanted to know who Mab had left everything to. I wanted to lay eyes on this mysterious M. M. Monroe and see if he or she was anything like the Fire elemental had been—and if he or she was a threat to me and mine.

Ah, my insatiable curiosity. Probably going to get me into trouble again—real soon.

Finn opened his mouth to argue with me some more, but I cut him off.

"Let's talk about something else. Did you get that information I requested?"

"I did, and you were right about Clementine's boss," he said. "I can't believe I didn't see it myself that night at the museum."

Finn leaned down, popped open the silverstone briefcase at his feet, grabbed some papers, and passed them over to me. "It took some doing, getting my hands on all the account information. The smarmy bastard's almost as well connected as I am. You wouldn't believe how many favors I had to call in, but I managed to dig up all of his dirt. There might be a few accounts I overlooked, but these are the most important ones, including the one he used to pay Clementine for her services. Looks like he gave her two million up front for the job, probably with another, similar payment to come once it was done. He also paid for that watch you noted, probably to sweeten the deal even more."

I skimmed through the papers and let out a low whistle. "He's one sneaky, black-hearted son of a bitch, isn't he?"

Finn nodded. "You have to admire that about him. It's a scheme that even I could be proud of. In fact, I may tuck this one into my back pocket for a rainy day."

"I wonder how long it was going on. Do you think he started before or after I killed Mab?"

He shrugged. "If I had to guess, I would say before. He would have had to in order to accumulate what he has. If I were him, though, I would have left Ashland the second Mab died. Not hung around for all these months. But the real question now is, how do you want to handle him?"

"Oh," I said. "I know *exactly* what I want to do about him."

Finn grinned. "That's the coldhearted girl I know and love."

"You have no idea."

"When?" he asked.

"Tonight," I said. "Let's go get the bastard tonight."

I sat in the dark and waited for my nemesis to come home.

According to the grandfather clock ticking away in the corner, it was almost midnight. I wondered what he was doing out so late. If I were him, I would have been packing my bags and getting out of town. But he was arrogant. Always had been, always would be. Oh, he'd probably been on edge these past few days, wondering if anyone would be able to trace Clementine and her crew back to him. But given that a week had passed and no one had come knocking on his door, he probably thought that he was finally in the free and clear.

I was going to enjoy showing him just how wrong he was.

It had been ridiculously easy slipping onto his sprawling Northtown estate. There were no giants roaming through the woods, no guard dogs to bark at the first hint of danger, no cameras zooming from one side of the lawn to the other. He didn't even have a decent security system on the house itself. No bulletproof glass, no iron bars over the windows, no reinforced silverstone doors. The pitiful locks that he did have on the doors were hardly worth the trouble of making a couple of Ice picks to jimmy them open with.

I suppose he thought that the stone wall and iron gate out front would deter most folks. Well, that and who he used to work for—but not me.

After I'd opened one of the doors, I'd gone from room to room to room, looking at all of his things, but the house was as cold and impersonal as he was. Oh, all of the furnishings were the absolute best that money could buy: antique desks and chairs, delicate china in stained-glass cabinets, expensive appliances done in polished chrome. But most of the furniture looked like it had never even been sat on, and there hadn't been any human touches in the house—no odd knickknacks, no stacks of books, no piles of magazines. I guess I shouldn't have been surprised. He'd been at Mab's beck and call so long he probably hadn't spent much time in his own house.

The only room that looked remotely lived in had been the master bathroom, and that was only because of all the beauty products inside. They were everywhere—in the medicine cabinet, clustered on the sink, even lined up like plastic soldiers around the rim of the sunken bathtub. Jo-Jo didn't have as many anti-aging creams, gels, and lotions in her beauty salon as he did in his bathroom. Then again, that didn't surprise me either. Not knowing what I did about him. He might have been a lackey, but he was a vain one at that.

The only other oddity I'd noticed had been all the mirrors. There was one on just about every wall, as though this was some sort of circus fun house instead of an upscale mansion. I wondered what exactly he saw when he peered into the glass. If he saw the smooth, confident figure he always tried to present to the world or the heartless monster lurking underneath that I did, maybe even if he saw Mab's ghost trailing along behind him. But it didn't much matter in the end. All that really mattered were people's actions, and he'd doomed himself long ago with his.

Those were my thoughts as I waited in his office. I'd decided to make my approach in here because I'd figured he'd probably stop by for a nightcap before heading to bed. Along with the desk I was sitting at, the other main feature of the room was a mahogany wet bar. Behind it perched a cabinet that was stocked with booze. A snifter and a bottle of brandy had been placed in the center of the bar, perpetually on call for their owner to come home and imbibe. I wondered how many drinks he'd had since that night at the museum—and if they'd been downed to calm shaking nerves or to celebrate his actions seemingly going undetected.

I might ask him—before the end.

Outside, a car churned across the crushed-shell driveway, and a pair of headlights sliced across the glass doors behind me that led out to a patio in the front yard. But I stayed where I was at his desk and waited, just waited.

Two minutes later, a key turned in the front-door lock, and a couple of footsteps sounded, scraping repeatedly across the rug inside the door. I admired his cleanliness, if nothing else. Home, sweet home.

He shut and locked the front door behind him, then made other noises as he moved through the house. The soft rustle of fabric as he shrugged out of his suit jacket. The clatter of his keys as he tossed them into a bowl on a table. The dull clang of his umbrella as he slid it into a brass tub. That was the other thing I'd noticed as I'd searched the house: he was very meticulous. Everything had a place, and there was a place for everything. Even Finn would have been envious of his walk-in closet, where the suits, shirts, ties, socks, and shoes were sorted by size and color.

It took him longer than I thought it would to go through his routines and make his way to the office, but I'm nothing if not patient, and he got here eventually. One light turned on in the hallway, perfectly outlining his trim silhouette. If I'd bothered to bring a gun, I could have easily put three bullets in his chest from here. But that would have been a waste of lead. Besides, I needed to talk to him first.

He stepped into the office and started to walk over to the light switch on the wall, but I picked up the remote I'd found earlier and hit a button.

The crystal chandelier above my head blazed with light. A startled gasp escaped his lips, and he whirled around. His eyes widened when he realized there was someone in his house—and that someone was me. His mouth dropped open, although the rest of his tight features remained where they were, like usual.

"Hello, Jonah," I said.

❊ 31 ❊

Jonah McAllister blinked and blinked, as if he couldn't quite believe that I was sitting in his office—in his own chair, no less.

I gave him a lazy grin, tilted back the chair, and propped my boots up on top of the desk. My shoes were not particularly clean, and McAllister's left eye twitched with fury as he realized that I was mucking up his pristine workspace. I crossed one leg on top of the other and leaned back a little farther, getting even more comfortable in his chair.

"What are you doing in my house?" he finally demanded.

"What?" I asked. "No 'Hello, Ms. Blanco'? No, 'You're looking well this evening'? Why, Jonah, wherever are your manners? I bet you were never this rude to Mab."

The lawyer's eye twitched again, but he stayed by the wall. I could almost see the wheels turning in his mind as he debated making a break for the door. Couldn't blame him for that. Late-night visits from the Spider tended to involve only one thing: blood, and a lot of it.

"Don't bother," I said. "You locked the front door behind you, remember? And I have no doubt that I can run faster than you."

He stared at me for several moments. Thinking.

"You're right. But since we both know that you're going to kill me, will you at least allow the condemned man one last drink?"

I gestured at the wet bar. "Be my guest."

McAllister moved behind the bar, his body stiff with tension, but he kept sneaking glances at me, wondering how he could get the upper hand and get out of this alive. Fool. He should have known by now it was far, far too late for that.

McAllister poured himself a brandy. I had to hand it to him, his fingers didn't shake at all as he fixed the drink. Then again, he'd worked for Mab for years. His nerves were probably as good as mine were—maybe even better.

McAllister carefully sipped the brandy, savoring each and every mouthful, instead of slugging it down the way I thought he might. It took him a few minutes, but he finished that first brandy and poured himself another one, adding more amber liquor to the snifter this time around. I wondered if he thought getting drunk would ease the pain of what I was about to do to him. Not the worst strategy, but it wasn't going to help him. Not tonight.

"What do you want?" he finally asked. "Or are you just here to kill me?"

"Well, as tempting as that thought is, I thought we might talk first," I said. "Chitchat a little bit."

He gave me a blank look. "And what do you think that we would have to talk about?"

Instead of answering his question, I asked one of my own. "You didn't really think you'd get away with it, did you?"

He tensed before he could stop himself. "And just what do you think it is that I've gotten away with?"

"Nothing much," I drawled. "Just hiring Clementine and her crew to rob the Briartop museum."

His eye twitched again, his shoulders shot up to his ears, and his lips pressed together so hard that they disappeared into the rest of his face. For a moment, I thought he might try to deny it, but McAllister had an entirely different reaction: he laughed.

He choked on that first laugh, trying to smother the harsh, barking sound, but he couldn't, and after a moment, he quit trying. It was like that one sound opened the floodgates of his emotions, because he just kept right on laughing, louder and louder, harder and harder, until tears streamed down his cheeks and he was almost bent over double from the force of his own mirthless chuckles.

I sat there and waited until he'd calmed down. It didn't take long. McAllister was a lawyer after all, used to tense, high-pressure situations. It didn't get any more tense or high-pressure than having an assassin appear in your office late at night.

"Forgive me," Jonah said, pulling a white silk handkerchief out of the breast pocket of his blue suit jacket and dabbing away his hysterical tears. "It takes a lot to surprise me, but you managed to do it. In fact, you've surprised me quite a bit since we first met last year, Ms. Blanco."

"Please. Let's not stand on formality tonight. Call me Gin."

"Very well, Gin," Jonah said. "As I said, it takes a lot to surprise me. I've been expecting you to be waiting for me in here for a long while now."

I shrugged. "I've been busy. Although you have been on my to-do list for quite some time."

He shrugged back.

We stared at each other, jaws tight, lips flat, eyes cold.

Finally, he sighed. "How did you figure it out? At least tell me that much."

"You made a couple of mistakes. Small things, really, but they added up to point the finger in your direction."

"Like what?" he asked, seeming to be genuinely interested in what I had to say. I supposed there really was a first time for everything.

"Your first mistake was when you confronted Clementine right after she took everyone hostage. It wasn't something I expected from you."

He raised an eyebrow, although the rest of his face didn't move with it. "How so?"

"One thing I admire about you, Jonah, is your sense of self-preservation," I said. "So why in the world would you confront a bunch of giants with guns? Oh, I could imagine you doing it if Mab had still been alive. You would have had to put on an indignant show to keep her from roasting you because someone ruined her exhibit. But she's dead, so why not let the museum director huff and puff instead? But no, you immediately shoved your way to the front of the crowd and faced down Clementine all by your lonesome. It just didn't make any sense."

"That's it?" he asked. "That's what you based your grand conclusion on?"

"Oh, no. There's more."

McAllister gestured with his brandy, graciously telling me to continue.

"Then there was the fact that Clementine didn't shoot you for standing up to her. Instead, she just slapped you around a little bit. It didn't make any sense that she wouldn't kill you, especially since I'd heard her talk about shooting someone in the face like it was no more important than getting her nails done. Sure, she wanted to keep the hostages calm, but you directly challenged *her*. She should have put you down just for that."

"So she didn't shoot me. So what?"

"So why didn't she just go ahead and kill you and make everyone else fall into line that much quicker? There was only one reason she wouldn't: because you were her boss. She wouldn't kill the person who'd hired her to pull the heist, or she wouldn't get paid the rest of her fee," I replied. "You really should have at least let her wing you with a bullet or two. But instead, you got away with only a bitch slap. Now, that seems to be something you excel at, so I didn't think too much of it at the time. But later on, it was just one more thing that didn't quite add up."

He eyed me. "And what were these other things that you found so troublesome?"

"Well, for starters, there was the fact that a woman was murdered—a woman who was wearing the exact same dress as I was," I said. "That made me think that I was the intended target, which I was. Now, I have more enemies than most, but there were a lot of bad people at the gala. So why come after me and not someone else? Because you knew that I was a threat to your plans to steal Mab's will. And, well, killing me would have been a nice bonus. You've wanted me dead for a long time now, and you saw a chance to finally make it happen at the museum."

"It would have worked too," he muttered. "If not for that damn dress."

This time, I nodded, agreeing with him. "Maybe. Although I imagine you were quite happy when Clementine dumped that body in the rotunda and you thought it was me."

"Ecstatic, actually. Too bad it didn't take. It never seems to, with you."

I grinned. He gave me a sour look, finished off his brandy, and poured himself another one. The first two rounds had already given his cheeks a ruddy flush—or perhaps that was just his anger finally showing through his too-smooth skin.

"Then there was Owen," I continued. "Since you were in charge of the gala, you knew exactly who was coming. When you saw his name on the guest list, you realized you could force him to help Clementine open the vault. Plus, you would never pass up a chance to hurt my friends and family. No doubt, you told Clementine to kill Owen immediately after he opened the vault for her."

McAllister shrugged. "You'd taken away my son. So yes, I wanted you dead, but I wanted the rest of your band of miscreants to suffer too. Killing Grayson seemed like an ideal way to do that, and I was going to make it look like he was working with Clementine the whole time. Just think of the problems that would have created for that sister of his. Everyone in Ashland would have been pounding on her door, demanding to know what her brother did with all of that stolen art. It would have been amusing to watch."

The brandy really must have bolstered his courage, because he was actually *bragging*—bragging about how he'd planned to hurt the people that I loved. Rage pulsed through my body. It had been bad enough that he'd put Owen in the line of fire, but to frame him after the fact . . . it almost made me rethink my plan for McAllister.

Almost.

"But the most interesting thing is exactly why you hired Clementine and her crew to break into the vault," I continued. "That's the really fascinating thing about all of this—what you wanted her to steal."

I reached down. McAllister tensed, but I wasn't going for one of my knives. Instead, I pulled the ebony tube out of a pocket on the front of my vest. I set it on the desk and scooted it forward, then turned it so he could see the sunburst rune glinting on the side.

"When I first went into the vault, I had no idea what Clementine was after," I said. "There were lots of treasures in there. Art, jewelry, paintings worth tens of millions. But all she wanted—all *you* wanted—was this. You didn't want anything else from the museum, not even the jewels that Clementine took from the partygoers. No, all you were after—all you *needed*—was this one little tube."

McAllister's face pinched even tighter than before, the

flush in his cheeks taking on a fiery tomato tint, and I could tell that he was struggling to control himself. So I decided to be a good guest and answer his silent questions.

"It took me a few minutes, but I figured out how to open it," I said. "And I know what's inside. In fact, I've spent the last few days reading and rereading Mab's will. Quite a bit shorter than I thought it would be. But fascinating all the same for what it says—and what it doesn't."

"And what do you think you've figured out from it?" he sneered.

"Why you wanted Mab's will so badly," I replied. "I must say I'm a little shocked that she didn't leave you a little something-something for all your years of loyal service. But you aren't mentioned in the will at all. She didn't leave you a nickel's worth of anything. No cash, no land, no personal property. Not even so much as a silverstone pen or a cheap gold watch. No wonder you were so pissed."

McAllister stared at the tube, his cold, furious gaze locked onto the sunburst rune. "You have no idea what it was like working for her. Being at her beck and call night and day for years—*years*. Constantly knowing that one wrong word, one wrong move, and she'd kill me with her Fire magic right where I stood with no warning and no sympathy. Mab wasn't even particularly clever. She was just strong. All that power, all that magic, all that money. She could have done so much with it. But she never could think big enough."

I'd thought Mab had dreamed plenty big, since she'd practically run Ashland, but I didn't contradict McAllister. Even he had a right to rant here at the end.

"But you know what the really ironic thing is? Mab actually had *me* draw up that will. I guess she thought she'd be around a lot longer than I would. Elementals." He snorted. "They all think that they're so much better than the rest of us. So much stronger, so much more powerful. But they die just like everyone else does."

He let out a dark laugh. "You definitely proved that to Mab."

I shrugged.

He raised his brandy glass to me. "I should thank you for that. For killing that bitch. For finally freeing me from her. I would have been content to do just that. Live and let live, if you will—if you hadn't killed my son."

McAllister moved to the end of the bar, reached down, and picked up a photo from a nearby table. A younger, larger, beefier version of himself stared out from beneath the glass—his son, Jake. McAllister stared at the photo a moment before setting it back down on the table. He nudged it with his index finger, making sure it was in exactly the same spot as before.

"Admittedly, Jake was an idiot and a colossal screwup. He wasn't worth all of the money I wasted bailing him out of one scrape after another over the years. But nobody fucks with a McAllister—not even you."

I tipped my head, telling him that I understood his sentiment. You didn't have anything, you weren't *worth* anything, if you couldn't protect your friends and family. But if you did fail them, the only thing left to do was get retribution. And in a place like Ashland, that was only paid out in one way: in blood.

"I have to admit that I was still a bit confused after

I found the will," I said. "I wondered who would hire Clementine to steal it. At first, I thought that maybe it was the mysterious M. M. Monroe who was mentioned in it, but then I realized that he or she had no reason to swipe the will, since Mab had left everything to him or her already. That led me back to you, Jonah. Although I wondered at the show you had Clementine put on. Why not quietly break into the vault after hours and steal the will? But then I remembered something Finn had said about the will being made public during the gala. You had to get the will before that happened, but you didn't want anyone to know what you were really after. The heist was the perfect cover for that. I imagine part of it was also payback."

"You're damn right it was payback," McAllister muttered. "Ever since Mab's death, everyone in the underworld's been thumbing their noses at me. Well, they weren't laughing at the museum, were they?"

"No. Nobody was laughing."

McAllister brooded into his brandy for a few seconds before raising his head to me again. "So tell me the rest of it. Why do you think I wanted the will?"

"Oh, the answer to that is simple: because you've been embezzling money from Mab for years."

He froze, shocked that his dirty little secret was finally out in the open after being buried for so long. For a moment, panic flared in his eyes, and his gaze flicked toward the doorway as if he expected Mab to storm inside and roast him on the spot for his betrayal. After a moment, he seemed to snap back to reality, because he laughed again, the sound even darker and harsher than before. But there was another emotion mixed in with all of the ugliness: relief. I wondered if it was because Mab was dead and couldn't hurt him or that he could finally share his secret with someone—even if that someone was me.

When his laughter finally faded away, I continued with my story.

"You see, when I started putting it all together, it only made sense that you would steal the will. You were Mab's lawyer, so of course you drew up it for her. That also meant that you knew exactly what was in it," I said. "So after I read it, I figured there was something you didn't want M. M. Monroe to find out about Mab's estate—something you'd done. Embezzlement seemed like just the sort of thing you'd want to cover up, so I had Finn do some checking. He said you hid your tracks very well but not quite well enough. Exactly how much have you skimmed from Mab over the years?"

He sighed. "Close to thirty million. With my investments, I've grown it into more than fifty. And it wasn't easy—it was the hardest thing I've ever done. That woman watched her money like a hawk, wanting to know where every little penny went. She had hundreds of millions at her disposal, and I still had to send her receipts for every dime I spent. Miserly bitch."

I wanted to point out that Mab had had good reason to be suspicious, given how much he'd swindled from her, but I graciously kept that thought to myself.

And now came the final question I had, the one thing that I most wanted an answer to. But I kept my voice light and casual. No sense in tipping him off about how important it was to me. It would be just like the lawyer to pick up on that and decide to mess with me, especially since he thought he had nothing to lose now.

"So who is the mysterious M. M. Monroe?" I asked. "The one you've gone to so much trouble to avoid."

For several seconds, the only sound was the *tick-tick-tick* of the grandfather clock. McAllister stared into the amber depths of his brandy. Brooding again. Just when I was about to ask the question a little more forcefully, he frowned and finally raised his eyes to mine.

"That's the problem," he grumbled. "I don't actually know. Mab kept whoever it is a secret even from me."

I watched him, studying his body language and listening to the tone and inflection of his words, but McAllister seemed to be telling the truth. His voice would have been sly instead of shaky, his eyes bright instead of dark, his posture confident instead of defeated, if he'd been lying. He really didn't know who Mab had left her millions to. Troubling, to say the least.

"But now you know why I had to act," he said. "Because if this person is anything like Mab, well, things will not go so well for me."

"No," I said. "I imagine the theft of millions of dollars would greatly upset anyone who came to Ashland looking to lay claim to his or her inheritance."

He sniffed. "Theft? *Please*. It wasn't like Mab didn't owe me that money anyway, given the pittance she paid me. Not as hard as I worked for her. Not after all the things I did for her. Not after all the things she made me watch her do." He shuddered at that last thought and the memories that came with it.

I didn't feel sorry for McAllister—not one little bit.

Yes, he had worked for a monster, had seen Mab do terrible things, and had been afraid that she might take her fiery wrath out on him at any moment. But like he'd said, he'd also done terrible things himself along the way. Besides, he could have always walked—or run— away. Left Mab, left town, gone someplace where nobody knew who he was or what he'd done. But instead, he'd stayed in Ashland all these years, enjoying all the bloody benefits of being Mab's lackey. McAllister wasn't upset that I'd killed the Fire elemental. He'd had no real affection for or loyalty to her. No, he was just pissed that people didn't kowtow and cower when he walked by these days.

McAllister didn't like the fact that no one was afraid of him like they had been of her.

"Well, I have to admit that it was a good plan," I said. "Rob everyone who's been thumbing their noses at you, tie up Mab's estate for as long as possible so you could steal even more from it before you finally skipped town, murder me on the side. I'll give you credit, Jonah. You always give it your all. Why, in your own way, you're even more devious than Mab was."

"I would have gotten away with it too," he muttered again. "If not for that damn dress. Who the hell in North-town sells two dresses exactly alike? Don't they know how gauche that is?"

Well, I guessed Finn wasn't the only man in Ashland who had a strange interest in women's fashion. My lips twitched, but I held back my laughter. At least I wasn't the only one who saw the irony of the situation. This time, it had actually worked in my favor.

McAllister pushed away his brandy glass and dropped his right hand down behind the bar. He straightened up to his full height and gave me a cold, sinister glare. "Very well done, Gin. Really. Quite impressive, how you put everything together. And all this time, I thought that you were just a coldhearted bitch. I didn't realize that you actually had a brain in that ruthless little head of yours."

I grinned. "What can I say? I'm full of surprises."

He gave me a thin smile. "And so am I."

McAllister raised his hand out from behind the bar, a gun glinting in his fingers.

❄32❄

Click.

   Click-click-click.

   Click.

McAllister pulled and pulled the trigger, cursing louder and louder when the gun didn't fire.

I reached into another pocket on my vest, pulled out the clip that went into the weapon, and waggled it at him. "Looking for this? I took the liberty of removing it from your gun, along with the round in the chamber. In fact, I went through the whole house and took all the ammunition out of every single one of your guns. You have quite the collection, Jonah. Revolvers, handguns, even a good ole-fashioned shotgun under your bed. Why, you've got enough firepower in here to start a small war, even by Ashland standards. Consider me impressed."

He looked at me a moment before his gaze dropped to the useless gun in his hand. "Dammit!"

He reared back and threw the weapon at me as hard as he could. His aim was lousy, and I didn't even have to duck as the weapon sailed on by me, hit one of the glass doors to my left, bounced off, and clattered to the floor. The fact that he'd missed me so badly only fueled his rage. McAllister slapped his snifter off the bar, not caring which direction it went or where it landed. A second later, the bottle of brandy shattered against the wall closest to him. One by one, he grabbed and threw and smashed everything he could get his hands on. Another bottle of booze from underneath the bar. A crystal paperweight on an end table. Even the photo of his son.

I grinned, laced my hands behind my head, and watched the show.

As suddenly as it had come, all of the rage went out of him, like a balloon that had popped under pressure. His entire body deflated, and he sagged against the bar, breathing hard, tiny drops of blood oozing out of the shallow cuts that dotted his knuckles. He looked at me again, his brown eyes dull and tired.

"All right," he mumbled. "Go ahead. Get it over with. Do your worst. I know you want to, and honestly, I just don't care anymore."

I removed my boots from the top of his desk, set them on the floor, and got to my feet. McAllister tensed as I walked toward him, and his gaze flicked to the doorway, like he was still thinking about making a break for it. No matter what he said, he wasn't ready to die. No one ever really was in the end. We all thought we had all the time in the world, and when we realized that wasn't the case, we did whatever we could to prolong the inevitable, if only for a few more precious seconds.

I reached the bar and stopped. I was directly in front of McAllister, with him on one side and me on the other, just like it had always been. I stared at him for a moment, then palmed one of my knives. He sucked in a breath at the flash of silverstone in my hand, and his body swayed from side to side like his legs were about to go out from under him. But I had to hand it to the lawyer. He bucked up, lifted his chin, and stared me straight in the eye.

The seconds passed. Ten . . . twenty . . . thirty . . . forty-five . . .

McAllister's breaths grew shorter and raspier, his left eye twitching in time to the rapid rise and fall of his chest. His body trembled, and his lips quivered, as he prepared himself to let out one final scream.

I stood there and let him sweat for a good three minutes. Then I tucked my knife back up my sleeve, crossed my arms over my chest, and leaned one hip against the bar.

"Relax, Jonah. I'm not going to kill you."

He blinked. "You're not?"

I shook my head. "Nope."

His whole body crumpled, and he barely managed to grab the edge of the bar to keep himself from doing a header onto the floor. For once, even his tight, smooth face had a bit of emotion in it: relief. Pure, sweet, unadulterated relief that he was going to get to keep on breathing.

His relief was going to be short-lived, though. I'd seen to that.

It took him a few moments, but McAllister pulled

himself together. He straightened back up and regarded me with cold eyes once more.

"What do you want?" he asked. "The money I stole from Mab?"

I laughed in his face. Laughed and laughed. And then I laughed some more.

McAllister's lips pinched together at my hearty chuckles, and more of that murderous rage glinted in his eyes, but he didn't say anything.

"Oh, Jonah, you are entertaining, I'll give you that," I said. "But no. I don't want Mab's money. Not one single *cent* of it."

"Then what? What do you want?"

I smiled at him. "Nothing—nothing at all."

I pushed away from the bar, walked out of the office, and headed toward the front door. My steps were light, and I whistled a soft, cheery tune, idly wondering how long it would take McAllister to come after me—

Ten seconds later, footsteps smacked into the floor behind me. I glanced over my shoulder. The lawyer had left the office and stopped in the middle of the hallway.

"What are you doing?" he called out, his voice high with surprise and puzzlement.

"What does it look like?" I said. "I'm leaving."

Silence. Then—

"You—you're just *leaving*? You're not going to kill me?"

I reached the front door, threw back the lock, and put my hand on the knob. I looked over my shoulder at him once again. "No, Jonah. I'm not going to kill you. Not tonight, not tomorrow, I'll even be generous and say not even this month."

His eyes narrowed. "Why? What are you up to?"

I gave him my most innocent grin. "I'm not up to anything, Jonah. You're the one who's been plotting, scheming, and embezzling this whole time. Not me. I think we can both agree that you've been a bad, bad boy. And now you're going to be punished for it."

His eyes narrowed some more. "What did you do?"

I shrugged. "Nothing much. Just told the cops all about your little scheme to rob the museum. Well, really just two cops, but they're good ones. Why, with all the information I gave them, I imagine that they're waiting right outside this very door, as eager as can be to come on in and arrest you. Shall we see?"

Before he could protest, I turned the knob and opened the door. Bria and Xavier stood outside. Behind them, their sedan sat in the driveway, the blue and white lights winking on and off in the darkness. I nodded at them and stepped to one side so they could enter.

"Why, look. Here they are. Right on time."

"The police? Please." McAllister sneered. "Do you know how many of those crooked bastards I've bribed over the years?"

"Of course I do," I replied. "So that's why I sent the information to all the local news media too. Anonymously, of course. Just for kicks."

"But—but why would you . . ." His voice trailed off as he thought about things. After a few seconds, shock and surprise filled his eyes, along with horror.

I walked back over to him so that we were standing face-to-face. "You see, Jonah, I could have killed you easily. But sticking my knife in your gut would have been a quick death—and far too good for the likes of you. So, in the end, I decided on a different punishment."

"And what would that be?" he asked in a wavering voice.

"To watch you *suffer*," I snarled. "You've spent the last few months planning how to take me out. You started back at Mab's funeral, when you hired those dwarves to try to kill me at her coffin. They failed, but you still managed to set me up as a target for every wannabe criminal in town. You painted a great big bull's-eye on my back, so I decided to return the favor and paint one on yours. What do you think will happen when all the crime bosses realize that you tried to rob them? Do you really think they'll let something like that just slide?"

I clucked my tongue in false sympathy. "Really, Jonah. You should know the answer to that as well as I do."

"They'll come after me," he whispered. "All of them. They'll all come after me."

I leaned forward, so he could see just how cold and wintry my gray eyes were. "Every . . . last . . . one."

McAllister kept staring at me, that horrified expression still on his face. Such a lovely, lovely sight.

"Now you know how I've felt these past few months. But you're exactly right. All the crime bosses will come after you—or send some of their goons to do the job for them." I paused. "Of course, this is assuming that Mab's mysterious heir doesn't get you first for cheating him or her. Either way, you're dead, Jonah. The only question is how long you can keep your head above water before one of the underworld sharks drags you under and gobbles you up. You know, it's probably a good thing you embezzled all of that money from Mab. You're going to need it. That might keep the sharks at bay, for a while."

McAllister choked, coughed, and sputtered for a few seconds before he finally got his voice back. "You won't get away with this. I'm Jonah McAllister! Nobody messes with me! Nobody!"

I shook my head. "Good luck with that. If I were you, I'd start working on your obituary. I'm looking forward to reading it in the newspaper real soon. Good-bye, Jonah."

Bria stepped forward, a pair of silverstone handcuffs in her hands. "Jonah McAllister, you're under arrest for the murder of Jillian Delancey, the attempted robbery of the Briartop museum and its visitors, and many, many other things. You have the right to remain silent . . ."

Xavier put a hand on McAllister's shoulder, holding him in place while Bria read the lawyer his rights, pulled his hands behind his back, and clinked the cuffs on his wrists. But McAllister ignored them and glared at me.

"You won't get away with this!" he hissed. "I'm the best lawyer this town has ever seen! I'll find a way to beat the charges! You know I will!"

"You're exactly right. I have no doubt that you'll find some way to wiggle out from underneath the long arm of the law," I said. "But I don't think even you can weasel away from every bad guy in town who'll be screaming for your blood. Enjoy the rest of your short, short life, Jonah."

I turned and headed toward the front door once again.

"Blanco! You can't do this to me! Blanco! Blanco!"

I grinned and walked outside, McAllister's screams ringing in my ears like the sweetest symphony.

*   *   *

I ambled down the driveway, through the open gate, and across the street. I opened the door on an Aston Martin parked at the curb and slid into the passenger's seat.

"How did it go?" Finn asked. "Did he cry? Please, please, *please* tell me that he cried. Or at least begged for his life."

"You should know," I replied. "You were listening."

I reached into a pocket on my vest and pulled out the digital recorder and microphone than Finn had outfitted me with. He took the device and plugged it into his laptop.

"Of course I was listening—and watching too, thanks to that spy camera we added to your vest," he said. "But I wanted to get your eye-witness take on things."

I rolled my eyes, but I watched as Finn checked that both the sound and the video recordings were okay and made several backup copies of them.

"I wonder if McAllister realized that you were getting him to confess for Bria," Finn said.

I shrugged. "Doesn't much matter now, since he sang his heart out."

That had been the plan I'd worked out with Finn, my sister, and Xavier. I'd told the two cops all about my suspicions that McAllister had hired Clementine and her crew and the information that Finn had dug up on the lawyer's embezzlement. But Bria had pointed out that she couldn't use any of the information—not legally—so I'd decided to get McAllister to confess to the whole scheme for her. That's why I'd broken into his house and confronted him tonight, and it had worked like a charm. Bria got to close the museum case, and I got to feed McAllister to the wolves. Win-win and then some.

Finn looked at me. "Are you sure you don't want to change your mind? Maybe you should have just killed him after all."

"Maybe," I said, leaning forward so I could stare past him out the driver's-side window.

Across the street, Bria perp-walked McAllister out of his fancy house and handed him off to Xavier, who stuffed the lawyer into the back of their sedan. McAllister was still screaming, although his voice was muffled at this distance.

Finn turned his head to watch the show. His grin matched the one that stretched across my face. We sat there until Bria started the sedan, and she and Xavier steered out of the driveway. Finn cranked the engine on his car and fell in line behind them. It was after one in the morning now, and the streets were quiet as we cruised over to the station.

"Well, that was certainly satisfying to watch," Finn admitted. "But I still think you should have just gone ahead and killed him. He's certainly caused you enough trouble."

"I know. But there's still a chance McAllister could be useful."

"Because of this mystery person Mab left everything to?" he said. "McAllister said he didn't know who it was, not even if it was a he or a she."

"I know. And I actually think he was telling the truth about that."

"But?"

"But if Mab actually had some family left, why weren't they here with her in Ashland?" I asked. "Why didn't they live with her? Or in some other mansion in Northtown?"

Finn shrugged. "Maybe they didn't get along. Maybe this other person hated her. I certainly wouldn't want to claim Mab Monroe as any sort of kin. Would you?"

"No," I replied. "But I would think that Mab would want to keep an eye on her family. There are only a few reasons I can think of for her not to have kept this person close. One, they are either too young or too old to be of any use to her. Then there's the other, more troubling reason."

"And that would be?"

"That this person was simply too dangerous to have around—too much of a threat to Mab herself."

Finn eyed me. "You think there's another Mab out there running around? Someone with the same sort of Fire magic she had? Someone as strong as her?"

I shrugged. "Maybe. Or at least strong enough to make Mab think twice about having them hanging around in Ashland, scheming to take her out, to have everything all to himself or herself."

He let out a low whistle. "Another Mab. Imagine that."

I didn't say anything. I didn't tell him that I'd imagined that in my dreams—in my nightmares—a thousand times. That the thought—the sheer *possibility*—kept me awake for hours on end, worrying in the darkness. That I'd even started scouring through Fletcher's files, going through every single one, every single photo and piece of paper, to see if there was any mention of Mab's mysterious relative and any clue to what kind of magic, if any, he or she might have.

Maybe there was another reason, a perfectly innocent reason, that Mab had kept this relative a secret from everyone, even McAllister. Maybe they just didn't get along, like Finn said.

Or maybe there was a whole new generation of trouble headed my way.

"We could speculate forever about Mab's relative," I said. "But if this person is anything like Mab, he or she will be plenty pissed to find out that McAllister was stealing from Mab—from them both—all these years. Maybe even pissed enough to come to Ashland and take care of him."

That was my hope anyway. I couldn't deal with a danger I didn't know about, and I was hoping that by using McAllister as bait—as another stalking horse—I could lure Mab's heir to the city. Maybe this person would just take Mab's money and run—or maybe he or she would be just as dangerous as the Fire elemental had been. Maybe the heir would thank me for killing her—or maybe he or she would come after me, wanting to avenge her death. Either way, I was going to get out in front of this person, instead of sitting around and waiting for the other shoe to drop.

"I'm on it," Finn said. "I've already spread money around to all the right people. We'll know everyone McAllister talks to, everyone he calls, even everyone he bends over for in the shower."

"I don't think we need to be quite that detailed," I drawled.

He smirked. "Anything worth doing is worth doing right. Don't you remember Dad telling us that?"

I snorted. "Sure, I remember that particular pearl of wisdom. But I don't think Fletcher intended that to mean getting the lowdown on McAllister's prison lovers."

Finn laughed.

We rode the rest of the way to the police station in silence, although I was still thinking about McAllister, Mab, and her long-lost heir. But there was nothing I could do about any of that tonight, so I pushed my worries aside and decided to make the best of the situation. After all, you usually only got to see your nemesis carted off to jail once.

Finn parked in front of the police station in a primo spot that gave us a clear view of the entrance. He'd tipped off his contacts at the local newspaper, TV stations, and radio stations, so there was already a passel of reporters waiting on the steps. The cameras started clicking and flashing before Bria even got the sedan parked. The media feeding frenzy reached a fever pitch as Xavier hauled McAllister out of the back of the sedan and led him toward the steps. Finn rolled down the car windows so we could hear the reporters' barrage of questions.

"Jonah! Jonah! Are the charges true?"

"Did you arrange the attempted robbery at the Briartop museum?"

"Why was Mab Monroe's will among the contents taken from the vault?"

McAllister winced and ducked his head, cringing against the sudden onslaught of light, noise, sound, and fury, but he clenched his jaw and kept his mouth shut. He knew that the court of public opinion could be the most damning. No doubt, he was already thinking about how he could spin things to his advantage. Let him try. It wouldn't save him. Not this time.

Finn pulled out his phone. "The newspaper's already posted it as breaking news on its website. It'll go viral in a few minutes. Come morning, this place will be swarming with press from all over."

"Good," I said. "So unless Mab's heir is hiding under a rock, he or she should see the story sometime in the next few days."

"That's the plan," he said. "*Your* plan. I would have just gone ahead and killed him."

"I know, I know. But I can always kill him later. This way, at least we get to humiliate him first."

Finn eyed me. "Sometimes I think you're even more devious, twisted, and vicious than I am."

I grinned. "You only *wish* you could be as ruthless as me."

"Absolutely."

We sat there and watched the flashes and lights of the cameras explode in McAllister's face over and over again, brighter than fireworks on the Fourth of July. Xavier got halfway up the steps, then dramatically paused and turned so that he and the lawyer were facing out toward the crowd of reporters. Bria stepped to one side, making sure that all of the reporters, photographers, and camera people got a good, long look at the lawyer. For his part, McAllister kept squinting into the glare. He seemed more shocked and frozen than a possum caught by a pair of headlights on a dark country road. I'd waited a long, long time to see that cringing, beaten, vulnerable look on his face, and I savored every single second of it.

After another minute, Bria grabbed McAllister's arm and led him up the rest of the steps and into the police station. Xavier stayed on the steps, holding his hands out wide and keeping the media vultures from storming inside.

"Now what?" Finn asked.

"Now we wait for Bria to take McAllister to booking," I said. "Maybe if we ask nicely, Bria will send us a copy of McAllister's mug shot. I think that would look marvelous matted, framed, and mounted on one of the walls in Fletcher's office or maybe even at the Pork Pit. Don't you?"

❊33❊

Life more or less went back to normal, although Jonah McAllister's arrest and alleged involvement in the Briartop heist dominated the news. The media didn't exactly convict the lawyer, but they raised enough questions to get all the crime bosses good and interested in exactly what had gone down that night and who had hired Clementine and her giants.

McAllister put some of Mab's embezzled money to use to pay his three-million-dollar bail. I saw him on the news a few times, giving press conferences where he proclaimed his innocence before quickly ducking back into his house. The lawyer looked pale, thin, and shaken, and even his thick coif of silver hair had lost its normal shiny luster. Even when the cameras were fixed on him, his eyes always darted back and forth, as if he expected a hail of gunfire to ring out at any second and put him down for the count.

Good. Let the bastard sweat. He deserved it. Actually, he deserved worse, but this would do—for now. Like I'd told Finn, if McAllister managed somehow to wiggle out of my trap, I could always come up with a more permanent solution. I sort of hoped he would, just so I could finally kill him myself. Time would tell.

Three days after McAllister's arrest, I was in the Pork Pit, chowing down on a cheeseburger that I'd made for my own supper, when the bell over the door chimed, and Bria stepped into the restaurant. She glanced around the storefront, looking over the diners. It was four in the afternoon. Too late for lunch and not quite time for the dinner rush to start, so there were only a few people sitting in the blue and pink vinyl booths next to the windows. The waitresses were in the back, taking a break, although Sophia Deveraux, Jo-Jo's sister and the head cook at the Pit, was standing at the counter that ran along the back wall, slicing sourdough buns for the rest of the day's sandwiches.

I was sitting on a stool behind the cash register, and Bria took a seat close to mine on the other side of the counter. Bria waved at Sophia, who grunted and waved back. The motion made the tiny silverstone skulls on the black leather collar around Sophia's neck tinkle together. Unlike Jo-Jo, who was the epitome of a sweet southern lady, Sophia had fashion tastes that ran more toward Goth. Today she had on black boots, jeans, and a black T-shirt embossed with a white rose dripping scarlet blood from its thorns. The silver glitter on the T-shirt matched the streaks in her black hair.

In between bites of my cheeseburger, sweet-potato

fries, and sweet iced blackberry tea, I'd also been reading through my latest book, as I so often did during lulls at the restaurant. In honor of the Briartop heist, I'd decided on *Plunder Squad* by Richard Stark. I grabbed a credit-card slip from underneath the cash register and used it to mark my place in the book before I set it to the side.

"Hey there, baby sister," I said, pushing away the remains of my burger and fries.

"Hey there yourself." Bria read the title on the spine. "What's that about?"

"An art heist."

She arched an eyebrow. "Okay . . . Is that our next book-club selection?"

"Nah," I said. "I'm reading this one just for me. Besides, it's Roslyn's turn to pick something, remember?"

A few weeks ago, Bria and Roslyn had both read *Little Women*, which I had been reading at the time. In an effort to cheer me up and take my mind off my breakup with Owen, they'd shown up at Fletcher's house one night, books in hand, along with some wine, cheese, and gourmet chocolates. The three of us had stayed up late drinking, eating, and talking about the book, along with everything else that was going on in our lives. We'd all had such a good time that we'd decided to make it into a monthly get-together.

Bria nodded. "I remember. Although next month, it's my turn. I already know what I'm going to have us read."

"And what would that be?"

"*The Maltese Falcon* by Dashiell Hammett."

"A detective novel, huh? Looks like I'm not the only one in an ironic mood. I approve."

She grinned. "I thought you might. And I thought it was appropriate, given what happened at the museum. You know, Clementine going after something that wasn't quite what it seemed, everyone's plans spiraling out of control."

I had to laugh. "Well, that's one way of putting things, I suppose."

Bria swiveled around on her stool and gazed out over the restaurant once again. "So how are things here? I'm sorry I haven't been around much lately, but I've been busy dealing with McAllister."

"I know. I've seen you on TV more than once."

She blanched. "I hate dealing with all those reporters. Sometimes I think they're more vicious and bloodthirsty than the criminals."

"Actually, to answer your question, the past few days have been quite relaxing," I said. "No one's come in and tried to kill me this week."

"They're all focused on McAllister right now," Bria said. "And with good reason. No matter how many times I listen to his confession, I still can't quite believe he arranged the museum heist and that he almost got away with it. That he *would* have gotten away with it, if you hadn't been there."

"And if Jillian hadn't been wearing the same dress as I was," I said in a soft voice.

Jillian's face flashed in front of my eyes the way it had so often in the past few days. Her warm eyes, her easy laugh, her soft smile. All gone forever—because of me.

"Yeah," Bria said. "That too. How are you doing with that?"

I shrugged. "Fletcher always taught me to avoid collateral damage. To focus on my target, hit that person, and not involve anyone else before, during, or after my crime. I know that Jillian dying wasn't my fault—not really—but I still can't help but feel responsible for it all the same."

She nodded. "I can understand that. But this is Ashland, Gin. People get hurt all the time in this city. You can't save everyone."

I'd told myself that more than once, but it still didn't keep me from waking up in the middle of the night, the image of Jillian's shattered face fresh in my mind, and me fighting the sheets twisted around my body, as if I could save her if only I could get free of them.

"McAllister would have still hired Clementine to rob the museum whether you'd been there or not," Bria continued. "Maybe Jillian would have gotten caught in the crossfire and still died. Maybe it would have been someone else. There's no way of knowing."

"Or maybe nobody would have died," I countered. "Maybe if I'd realized what Clementine and the others were up to, I could have stopped them before things got so out of hand."

Bria reached over and squeezed my fingers, telling me that she understood my troubled, turbulent thoughts. We were silent for a few moments, then she let go of my fingers and leaned back. She gestured at the cake stand that featured the dessert of the day: a peach pie.

"Is there any chance of me getting a slice of that?" she asked. "And maybe a few other vittles to whet my whistle with?"

I grinned. Bria knew that cooking always helped take my mind off my troubles, and asking for the food was her way of trying to lighten my mood. "Sure thing, baby sister. One fine meal, coming right up."

Bria ordered a burger topped with spicy chili and sharp cheddar cheese, onion rings, potato salad, and a vanilla bean milkshake to go with her slice of peach pie. I moved back and forth behind the counter, grilling the burger and dropping the batter-dipped Vidalia onions into the french fryer to crisp up. Sophia stopped slicing buns long enough to put the ice cream, milk, and a splash of vanilla syrup into the blender to make the shake.

A few minutes later, I set Bria's plates in front of her, and she dug into her meal. As she ate, she caught me up on the latest developments regarding McAllister.

"I still can't believe they let him out on bail," Bria said. "Even if it was three million dollars. At least the judge agreed to make him wear a tracking anklet so there's less chance of him skipping town before his trial. It's been set for later this year."

She dragged half of an onion ring through the ketchup on her plate and popped it into her mouth. "Although I have to wonder if he'll actually live long enough to make it to trial."

Despite the plethora of crimes in Ashland, the court system actually moved along at a fairly quick pace. Normally, there were never that many cases on the docket, since most folks who committed said crimes were usually found toes-up before their trial dates. Revenge was a bitch, especially in Ashland. Justice wasn't blind here so much as it was swift—and permanent.

"Even if he does go on trial," she continued, "there's always the chance that he could walk. It's not like judges and juries haven't been bribed before in this city, and McAllister knows how to work the system better than anyone."

"Well, if McAllister pulls that particular rabbit out of his hat, I may have to revisit my original plan for him."

Bria took a drink of her milkshake and looked at me. "You really think all the news stories about McAllister and the museum heist will bring Mab's relative to Ashland?"

I shrugged. "It can't hurt. The will was made public, what, two days ago? If I were in line to inherit all those millions, I'd be making a beeline to town lickety-split."

Worry tightened her pretty face. She fiddled with the primrose rune around her throat a moment before dropping her hand and twisting around the two rings that she wore, the ones with snowflakes and ivy vines carved into them. "Who do you think this person is? Do you think he or she is anything like Mab?"

I knew what she was really asking—if Mab's relative was going to be as big a threat to us as the Fire elemental herself had been.

I'd gone over it a thousand times in my mind, but the truth was that I had no way of knowing. Maybe this person would take Mab's money and go back to wherever he or she had come from. Maybe he or she would stick around in Ashland and live the high life. Or maybe the heir would be just as cruel and power-hungry as Mab had been. But the carrot had been dangled out there. Now all that was left to do was to see who snatched it off the stick.

"I don't know," I said. "But no matter what happens,

we'll be ready for M. M. Monroe, and we'll face him or her down—together."

She nodded. "That we will."

Bria finished up her food. One of the other diners needed a refill on his water, so I left my sister at the counter while I moved through the restaurant and made sure that everyone had everything they needed. I had put the pitcher of water down and was sliding back onto my stool when the bell over the front door chimed. I looked past Bria, wondering who my latest customer might be.

To my surprise, Owen strolled into the Pork Pit.

❃34❃

Owen must have left work for the day, because he wore a light gray suit and a pair of polished black wing tips, although he'd already taken off his tie and unbuttoned the top of his white shirt.

My eyes traced over him from head to toe, drinking in the sight of him. We hadn't talked since that night at Briartop. I'd thought about calling Owen a dozen times, but I didn't know what to say to him, especially since his friend was dead because of me. Even if it had been a cruel twist of fate. I'd hoped that he might call, but he hadn't, and I hadn't seen or heard from him—until now.

Bria noticed me staring over her shoulder and turned to see who I was looking at. After a moment, she swiveled back around to me. "I take it that you and Owen are still up in the air?"

I grimaced. "Something like that."

"You should go talk to him."

I watched as Owen walked over to one of the booths in front of the storefront windows and took a seat. Since the waitresses were still on break in the back, Sophia grabbed a menu, walked around the counter, crossed the restaurant, and handed it to Owen. He took it and gave her a smile before his gaze drifted over to me. After a moment, Owen lifted his hand and waved at me. I returned the gesture before turning my attention back to Bria.

"Even if I don't know what to say?"

"Even if," she replied. "The two of you are good together, Gin. All I'm saying is don't give up on him just yet. He may still surprise you."

"It's hard, though," I said in a soft voice. "So hard. He broke my heart."

It was something I hadn't admitted to anyone. I'd barely acknowledged it myself. But Owen keeping his distance from me after I'd killed Salina, well, it had hurt. I hadn't expected him to be happy about what I'd done, but I hadn't expected him to go completely radio-silent either. Oh, I knew why he'd done it, and I probably would have done the same if our positions had been reversed. But it had still broken my heart and brought all of my old fears and worries roaring back to the surface. Fears that Owen wouldn't be able to accept me any longer for who I was and what I'd done to the woman he'd loved—even if I'd had reasons for my brutal actions.

"Go on," Bria said. "You're not going to solve anything just standing there staring at him."

"Since when are you playing the part of the big sister?"

"Since now." She grinned. "Now, get."

"Yes, ma'am," I said, giving her a small salute with my hand.

Then I squared my shoulders, lifted my chin, and went to see what he wanted.

I followed the faded, peeling, blue and pink pig tracks on the floor all the way over to Owen, who sat in a booth in the back close to the restrooms.

"Hi," I said.

"Hi." He smiled. "Can you sit for a minute? I'd like to talk—if that's okay."

"Sure."

I slid into the opposite side of the booth from him. Sophia raised her eyebrows and gave me a questioning glance, but I waved, telling her to finish what she was doing. Owen wasn't here to eat. Instead, he stared at me, and I looked back at him. Perhaps it was my imagination, but his violet gaze seemed clearer than I remembered—calmer too. As if he'd finally made peace with some of his demons. I wondered if any of them were Salina—or maybe even me.

"I went to Jillian's funeral yesterday," he finally said.

I nodded. I hadn't gone to the service, although I'd sent flowers and made a hefty donation to Jillian's favorite charity. I also had Finn working on a way to quietly slip Jillian's family enough money so they wouldn't have to worry about anything for the rest of their lives. But I hadn't thought it was right for me to show up at her funeral when I was the reason she'd been killed to start with. I knew the money wouldn't make up for anything either, but it was all I could do to help those she'd left behind.

"It was a nice service, as far as those things go," Owen said. "She was well liked. Lots of friends there, along with her brother."

I nodded again. There was nothing I could say to make Owen feel better or ease my own guilt.

"The folks who were there were happy that McAllister had been arrested," he continued. "Especially her brother. He was glad that Jillian was going to get the justice that she deserved, and so am I."

"Are you upset that I didn't kill McAllister?" I asked. "Because I thought about it. I thought long and hard about it."

He shrugged. "I'd like to see the bastard suffer for everything he's done to all of us. I'm okay with your decision."

I hadn't spoken to Owen, but I knew that Bria and Xavier had filled him in on everything McAllister had said, including the lawyer's plan to implicate him in the robbery.

"But I didn't come here to talk about McAllister," he said.

"Then what did you come here to talk about?"

"Salina."

"Oh. That."

"Yeah. That."

He stared at me, his eyes steady on mine. "I'm okay about Salina. I understand why you did what you did, Gin."

Those were the words I'd hoped to hear, but that sad, dull, resigned tone still clouded his voice. The one that told me that he might understand, but he hadn't really accepted it yet. Still, I wanted to hear what he had to say.

"What changed?"

Owen shrugged. "Nothing. Everything. I don't know. I've spent the last few weeks thinking about Salina and everything that happened. Replaying it over and over again in my mind. I told you that at the museum."

I nodded.

"But no matter what I think, I can't see things ending any differently from how they did. I even hired a private investigator to dig into her past for me, everything that she'd done since she'd left Ashland. He gave me the report a few days ago. It wasn't pretty. She was married several times. Did you know that?"

"Yes. Finn found out."

"Why didn't you tell me?" he asked. "Especially that all of her husbands looked like me? And that she killed every single one of them with her water magic?"

I shrugged. "I thought about it. But after everything that happened, I wasn't sure how to tell you. I wasn't sure that you'd want to know."

I wasn't sure that it would have made any difference, since you loved her so much.

I didn't say the words, but that had been my main fear. That Owen had loved Salina so much that he would forgive her even that. That he would never get over what I'd done to her. That he could accept all of her awful actions but not mine. That she'd always have more of his heart than I ever would, despite all of the terrible things she'd done.

He nodded. "I suppose I can understand that too."

"So what changed?" I asked, repeating my earlier question. "Why are you here now?"

He stared down at the tabletop for several seconds before finally lifting his gaze to mine. His violet eyes burned with emotion. "Because part of me shattered when I thought that you were dead."

My breath caught in my throat, even as hope blossomed in my chest. There were so many things I wanted to say to him, but I held my tongue. This was Owen's chance to speak, and I wanted to hear what he had to say, all of it—no matter how good, bad, or ugly it might be.

"When Clementine threw Jillian's body into the middle of the rotunda, and I thought it was you, when I thought that you were dead . . ." Owen's voice trailed off, and the memory and pain of that moment etched lines of anguish into his face. "It ripped me apart inside. Not just that you were gone but how things were between us. How I'd left things between us. I couldn't believe that I'd never get the chance to tell you how I felt about you."

"And how is that?" I whispered.

He looked me in the eye. "I love you, Gin. That hasn't changed, even with everything that's happened between us. I love you. I'll always love you."

"But?"

He sighed. "But every time I close my eyes, I still see Salina lying there, reaching for me, asking me to save her. And I feel guilty that I didn't."

"You didn't have a choice. I took that away from you when I had Finn hold you at gunpoint."

He nodded again. "Maybe you did, but I still felt like I should have tried harder, fought harder. Can you understand that?"

I let out a tense breath. "I do, because I feel the same

way about Jillian. Like I should have been able to save her, even though I didn't know anything about McAllister's plans."

"It wasn't your fault," Owen said.

"And Salina wasn't yours. Not what she did to Eva or Phillip or Cooper. Not what she did to those ex-husbands of hers or what she tried to do to everyone at her estate."

We fell silent, lost in our own thoughts, in our own guilt about everything we'd done and all the regrets we had. Finally, after a few minutes, I spoke once more.

"Salina might be dead," I said, "but that doesn't change things. It doesn't change *me*."

"What do you mean?"

"I mean that Salina's not just a onetime thing. It could happen again. I could choose to do something that you don't approve of. You might disagree, you might tell me all the reasons not to do something, and I might just do it anyway, because I think it's the right thing to do."

It was something I'd been thinking about ever since I'd had those dreams about the Delov hit all those years ago. Fletcher had been right when he'd said that I'd hurt the people I cared about. That's what I'd done to Owen when I'd killed Salina. But the old man had also been right about something else: that I'd rather have Owen alive and hating me than dead by Salina's hand.

This simple fact had helped me make peace with the water elemental's death and my part in it. More than that, it had helped me come to terms with what was happening between me and Owen now. I would always love him, but I would understand if he couldn't get past this. I would understand if I'd ended us when I'd killed Salina.

It hurt—it would *always* hurt—but I would accept it and move on. Because no matter what, Owen was alive, and Salina wasn't, and that was all that I really cared about.

"What do you mean?" he asked.

"Because if things are going to work between us—*really* work—then you need to understand this about me," I said. "I will do whatever I have to in order to protect the people I love—even if they don't like my actions. Even if they hate me for them."

He sat there and studied me, his gaze tracing over the smooth set of my shoulders, the determination in my face, and finally, the certainty blazing in my eyes.

"And what if you're wrong about something?" he asked. "What then?"

"Then I'll be wrong. And I'll live with that—and all the consequences of my actions."

He studied me a moment longer. "I think I understand what you're trying to say."

"So where do we go from here?"

Instead of answering me, he tapped his fingers on the table for several seconds before abruptly stopping. He hesitated a moment longer before answering me. "I don't know. I just don't know yet."

I didn't say anything else. I didn't know what was left to say. We weren't back together, but maybe we weren't as far apart as we'd been. And for the first time, that spark of hope in my heart didn't snuff itself out. Oh, it flickered and sputtered, but it kept right on burning, and I knew that it would until things were finally settled between us—one way or the other.

After a moment, Owen smiled at me. "I actually had

another reason for coming by today. I wanted to give you something."

"What?"

He reached inside his jacket and drew out a long, rectangular black velvet box, the sort of box you'd think would contain expensive jewelry. I wasn't much for jewelry, other than my spider rune ring, so the box probably held something else. Perhaps a knife or some other small weapon that Owen might have crafted. Although I had no idea why he would hand me a weapon now, given that I'd killed Salina with one of the knives he'd made for me.

"What is it?" I asked.

"Just something I thought you should have."

I wondered at his mysterious words, but before I could ask him what he meant, Owen slid out of his side of the booth and got to his feet.

"Anyway," he said, "I'm headed over to the riverboat to check on Phillip and Eva."

"How is Phillip?"

Owen shook his head. "Complaining like usual, even though Jo-Jo fully healed him at the museum. Eva's been on the boat all week, staying right by his side."

I arched an eyebrow. "And what are you going to do about that?"

He sighed. "I haven't decided yet. Got any ideas?"

"Is Eva too old to send to a convent?"

Owen laughed—the first genuine laugh I'd heard from him in weeks. He grinned at me, and for a moment, everything was perfect, and I felt like we were the Gin and Owen of old.

His laughter and his smile slowly faded away, the way these things always do. But the warmth lingered in his eyes, and there wasn't as much tension between us as there had been before.

He nodded at me once, then turned and left the restaurant.

I stayed where I was, reached out, and picked up the box. I hefted it, and it felt surprisingly light in my hand. Probably not a weapon after all.

I put the box back down on the table and slowly cracked open the top. A surprised gasp escaped my lips.

My mother's and sister's rune necklaces lay inside the box, Eira's snowflake and Annabella's curling ivy vine.

Sunlight slanted across the table, making the silverstone runes gleam. Both necklaces looked absolutely perfect, as though they'd just been made a moment before. Even the chains looked brand-new, as though they and the runes had never even been touched, even though my mother and my sister had worn them every single day, just like Bria did her primrose necklace and I did my spider rune ring. All the black, ashy, sooty remains of Mab's elemental Fire had been scrubbed off the runes, making them bright, shiny, and clean.

"How—when—" Words failed me, even though I was only sputtering to myself.

I hadn't told anyone about seeing the rune necklaces at the Briartop, because I hadn't thought there was a chance that I could somehow find them. I hadn't wanted to get Bria's or even my own hopes up, so I'd kept quiet, although I had asked Finn to get me a list of all the items from Mab's exhibit that had been recovered. But the necklaces hadn't been on it, so I'd figured that someone had swiped them in the confusion and chaos.

I'd never thought that someone would turn out to be Owen.

My head snapped up, searching for him, wondering if I could run out the door, catch him, and tell him how much the runes meant to me.

But I didn't have to, because he was standing right outside, watching me through the window. We stared at each other for a moment.

"Thank you," I finally mouthed.

I pressed my palm against the window, and I let him see the hope in my eyes—my hope for us. Owen smiled for a moment, and I saw the answering warmth in his gaze. He leaned over and pressed his hand to mine, even though the glass separated us.

We stayed like that for the better part of a minute, staring at each other, before Owen slowly drew his fingers away. He winked at me, then stuck his hands in his pockets and strolled away. A second later, he was gone.

But for the first time, it didn't feel like I was losing him—it almost felt like he'd left part of himself behind with me.

It wasn't the reunion I'd hoped for, but it was a start. Like Bria said, we had to start somewhere, even if our end destination seemed impossibly far away.

I sat there in the booth, my heart lighter and more hopeful than it had been in weeks. Owen and I weren't back together, but I felt like we'd at least turned a corner. That maybe there was a chance for us after all.

I stared at the pendants. Maybe it was my imagination, but for a moment, they seemed to gleam even brighter than before, as if the metal shared my hopeful thoughts. I reached out and traced over the runes with my finger, just as I'd done countless times before as a child. Owen had found them and brought them back to me. I couldn't quite believe it. That the runes were whole and with me once again. He'd given me such a lovely, thoughtful gift, such an important gift. Despite everything that had passed between us, my heart swelled with love for him—and also with hope for our future.

Smiling, I grabbed the runes, slid out of the booth, and went over to the counter to show Bria the gift that Owen had given to both of us.

One of friendship, family—and love.

Turn the page for a sneak peek at the
next book in the Elemental Assassin series

HEART OF VENOM

by Jennifer Estep

Coming soon from Pocket Books

1

"What do you mean, I can't come?"

I jerked my head down at the heavy weight swinging between us. "Do you really want to talk about this right now?"

"I can't *think* of a better time," he replied, then dropped his half of the load onto the ground.

I let go of my half of the weight, put my hands on my hips, and rolled my eyes at the whiny, petulant tone in my foster brother's voice. "You can't come because it's a girls' day at the salon. No guys allowed. That includes you."

Finnegan Lane sniffed, straightened up to his full height, and carefully adjusted the expensive silk tie knotted around his neck. "Yes, but I am not just *any* guy."

More eye rolling on my part, but Finn ignored me. His ego was pretty much bulletproof, and my derisive looks wouldn't so much as scratch his own highfalutin opinion of himself.

"Besides," he continued, "I'd get more enjoyment out of a spa day than you would."

"True," I agreed. "I don't particularly care how shiny my nails are or how well conditioned my hair is."

Finn held out his manicured nails, studying them with a critical eye, before reaching up and gently patting his coif of walnut-colored hair. "My nails are good, but I could use a trim. Wouldn't want to get any split ends."

"Oh no," I muttered. "We wouldn't want such a horror as *that*."

With his artfully styled hair, designer suit, and glossy wing tips, Finn looked like he'd just stepped out of the pages of some high-end fashion magazine. Add his intense green eyes, chiseled features, and toned, muscled body to that, and he was as handsome as any movie star. The only thing that ruined his sleek, polished look was the blood spattered all over his white shirt and gray suit jacket—and the body lying at our feet.

"Come on," I said. "This guy isn't getting any lighter."

The two of us were standing in the alley behind the Pork Pit, the barbecue restaurant that I ran in downtown Ashland. A series of old, battered metal Dumpsters crouched on either side of the restaurant's back door, all reeking of cumin, cayenne, black pepper, and the other spices that I cooked with, along with all of the food scraps and other garbage that had spoiled out here in the July heat. A breeze whistled in between the backs of the buildings, bringing some temporary relief from the sticky humidity and making several crumpled-up white paper bags bearing the Pork Pit's pig logo skip down the oil-slicked surface of the alley.

I ignored the low, scraping, skittering noises of the bags and concentrated on the sound of the stones around me.

People's actions, thoughts, and feelings last longer and have more of an impact than most folks realize, since all of those actions and feelings resonate with emotional vibrations that especially sink into the stone around them. As a Stone elemental, my magic let me hear and interpret all of the whispers of the element around me, whether it was a jackhammer brutally punching through a concrete foundation, weather slowly wearing away at a tombstone, or the collective frets of harried commuters scurrying into an office building every day on their way to work, hoping that their bosses wouldn't yell at them for being late again.

Behind me, the brick wall of the Pork Pit let out low, sluggish, contented sighs, much the way the diners inside did after finishing a hot, greasy barbecue sandwich, baked beans, and all of the other southern treats that I served up on a daily basis. A few sharp notes of violence trilled here and there in the brick, but they were as familiar to me as the sighs were, and I wasn't concerned by them. This wasn't the first person I'd killed inside the restaurant, and it wouldn't be the last.

"Come on," I repeated. "We've had our body-moving break. You grab his shoulders again, and I'll get his feet. I want to get this guy into that Dumpster in the next alley over before someone sees us."

"Dumpster? You mean the refrigerated cooler that Sophia hauled in just so you could keep bodies on ice close to the restaurant with at least a *modicum* of plausible deniability," Finn corrected me.

I shrugged. "It was her idea, not mine. But since she's the one who gets rid of most of the bodies, it was her call."

"And why isn't Sophia here tonight to help us with this guy?"

I shrugged again. "Because there was some James Bond film festival that she wanted to go to, so she took the night off. Now, come on. Enough stalling. Let's go."

"Why do I have to grab his shoulders?" Finn whined again. "That's where all the blood is."

I eyed his ruined jacket and shirt. "At this point, I don't think it much matters, do you?"

Finn glanced down at the smears of red on his chest. "No, I suppose it doesn't."

He grumbled and let out a few put-upon sighs, but he eventually leaned down and took hold of the dead guy's shoulders, while I grabbed his ankles. So far, we'd moved the guy from the front of the Pork Pit, through the rear of the restaurant, and outside. This time, we slowly shuffled away from the back door of the Pit and down the alley.

Finn and I had moved bodies before, but the fact that this dead guy was a seven-foot-tall giant with a strong, muscled figure made him a little heavier than most, and we stopped at the end of the alley to take another break. I wiped the sweat off my forehead and stared down at the dead guy.

Half an hour ago, the giant had been sitting in a booth in the restaurant, chowing down on a double bacon cheeseburger, sweet-potato fries, and a big piece of apple pie and talking to the friend he'd brought along. The two giants had been my last customers, and I'd been waiting for them to leave before I closed the restaurant for the night. The first guy had paid his bill and left without incident, but the second one had swaggered over to the cash register and handed me a fistful of one-dollar bills. I'd counted the bills, and the second my eyes dropped to the cash register, the giant had taken a swing at me with his massive fist.

Please. As if no one had ever tried that trick before.

But such were the job hazards of an assassin. Yep, me, Gin Blanco. Restaurant owner by day. Notorious assassin the Spider by night. Well, actually, it was more like I was the Spider all the time now. Ever since I'd killed Mab Monroe, the powerful Fire elemental who'd owned a good chunk of the crime in Ashland, everyone who was anyone in the underworld had been gunning for me. I was a wild card in the city's power structure, and lots of folks thought that arranging my murder would prove their mettle to everyone else. Tonight's giant was just the latest in a long line of folks who'd eaten in my restaurant with the intention of murdering me as soon as they'd sopped up the last bit of barbecue sauce on their plates.

Since Finn had been sitting on a stool close to the cash register, he'd pulled a gun out from underneath his suit jacket and tried to put a couple of bullets into the giant, but the giant had slapped Finn's gun away. The two of them had been grappling when I'd come around the counter, palmed one of my silverstone knives, and repeatedly, brutally punched the blade into the giant's back, side, and chest until he was dead. Hence the blood that had spattered all over Finn—and me, too, although my long-sleeved black T-shirt and dark jeans hid most of the stains.

"All right," Finn said. "Let's lug this guy the rest of the way. I need to go home and get cleaned up before my date with Bria tonight."

I'd just started to bend down and take hold of the giant's ankles again when a mutter of unease rippled through the stone wall beside me—a dark whisper full of malicious intent.

I stopped and scanned the alley in front of us. Sophia's rusty cooler stood at the far end, although several more Dumpsters and smaller trash cans crouched in between like tin soldiers lined up against the walls. It was after nine now, and what little lavender twilight remained was quickly being swallowed up by the shadows creeping up the walls. Another breeze whistled down the alley, bringing the scents of cooked cabbage, grilled chicken, and spicy peanut sauce with it, since a Thai restaurant was among the businesses on this particular block.

Finn noticed my hesitation. "What's wrong?"

I kept scanning the shadows. "I think we have company."

He adjusted his tie again, but his eyes were flicking left and right just like mine were. "Any clue to who it might be?"

I shrugged. "Probably the guy who was eating with our dead friend earlier."

Finn shook his head. "But that guy left before the giant attacked you. Even if they were partners, once he saw what happened to his buddy, the second guy would have hightailed it out of here as fast as he could, if he had even the smallest *shred* of common sense—"

A bit of silver stuck out from behind a Dumpster off

to my right. I immediately lunged forward and threw my body on top of Finn's, forcing us both to the ground.

Crack! Crack! Crack!

The bullets sailed over our heads, but I still reached for my Stone magic and used it to harden my skin into an impenetrable shell. I also tried to cover as much of Finn's body as I could with my own. I might be bulletproof when I used my magic, but he wasn't.

Footsteps scuffled in the alley behind me, indicating that our attacker felt bold and confident enough to move toward us. Then—

Crack! Crack! Crack!

More bullets zipped down the alley. The guy must have adjusted his aim, because I felt all three of the projectiles punch against my back before rattling away in the semidarkness. One of the bullets would have blasted out through my heart, killing me and maybe Finn too, if I hadn't been using my Stone power to protect both of us. My body jerked with the impact of the bullets; then I let my limbs go absolutely slack and still as I sprawled over Finn, as though I were as dead as the giant lying next to us.

I looked at Finn, who gave me a saucy wink, telling me that he was okay. I felt his hand reach up, then drop from my waist, taking a light, thin weight with it. Finn brought his hand back up, and I wrapped my fingers around his. He pulled his hand away, leaving me holding the knife he'd grabbed from against the small of my back. I slid the knife partially up my sleeve, hiding the blade from sight, then closed my eyes and waited—just waited—for my enemy to come close enough.

More footsteps scuffed in the alley, followed by the harsh,

raspy sound of someone breathing in through his mouth. I opened my eyes just a crack. A pair of mud-covered boots were planted right next to my face. As I watched, one of the boots drew back, and I knew what was coming next.

Sure enough, a second later, the giant's boot slammed into my ribs.

Despite the fact that I was holding on to my Stone magic, the blow still hurt, like getting beaned in the chest with a fastball, but I kept my body loose and floppy as though I couldn't feel it at all.

But the force of the blow knocked me partially off Finn, who grunted as my elbow dug into his shoulder.

Silence. Then—

"Open your eyes, pretty boy, or I'll put a bullet through your skull," the guy threatened.

Finn sighed, and I saw him open his eyes and slowly hold his hands up. "All right, all right, you got me. I'm still alive."

"I don't care about you," the giant snapped. "Is she dead? Or is she faking?"

"Of course she's dead," Finn snapped back, holding his hands out so the giant could get a better look at the bloody smears on his clothes. "Do you not see the blood all over the two of us? I'm lucky the bullets stopped in her instead of going on through and into me." He shuddered. "And now I think I'm going to be sick. So can you please just roll her off me or something? I can't *stand* the sight of blood."

If it wouldn't have given me away, I would have snorted. Finn didn't have any more problem with blood than I did. He just didn't like it being splattered all over one of his precious Fiona Fine designer suits.

"But you're her partner," the giant said. "Everyone knows that. Shouldn't you be, you know, more upset that she's dead?"

"Actually, I'm more like her henchman," Finn corrected. "As for being upset that she's dead, well, she's not exactly the kind of woman you say no to, if you know what I mean. Trust me. I'm happy that she's gone. Thrilled. Ecstatic, even."

Silence. Then—

The giant kicked me in the ribs again. Once more, I pretended that I couldn't feel the sharp, brutal blow. The giant kept up with his attacks, plowing his foot into my ribs, my shin, and even my shoulder. I thought he might lean down, press his gun against the back of my skull, pull the trigger, and put a couple of bullets into my head just to make sure that I was dead. But for once, my luck held, and he didn't take that final step. Maybe he was out of bullets. Or maybe he just wasn't that smart. Either way, after about three more minutes of dithering around and petulant pleas from Finn to move my body off him, the giant seemed to buy my playing possum.

"I did it," the guy finally said. "I did it! I killed the Spider! Woo-hoo!"

Okay, I thought the *woo-hoo* at the end was a little much, but I let the giant enjoy his moment of victory.

It was going to be the last thing he ever enjoyed.

"All right, all right," Finn groused again. "Now, can you please just get her off me? Seriously, dude, I'm about three seconds away from throwing up here. I know you don't want that all over your boots." He started making choking sounds.

"Fine, fine," the other man muttered. "Just quit your damn whining already."

The giant reached down, grabbed my shoulder, and turned me over.

I surged up and stabbed him in the chest for his thoughtfulness.

The giant screamed in surprise and jerked to one side, making my knife skitter across his ribs instead of slicing into his heart. He staggered back, and my knife slid free of his chest, blood spraying everywhere. The giant brought his revolver up between us and pulled the trigger.

Click.

Empty. Just like I'd thought. Too bad for him. Fatal for him, actually.

I scrambled to my feet, raised my knife high, and threw myself forward, but the giant was anticipating the move. He caught my arm in his hand. Given his enormous strength, it was easy for him to keep me from plunging my knife into his chest a second time. So I brought my free hand up, curved my fingers, and clawed at his face. The giant craned his neck back, trying to protect his eyes from my prying fingers.

"Gin! Down!" I heard Finn yell behind me.

I immediately stopped my attack on the giant and dropped to the ground.

Crack! Crack! Crack! Crack!

Bullets punched through the air where I'd been standing, and the familiar acrid burn of gunpowder mixed with the stench of garbage in the alley. A second later, the giant's body hit the alley floor with a dull *thud*.

Knife still in my hand, I got to my feet and hurried over to him, but there was no need. Finn had put a couple of bullets through the giant's right eye and up into his brain, killing him. His body had already shut down, and he wasn't even twitching.

I turned to look at Finn, who had a gun clenched in one hand. With his other hand, he was picking a piece of wilted cabbage off his jacket sleeve. He tossed the cabbage aside with a disgusted expression and moved over to me.

"You okay?" I asked.

Finn nodded. "You?"

I nodded back and gingerly touched my side. "I'll have some bruises from where he played kick-the-can with my ribs, but I'll stop by Jo-Jo's on the way home and get her to patch me up. No worries."

"Speaking of Jo-Jo's, I still say that I should get to come to your little soiree," Finn said. "Especially after I was so helpful here tonight."

I narrowed my eyes. "You start up with that again, and I'll be dealing with three bodies instead of just two."

Finn gave me a wounded look, but after a moment, he sighed and holstered his gun. "Well, at least this one's already halfway to the cooler," he grumbled.

I grinned at him. "See? We're nothing if not efficient."

Finn muttered some choice words under his breath, but he reached down and took hold of the dead giant's shoulders, and I grabbed his ankles again. We lugged the two giants over to the cooler to await Sophia and her body-disposal skills.

Not the first body dump we'd done—and certainly not the last.